12/96

DATE DUE			

F   Rodi, Robert.
ROD
      Kept boy

Kept Boy

robert rodi

Kept Boy

A DUTTON BOOK

DUTTON

Published by the Penguin Group
Penguin Books USA Inc., 375 Hudson Street, New York, New York 10014, U.S.A.
Penguin Books Ltd, 27 Wrights Lane, London W8 5TZ, England
Penguin Books Australia Ltd, Ringwood, Victoria, Australia
Penguin Books Canada Ltd, 10 Alcorn Avenue, Toronto, Ontario, Canada M4V 3B2
Penguin Books (N.Z.) Ltd, 182–190 Wairau Road, Auckland 10, New Zealand

Penguin Books Ltd, Registered Offices:
Harmondsworth, Middlesex, England

First published by Dutton, an imprint of Dutton Signet,
a division of Penguin Books USA Inc.
Distributed in Canada by McClelland & Stewart Inc.

First Printing, November, 1996
1 3 5 7 9 10 8 6 4 2

 REGISTERED TRADEMARK—MARCA REGISTRADA

Library of Congress Cataloging-in-Publication Data
Rodi, Robert.
Kept boy / Robert Rodi.
p. cm.
ISBN 0-525-93926-1
I. Title.
PS3552.L8415E96   1996
813'.54—dc20   96-34034
                                           CIP

Printed in the United States of America
Set in New Baskerville

For J.P.S. with L.U.V.

*With special thanks to the
Christopher Schelling/Jim Hoffman/Peter Borland/
Robert Drake/Mary Herczog Brain Trust*

Kept Boy

chapter

1

The surface of the moon, it looked like. Or a fractured auto windshield. A network of spidery lines, crisscrossing themselves with a mad and maddening randomness. And no matter how much Clinique M lotion he applied, they refused to go away.

The two deepest lines—ravines, really; spelunkers could investigate them—were on the same side of his face, craning out from his left eye toward his temple before dipping down to touch his cheekbone.

Why just on the *left* side? If wrinkles must disfigure one's face, they might at least do so symmetrically. This was almost certainly the result of having driven for so long without sunglasses; his left eye, being closest to the driver's-side window, surely squinted more than his right. Irony, there; the only reason he'd refused to wear sunglasses in the first place was that on warm days, the sweat that developed beneath them caused pimples on the bridge of his nose. Given a choice of catastrophes—wrinkles or pimples—he'd certainly have chosen pimples; pimples fade. Or maybe he was just feeling that way now, because he had wrinkles and not pimples. With a face full of acne, wouldn't a splaying of innocent hash marks seem innocuous, even dignified?

But it should be neither, damn it. *Neither.*

He stepped back from the full-length mirror. Just a bit of distance and the wrinkles disappeared. His familiar self-image now registered without a single discordant blip. There it all was: sandy hair hanging slack across his forehead, pectorals moving across his chest as if illustrating the theory of plate tectonics, abdominal muscles displaying the shape and texture of a John Deere tire tread, and smooth, long legs boasting French-bread-sized calves. Dennis Racine may have been thirty-one years old, but at this distance he looked a robust twenty-three.

Still, even twenty-three was a bit long in the tooth for a concubine. And that's what he was, wasn't it? Happy, humpy concubine to the brilliant, obscenely rich, sixty-whatever theatrical impresario Farleigh Nock (a.k.a. the "Papp of the Provinces").

He looked away from the mirror—tore his gaze away, really; it required tearing—and glanced through the bedroom window to the deck of the pool, where Farleigh sat hunched over a script, pear-shaped and pale in a seven-hundred-dollar silk bathrobe. As usual, Farleigh's concentration was marked by his steady scratching of his left instep with a ballpoint pen. He'd suffered a perpetual, irritating itch on that instep for years, but refused to see a doctor about something so silly and trivial; had instead spent hours upon hours of time scratching, scratching, scratching it.

The act both annoyed and frightened Dennis. Annoyed him, because it was such a repulsive habit, and weren't doctors accustomed to silly complaints? Frightened him, because this one might not be so silly. He'd developed the itch only after a coronary bypass operation, which to Dennis meant that there might still be something wrong with his circulation. But he was thirty-one years old, and his nagging Farleigh about seeing a doctor was now less likely to be offset by any irresistible boyishness.

Farleigh looked his way, and caught Dennis staring at him. He grinned, winked, and went back to his reading.

Dennis smiled. He'd been with Farleigh for virtually half his

life—ever since the producer had plucked him off the street
when he was fifteen. Dennis had wanted to be an actor then,
but had appeared in nothing, couldn't even pass the audition
to a decent acting class. In that sense, Farleigh was his rescuer.
His existence, once absorbed into Farleigh's, had been a never
ending round of parties and travel and glamour, going everywhere and anywhere on Farleigh's arm, being showered with
gifts. And in return, all he'd ever had to do was welcome Farleigh's body on the infrequent occasions he offered it, and fetch
him an odd vodka and tonic. Although Dennis had had a few
outside affairs—torrid thrashings against bodies as firm and
beautiful as his own—he'd kept them very much a secret, and
therefore had every reason to expect that when Farleigh died,
he would inherit his fortune.

Not that he wished Farleigh dead; in fact, he looked forward
to the day with no small amount of dread. He loved Farleigh.
Farleigh protected him. Farleigh made him feel both desirable
and desired. Farleigh and he laughed together, and often. They
enjoyed each other's company. But facts were facts: Farleigh
would almost certainly die before Dennis, and Dennis had to
think of how he'd get along after that. After the bypass operation, he'd even been so bold as to ask Farleigh for certain as-
surances on the matter . . . but he hadn't done so lately. Not
since the surface of the moon began replacing his previously
eggshell complexion. Best not to push a good thing.

While Dennis had leaned against the mirror frame and let
his mind wander thus, the new, young pool boy had been busy
sweeping the Tiffany blue pool bottom; now he squeezed past
Farleigh, who looked up and spared him a few quiet words.
Actually stopped scratching his instep for a moment.

Dennis, who ordinarily didn't dare interrupt Farleigh while
he was busy with a script, took this as a sign that Farleigh really
wouldn't mind having some company. Accordingly, he padded
down the hall to the sliding glass door and stepped outside to
the deck. When they saw him, both Farleigh and the pool boy
stopped talking and turned their heads his way.

He waved. "Hey."

The pool boy waved back. "Hey!"

Dennis frowned. "I wasn't talking to *you*," he muttered

under his breath. He had little use for what he called "the help" . . . perhaps because some of Farleigh's bitchier friends had a habit of treating him as though he were little more than "help" himself.

Ignoring the pool boy, he sauntered over to the chair next to Farleigh's and lowered himself into it.

"*Gaw*-juss day," he said.

"*Gaw*-juss," replied Farleigh, and they shared the requisite laugh at the use of their special language.

The pool boy, pointedly excluded, moved away, sweeping as he went.

Dennis stretched his arms over his head, then rested his wrists on the top of the chair. "What've you been up to?"

Farleigh grunted. "Work."

"On a day like this?"

"No one's come along to make me stop."

Dennis swiveled his head and peered at him with one eye. "Is that a complaint or an invitation?"

"I think it's more of a cry for help." He put aside the script. "You feeling Samaritan at all?"

Dennis drew his knees to his chest. "Oh, very Samaritan," he said with a depraved grin. "*Drippingly* Samaritan."

Farleigh got to his feet with surprising ease. Despite the degradations of age, weight, and illness, there were still times he resembled the dashing forty-eight-year-old who'd swept Dennis off his feet.

"After *you*, my dear Alphonse," he said as he held his arm toward the door.

Dennis giggled and hopped off the chair. "No, after *you*, my dear Alphonse." Another of their pet phrases—never less than wildly witty, to them.

As Dennis passed Farleigh, he noted that the pool boy was still watching them. It gave him a kind of kick to be the object of some young stud's voyeurism, although he hated to admit it to himself, and put it out of his mind at once.

"You know," said Dennis lazily as they slipped into the house, "I was thinking maybe we could retile the pool next spring. A different color or something. That Tiffany blue is . . . I don't know. So eighty-eight. I was thinking, maybe . . . peach."

He looked at Farleigh and smiled, but Farleigh wasn't smiling back.

"Oh, you were thinking *we* could do that, huh?" he huffed. "With all *our* money?"

Dennis was stung for a moment, then instantly recovered his poise. He didn't reply; his best bet was just to drop it. He still did this, on occasion—stepped over the line from love-slave to lover. The only smart thing to do was take a swift step back.

He put his arm around Farleigh's neck, kissed him, and led him up the stairs to the bedroom.

Little pinpricks of mortification were a small price to pay for such a serene life as this, he thought. Sequestered away in seraglio-like privacy on Chicago's near-north side, with a brilliant and famous patron and a battery of servants, pampered and cooed over like a rare treasure, a carnal, feline sprite kept in luxurious captivity. He could live this way forever.

If only the wrinkles would go away. Nothing but trouble there.

Nothing but trouble at all.

chapter
2

Summer began to wane. Farleigh and Dennis dined *á deux* at Alain's, an impeccable Franco-Asian restaurant tucked behind an unremarkable Halsted Street facade. The dinner restored their spirits—or Dennis's, anyway; six days of solid, drenching rain had combined with his ongoing uneasiness about aging to make him feel downright paranoid.

But the ministrations of the ever effervescent Widow Clicquot, followed by a china platter positively illuminated with multicolored seafood ravioli, had made the world seem a safe and lovely place again, so that when he and Farleigh exited the restaurant and found themselves face to face with Bix Zimmer, Dennis actually smiled and said, "Bix! Good to see you!"

Bix, his filth-encrusted poncho dripping black water onto the sidewalk, held his hand aloft and said, "HELLO, MY FRIENDS!" Everything Bix said sounded as if it were coming through a megaphone. He was a sad, rather archetypal 1990s story; a petty coke dealer during the previous decade, he'd suffered a double whammy around the time of the Gulf War (stroke *and* aneurysm), and had been left a virtual half-wit. Now, homeless and repentant, he roamed the streets of Chicago per-

forming good deeds—or, rather, one good deed endlessly repeated: he put quarters in expired parking meters so that the
cars parked there wouldn't greet their owners bearing tickets.

Dennis began digging into the pockets of his linen trousers.
Years ago, he'd been one of Bix's biggest customers. Now, although coke-free for nigh on six years, he felt obliged to supply
Bix with whatever quarters he'd accumulated during the day,
and in fact sometimes found himself consciously collecting
them for that reason, to the point that he'd use dimes and
nickels in a soda machine to preserve his quarters. For whatever
reason, he seemed fated to spend his life handing cash over
to Bix.

Farleigh mumbled a greeting to Bix, then said, "I'll get the
car," popped his umbrella, and trundled off into the rain.

A breeze eddied underneath the restaurant's awning and
tugged a strand of Bix's greasy hair into his mouth. "HOW
COME FARLEIGH DON'T LOVE YOU ANYMORE?" he asked.

Now, Dennis was in every way a modern man, which meant
he was heir to the unfortunate Romantic notion (perpetuated,
if not immortalized, by decades of Hollywood movies) that im-
beciles had gifts of perception the rest of us lack. So Bix's question jolted him not a little. He squinted his eyes and scanned
the bum's spotty face and matted hair, and told himself sternly
that there was absolutely nothing oracular about him, and thus
no reason to take him remotely seriously. Still, the pity in Bix's
eyes was palpable. Dennis cleared his throat and said, "What
makes you think Farleigh doesn't love me?"

Bix kept his gaze fixed steadily on Dennis's face. "HE
DI'N'T LOOK AT YOU. HE SAID HE'D GET THE CAR, BUT
HE DI'N'T LOOK AT YOU WHEN HE SAID IT."

Dennis, relieved that this was the extent of Bix's insight,
shook his head. "That's nothing. Farleigh just has a lazy eye.
Sometimes when he's looking at you, it seems like he isn't. It
confuses a lot of people."

"NO," said Bix, shaking his head. "HE DI'N'T EVEN
TURN HIS HEAD TOWARD YOU, MAN. HE JUS' WALKED
AWAY." He put his filthy hands around Dennis's palm, still
outstretched and filled with quarters, and closed it into a fist.
"YOU KEEP THAT MONEY," he said, patting Dennis's newly

clenched fingers. "YOU'LL PROB'LY NEED IT 'FORE I DO."
Just as Bix blared this, a pair of suntanned teenage boys walked
by under a single hangar-sized umbrella. Dennis smiled sheepishly at them and then turned to reply to Bix, but he was already
moving away, leaving behind him an aroma of urine and a
stench of fear—the latter emanating from Dennis.

Dennis heard the toot of a car horn, and turned to catch
Farleigh pulling his Saab convertible out of Alain's parking lot
onto Aldine, which was a one-way street heading east—away
from the restaurant. Farleigh's usual custom was to pull into the
nearby alley, drive around the back of the restaurant to Halsted,
and pick up Dennis in front, but tonight he simply tapped the
car horn and motioned Dennis to run over.

Which, of course, Dennis did. What choice did he have?

His shoulders were heavy and wet when he stumbled into
the passenger seat. Rainwater ran down his forehead and alongside his nose. He wished he could scream. But he forced himself to smile at Farleigh, who appeared to be looking at him
fondly . . . or was he? That lazy eye . . .

During the drive home, Farleigh steered with his right hand,
resting his left elbow against the window and thrumming his
lower lip with his free forefinger. He hummed quietly—a tune
Dennis couldn't quite make out beneath the patter of the rain
on the canvas roof and the metronome clicking of the windshield wipers. A week ago—an hour ago—he would've deduced
from this that Farleigh was sated and happy, a man in a fugue
state, close to purring, but tonight Dennis thought, *He's a million
miles away—I'm not even on the fringes of his thoughts.*

He reconstructed Farleigh's behavior during dinner: he'd
sat quietly and consumed his saddle of lamb with mushroom
strudel, only occasionally looking up to pour more Chateauneuf
du Pape or to nod absently at Dennis's breathless retelling of
all the day's gossip. He hadn't once responded with anything
more substantive than a muttered "Is that right." Spoken as a
statement, not a question. In fact, Dennis now realized, the tone
of that "Is that right" was faintly patronizing—as though Farleigh was giving him just enough encouragement to keep him
babbling on so he could occupy his mind with other things.

What things could those be?

They turned onto Lake Shore Drive, and Farleigh heaved a heavy, but happy, sigh. Good food always acted on him like a drug. Probably shouldn't even be driving, but of course, it wouldn't be wise to tell him that.

That contented sigh was like a single note that shifts a piece of music from a minor key to a major. Dennis felt suddenly ridiculous for having suspected him of some kind of dangerous secret. Damn Bix Zimmer! If he was fated to spend his life handing money to Bix, Bix seemed likewise fated to keep handing him back bad goods—whether diluted coke or screwy advice.

Learn from this, he commanded himself, even as he suspected he never would.

chapter
3

The next day, Dennis had to put his insecurities aside because of a panicked call from Paulette Ng summoning him to the War Room.

The War Room was a Bucktown grunge bar where he, Paulette, and Lonnie Roach could rest assured they'd run into no one who would know them—or, more important, know their respective keepers. For each of them was kept; that, in fact, was the genesis of their little fellowship.

They'd met by chance at the East Bank Club, a tony River North health complex patronized by various Chicago notables and wanna-bes. Paulette, Ronnie, and Dennis were in the same aerobics class—a class that, by virtue of its late-morning place on the schedule, could be attended only by persons for whom time wasn't money. Dennis had been a regular for two weeks before he worked up the nerve to approach the blond, lean, bedroom-eyed Lonnie, who, at the moment Dennis chose to make his move, was leaning over in the locker room unlacing his shoes, presenting, Dennis thought, his best face to the world.

Lonnie laughed at Dennis's nervous attentions before slapping him on the back and whispering, "I'm straight, sport. But I'll buy you a drink after you shower."

Dennis was bewildered by this reaction; he'd been accustomed to being rudely rebuffed by the occasional gaydar-confusing straight guy. Intrigued, he followed through and met Lonnie in the club's bar ten minutes later, where he was seated next to a tall Eurasian beauty with ivory white hair. Paulette, of course. Over a Kir aux Sauvignon, Dennis learned that Lonnie had met Paulette in the exact same way—she'd made a pass at him—more than a year ago. And that they'd both noticed Dennis on his first day of aerobics and had been dying to know his story.

Which implied that they already knew it. And in a sense they did. Lonnie Roach revealed himself to be the kept man of the gossip columnist Dierdre Diamond ("Not," Lonnie added with an eyebrow arched, "her real name"), and Paulette Ng was the kept woman of an Illinois congressman she refused to identify but whom, in honor of his favorite fetish, she referred to instead as the "Spanker of the House."

Dennis had at first felt a flush of irritation that he'd been so easily spotted as the spoiled house pet he was, but this was almost immediately overridden by a growing delight at having two comrades with whom he could share the difficulties and trials unique to their rather rare situation. After a few more drinks (the last several accompanied by lunch), they were well on the way to a fast friendship.

One of their pledges to each other was to make themselves available whenever any one of them was in crisis and needing advice and support. Over time, their venue for these meetings came to be the War Room, as much for its name as for its demimonde clientele.

Paulette had already claimed one of the bar's tiny tables by the time Dennis arrived there; in fact, she was in the process of *re*claiming it. A ratty-haired blonde standing with a group of her friends had dared to set her purse on Paulette's otherwise empty tabletop; Paulette shoved it to the floor, then snarled at the astonished blonde, "Do I haveta *piss* on the table to get it through your skull it's mine?"

The blonde quietly retrieved her purse; she and her chas-tened friends then edged themelves across the bar.

Dennis chuckled and threw himself into one of the free chairs next to Paulette. He gave her a perfunctory kiss on the cheek and said, "Hi, sweetie," then sat back and appraised her outfit: sapphire necklace from Cartier (Dennis had seen it be-fore), a phony college sweatshirt reading FUCK U., black tights, and authentic wrestling boots she'd gotten from her maternal aunt, 1969 Regional WWF Champ "Glorious" Gloria DiMott.

"Lookin' good," said Dennis with a wink.

"Better be," she said as she lit up a Tiparillo. "Where the fuck's Roach?"

Dennis thought she was never so beautiful as when puffing on one of those foul-smelling monsters. He felt a shiver of love for her. "Late as usual," he said. "Probably didn't mousse his hair just right the first time."

"That guy hadn't banged me silly for one month straight, I'd swear to Christ he was a fruit." She blew smoke out one side of her mouth.

This wasn't the first time Paulette had let slip that her own pass at Lonnie had been more successful than Dennis's, but it was a rare enough admission for him to get a secret charge out of it. He knew better than to ask for further details; her lips would instantly sprout shrinkwrap.

And anyway, here came Lonnie, looking incredibly delicious as usual, in a floppy plaid shirt and jeans so big that no belt should've been able to keep them hitched to those spectacularly lean hips. A great big cuddly cotton sex god.

He whirled his chair around and sat astride it, backward—something Dennis had to this day seen no gay man do. He ran his fingers through his hair and said, "Sorry I'm late. Miss anything?"

"Yeah, the first drink," said Paulette. " 'Nother Stoli for me, please."

Dennis turned to see that their waitress had arrived at the table. "Pimm's Cup," he said to her with his most winning smile.

Paulette whispered *"Fag"* at him and he whispered back, *"Duh."* They giggled at each other.

Lonnie ordered a Samuel Adams stout, and the waitress retreated. Then he and Dennis turned their attention to Paulette, who gave another nervous chomp to her cigar, crossed her ankle over her knee, and said, "Okay. It's the wife again."

"Mrs. Spanker?" asked Dennis. "I thought she was into her whole New Age live-and-let-live thing."

"She was. But then she got into this car accident—it was raining, freeway was slick, car in the opposite lane slid right into hers—and, dig it, both cars are totaled. Well, Mrs. Spanker gets out, walks away without a scratch on her."

"How very unfortunate," said Lonnie as he grabbed a handful of salted peanuts from the dish the waitress was just now placing on their table. He shoved them in his mouth and let the salt and skins flutter into his lap.

"Yeah, well, bitch'd survive the Great Flood, I know that now," said Paulette. She sucked in some more smoke and said, "Watch this," and released it out her ears—a favorite trick of hers.

"Amazing," said Dennis without enthusiasm. "Mrs. Spanker . . . ?"

"Just a pause for genius, Philistine. Okay, so Mrs. Spanker sees her miraculous survival—the other driver has a leg sheared off, I tell you that?—she sees her survival as a sign from God to stop dealing in satanic arts, so she goes home and throws out her Ouija board and her Tarot cards and all her J. Z. Knight books."

"Oh, hell," said Dennis with a pout of disappointment. "I'd've taken those off her hands."

The waitress returned to the table and set their drinks before them, then melted back into the crowd without another word.

"Friendly," said Lonnie disdainfully. He downed a mouthful of beer.

Paulette refused to extinguish her Tiparillo, but alternated between that and her vodka, all the while continuing her tale of woe. "So, anyway, Mrs. Spanker doesn't dare say a word about *me* . . . I mean, officially she doesn't know I exist. But she comes up with this brilliant plan to save her husband's soul from my damning influence. See, his first term of office is up next year, and she's all of a sudden on him like a ton of bricks not to run again, to retire to Florida."

"To *Florida?*" Dennis said, aghast. "How old *is* the Spanker?"

"Not that old—yet. Which is what he tells her: 'Hey, bitch, I ain't old enough to retire.' Well, words to that effect. But she's ready for 'im: 'Oh, I don't mean retire,' she says. 'My sister's husband, Vic,' or Vinnie, or whatever the fuck his name is, 'is selling his newspaper, and you could buy that and get back into publishing'—that's what the Spanker did before; he had a magazine he had to sell when he went into office—'and that way the paper would still be in the family and we'd be closer to the children and blah blah blah.' "

"Where do the children live?" asked Lonnie before filling his mouth with more peanuts.

Paulette almost spat her vodka at him. "Mind your own goddamn business, that's where."

"So," said Dennis as he swirled his Pimm's Cup in his hands, "the pressure is on the Spanker."

"Oh, big time. Damn kids callin' him, beggin' him to do it . . . wife treating it like it's a done deal . . . yeah, major pressure." She took another drag off the cigar.

"What about convincing him to take you with him?" asked Dennis.

She gasped, then started coughing convulsively into her hand. "Like I'd agree to fucking live in goddamn Marina Del Whatever for the sake of the Spanker!" she said when she'd recovered from the initial horror of the idea.

"What's his approval rating?" asked Lonnie, his eyes narrowing with sudden intensity.

"*Great,*" she said, with a telling hint of pride. "That's just the thing. It'd *kill* 'im to have to walk now. Just when he's doin' so much good." The jukebox suddenly blared to life; someone had selected "To Sir With Love" by Lulu. Paulette stuck her finger down her throat and made a gagging sound.

"Well, then, the answer is simple," said Lonnie. "Have him agree."

Paulette actually stood up; for a moment Dennis thought

she was going to throw her Stoli at him. "I'm *serious* about this, you piece of stringy dogshit!"

"So am I," said Lonnie calmly, but leaning back a bit just in case. "Listen. Election's not for a year, right? So if the Spanker announces right now that he's not running—I mean, think about it. No challenger is gonna be ready to jump in and say they'll take his place; not this early. So they'll start scrambling, like a bunch of starving dogs . . . and that'll make the Spanker look like George Washington in comparison. Above the fray, doncha know. And if he's really as popular as you say, there's bound to be a groundswell of support for him . . . people standing in the streets with placards saying Don't Go, Spanker, and stuff."

Dennis was, as ever, amazed by the sleepy-looking Lonnie's gift for outright manipulation. No wonder he'd been able to hang on to so public a figure as Dierdre Diamond. "Lonnie's right," he said to Paula now. "It's the only answer. The Spanker can't fight his wife *and* his kids *and* his in-laws. So have him agree to quit. Then have him go public with the news on a talk-radio show."

"Oh, talk *radio*," said Lonnie, wiping beer foam from his lips. "*Nice*, Denny."

"You know damn well," Dennis continued, "by the time that radio show's over, he's going to have so many call-ins from people saying, 'Don't quit,' he'll *have* to agree to stay on."

"He could even call his wife on the air," added Lonnie, his eyes brightening. "Tell her, 'Honey, you've heard the voice of the people. But it's up to you. I won't serve another term if you don't want me to.' She'll have to say yes, or she'll look like a selfish bitch to the whole damn state."

"Amazing," said Dennis to Lonnie. "You are as devious as any character Bette Davis ever played. You *sure* you're not gay?"

"Who's sure of anything these days?" said Lonnie, his eyes twinkling—the big tease.

Paulette had pursed her lips; the cigar rested between her fingers, forgotten, trailing smoke into the air. "Yeah, well, that could work," she said at last. "That could maybe do it. I don't know. Any other ideas?" She asked this halfheartedly, as though she really didn't expect anything to top the suggestion she'd already heard.

Lonnie and Dennis looked at each other and shrugged.

She leaned over the table and stubbed out her cigar. "Okay, then. Next plan of action: how do we fuckin' murder the slob who started up the jukebox?"

Over Lulu's climactic chords, Dennis said, "I'd be willing to let him live if he agrees to play the B-side."

chapter
4

Farleigh, of course, couldn't know about Lonnie and Paulette and the War Room. That was the whole point of
their existence . . . that they should be a resource which
Dennis could tap behind Farleigh's back. But the administra-
tion of Paulette's crisis (which was going well—she had convinced the Spanker of the House to give Lonnie's plan a shot)
had so depleted Dennis's social energy that he found himself
with nothing else to gossip about with Farleigh at dinner.

Which made for rather quiet dining, as Farleigh was moody
and withdrawn himself. Dennis guessed that this was because
he was busy putting together a new production—an updated
version of Oscar Wilde's *Lady Windermere's Fan*—and any new
show was always occasion for this kind of mute anxiety. Farleigh
had a lot to work through in his head.

Fortunately, their housekeeper, Christos—a strapping,
handsome, fortyish Greek expat who some years earlier had
himself been Farleigh's boy toy—was in one of his typically gar-
rulous moods. He scooted around the table in his apron, serving up successive courses, beginning with a Belgian endive salad
with walnuts, fresh mangoes, sun-dried tomatoes, and vinai-

grette, and as he served he related the story of his dazzling run-in with a fabulous celebrity.

"*Leona,*" he said breathlessly as he set the salad plate before Farleigh. "Remember her? Star of *The Money Movie With Leona* back in the early seventies?"

"Oh, wait a minute . . ." said Dennis, pressing his forefinger to his chin.

"Don't bother, hon, you're too young. *You* remember," he continued to Farleigh, who showed absolutely no interest in the story, but used the opportunity to scratch his instep with his salad fork. "She'd show old Alice Faye or Betty Hutton movies, and during commercial breaks she'd play snatches of old records, and whoever called in with the name of the song would win twenty dollars. And every half hour she'd have an exercise break, where she'd put on leotards and do some stretches. 'Member? . . . Hold that thought, if you do."

He sailed back into the kitchen to look after the next course, and silence loomed in the dining room . . . a silence that was reflected by the stillness of the enormous Helen Frankenthaler canvas set on the adjacent wall.

When he could stand it no more, Dennis said, "So, how are rehearsals going?"

Farleigh snickered at him, as though disdaining his ignorance. "What do you mean, 'rehearsals'? I haven't even got a cast yet."

Dennis felt his face flush. "Well, then, how's casting going?"

Farleigh waved a hand, as if to say, How *should* it be going?

Christos reappeared with the wine, apologizing that he hadn't brought it sooner, but he'd had to decant it and let it breathe a sufficient time. As he poured Farleigh a glass, he said, "A 1988 Ruffino Chianti Classico Riserva Ducale. You will never drink a finer Chianti, this I swear."

He shimmied around the table, and as he filled Dennis's glass he said, "Anyway, my favorite Leona moment was one Halloween where she did the show all done up in gypsy garb. Looked positively bronzed. Midway through the movie, she confessed she got her skin that way by taking a bath in coffee. HAH!" He hopped out of the dining room, giggling to himself.

Dennis wolfed down his salad while Farleigh toyed with his. It was unusual to see him so indifferent to food.

"Anything wrong?" Dennis asked.

Farleigh put down his fork and looked Dennis in the face. Dennis suppressed a sudden spasm of fear.

"It occurs to me," said Farleigh, "that you might help pay your way around here."

No more fearsome words could have issued from Farleigh's lips. Not "I have cancer." Not "You have cancer." Not "We lost the summer house in Saugatuck." Nothing more fearsome than what had actually just been said.

Dennis blinked at him. "Wh—wha—I mean . . . how am I supposed to . . . to . . ."

Farleigh shrugged his shoulders. "Get a job," he said. "There's a radical notion for you."

Fearsomer and fearsomer.

Dennis looked at his salad plate and thought carefully over how he should respond to this. Whatever he said now would determine Farleigh's future course of action. If Dennis laughed it off, as if Farleigh were joking, he risked offending Farleigh's obvious seriousness; if he got angry and refused, he'd encourage Farleigh into intransigence. If he burst into tears, he might disgust him.

What, then? The seconds were ticking away . . .

Mercifully, Christos reappeared, bearing plates of pasta. "First course," he announced merrily, "*orrichiette* with a butter-sage sauce and a hint of saffron. Mmm-mmm! Smell that, now!"

He set the dish before Farleigh and Dennis without ever noticing the powerful tension between them. Instead, he picked up the thread of his narrative. "So, anyway," he said, wiping his hands on his apron, "there she was—Leona—right at the Marshall Field's silver counter. And I was just about to go up to her and say, 'I have adored you for *decades*,' when some old bat beats me to it, goes up to Leona and starts fawning in the most repulsive manner possible. 'I caught your show every single day it was on.' The show ran eleven years, and she caught it every day? *Sure* she did. Suck my sweat socks, bitch."

While Christos rattled on, Dennis thought that perhaps this

was a crisis worthy of a summit at the War Room. But no, not so soon after the last one; he'd feel silly. Especially since Farleigh commanding him to get a job was but a trivial matter compared to Mrs. Spanker's attempt to spirit her husband one full time zone away from Paulette.

In fact, for now the best thing he could do was probably follow the same advice he and Lonnie had given Paulette on that very matter: when there's no possible means of saying no, say yes. As the Spanker would have to bow to his family's wish that he retire from government, so too must Dennis bow to Farleigh's wish that he take employment. Then both the Spanker and Dennis could use their temporary reprieve to plot a way to subvert it.

He looked up at Farleigh, eyes moist, and said, "Okay. Guess you're right. High time I became a little more responsible."

Farleigh, never one to mask his feelings, let his face contort with surprise. Dennis had clearly taken the wind out of his sails.

Wish I could hear the speech he had planned if I'd fought him, Dennis thought.

Farleigh grinned, winked at him, and began digging in to his *orrichiette.*

The grin bolstered Dennis's spirits, and he set his mind to work.

chapter
5

The next morning, Dennis made a great show of going over the Help Wanted ads as he sipped his coffee at breakfast. Farleigh, who was at his most grizzly and unsocial just after rising, grunted several rote pleasantries before kissing Dennis perfunctorily atop the head and staggering out to the car.

Dennis immediately shoved the newspaper aside and darted to the window in Farleigh's office, which overlooked the garage exit three floors below. He opened the window and stuck his head out. There was a damp morning mist; he risked frizzing his hair, but this was important.

A few moments later, Farleigh's Bentley rolled sedately out of the garage. From this vantage point Dennis could just make out Farleigh slumped in the backseat, his hand over his eyes, and Christos in the front, steering with two fingers and already jabbering away.

When the Bentley had passed two traffic lights and was receding from view, Dennis pulled his head back into the house and shut the window.

Farleigh would be busy all day with the new production.

That was time aplenty for—well, *something*. Something drastic, something totally unexpected that would make Farleigh give up this ridiculous insistence that Dennis pay his own way.

Lost in thought, he walked down the hallway to the bathroom, where he slid open the glass door to the shower and started the water running. Then he slipped out of his silk bathrobe and was about to step in when he noticed that the last of the bath towels were strewn about the floor, wet with Farleigh's residue. Since Dennis couldn't call Christos to fetch him new ones, he padded down the hallway to the linen closet himself. On the way he passed a full-length mirror and for a moment caught sight of the slight beginnings of a spare tire around his midsection.

He stopped short.

What was that? That hadn't been there the last few times he'd appraised himself!

Genuinely alarmed, he stood before the mirror and gave himself a good, hard look. Maybe, he considered as he poked a handful of fatty residue adjacent to his navel, he had been subconsciously preparing himself for every visit to the mirror . . . sucking in his stomach, flexing his biceps, rolling back his shoulders. Maybe when he was *away* from a mirror, he let everything slide, so that Farleigh would see him as he had just caught himself unawares: round, plump, soft . . . still beautiful, but in a fleshy way, like an indolent Italian contessa or something.

And all that body hair—that couldn't help. Back when he'd met Farleigh, he'd been as smooth as an apple. Now he noticed, as if for the first time, the rivulets of dark, wiry hair running up from his crotch to the gulley between his pectorals and madly circling his nipples like whirlpools.

When did I become such a *gorilla?* he wondered.

He stood a moment longer, truly dismayed by his appearance.

But at least it gave him a starting point; at least it gave him a direction for his energies.

Within minutes he was on the phone, making an emergency appointment for a full body wax, plus a haircut and a facial.

After a moment's hesitation he threw in a manicure and pedicure too.

Then he returned to the shower and turned off the water. Far better that he shower at his gym, after a good, solid two-hour workout consisting of high-impact aerobics and a trip around the free-weights circuit.

Then he could return home, buffed, waxed, and humming like a fine-tuned sports car. A little candlelight, a little champagne, and—well. He'd see what he'd see.

He'd been neglectful, that's all. Cheating on his diet. Cutting corners off his workout. Letting the magic, the romance, trickle like sand out of his relationship with Farleigh.

So, he'd just put the magic back in. Nothing to it. Piece of cake.

Or was it? That look of indifference in Farleigh's eyes over dinner last night . . .

Maybe he'd better go the extra mile. Give Farleigh a little kick-start. Get him humming too. And he knew just how to do that.

"*I'll get by with a little help from my friends,*" he sang as he grabbed the phone once more.

He dialed Lonnie's private number. When he got the answering machine, he knew better than to leave a message; Ms. Diamond had been known to snoop. Instead, he hung up and dialed Lonnie's pager number, then sat down to wait for him to call back.

As he sat, he ran over his battle plan in his mind, and everything fitted perfectly. But he'd have to keep going over it, examining it for any potentially fatal fallacy or flaw. Or, conversely, for any room for improvement.

After Lonnie returned his call, and Dennis had explained what he wanted from him, it was time to hit the gym. And it was there, on the bench press, beneath a barbell bowing from a surfeit of stupendous weights, that Dennis did indeed uncover a flaw in his plan, and became so alarmed that he momentarily lost the strength in his arms and found himself pinned, his legs flailing, the barbell poised a hair's width from his windpipe.

"*Could someone please help me?*" he whined through clenched teeth.

An enormous and startling-looking woman—African-American but albino, with white corn-rowed hair and a nose ring—took two loping leaps over to him and lifted the weights with arms that made Dennis's look like fettuccine. She grunted, dumped the barbell back in its cradle, then shook her finger at Dennis like some kind of mutant schoolmarm. "You shouldn't be doin' this without a spotter, Ace," she said with just a hint of menace.

Dennis sat up, thoroughly abashed, and rubbed his neck. "I know, I know," he said, wishing that everyone in the weight room would stop looking at him. "I don't have a partner, though."

"You got one now," the woman said, and she extended her steel-cable arm. "Fatima Howitzer. I just got into town an' don't know a soul, so I'm lookin' for a partner myself. How 'bout it?" She grabbed his hand and shook it. "Put some muscle on them bones."

Dennis was shocked. Put *some* muscle on them bones, she'd said; not some *more*, just *some*. Was he really as far gone as that?

"Thanks," he said, "I'd like that myself. Been a while. See, I *did* have a partner for a while, but he died." Dennis didn't like to bring up Ricky so casually, but he did want Fatima Howitzer to know that he wasn't a novice at weights.

The woman slugged him in the shoulder. That was what it was: a slug. No other word for it. "Aw," she said, "what a damn shame. You poor kid. AIDS, huh?"

Dennis nodded. Now he was beginning to feel guilty that he hadn't known Ricky as well as this woman thought he had. "Didn't even know he was sick," he said, trying to backpedal a little. "One day he just stopped showing up for our workouts. I was pissed, thought he was blowing me off. Then a couple weeks later, I heard—well, he was in the hospital." And I never went to see him, he almost added, but he didn't like admitting that, not even to himself.

Fatima clicked her tongue. "Well, hell. Explains how you got to be such a string bean, then. But don't worry, Ace. Fatima's here. Have you hardbody in no time."

He got to his feet, fetched his towel from the floor and

wiped his face. "Well, great," he said. "By the way, my name's Dennis. Dennis Racine."

"Fine by me, Ace. I'm here every day, eleven sharp. Can't be hard to miss me." She chuckled as she displayed her translucent-looking legs and midriff. "That work for you?"

He shrugged. "Well, I'm looking for a full-time job, but for now, yeah."

"Beauty. Might as well start now, then. Get back down there and do that thing right." She tugged on his shoulders, and he dropped back onto the bench press.

By the time Fatima had finished with him, he could count the places he didn't feel pain on the fingers of one hand: only his earlobes, his lips, his scrotum, and the tip of his nose didn't know agony. Everything else burned like hellfire. But people had stared at Fatima—at this great Amazonian person-of-no-color—and some had stared openly at Dennis, too, obviously wondering who he was to warrant the acquaintance of such a mythic apparition. And Dennis dug attention—*any* attention—quite a bit.

"Good workout!" said Fatima as she toweled down her massive, ivory thighs. "Next time, though, we get serious and stop with the wimp weights. All right by you, Ace?"

"Dennis, it's Dennis."

She grabbed him by the neck and shook him. "That's the spirit! See ya *mañana!*" And she loped off to the women's locker room.

Dennis felt as though he might be concussed; she'd given him quite a shaking. But as he shuffled down the hallway to the men's locker room, he thought that Fatima might be just what he needed—extra incentive to get into really terrific shape, the better to keep Farleigh in line.

That reminded him of the big flaw in his plan for tonight . . . the one that had caused him to need Fatima's aid in the first place.

He leaned against a wall and thought it all through.

He'd worked out a carefully laid strategy to seduce Farleigh tonight—to reinvigorate their stale sex life with a new layer of polish and some dangerous new sparks. But that wouldn't be enough.

Farleigh wasn't stupid. If he showed up and Dennis jumped his bones at the door, all waxed and oiled up for hell-raising, he'd *know* he was being seduced. And he'd know why.

The only way this would work was if Dennis first greeted him with some kind of news about his employment search. Like, "I've got an interview at Ooga Booga Corporation tomorrow at ten. Let's celebrate with champagne!" And then, after a bottle or two, could come the unveiling of Dennis's newly waxed body. And of course, there was still Lonnie's contribution to the effort . . . the fail-safe.

But how was Dennis going to get an interview before tomorrow?

He checked the gym clock. Three-thirty p.m.

He'd wasted too much time here with Fatima.

Well, shit. Double shit. Flame-broiled shit on a stick.

He was in the shower when he realized that all was not lost. As he soaped up his crotch for the benefit of a peeping-tom closet case in the adjacent stall, he remembered that there were places that ordinary people went to get jobs. You registered for them, as if you were a bride or something. Except *you* were the merchandise. What were those places called?

That's right: employment agencies.

chapter
6

Cindy Bassey-Esterhazy was a wiry, gnome-faced woman in a navy blue Chanel-suit knockoff who kept a pitcher of water and a box of foil-wrapped Alka-Seltzer tablets atop her desk. She poured herself a glass of water now, spilling some onto her blotter and her stack of pink WHILE YOU WERE OUT messages, so that she had to put the pitcher down, blot the spill up with her Hermés scarf, and then pick up the pitcher and finish pouring.

"Such a klutz," she muttered during the operation. "Hold on, be with you in a millisec."

She was setting down the pitcher when an older, rather feline man passed her desk and said, "Cindy! Thought you'd left for vacation."

"Ha-ha, you know how tough it is to cut the cord," she said nervously, tearing open an Alka-Seltzer packet and flicking the tablets into her hand.

The feline man looked at Dennis, who was sitting on the far side of Cindy Bassey-Esterhazy's desk. "She didn't make top agency biller last month," he said to Dennis with a smirk, tossing his head in Cindy's direction. "Thought she'd need oxygen." Then he turned back to Cindy and said, "Bermuda, isn't it?"

Cindy nodded furiously and said, "Six-twenty flight out of O'Hare."

"Well, it's ten to five now," the feline man said, appropriately cattily. "Hope Mr. Greed hasn't screwed us out of our tropical jaunt." He darted away.

Cindy smiled an agonized smile and dropped the Alka-Seltzer into the water glass. "Plop plop, fizz fizz," she said mechanically. Then she pulled a pencil from behind her ear and, looking at Dennis's application form, said, "So you don't have an up-to-date résumé."

"I don't have a résumé, period," said Dennis with a little fluttery laugh.

She smiled at him as though he'd stuck her with a spear. "Yes, ha-ha," she said. "Well, okay. Probably a good idea to make one up while I'm away. Let's get through this, okay?"

"Okay," said Dennis.

An elegant Latina woman in a red hat passed Cindy's desk carrying a Diet Coke. "Be glad to take this guy for you, Cindy," she said. "Let you catch your plane."

Cindy spread her arms protectively over Dennis's application form. "That's okay," she said with a smile like death. "No trouble. Oodles of time. Lots of cabs and everything."

The woman shrugged, and as soon as she was out of sight, Cindy pulled her hair back behind her left ear and craned her neck over Dennis's application. "Last employment listed here is—what? Lasher? What's this word?" She shoved the application toward Dennis, who raised an eyebrow and regarded it.

"Cashier," he said, nodding.

She took a swallow of the Alka-Seltzer, yanked the application back into her personal space, and, after clearing her throat, said, "Cashier? As in taking money?"

"That is correct," said Dennis with what he considered an air of cool professionalism. He smiled.

She kept one hand around the glass of Alka-Seltzer and regarded the application for a moment, as if suddenly disconcerted by it. When at last she raised her head, she said, "The date you have down for that job is 1979." She poised the pencil over the application, as if preparing to make an alteration to this figure. "What is the correct date?"

"The correct date is 1979," said Dennis, reddening.

Cindy dropped the pencil, looked at him, took another swig of Alka-Seltzer, then picked up the pencil again. She had just opened her mouth to say something, when a balding man in a blue suit walked by and said, "Still here, Cindy?"

"*Yes! Yes,* I'm still here! Tell *everyone* I'm still here!" She waved her arms at him, and he ran away.

Cindy pressed the bridge of her nose with her thumb and forefinger, then checked her watch and looked back at Dennis. "You haven't had a job since 1979."

Dennis shook his head. "Not exactly, no."

"What have you been doing since you were"—she regarded Dennis's birthdate and then moved her lips as she counted backward—"since you were fifteen years old?"

Dennis shifted in his seat and suddenly wished he hadn't come to this meeting in khaki pants and a Jane Siberry concert T-shirt. "Well, I've sort of functioned as an unofficial . . . well . . . not a majordomo exactly, more of a personal counselor . . . a kind of . . . um . . ." He could sense her looking at him, and started gazing at the ceiling and making spiraling motions with his right hand. "I guess I'd call myself a kind of companion-cum-physical therapist for a . . . a major theatrical impresario." Pleased with this description, he lowered his head and smiled at Cindy, who was staring at him with the exact gaze the American Indians must have used on Columbus.

"What the hell are you talking about?" she said.

Dennis flushed bright red. "I'm a member of someone's household," he said in a low voice as two people passed behind him, carrying briefcases and heading for the door. "*Sans* pay."

Cindy stared at him a moment longer, then took another swig of Alka-Seltzer and looked at her watch again. "This is an employment agency for professional persons, Mr.—Mr. Racine," she said, checking the name on Dennis's application. "Not a lot I can do for someone whose experience doesn't run beyond cash registers."

"Oh, I can't operate a cash register," he said, shaking his head.

Her shoulders slumped. "You're kidding."

"No, no. I mean, the place of business I've listed there," he said, pointing at his application, "was a head shop. You know? Like in, roach clips and stuff? Hole-in-the-wall place on Wells and North. Old Town, the seventies—that kind of place." He giggled. "I mean, we had a cash *box.*"

A portly older woman came around the corner briskly, spotted Cindy, and said, "Thought you'd have been on a plane by now!" Cindy turned and looked out the window and pretended not to have heard her.

When the portly woman had gone, Cindy turned to Dennis with the most incredibly artificial smile he had ever seen splayed across anyone's face. "Okay, Mr. Racine. I think I get the picture. We'll call you if anything comes up." She rolled her chair away from her desk and stood up.

Dennis got to his feet as well, and said, "Thank you for your time, Ms. Bassey-Esterhazy. I just want to add, though, that I think I might be good at jobs in theater-related businesses, if you have any, because of my long association with Farleigh Nock."

Cindy's grip on his hand tightened to the point of nearly crippling him. "Farleigh Nock? He's—*he's* the—" She dropped his hand and started scanning Dennis's application.

"He's the owner of the household to which I've been attached," said Dennis airily as he massaged his wounded hand. "That's correct."

Cindy shot him a reappraising look. "And he'll provide references?"

"Of course."

She yanked open the top drawer of her desk and pulled out a photocopied piece of paper. "This is my vacation itinerary," she said in a low voice, handing it to him. "Feel free to call me abroad at any time. Also, I'll be in contact with the office daily, and I have your number here on your application . . ." She made certain of this by nearly piercing the number in question with one of her saber-like fingernails. ". . . So I think we're all set, Mr. Racine. We have a number of public relations and events-management clients, and with Farleigh Nock as a reference I'm sure we can place you in a position that will meet with

your satisfaction." She smiled at him, this time almost genuinely, and said, "Now if you'll excuse me, I have a plane to
catch."

She chugged the rest of her Alka-Seltzer, moved two gigan-
tic Louis Vuitton suitcases from behind her desk, then shook
Dennis's hand again and pointed him toward the exit.

Dennis waited for the elevator in the reception area, where
the pert Japanese receptionist had just taken an application
from a young Wall Street type and was now buzzing someone
on the intercom. As the doors to the elevator slid open, Dennis
heard the receptionist say, "Cindy, you're the only one still
here. Do you have time for one more applicant?"

He could actually hear Cindy yell from her desk, "*Send 'im
on back, then call me a cab, and TELL IT TO WAIT!*"

The elevator doors rolled shut, and Dennis began his
descent.

chapter
7

Dennis arrived home from his depilatory appointment smarting with pain. Perhaps having his body hair ripped from his skin with hot wax hadn't been the best idea on the night he wanted to engage Farleigh in hot, acrobatic sex.

He flipped on the front hall light and dropped his gym bag into the quilted chair next to the door. As soon as he'd done this, Christos appeared at the other end of the hallway, wearing a lime green leotard under an apron that said HOUSEHOLD GODDESS and waving wooden spoons in both hands.

"Oh, Miss Denny," he squealed in a plantation accent, "thought you was the massuh!" He grinned. "Wait'll you wrap your yap around what I'm whippin' up tonight! Doing things with stir-fry ain't never been done before."

Dennis could barely hear him; a furious soprano was shrieking her rage over every one of the house's several, strategically placed stereo speakers. Christos was in the habit of blaring opera discs whenever Farleigh was away (it had used to be rock, till he suffered a humiliating breakup with a young grunge-rock god in a local group called Pants for Nancy; since then Christos disdainfully referred to all music later than Benjamin Britten as "jungle din").

Dennis started toward him, stiffly doffing his windbreaker. "Actually, Christos," he said, striving to be heard above the singing, "I'd kind of appreciate it if you'd vacate the premises tonight. I know Farleigh's getting a ride from that bitch assistant of his, so since you don't have to pick him up, it shouldn't be a problem for you to just, you know . . . vamoose. Go see a movie or something."

He put his hands on his hips so that the wooden spoons were pointing at Dennis like cannons. "Like hell I'm gonna do that! Why are you walking so funny?"

"I just—*ugh*—got a full body wax," he replied, depositing the windbreaker on a doorknob. "I'm a little sore, is all. Seriously, buddy, scoot. I kind of need to be alone with Farleigh tonight."

Christos cocked his eyebrows and partially turned his head. "Oh, and I'm supposed to dump forty minutes' worth of hard vegetable labor down the disposal because you're feeling a tad randy? I really don't think so. I take my orders from Farleigh, who happens to be my employer."

Dennis let his head fall back; he sighed in exasperation. "Come on, man. I won't let him go hungry. I've already ordered pizza."

"*Pizza?*" shrieked Christos. He shook his head, and his coal black hair went tumbling around his face. "When Farleigh is working, he demands healthful, *low-fat* foods, so he can stay alert. You know that perfectly well. What are you thinking? Do you know what he'd say to you if you put some slobbery old pizza in front of him when he got home?"

Dennis stripped off his T-shirt. His flesh was now tinged a dark tanning-parlor rose, except where bright red welts had sprung up in homage to the departed body hair. "He'd probably thank me," he said to Christos as he dropped the shirt onto an empty knee-high vase. "He may ask for that macrobiotic stuff, but that doesn't mean he looks forward to it."

"I'm still not gonna go against orders, and you can just pick up those clothes yourself, young master Dee."

Dennis stepped into the adjoining bathroom and took a jar

of moisturizing lotion from the medicine cabinet. "Christos, I'm not trying to get you to disobey orders," he said. "I'm just asking for a favor. I need a little time with Farleigh alone, that's all. I *need* it."

He started rubbing the luxuriously cold lotion into his smarting chest. A moment later, Christos peered around the doorjamb. "Things not going well, is that it?"

Dennis grimaced and continued applying lotion. "I didn't say that."

"Didn't have to." Christos slung his back into the door frame and leaned against it. "Now that I think about it, there *have* been fewer fireworks than usual between you two."

"That's stupid. Get out of here. I need my privacy."

Christos crossed his arms. "In fact, every time I bring you boys dinner, I seem to find you sitting in complete silence. Used to be I'd listen at the door beforehand, in case I was interrupting anything important. Haven't had to do that in a long time."

Dennis felt his face redden. "If you're going to stay here, make yourself useful. I had my back waxed, too." He handed the lotion to Christos, who set the wooden spoons on the toilet tank to free up his hands.

As he worked the lotion into Dennis's smarting back, he said, "Hell, happened to me, too, you know. I was Farleigh's hunka hunka burnin' love once, 'member. Sun rose and set on me. Then one day, it seemed like overnight, I woke up in a suddenly strange house with this man who kept *staring* at me like I was someone he'd invited to a party the night before and he couldn't understand why I was still there."

"Oh, shit," Dennis croaked, and he buried his face in his hands.

Christos kneaded his shoulders with his strong, wide fingers. "Aw, come on. You're not me, and my story's not your story. Look," he added, giving Dennis's neck a squeeze, "I'll do you this favor, this *once*." He wiped the excess lotion onto his apron and began untying it. "But you owe me, okay, girlfriend?"

They looked at each other's reflections in the mirror. "Deal," said Dennis. "Thanks, sweetie."

"And if Farleigh gets all purple in the face about the pizza, well . . . you know." He picked up the wooden spoons and shook them at Dennis in warning. "I'm gonna send him back your way to wreak his terrible revenge."

Dennis nodded, sniffed back the beginnings of a sob, and smiled gratefully at Christos. "You can turn off the music before you go. Who is that, anyway? Janis Joplin's great-grandmother?"

Christos scoffed at him. "Birgit Nilsson in *Tosca*, you Philistine! Although the principle is the same: a bitch you don't mess with."

Dennis nodded. "Well, I'm sure she would've been my next guess."

Christos clicked his tongue at him, then traipsed away. For some moments afterward, Dennis appraised his torso in the mirror. Then he stripped down to his boxer briefs and gave the rest of him the once-over.

Not bad; he was as smooth and as taut as a stealth bomber. He'd lube up with a little Johnson's baby oil later, the better to catch the candlelight. And the better to hide the big red welts.

As for the pain of lovemaking, of having Farleigh skimming and scraping his bulk across Dennis's recently tortured skin, well, he'd just have to endure that, wouldn't he? And if he lost control and screamed—

Hell. Maybe Farleigh *liked* screaming.

Tonight, he thought, could very well be the start of a whole new phase in their life together.

chapter
8

Fortunately, all the lights in the house were controlled by dimmer switches. In five short minutes Dennis had every room in the place looking as though it were powered by a fat man on an Exercycle.

Up in the bedroom, he pulled back the covers and sprinkled a few drops of an off-brand musk oil he'd been given some years before and never worn. Farleigh disliked scents of any kind, but the tiny dribbles of essence Dennis now let spill on the sheets weren't even enough to intrude on his conscious mind. His unconscious mind, though!—now, *that* might just be turned on.

He then popped a spearmint Lifesaver into his mouth, slipped back downstairs, and turned on the stereo. He dug out the most romantic CD he knew: Sarah Vaughan's eponymous 1955 album, where she gently croons her way through "Jim," "September Song," and "Embraceable You," backed only by the sparest and most muted of trios.

The mood was set to his satisfaction, so he took two champagne flutes from the crystal cabinet and put them in the freezer, to chill them in preparation for their first gust of Bollinger. He then filled the crystal ice bucket, placed it on the kitchen counter, and sighed nervously.

What else? What else was there to do? *Think!*

He checked himself in the hallway mirror one last time. He hadn't really dressed the part of seducer; after all, he wanted Farleigh to think that this particular event was an eleventh-hour thing, a thrown-together celebration of his encouraging interview with Cindy Bassey-Esterhazy. So he'd left on his worn khakis, but put on a crisp white oxford shirt, so that his newly bronzed, newly smooth chest would peek out suggestively. Now, however, he decided against showing so much skin; it was too blatant a come-on—Farleigh wasn't stupid. Fingers flying, he fastened every button but the topmost. Then he mussed his hair a bit, lest he look too enticingly groomed. He must seduce without the *appearance* of seducing—without letting Farleigh *know* he was being seduced.

It was a challenge, this. How do you act unknowingly sexual with someone you've been sleeping with for a decade and a half? Who knows your whole repertoire of lovemaking gestures as well as you do? If not better?

He was just musing on this when the lock in the door began to turn.

Slooowly.

One dull tumble after the next.

A bad sign; Farleigh moved this deliberately only when achingly tired.

And sure enough, when the door swung open ("swung" being altogether too active a term for the way it arced listlessly across the floor), Farleigh stood revealed, a hunched, baggy-eyed figure, brow knotted with tension.

He stepped inside and dropped his briefcase the way a prisoner would drop a ball and chain. "What's with the lights?" he asked.

Dennis skipped over to him and hugged him fiercely; he smelled sour, and his neck was cold with stale sweat. "Hi, babe!" Dennis cooed, ignoring the inquest into the lights. "I'm so happy to see you! Got great news!"

"Tell me over dinner," Farleigh said as he gently, but

firmly, disentangled himself from Dennis's arms. "I'm half famished. Where's Christos? Tell him I'm ready to eat."

Dennis smiled brightly through his fear. "Um—honey? I gave Christos the night off."

Farleigh paused, then took a great deal of air into his lungs, and let it out slowly. He regarded Dennis without a trace of affection and said, "Now, what made you go and do a thing like that?"

Dennis reached out to take his hand, then thought better of it and just patted his shoulder. "I wanted to be alone with you tonight," he said. Before Farleigh could get any ideas about being manipulated, he hurried on: "I ordered us a pizza, to celebrate. 'Cause I went to an employment agency today, and they—"

"You got a job?" Farleigh asked as he removed his tie.

"Not yet. I haven't really got the kind of experience that gets a job immediately. But my agent, Cindy Bassey-Esterhazy" —and here he produced Cindy's business card from his pants pocket, to quell the dubious look that had crept into Farleigh's eyes—"she says she's sure she can get me a job. And a *good* one."

Farleigh examined the business card, and seemed somewhat appeased. "Well," he said, one eyebrow arched. "Glad to hear it."

Dennis put his first gambit immediately into motion. He sidled up to Farleigh and gave his ear a nibble. " 'Course, I need a big favor from *you* to make it happen."

Farleigh stiffened. In a voice encrusted with ice, he asked, "And what exactly would that be?"

A car to get to the office? A new wardrobe of Italian power suits? Dennis could only imagine what Farleigh was expecting to hear. He gleefully shattered these expectations by whispering, "A reference."

Farleigh's head spun around like a desk globe. "A *what*?"

"A *reference*, honey!" Dennis tweaked his love handles. "Cindy says my connection to you is what's going to get me placed somewhere exciting. So will you do it? For me? If someone calls and asks what kind of employee I am, will you give me the benefit of the doubt and tell them nice things?" He gazed imploringly into Farleigh's eyes.

Farleigh didn't bother to disguise his astonishment. To have the boy he'd showered with diamonds and gold, reduced to pleading with him for a kind word to a stranger! Maybe he suddenly felt a little ashamed of himself; all Dennis knew for certain was that he melted. He actually returned Dennis's hug and said, "Now, why wouldn't I do that? Everything I know about you tells me you'll be a marvelous employee!" He leaned back and said, "After all, you've always done everything I've asked you to."

"And always will," Dennis growled provocatively. Overcome with grateful relief, Farleigh craned his neck forward for a kiss; after one taste of Dennis's mouth, he said, "Mmm, spearmint," and moved in for more.

But Dennis bit him lightly on the lip and said, "Oh, no you don't! I have champagne chilling and a pizza on the way!" He sauntered down the hallway to the kitchen, gesturing for Farleigh to follow him. "We're going to have a little celebration of my first step on the road to financial independence. And because I owe it all to you—because I owe *everything* to you—I even bought the champers myself!"

Farleigh followed, slowly shaking his head, as if to ask, Who *is* this creature?

It was all going so well that Dennis didn't even mind Farleigh dialing the lights up to their full intensity the moment he entered the kitchen. Dennis produced the chilled flutes from the freezer, pulled the bottle from the fridge, removed its wire cage, and twisted its neck so that the cork was released with a barely audible hiss.

He then filled both flutes, handed one to Farleigh, and lifted his own to eye level. "To Farleigh Nock," he said, "my mentor, my friend . . ." He paused wickedly here, before delivering the final tribute, a tribute that could not be contested—not here, not now. ". . . my lover."

Farleigh balked only a moment; less than a moment. A shard of a moment. But he then drank to the sentiments expressed with no small amount of gusto.

Victory, victory, victory was in the air.

Farleigh even reached out to hold Dennis's hand, but just before contact could be made, Dennis pulled away and snapped his fingers. "Almost forgot," he said, fetching the champagne bucket from its place near the sink. "Don't want it to get warm, now, do we?" He plunked the enormous bucket between Farleigh and him, and stuck the Bollinger into it, twisting it to embed it firmly in the ice.

Then he stood back and folded his hands around his flute, a safe distance from Farleigh's reach. He mustn't let Farleigh touch him . . . not until he was absolutely dying to. Which wouldn't be long, if he kept putting him off like this.

To show Farleigh that he wasn't completely self-obsessed, Dennis now leaned forward and, twirling his flute suggestively between his forefingers, said, "But enough about me; let's hear about the *real* success in the family. How went casting today?"

Farleigh actually smiled (how long had it been since Farleigh had just plain *smiled*?) and said, "Oh, not badly, I suppose." Not badly! He'd walked through the door tonight like Napoleon after Moscow. "The male lead's cast, the ingenue's cast, but the leading lady . . . oh, honey." (Honey! He called Dennis *honey*!) "Don't know what it is about high melodrama, but even Stanislavskians end up playing it like drag queens."

Dennis laughed at this. "I don't know much about the play," he confessed. "What's it called? *Lady Something-or-Other's Whatchamagig*? Tell me the plot." He put his elbows on the kitchen counter and lolled his head back, expectantly.

Farleigh chucked with delight. This was what Dennis should have been doing all along—what he'd done when he first met Farleigh: been the dizzy, worshipful face at the door at the end of a hard day . . . the doting boy toy who could amuse in one moment and be instructed the next. Make Farleigh feel like both Desired Daddy and Sage Professor. "Play's called *Lady Windermere's Fan*, you dumb blonde!" Farleigh said now, affectionately. He reached over to pinch Dennis's nipple; Dennis decided to allow it. Only as a tease. "Oscar Wilde. About a world-roaming, free-thinking woman who returns to see the respectable daughter she left behind—a daughter who has no idea that the scandalous new arrival is actually her mother."

Dennis raised his eyebrows. "Well, it does sound a bit Charles Busch, doesn't it?"

"Everything to you sounds like Charles Busch." He stared briefly into space. "Tell the truth, I think if he walked in today, I'd *hire* Charles Busch. But I have to hold out; somewhere out there is an actress who can pull off this character without descending to camp or resorting to histrionics."

"Well, here's to finding her," Dennis said, refilling his glass and raising it anew.

They toasted the elusive actress, then stared at each other for a happy, lusty moment.

The doorbell rang.

"That'll be the pizza," said Dennis gaily. He put down his flute and headed out of the kitchen. "Be right back."

Farleigh called after him. *"How'd you get Christos to agree to pizza on one of my low-fat nights?"*

Dennis called back, *"Deep down, he knows what's best for you. And so do I."*

He raced down the hallway and flung open the door, not daring to breathe lest it not be Lonnie.

But it was indeed Lonnie. Although at first Dennis almost didn't recognize him. He was wearing an open windbreaker, black Converse high-tops, tattered cutoffs, a baseball cap (backward)—and nothing else. His skin was the color of medium-rare prime rib, and a polite wedge of auburn chest hairs perched atop his pecs like an owl. He winked at Dennis. "Pizza, sir?"

"*Sir?*" Dennis repeated, almost choking. "What's with this *look?*"

Lonnie whispered, "You said Farleigh likes 'em young. Well, this is what kids wear these days. Except usually more of it." He flashed a grin at Dennis, who felt suddenly very old.

"Never mind," he said, closing the door behind his friend. "It's not like you're going to have it on for very long, or anything. Okay, give me the pizza and I'll be right back."

Lonnie handed him the enormous cardboard box, and Dennis trotted back to the kitchen, where Farleigh was waiting patiently, running his fingers around the rim of the flute.

Dennis slid the pie onto the counter and said, "Honey, you

got some singles for a tip? Our delivery boy deserves them for being so cute."

Farleigh's eyes lit up. He immediately stood erect and started pawing through his pockets. "Singles, huh? No problem," he said, and as he searched for them, he trundled out into the hallway to give them to the boy himself—as Dennis knew he would.

Dennis followed him all the way down the corridor, which suddenly seemed the length of a standard Olympic field. Everything depended on the next few moments.

Suddenly Farleigh stopped short. Dennis allowed himself to bump him. "*Far*leigh," he said, "what's—what's the—" He peeked over Farleigh's shoulder, and there was Lonnie by the door, his mouth agape, naked as a sheared lamb. He'd even doffed the baseball cap.

"What's going on here?" Dennis asked, in a very real imitation of alarm.

Lonnie didn't take his eyes off Farleigh. "Oh, hey, man, who's this?" he drawled.

"My lover!" Dennis retorted. "Who are you to ask who he is? What *is* the meaning of this?" He was feeling a bit like a melodramatic actress himself, all of a sudden.

Lonnie started grabbing his clothes from the floor, balling them into his crotch. "Sorry, man, I thought you were—like, *alone*, and that we—that you wanted us to—*you* know, man . . ."

"I certainly don't," said Dennis in his most affronted Victorian-lady tones. "I left you for not thirty seconds, to go get change, and—"

Lonnie held a finger up. "Oh, hey," he said, "way huge misunderstanding. I, like, thought you said you were gonna go get *changed*—like into a bathrobe or somethin'." He reached behind him, his hand searching for the doorknob.

"Why would I do that?" Dennis fairly shrieked.

Lonnie found the door and pulled it open. "Sorry, man, but I thought—you know, our eyes met for a sec, an' I thought maybe—you know—maybe you liked me, and—" He kicked his shoes out the door and then slipped through it after them, still clutching his clothes to his groin. "Look, it was just wishful thinking. You're very fuckable, is all." He pulled the door shut from the other side. His parting words were, "Please don't tell my boss about this."

Dennis looked at Farleigh, who had gone blood red; he was still staring at the door, as if he might catch an after-image of the departed delivery boy, like the ghost that remained when you turned off an antique TV set.

"*Well*," said Dennis, in what he hoped sounded like good-humored relief. "Must be hard to get good help these days!"

Farleigh turned to look at him; his breathing was labored. Exactly the effect the naked Lonnie had been designed to have on him. "You get hit on by these young kids often?" he asked Dennis, almost hoarsely.

Dennis shrugged. "Who pays attention? Let's forget about it. Pizza's getting cold."

He started back to the kitchen, but Farleigh grabbed his shoulder and held him in place. "My irresistible little love monkey," he said playfully, and he drew Dennis to him. Dennis allowed himself to be ensnared in Farleigh's arms; Farleigh kissed him on the ear. "You know what? I *like* my pizza cold."

He led Dennis to the stairway, and they began to climb toward the bedroom. Dennis, delirious with the thoroughness of his victory, allowed himself to relax and prepare his mind for carnal pleasures.

But in all of Dennis's planning and plotting, the one thing he hadn't counted on was a guest appearance by rogue Fate. Near the top stair, Farleigh tripped on something, fell heavily down to the landing, and broke his foot. He demanded to see what he had slipped on, and when Dennis, after a panicked search, at last produced the offending item from the far side of the landing, it turned out to be a roll of Lifesavers. Spearmint Lifesavers.

Dennis spent the rest of the evening in a hospital waiting room, watching CNN with the glassy-eyed families of other emergency room inpatients. Whenever he asked the admitting nurse if he could see Farleigh, she told him that Farleigh insisted he was too ill and upset to see anyone. Anyone at all.

chapter
9

Dennis started work four days later.

With the mood Farleigh was in (his ankle entombed in a cast and his now inaccessible instep itching worse than ever), it had seemed wise not to wait for Cindy Bassey-Esterhazy to return from her vacation, but to find some sort of employment immediately. And when Dennis saw the HELP WANTED sign in the window of the Newtown Copy Shop, he'd thought, Hell, anyone can run a copy machine.

So he applied. Fortunately, the manager of the shop turned out to be a slight, mustachioed little man whom Dennis would've recognized as gay from a distance of half a mile. Dennis decided at once that his best shot at being hired was to flirt with him outrageously. (At one point the manager asked, "Have you had any experience?" and Dennis throatily replied, "Don't I look it?"—at which the manager suffered a short coughing fit.)

So after a firm and rather too-lengthy handshake, Dennis was hired. He was to start the next morning, because even though it was Friday, it was the first of the month, and thus the beginning of a pay period. The manager—Todd by name—

liked to keep things tidy that way. Todd ended by saying he'd
be there to show Dennis the ropes.

But Dennis had arrived at eight-thirty sharp, and now it
was ten, and there was no Todd in sight. He'd introduced himself to the only other employee on the premises, a tall woman
named Anna who wore bell-bottom jeans and a flowered blouse.
Anna had been completely unfazed by his sudden appearance
as her colleague, and was now busy chattering away to him as
she colored strands of her long blond hair with a purple water-
color marker.

"I had this wild dream last night," she said. "It's really personal, but I feel like I can tell you. Maybe we knew each other
in a past life or something." She wrapped her tongue around
her cheek and dyed a swatch of hair near her temple with two
swift strokes. "It was, like, World War Two, okay? And I'm in a
concentration camp, but all the other internees are animals.
Two of each, like in the ark? Except there's no other human
being; just, like, *me*. And we get marched to this gas chamber,
and I'm so sad, because I'm dying like *alone*, and I'm the only
species that has to do that. What do you think it means?"

Dennis checked the clock again, and willed Todd to appear.
He had no intention of helping Anna interpret her dreams.

A fresh-faced college student came up to the counter to pay
for a half-hour's work on one of the shop's bank of Macintosh
computers. Anna put down the purple marker and rang up the
charge, then took the student's money and sent her on her way.

"You speak Spanish?" she asked as she picked up the
marker and resumed highlighting some locks at the back of her
head. "I learned in school, but, like, my boyfriend? He's Mex-
ican. And he says I speak Spanish with a Dutch accent. Like,
I'm not Dutch, okay? I've never even met anyone Dutch, I'm
pretty sure. So, like, how can I speak Spanish with a Dutch
accent?"

"Listen," said Dennis a bit impatiently, "isn't Todd supposed to be here?"

"Oh, Todd," Anna said gravely, as if this were a terrible
secret. "Todd never comes in till noon on Fridays." She put
her forefinger to her lips and said, "Sssh!"

Dennis glanced again at the clock and sighed. He was becoming increasingly aware of the frightening array of imposing, iron lung-sized machines that filled the room behind him. None of them looked a thing like the polite little copy machine he'd remembered from the back office at his father's furniture store—the kind of machine even a kid could operate. In fact, he *had* operated it as a kid; he'd used it to make copies of the centerfolds of the office stash of *Playboy* magazines, which Dennis's father had caught him doing once. "Not a word to Mom, from either of us, eh?" he'd said genially, and patted Dennis on the back. Dennis didn't dare tell him he only wanted to copy the nude models so he could take them into an empty office and draw exciting new swimsuit designs onto them.

Anna had finished coloring her hair; it looked like a floor mop someone had used on spilled ink. She was shaking her head dry now. "In my therapy group," she said, "there's this woman who has a birthmark that takes up almost half her face. And *nobody ever talks about it!*" She fluffed her hair above her shoulders. "I mean, it's clear that all her problems come from having a birthmark covering half her face, but everyone sits there politely and, like, *listens* to her while she goes on about how it's because her dad committed suicide when she was fourteen that her life's such a mess. And I just want to go, you know, lady, you're disfigured—like, how important is *that?* But if I did, everyone would be really down on me and, like, maybe even kick me out?" She stopped fluffing her hair and looked deeply into Dennis's eyes. "So, I'm, like, trying to help her by every time I go in there, just staring at her birthmark as soon as I sit down and not stopping till it's time to go. I just stare harder and harder, and sometimes I touch my own cheek where her birthmark is. And I know she's gotta know I'm staring at her birthmark, because—like—*duh.* But I have to, 'cause I care so much for her, you know? She's my sister."

"You're in the same therapy group as your sister?" Dennis asked, not quite believing it. "Is that wise?"

She started spinning around on her stool. "Not my, like, *sister* sister," she said merrily. "My, you know . . . my *feminist* sister."

Another Macintosh user came up to pay his bill, and Dennis offered to conduct this transaction—his first since arriving at the store. Anna guided him through the first part of this, then faded into the background behind him; at one point he thought he heard her mutter something like, "My life is shit," but he was too busy waiting on his customer to respond.

When he was free again, he turned and found her again on her stool, but facing away from him. Her back was shaking; she must be either laughing or crying.

He approached her, but stopped short of actually touching her. "Anna?" he said. "You okay?"

She swept her hair from her face and could see that her cheeks were wet with tears. She let a breathy sigh escape her, then said, "Today, okay, I just *cannot* deal." And she grabbed her purse and fled the store.

Dennis now found himself alone behind the counter of the Newtown Copy Shop, where he had been employed for just shy of two hours.

He swallowed his first panic attack, then tried to assess the situation rationally. It was the middle of a workday morning, and it therefore seemed unlikely that there'd be a rush of customers till at least lunchtime. There were only three more people here at all, every one of them working on the Macintoshes, and they seemed to know what they were doing. So maybe, just maybe, Dennis could get by till Todd wandered in.

This shaky confidence lasted until a quarter to eleven, when one of the Macintosh users called out to him that her printer had a paper jam.

"What?" Dennis asked.

She appeared exasperated, rolled her chair away from the computer, and pointed at a kind of beige box with cables running out of it. "The *printer's* jammed," she said with excessively precise elocution.

Dennis was dizzy with confusion and helplessness. "So—I should, what . . . call someone, or—"

The woman rolled her eyes. "Hell, *I* can fix it, if you say it's okay."

"Oh, sure—go ahead. Do."

"You guys just usually don't let customers touch the printer, is all."

"We have a new policy," he said, a little too giddily. "Customers may now touch the printer to their heart's content." He laughed, and was immediately appalled by his behavior.

The woman rolled her chair over to the printer and with great authority began disassembling it.

Dennis was just about to collapse into his chair with relief when a young, handsome, dark-haired man in a business suit appeared before him and thumped his briefcase onto the counter. "Morning," he said with almost military peremptoriness. "I have a rush job that I need finished no later than three this afternoon."

Dennis leapt to his feet, propelled more by terror than a desire to be of service. "Uh-huh," he said.

The man opened his briefcase and produced a collection of typeset pages and graph charts, which he spread across the counter before Dennis. "These are to be offset printed and collated into a booklet. Double-sided pages, spiral bound. That is, unless by some odd chance you do perfect binding?"

"Everything we do here is perfect," Dennis said because he thought he ought to.

The man grinned attractively. "Well! Pleasant surprise. Anyway, the pages are enumerated, so there's no excuse for a mixup in order. As for the cover, I want the following on Bristol stock, you understand?" He produced a mounted piece of artwork from the pile, pulled pack the waxlike paper that covered it, and showed it to Dennis; it was a colorful logo reading WYMARK, INC. "This is the original, okay?" the businessman said. "So be careful with it. It's camera-ready, so you can just take it and center it at the top of the cover page. And this," he continued, producing a slick picture of the Earth rendered in Day-Glo colors, "should be centered directly beneath it. I know you've got the capability to scan images here, so it should be no problem. Okay?"

"Huh?" said Dennis, completely lost.

But the businessman apparently heard this as "*Uh*-huh," because he smiled and said, "Wymark has an account here, so you shouldn't need a deposit. My name's Scott Pittman. Call me if you have any questions at all." He clamped shut his briefcase (Coach, Dennis noticed) and said, "I'd get started, if I were

you. You're going to need every spare second." Then he nodded good morning and strode out.

Dennis looked at the ungainly mass of paper that was sitting
before him. What the hell was he supposed to do with it?

From behind the bank of Macintoshes there came a sudden
yelp; then the woman who had been taking apart the printer
leapt into the aisle, holding her hand as though a bee had stung
it. "The goddamn thing shocked me!" she barked.

Dennis pretended not to have heard her and, trying to be
the very picture of brisk efficiency, he took the Wymark, Inc.
logo and trotted over to a machine at the back of the shop.

"Hey! Don't ignore me, asshole! The printer *shocked* me!"

Dennis, running on sheer animal fear, put the logo board
under what looked like the lid of a certain machine, and
pressed several buttons. Whatever it did, it'd give him precious
time to consider how to handle the snarling shock victim, who
was even now storming toward the counter, growing more in-
cendiary with each step.

The machine came to life, moving a part of it that Dennis
hadn't considered might move, and producing a grinding, tearing sort of sound, which, when it had retreated to its starting
position, Dennis discovered had come from the Wymark, Inc.
logo board, now a mass of ribbony strips.

"*God damn it, I want attention!*" the wounded customer was
shrieking. The two others were now leaning out of their cubi-
cles, staring at her . . . and at him.

Dennis knew there was only one thing left to do. He turned
to her and said, "I'm new here. Let me grab our policy book
from the office, and I'll be right back."

"*Screw your policy book!*" the woman screamed at him. "*I've
been shocked!*"

Dennis ducked into the tiny office behind the equipment
room and found the desk at which Todd had sat during yesterday's interview (had it only been yesterday? It seemed an ice
age had passed). Fortunately, he found his application and all
his employment forms still sitting atop Todd's desk, awaiting
processing. He took them, folded them into quarters, and
slipped them into his back pocket.

Then, feeling reasonably certain that he'd just wiped the place clean of any traceable evidence of his identity, he slipped out the back door into the parking lot, jumped into the Saab convertible, and zoomed away from the Newtown Copy Shop, never to return.

chapter
10

His next job was not quite as long-lived as his first.
As a counter-clerk trainee at the Coffee Brakes, a
drive-up gourmet coffee service, Dennis managed to
spill a not quite scalding Decaf Latte Lite Supremo with Vanilla
Booster right into the outstretched hand of the Wilmette matron who had ordered it. She sat in her Cadillac Allanté screaming lawsuit until the manager placated her first by offering her
free product for an entire year, then by firing Dennis, who was
only too glad to go. As he doffed his apron and departed, he
could hear the manager negotiating with the matron over the
replacement of the latte-warped Allanté upholstery; and while
Dennis thought that the establishment had done more than
enough in the way of atonement, the number of cars he found
outside, backed up in the stalled Coffee Brakes service line to
the point of snaking around the corner, told him that the Wilmette matron had quite a lot of bargaining power, and un-
doubtedly knew it.

His next job was a lengthier affair: three days, all told, by
the end of which he felt qualified for a gold watch—or would
have, had he not been forcibly ejected from the premises.

The position was inventory clerk at the Colebay Rock Salt Company, in which capacity he was required to log in deliveries of road salt to the company's hangar-sized stockroom, match up the invoices with purchase orders, sign the whole package, and send it on up to Accounting. An idiot could have done the job. But it was so spectacularly dull that Dennis, forbidden books or magazines even during the most arid, activity-free stretches, found himself resorting to any kind of distraction to preserve his sanity—such as counting the panes of glass in the ceiling. Or charting, with his desk stopwatch, the exact rate by which the stockroom clock was slow (it lost one minute every nine hours, he calculated).

Or, fatefully, examining the blue-jeaned derriere of one Xavier Ybarba, a loading-dock worker of no more than twenty-two years and a twenty-seven-inch waist. Xavier's charms were not so evident that he would suspect himself of being visually ravished by a coworker, Dennis thought, and yet so bored was Dennis that this ravishment began to inch toward the realm of the great carnal obsessions of epic poetry, and even Xavier Ybarba—married, with a baby girl not six months old—could not remain unaware of it. Nor, apparently, resist it; as who *could* resist being looked at as though he were the first course in the most sumptuous dinner ever served?

Dennis and Xavier were discovered in Storage Aisle 12 by the office manager, Annetta Clarke, who took one look at them standing there with their pants around their ankles and their cocks in each other's hands, and with a devastating air of imperturbability asked if either of them had seen the foreman, Mr. Vasquez; after learning that they hadn't, she returned to her desk, sat her ample bottom in her chair, and immediately dialed Human Resources.

Dennis was escorted from the company's facility by armed security guards whose smirks were as big as their holsters. He didn't know what had happened to Xavier . . . and, now that he'd had his way with him, he didn't particularly care.

It being late in the day, the only thing left to do was go home. Farleigh, however, was under the impression that Dennis had been gainfully employed since his first morning at the Newtown Copy Shop; Dennis hadn't dared tell him any different.

So Dennis called Christos and asked if Farleigh was at home. Christos said he was still at the theater, so Dennis felt it safe to return.

When he walked in, he caught Christos kneeling in the living room wearing nothing more than his HOUSEHOLD GODDESS apron, while another soprano wailed desperately over the stereo. Sweat was running down his broad, hairy chest like tributaries of some steamy river, and he lip-synched the Italian lyrics with his eyes clenched shut. He held his dust mop away from him as though it were a weapon. Dust motes were everywhere.

Suddenly, Christos executed an anguished, Martha Graham wave of his arms, which brought him face to face with Dennis. He shrieked, dropped the dust mop, and sprang over to the stereo, which he unceremoniously turned off.

Dennis doffed his jacket and shook his head. "Oh, come on, Christos," he said. "Not like it's the first time I've caught you doing your diva thing."

"That is not the *point*, palomino," the burly manservant said, his nostrils flaring. "The shattering of one's fantasy is unwelcome no matter how many times it occurs. My God! How'd you like it if *you* were caught up in pretending to be Renata Tebaldi singing Madama Butterfly's suicide aria, only to have someone throw up a mirror so you know you're just a dull domestic shirking her duties? You should've called first!"

Dennis sauntered down the hallway. "I did. Why'd you think I asked if Farleigh was home?"

"I thought you just wanted to know where to reach him."

"Nah." He entered the kitchen, flung open a cabinet, and pulled out a jar of peanut butter and some pretzels. He proceeded to dip the latter into the former and munch away.

Christos strode after him. "Don't tell me you got axed again," he said.

"Yup. Axed to leave," he chuckled. He never tired of this little pun, and there had been plenty of opportunity to get tired of it, given the way his life was going.

Christos got a damp dishrag and stood next to Dennis so that he could wipe up the pretzel crumbs at the same time he offered advice.

"How's your money holding out?" he asked.

Dennis shrugged. "Well, not great. I mean, I'm used to spending everything I get." He wiped a thread of peanut butter from his chin and grabbed another pretzel. "I've stopped doing that, of course, but I've still got old bills from Field's, Neiman-Marcus, Mark Shale, Tiffany—all those charge accounts, you know." He let a dollop of peanut butter fall on the far side of the counter so that the aproned Christos would have to bend over to wipe it up, revealing those deliciously furry buttocks of his. No one wore body hair better than Christos. On him it looked like filigree, or the swirls and arabesques on a Mideastern mosque.

As he dutifully wiped away (gingerly lifting one foot as he leaned into the task), the housekeeper said, "You haven't got around to pawning your jewelry, have you?"

Dennis cast an appalled look in his direction. "Never! My God. What a thing to say!"

"Well," said Christos matter-of-factly as he rinsed the dishtowel under the tap, "that's what *I* had to resort to before I finally got Farleigh to take me on as his houseboy. I was down to just my gold cuff links and my diamond earring, no shit." He wrung out the towel and stood at the ready for further crumbs. "Fortunately, he bought the house in Mykonos that same summer, so my bilingual abilities clinched the deal, and after I was hired I was able to get most of the stuff he'd given me back out of hock. But it was scary for a while. And then, of course, there was the stuff he just *took* back."

Dennis's heart sank. "What—what do you mean—*took* . . ."

"*Took* back," said Christos, his eyes fogging over with memory. "A diamond tennis bracelet; a gold Rolex; anything he'd ever just handed me, as opposed to gift wrapping, he claimed was only a loaner, and wasn't it too bad I hadn't realized that, but shit happens." He shrugged.

An awful thought seized Dennis's mind. "Some of that stuff . . . some of that stuff he gave to *me*."

"*Lent* to you, sweetie. You finished eating, or am I holding this towel for nothing?"

Dennis shoved all the food aside. "Christos, you mean to tell me, I waltzed in here wearing all this jewelry Farleigh once gave *you*, and you've actually been *nice* to me all these years?"

He made a face and snapped the towel at him. "Oh, come on! What was I supposed to do, blame you? Besides, I *liked* you. You treated me like one of the family."

Dennis shook his head. "I can't believe this. It's a nightmare."

Christos opened his arms and enfolded him in a big bear hug; Dennis could feel the damp dishtowel at the base of his neck. When they came out of the hug, Christos said, "I told you before, my story isn't your story. You want to keep Farleigh, you *fight* to keep him, you hear? Truth is, I didn't want him so much anymore; when I said that our relationship ran its course, I meant from both sides. But you, you made him happier than anybody, and if he still makes you happy, don't you give up. Okay?"

Despite being sensually distracted by Christos's soothingly large, downy, musk-smelling chest, Dennis's mind was feverishly at work. He kissed Christos on the cheek and said, "Thanks, you're right. I'll do that. Love you, honey."

"So you *say*," said Christos provocatively. He'd never made a secret of his attraction to Dennis, and Dennis, of course, was perpetually hot for Christos. But he knew instinctively that while Farleigh might forgive an occasional affair, he'd never forgive one quite this close to home.

Dennis said nothing, but smiled affectionately and ran a finger down Christos's sweaty chest. "You're too big a mess to flirt," he said. "Go take a swim or something."

"Yuck," Christos replied, tossing the dishrag into the sink. "You seen the pool lately? Algae Disneyland." He picked up the feather duster he'd left on the table and said, "I get reamed for missing a spot on the banister, but the fucking pool boy gets away with bloody green murder. Go figure."

Dennis knew Christos wanted to dish the other, part-time help he was forced to endure on Farleigh's behalf, but Dennis, who ordinarily would've loved this type of thing, was too restless to stay and listen. He tweaked Christos's nipple, then scooted up to his dressing room. He dumped everything out of his gym bag, then took his entire jewelry box, stuffed it inside, and zipped it up. It was just past three o'clock. He'd have plenty of time to get to a bank and open a safe-deposit box.

chapter
11

Over the next few days, Farleigh took an occasional, per-plexed glance at Dennis's naked wrist, throat, and right earlobe, but said nothing about the sudden absence of gemstones and precious metals there. Having at long last found his leading lady, he had begun rehearsals, and was therefore too distracted by busyness to spare much wonderment at the new, un-adorned Dennis. And when he did find time to speak with his os-tensible lover, his subject was invariably the great difficulty he had getting around with a busted foot, and the painful, itchy misery endured by his walled-up instep. Which made Dennis more than content to just stay the hell out of his way . . . and having his imaginary job to go to every day made doing so all the easier.

He was running very low on funds, but despite this he re-fused even to consider going after another nonprofessional job. The only reason he'd done so in the first place was that he'd expected Cindy Bassey-Esterhazy to rescue him at any moment with a glamorous, high-profile, high-salary career. But he'd heard nothing from "his agent," as he liked to call her, since their initial meeting.

In something close to desperation, he dug out her vacation itinerary, plopped down on the chaise longue in his changing room, and placed a call on his private line to her hotel in Bermuda. He really couldn't afford it, but he didn't dare use one of Farleigh's lines; Farleigh might think he was trying to sneak it past him. And he'd be absolutely right.

He crossed his foot over his knee and tugged at the toe of his sweat sock for the duration of several odd-sounding rings; then a man with a musical baritone answered and made his connection for him.

"Hello?" said someone who sounded very unlike Cindy Bassey-Esterhazy.

"I'm—I'm sorry," he said, thinking he might have been connected to the wrong room. He uncrossed his legs and sat up. "I'm sorry, I'm looking for—is this Cindy?"

"That would be me." There was languor in this voice, as if its owner was swinging in a hammock. Maybe she was; Dennis could hear the gentle breaking of the surf.

"Cindy, hi," he said brightly, trying to disguise how taken aback he was. "It's . . . it's Dennis Racine."

"Who?"

"Dennis Racine. In Chicago." Silence. "One of your, uh, whatever you call them." He waved his free hand in the air. "Your people. I met you just before you left." Even stonier silence. "I'm Farleigh Nock's . . . uh, associate."

A breathy sigh. "Uh-huh."

Dennis looked at the receiver a moment. "This is Cindy *Bassey-Esterhazy*, right?"

"Yes. Why are you calling me, please?"

He inhaled sharply. "Well, you *said* I could. You gave me your itinerary." He actually held the document in question up to the phone, as though she might see it. "You told me you'd be in touch with your office on a daily basis . . ." (Dennis thought he heard a laugh burble across the line.) ". . . and that you'd work on finding me a jo—a position."

Either there was static on the line, or Cindy Bassey-Esterhazy clicked her tongue. "Yes, well, I was a little overly optimistic about that, wasn't I?"

Dennis frowned. "But I couldn't know that! If someone tells
me she's going t—"

"*For Christ's sake, kid, I'm on vacation,*" she hissed. "I'll call
you when I get *back.*"

Dennis found himself listening to a dial tone.

He replaced the receiver in the cradle, a trifle shaken. Apparently, the tropical sun had dissipated all of Cindy Bassey-
Esterhazy's considerable ambition as though it were just
another layer of morning haze. And it was still a full week before
her scheduled return.

And here was Dennis, without a job. Worse: without a job
while pretending otherwise to Farleigh. So he couldn't exactly
ask him for a few hundred bucks to help him get by. (Not that
a few hundred bucks would have as much as kept him in skin-
care products.)

He lay back on the chaise and folded his arms across his
chest sternly. There was only one course of action left to take.
First, he had to admit to himself that he was unemployable, and
end this stupid charade. Second, he must turn his efforts back
to solving his real problem: Farleigh's sudden disenchantment
with him. Since Dennis clearly couldn't support himself, it was
all the more imperative that he get back in Farleigh's good
graces; his place in Farleigh's will was now not only desirable,
it was downright necessary for his survival.

But in order to get back in Farleigh's good graces, he had
to figure out what had caused his fall from favor in the first
place. Christos was no help there; although he'd been through
roughly the same ordeal, all he had to say about it was "Gosh,
it was weird the way Farleigh changed overnight." It wasn't like
Christos to wonder why this had happened; he was more reac-
tive than analytical. But if Dennis was going to pass safely
through this sudden cold front, he'd have to figure out what
had brought it on.

Could it really have been something as prosaic—and as
insurmountable—as his age? That had been his initial fear, but
since then he'd been spending his days at the gym under the
drill-sergeant eye of Fatima Howitzer, and had shed a good deal
of the fat around his midsection, not to mention adding an

equal or greater amount of bulk to his overall musculature. The tanning parlor added the finishing touch. He was looking increasingly like the golden-haired beach boy he'd been at eighteen . . . well, maybe twenty-six. (He couldn't expect *miracles*.) Now when he caught sight of himself in the mirror, he liked what he saw. In fact, he was spending an increasing amount of time in front of mirrors. And if he could re-seduce himself, wouldn't Farleigh be as likely to swoon—or at least sway?

Of course, there was always the possibility that Farleigh's sudden disdain for him had a more sinister cause. What that might be, he couldn't imagine.

Unless, of course, it was someone new. Someone younger. Someone *really* eighteen.

But who? Dennis knew everyone on Farleigh's staff; they were all at least thirty. He'd already taken the trouble to check out the cast of characters of *Lady Windermere's Fan* . . . no role there for a male ingenue, so it couldn't be that Farleigh had hired himself some sweet little actor boy. And except for the time he spent at the theater, Farleigh went nowhere without Dennis. Not even now, when things between them were so barren and tense.

Christos, who drove Farleigh to and from nearly every rehearsal, confirmed that there had been no stops anywhere, of any kind, since *Lady Windermere* began. Every night it was the same routine: straight to the theater, then straight home again, exhausted. Especially so, now that Farleigh was on crutches.

So it just wasn't possible. There couldn't be a younger man in the picture, because Farleigh had simply had no opportunity to meet one.

But if not that—and not Dennis's age—then what? *What?*

The phone rang. He rolled over, grabbed the receiver, and said "Hello" in a voice plaintive enough to wring pity from whoever heard it.

Worse luck, then; it was Paulette, sounding completely absorbed in traumas all her own. "Hey, candy ass," she said hoarsely. "War Room, forty minutes. Do-able?"

Oh, hell, thought Dennis, *last thing I need is to shovel up someone else's shit.* But he was committed to the War Room conferences. And besides, he hoped that once Paulette was through this Mr. Spanker-Goes-to-Florida scenario, he could recruit Lonnie and her to help him with his Farleigh crisis.

"Sure, do-able," he said, and he hung up without another word.

He rolled onto his back, kicked his legs in the air, and peeled off his jeans; then he hopped out of bed and pulled off his shirt. The War Room was only a fifteen-minute drive; he'd have time for a quick swim beforehand. It would clear his head, make him more alert.

He slipped out of his briefs, then trotted down the hallway naked, stopping at the linen closet to grab a towel.

Outside, at poolside, he stretched his arms high, flexed his leg muscles, and was about to dive in when he noticed the slick spread of blackening algae covering the bottom of the pool like ooze from the Exxon *Valdez.*

"*Ugh,*" he grunted, staggering back a few inches.

He turned on his heel and went immediately back inside.

Christos was right; the pool was a fucking mess. Farleigh *had* been letting the pool boy get away with it.

Or had he? Dennis couldn't actually remember having seen the pool boy lately. Maybe Farleigh had in fact fired him and just forgotten to tell Christos.

Whatever.

Within ten minutes, he was dressed again, strapped into the Saab, and on his way to the War Room—trying to coast as much of the distance as possible, since he couldn't afford to keep filling the car with gas.

chapter

12

Paulette was tucked into her waist-hugging chinchilla jacket, not because of any chill in the air (she was wearing a skirt so short that a drop in temperature would've turned her thighs blue), but because it was furry and soft and comforting. Dennis had seen her wear it only a few times before, always when she was feeling insecure or anxious—as when it had seemed Mrs. Spanker might be pregnant again, perhaps with the longed-for Spanker son (it turned out her new all-legume diet had merely halted her menstruation), or when the Spanker was being talked up as possible gubernatorial material (the talk, thankfully, never got farther than Springfield). That she was wearing the jacket again tonight signaled to Dennis that she was afraid the Spanker was once again being pulled away from her.

Lonnie had already arrived, looking dapper and damp in a sweaty T-shirt and linen trousers that must have set Dierdre Diamond back at least four hundred smackers. The T-shirt clung to his enormous, granite-hard chest as he raised his arm, slugged down a designer beer, and burped. He was beyond a doubt the perfect synthesis of Apollonian form and Dionysian function. If only he wasn't so *straight* about it.

The War Room wasn't very crowded tonight, but all the same, Paulette was fidgeting and craning her neck when Dennis came in, as though afraid she might miss him. The moment she caught sight of him, she waved him over and into a chair. "Sit, sit," she said peremptorily. "You fuckers better be right about all this," she continued, wasting no time on pleasantries. "The Spanker's goin' ahead with it. Radio show's tomorrow."

"What station?" asked Lonnie.

"What time?" Dennis added.

She kicked them both beneath the table—and with her torpedo-toed shoes, this was no coy admonition. "Never the fuck you mind," she said. "Bad enough you slobs'll prob'ly figure it all out before the end of the week, but for right now I want your promise that you'll stay away from the radio tomorrow."

Lonnie set his beer on the table and ran his hands through his hair, casting a disappointed look at Dennis. "I don't know about you, pal," he said, "but stay away from talk radio for a whole morning? Hell of a sacrifice, you know?"

Dennis nodded gravely. "Does kind of leave a big hole in my day."

She flashed her middle finger at them—a middle finger adorned with a sapphire the size of a small raspberry. "Oh, *très sarcastique*," she said in a pitiful French accent. "I'm sure I'll laugh when I get home. But seriously, thanks. Um, I—" She clearly had something more on her mind, but was having trouble verbalizing it. A waitress arrived to take Dennis's drink order, and derailed Paulette's train of thought completely.

The jukebox was playing an old Gino Vanelli tune. "Where do they *get* this crap?" Lonnie asked.

"You got a dollar?" Dennis asked after his first sip of Pimm's Cup. "I could go punch in some good stuff."

Lonnie had his hand halfway into his pocket before he knit his brow and said, "Hold on—I just remembered what you call 'good stuff.' All that Nancy Sinatra and Petula Clark crap."

"And Lesley Gore," Dennis said, nodding enthusiastically.

"They've got Lesley Gore, too. I've heard her being played here."

Lonnie made a gagging noise, then pulled out a roll of bills big enough to choke a sperm whale. Dennis almost wept at the sight; once, not all that long ago, he himself had carried a wad that size.

Lonnie flipped through the mass of twenties and fifties, saying, "I know I've got a single in here somewhere." He finally found it, gently pulled it from the roll, and handed it to Dennis. "It's yours on the condition that you play a Bruce Hornsby number, too."

Dennis winced in disdain and said, "How *muy, muy macho.*" He slid his chair from the table, got up, and trotted over to the mammoth jukebox, where his dollar bought him four selections. He chose Lesley Gore's "Sunshine, Lollipops and Rainbows," the Fifth Dimension's "Stoned Soul Picnic," and Freda Payne's "Band of Gold." Then he got bored looking for a Bruce Hornsby number and settled for Bob Seger's "Against the Wind," figuring it was pretty much the same thing.

On his way back to the table, he was distracted by the arrival of an achingly gorgeous man at the front door—a black-haired, blue-eyed dreamboat with cheekbones that could shelter small children from a rainstorm. Dennis, whose favorite hobby was "window shopping," as he called it, let himself ogle the newcomer unashamedly as he crossed the bar, so that it wasn't till he'd taken his seat again that he noticed the look of acute dismay on Paulette's face.

"Paulette?" he said. "Something the matter?"

Lonnie, who was busy ordering another beer, heard the tone of consternation in Dennis's voice, and turned to see what was wrong. "What is it, Paulette? There something else?"

Paulette put her hands over her forehead and ducked her face into her chest. "Ah, shit," she said, "I told myself I wouldn't cry. You guys aren't fucking seeing this, you understand?"

"What *is* it?" Dennis asked, scooting his stool closer to hers.

"Just—just—I'm so *nervous*," she said, slightly trembling. "What if this doesn't work, y'know? What if the Spanker pulls

up stakes and heads south?" She looked up, and her eyes were
spattered with mascara-stained tears. "I mean," she continued,
counting on her fingers as she spoke, "I got no education, I
got no skills, I got no job history, I got no—*anything.*" She threw
her hands in the air. "The Spanker walks, I might as well pack
it in. Start hooking or whatever." She immediately shook her
head and started tearing up a damp paper cocktail napkin.
"Nah, that'd kill me," she said in a low voice. "Funny, ain't it
—I'll do it for diamonds, I'll do it for plane tickets, I'll do it
for a new car—but for *money?*" She shuddered in disgust, pulled
the chinchilla jacket tighter about her, and lit up a Tiparillo.

Lonnie reached over and patted her arm. "Don't worry,
hon. Not gonna come to that. And if it does—which it won't
—we'll be here for you. Help you out financially till you get
back on your feet. Find yourself another Spanker." He grinned
his irresistible grin at her, then turned to Dennis. "Won't we,
buddy?"

Dennis wanted to tell him that instead of helping Paulette,
he'd be far more likely to join her on the Dierdre Diamond
breadline, but he bit his tongue and smiled. "Sure," he said
comfortingly.

This, of course, was all it took to send Paulette into a full-
scale sobbing fit. Lonnie and Dennis sat quietly, pulling the
soaked labels off Lonnie's empty beer bottles, waiting for her
to wind down.

Finally, Paulette sniffed herself back into composure, put
her as yet unsmoked cigar in the ashtray, and took both their
hands. "Thanks. For a couple of assholes, your shit don't stink."

Dennis knit his brow. "I can't decide if that's mixing met-
aphors or not."

She dug her nails into his hand playfully. "Just remember,
now—you promised, no radio tomorrow morning."

Lonnie crossed his heart. "Scout's honor."

Dennis shrugged in compliance. "Sure, sure. But, honestly,
Paulette, it's not like you can't trust us with the Spanker's secret
identity. You ought to know that by now."

"I do, I do," she said. "I'm just not ready yet. Humor me."

Dennis winked at her. "It's okay. As far as big revelations

go, I'm much more excited that I actually got to see Lonnie's willy last week."

Paulette feigned shock, and whirled to look at Lonnie, who blushed at this mention of his pizza boy performance. Then she whirled back on Dennis and said, "Wait a minute . . . you've seen that big old trouser snake before, haven't you? In the locker room, that first time you met."

It was Dennis's turn to blush. "Well, you might think so. But, see, I was flirting with him then, so I was too nervous to actually look."

Paulette leered at him and nudged his shoulder. "And now that you've finally had a gander, what do you think?" She cast her sparkling black eyes at Lonnie, enjoying his discomfort.

Dennis parted his lips to answer, then stopped short. "Actually," he said, looking thoroughly nonplussed, "because of the circumstances, I was *still* too nervous to look."

Paulette groaned, and Lonnie smiled broadly.

"Tell you what," Paulette said to Lonnie, "after my problem's wrapped up, we take care of Dennis's."

That's exactly what I'm counting on, Dennis thought.

chapter
13

Dennis, down to his last three hundred, was forced to beg Farleigh for a loan, subsequent to coming clean about his litany of employment disasters.

Farleigh listened politely, finished stirring his breakfast coffee, then bent down and stuck the spoon into his ankle cast in a vain attempt to scratch his instep. "What about that employment agent whose card you showed me?" he asked. "Sassy Shirley Bassey, or whoever."

"Cindy Bassey-Esterhazy," said Dennis humbly. "Actually, she flaked out on me. I called her office in desperation just now; they told me she's gone on official and indefinite leave of absence in Bermuda."

Farleigh's eyes twinkled amusedly. "Must've met a native Lothario," he said. "She'll be back. Meantime, hook up with one of the other agents at her office. She wasn't the only one who could find you a job."

This was such a simple solution to his dilemma that Dennis was amazed it hadn't occurred to him. He was likewise amazed by Farleigh's offhand manner; he'd expected fireworks.

"I'll do that," said Dennis, appropriately contrite. "But in the meantime, if—you could just see your way clear, I'd—I'd be grateful beyond—beyond anyth—" Appalling even himself, Dennis lapsed into a crying jag.

Farleigh smiled widely and, leaving the spoon wedged firmly in his cast, he leaned over and tweaked Dennis's chin. "Look at you," he said mirthfully. "Last time I saw you like this was at the end of that Disney film about the otter."

Dennis suffered an instant surge of outrage. "I've told you before," he said, his nostrils flaring, "I was *high* at the time. I wish you'd stop bringing it up."

Farleigh chuckled and resumed his manipulation of the spoon. "How about, after breakfast, I write you a check for twenty-five hundred? Average man feeds and clothes a family of four for a month on that, so it should last you till at least Friday—by which time I hope to hear of a job."

Dennis leapt from his chair and tried to fall upon Farleigh with a hug, but Farleigh pointedly lifted his coffee cup to his lips, making such a maneuver impossible.

Farleigh left for the theater shortly thereafter, and Dennis drove to the gym for his thrice-weekly workout with Fatima Howitzer. As he drove, he reflected on Farleigh's avuncular manner during the breakfast revelation; might the frosty, off-putting Farleigh of recent weeks be melting back into the loving, generous one Dennis had known for so long?

It wasn't likely; he was still a bit distant and patronizing. Dennis felt less like a lover restored to good graces than a servant handled with kind indulgence. This reminded him that Farleigh's last lover had in fact *become* his servant, which gave him a chill of fear he couldn't shake even with the convertible's top up and the heat turned to high.

He was just pulling into the gym's parking lot when his cellular phone rang. It was Lonnie.

"*I* know who the *Spanker* is," he sang.

Dennis was shocked. "You listened? After promising you wouldn't?"

"I didn't promise," he replied merrily. "I said 'Scout's honor.' Well, I was never a scout. So I felt free to tune in. Took me half the morning, spinning the A.M. dial, to find it, too."

Dennis pulled into a parking space and shifted out of gear. "You're capital-E evil, you know that?"

"Not evil, amoral. More fashionable. Anyway, turns out we're talking about Representative Patterson Dance, Republican. Ever heard of him?"

Dennis had to admit he hadn't. "Politics don't much excite me."

"Politics don't *at all* excite you. Anyhow, Dance sounded pretty patrician . . . and all this time I thought Paulette was humpin' a hick! But his voice—all veddy veddy so and so. Gonna do some digging, see what I can find out about his background."

"Whatever blows your skirt up." Dennis remained in the car, unwilling to turn off the ignition till he'd heard the full story. "So how'd it go? The show, I mean. Like we expected?"

"Well," Lonnie said, "to an extent. Like I said, the guy makes George Bush sound like a yokel, so his appeal to the common man wasn't all it could be. But after twenty minutes of open phone lines, the public had worked itself into a pretty decent pitch over the announcement. Lots of pleas for him to change his mind, stay on. And when the Spanker—'scuse me, force of habit—when Dance said he couldn't alter his decision without consulting his wife, the host called her up right then and there, just like we thought. But the bitch had been listening, and wouldn't come to the phone; had the maid say she was on another line."

"Ouch," said Dennis. "Still, makes her seem like some kind of prima donna."

"Yeah, I figure it's not all bad. Heat's really on her now. Wouldn't surprise me if the Spanker's constituents started picketing the house. Presuming it's possible to make it across the front lawn before the primary rolls around. And that the Dobermans don't get you."

"Well—hell. Guess I'll be watching the news tonight."

"That'll be a first." Lonnie snickered, and Dennis felt like slugging him. "Meantime, you keep it cool, party boy."

"You do it too, homey."

Fatima was merciless with Dennis this morning, pushing

him beyond his comfortable rep-sets routine into greater and more harrowing endeavor. He loathed it while it was going on, but he had to admit that the results were pretty great. Now that his pecs, abs, neck, and thighs were beginning to swell with granite-hard glory, he was even getting off on being watched during his workouts—as no one, it seemed, could turn away from the albino Amazon and her studly young charge for more than four seconds at a time. Fatima appeared oblivious to all the furtive glancing . . . from bitter experience, Dennis supposed. Dennis himself was aware of every slight rotation of a head, and dug it big-time.

After the workout, Fatima announced she'd be missing a few sessions the following month. "Just want to let you know in advance, Ace, so you can find a substitute partner," she said, placing her palms on her lower thighs and going low for a stretch.

"As if I'm not just gonna sleep in those days," he joked. "But what's up? You going on a trip?"

"Little one, yeah," she said, righting herself and toweling down her neck. "See, I work at a travel agency, and we occasionally get offered trips to resorts and stuff—supposedly to show us what they've got to offer so we'll book them, but really to schmooze us into it." She grinned and hung the towel around her shoulders. "It's pretty cool. Anyway, we got an offer to see this resort in the Ozarks, and I'm the only one in the office who said, 'Yeah,' so it's mine."

Dennis tossed his own sweaty towel into a bin. "But you'll be here next time, right? You're not leaving me cold just yet."

"Would I do that?" she asked, punching him in the arm. "Nah, I don't leave for another week yet."

After showering and changing, Dennis felt worlds better, and decided to go immediately to his bank and deposit Farleigh's $2,500 check. He was four blocks into the trip when he was approached at a red light by Bix Zimmer.

"HEY, DENNIS," the bum said in his habitual holler. "ANY QUARTERS TODAY, OLD BUDDY, OLD MATE?"

The light changed to green, so Dennis said, "Meet me on the other side," and proceeded to drive through the intersection and into the parking lane on the right side of the street.

As he dug through his pockets for loose change, he heard a flurry of car horns behind him, and turned to see Bix loping blindly through traffic, signaling wildly for drivers to stop for him.

"*Jesus,*" muttered Dennis, "must be out of his head." Then he reflected that, well, yes, Bix was.

Bix was panting through his greasy beard when he reached the Saab. Dennis handed him $1.75 in quarters—all he had on hand. Bix was embarrassingly grateful. "WOW, THANKS!"

"Don't mention it," said Dennis, shifting into gear again.

"HOW'S THINGS WITH FARLEIGH, MAN?"

"Oh, better, better," Dennis said, not wanting to meet Bix's eyes.

"YOU SEEM NOT SO SURE."

Damn this man and his lunatic's hypersensitivity! "Well, I said *better,* but not *great.*"

"YOU GOTTA MAYBE PUT MORE SURPRISE BACK INTO HIS LIFE," said Bix. "MAKE HIM THINK HE DON'T KNOW YOU MAYBE AS GOOD AS HE THINKS."

"Yeah, Bix, thanks. Tried that." He tapped the accelerator with his foot, willing Bix to get out of the way.

"KEEP TRYIN', OLD PAL, BIX IS ROOTIN' FOR YA!" He raised his filthy sleeve and shook it in the air. "LET LOVE RULE, RIGHT, MAN?"

"Oh, sure, let love rule." Dennis smiled and nudged the car into the traffic lane ever so gently, and Bix, instantly picking up on the hint, shuffled out of the way and onto the sidewalk, where he paused to slug a quarter into the meter Dennis had parked against.

"JUST 'CAUSE WE DI'N'T PAY WHILE WE WERE TALKIN'," he called out by way of explanation. Dennis nodded wearily and zoomed back into traffic.

While he was in line at the bank, he found himself reluctantly considering Bix's advice. When was the last time he'd done anything to surprise or delight Farleigh? When had he done anything that Farleigh couldn't have predicted with a calendar or a stopwatch? If he wanted to remain Farleigh's lover, maybe he'd better start acting like one.

At this point, anything was worth a try.

He hopped back into the Saab and drove to the theater, determined to pay an unexpected call on Farleigh during rehearsal.

That ought to shake *something* up, he felt certain.

In a final burst of inspiration, he bought a rose for a dollar from a religious fanatic on the corner of Dearborn and Balbo. He felt almost courtly, bringing this humble token to lay at the feet of his beloved.

It wasn't till he entered the timeworn lobby of the Pruitt Theater that he began to suffer anxiety. His little gesture seemed suddenly silly in this place that over the decades had seen so many huge and heroic ones. But he soldiered on, past the yellowed marble doors to the darkened lobby, on into the chill, damp, mote-mad theater itself.

He hadn't often visited Farleigh at work, as he felt uncomfortable around what Farleigh called "show people." Especially actors, who intimidated him—he suspected intentionally—with either their physical beauty or their grandness. Or, occasionally, both. There was nothing in the world more fearsome to Dennis than a cocktail party filled with self-enchanted thespians, lobbing barbs like hand grenades and declaiming like bishops.

And this was no mere party; this was their temple, their home turf. So Dennis entered anxiously, keeping to the far wall of the theater so as to proceed as unobtrusively as possible.

So focused was he on his tiptoed progress that he didn't at first notice the amazing spectacle set before him on the stage. It wasn't until he'd slipped behind a waxy pillar and looked to the front of the theater for Farleigh's silhouette amongst the smattering of visible heads that he saw that the stage itself had been bisected horizontally. A platform had been constructed, some six feet high, atop which a middle-aged actress and a blue-jeaned young actor paced around each other like a mongoose and a cobra, wielding thick, folded-back scripts and reciting Oscar Wilde's crystalline lines. Beneath the platform, on the actual stage itself, a quintet of actors, all but one male, staggered or crawled about in what appeared to be abject misery. One of them—the largest and broadest of the group—hauled a rope attached to a dirty roll of what looked like leftover carpeting. They did not speak, but uttered a continuous series of moans and low cries, the din which Dennis had heard but not registered.

Dennis watched in almost stupefied fascination at the spectacle on the stage. He also caught sight of Farleigh's unmistakably pepper-shaped head in the fourth row, nodding briskly as it conferred with another head next to it that Dennis didn't recognize.

Within a few moments, the actress—who by her imperial manner and House of Windsor enunciation Dennis assumed must be the long-sought leading lady—halted the proceedings by breaking character in a rather startling manner.

"*No,*" she had begun, her eyes fixed on the script, "*what consoles one nowadays is not repentance, but pleasure. Repentance is quite out of date. And besides, if a woman really repents, she has to go to a bad dressmaker, otherwise no one believes in her. And nothing in the world would induce me to do that.*" Then she suddenly stopped, peered over the platform with an eyebrow arched like a dagger, and continued in her own voice. "Farleigh, darling, would the peasants below perhaps consent to still their moans for the duration of this line alone? It's perhaps my favorite of the lot, and I'd like it to get a laugh." She punctuated this remark by snapping her head forward and barking, "*Sodomite.*"

Dennis felt a flourish of fear play itself up his spine, but Farleigh seemed almost bored by the woman's unheralded insult. "We've been through this, Mercedes," he said in his own, far less imposing voice.

The young actor, also unfazed by the attack, dropped into a folding chair, plunked the script into his lap, and extended himself into a luxurious stretch. The actress remained standing. "Yes, yes, I know, do forgive and humor me," she continued. "I do know that you are the genius and I a simple artisan. *Vile uranian.* But may I dare to suggest—well, I *will* dare—that a full forty minutes of vocalized anguish is more than enough to convey the point even to an audience of lower-order primates. A pause now and then, carefully placed, can only help those of us who toil away *up here.*" The way she bit off the words "*up here*" implied that not enough attention or thought had been granted the topmost players, as opposed to those below.

Before Farleigh could answer, the blue-jeaned young actor

plucked at the seam of his crotch and said, "Hey, Farleigh, I've gotta take a quick wizz."

"Fine," said Farleigh. "Ten minutes."

At that, the dozen or so persons in the theater began milling about and chatting. The actress—Mercedes—descended the platform rather hesitantly, as if she didn't quite trust its construction, then strode over to where Farleigh sat in heads-together conference with someone Dennis now thought looked oddly familiar. He stepped from behind the pillar and approached Farleigh as well, but allowed Mercedes to get there first; her habit of bursting into epithets frightened him too much to allow him to cross her.

She sailed into Farleigh's presence on a wind of righteous indignation. "So sorry to interrupt, Farleigh, dear," she said, "but alas, you never did acknowledge the value of my suggestion." Her lips twisted into a snarl. *"Pervert. Pederast."*

"This is only our second week, Mercedes," he said patiently. "We're still working things out. I assure you I'll give full weight to your—"

"Sorry, sorry, everyone," said a lumpish blonde with a clipboard who darted in front of Dennis to Farleigh's side. This was Debbie Stebbe (she insisted in vain that she be called "Deborah" to avoid the embarrassing rhyme), Farleigh's production assistant—though she magically transformed that title, behind his back, to Assistant Producer. "Farleigh," she said now, breathlessly, "I got five fans in to look at, but *not one* of them is what we've been askeen for and I think—"

Dennis, who had never remotely liked Debbie Stebbe, now braved his way into the circle and cut her off by sticking the rose between her face and Farleigh's. Both turned to look at him—with, he was appalled to see, about the same dearth of delight.

"Dennis," said Farleigh, his voice empty of feeling. "What are *you* doing here?"

"Just came to see how it's going," he replied, attempting a smile and a wink. "Brought you a flower for good luck."

Farleigh took the rose from him, looked at it blankly, and said, "I wasn't aware roses conferred good fortune."

There was a terrible silence for what seemed like an eon.

Then Debbie Stebbe continued her spiel. "I think we should return all the fans and write them a letter demandeen that the supplier account for why they couldn't meet our origina—"

"Guess I'll be going," said Dennis disgustedly, interrupting her again and turning on one heel. Among other things, he'd never been able to endure the way she dropped her g's.

"Oh, no, you don't," said Mercedes as she grabbed his arm and held him in place. "Farleigh, you beast, this young man has brought you a rose and wished you well. Don't you *dare* treat him like—like—he's one of your *actors.*" She gave Dennis's arm a squeeze. "How do you do? I'm Mercedes St. Aubyn. I'm playing Mrs. Erlynne. *Masturbator!*"

"Dennis Racine," said Dennis with a break in his voice. He'd done it again . . . walked right into an off-putting scenario devised by an actor. And this one about ten times more erratic than the usual lot! At least she *appeared* to be on his side.

When Farleigh still didn't respond, Mercedes cleared her throat and pointedly turned her back on him. Still gripping Dennis's arm, she led him over to where the blue-jeaned young actor was sipping coffee with a skinny redhead over a card table brimming with bagels and cream cheese. "Allow me to introduce you to the other principals in the company," she said. "This is Miss Judy Shapiro, who has the role of my daughter, Lady Windermere. *Temptress. Carnal filth.* And this charming gentleman is Mr. Robin Allen, who is to play her husband, and my adversary. *Whoremonger.* Do you know the play?"

"How do you do . . . how do you do . . . uh, no," said Dennis, who, thrown as he was by Mercedes's bouts of virulence, was momentarily thrown back by Robin Allen's puckish handsomeness. Another actor doing it to him. He turned to Mercedes and, wincing at what she might say in reply to him, admitted, "No, I've never read it."

"Not the divine Oscar's finest," she confided, leaning in to him, as though not wanting her opinion to be overheard. "But a fair piece of melodrama, and I'm sure we'll all do well by it, despite the rather alarming conceit inflicted on us by the Boy Wonder."

He knit his brow and said, "What 'boy wonder'?"

"Our *director*," said Mercedes, somehow managing to hiss despite the absence of any sibilants. "Surely you've heard. *Homosexualist.*" She jerked her head violently as she snarled this accusation at Dennis, then just as suddenly turned a brilliant smile on him.

He took his cue from the others and ignored the verbal assault, then nodded and tried to smile back. Suddenly he felt a hand grip his shoulder, rather too tightly. He turned and found Farleigh's eyes boring into his.

"That's enough, Mercedes," Farleigh said. "I'll see to Dennis now."

The actress shrugged. "Just as well that you see to something. *Wretched onanist.*" She threw her head back and—there was no other way to describe it—made an exit.

"Sorry you had to meet her with no warning," said Farleigh. "She suffers from Tourette's syndrome, but because she had such a sheltered upbringing, in a convent up in Toronto, the only obscenities she ever learned are these old Edwardian ones." He chuckled. "Once she's on stage, though, she's syllable-perfect . . . every line as written. We were so desperate, we decided to take a chance on the old witch." He sounded conspiratorial and happy; he'd obviously moderated his tone now that he'd gotten over the surprise of Dennis being here. But it was too late; Dennis had seen his initial reaction, and it had not been one of pleasure. He decided to waste no more time on courtship games; they were clearly hopeless.

"I thought *you* were directing this play," he said a touch too accusingly.

Farleigh stuck out his lower lip in displeasure, and, as quickly as he could in his calf-high cast, escorted Dennis back to the far wall. "I've decided to simply produce this one," he said in a low voice. His bulk, which had once seemed so soft and welcoming to Dennis, now pressed in on him like a threat.

"If you're just the producer, how come you have to be here every day?"

Farleigh folded his arms. "Go home now. I'll explain everything later."

Dennis felt tears spring to his eyes. He blinked in an effort
to hold them back. "Who's the 'boy wonder'? What's going on
here."

"I said, go *home*," Farleigh repeated, jabbing his finger at
Dennis. "I'll explain *later.*"

Dennis withered before this blast of sheer uncaring. "Yeah,
well," he muttered, "that'd be nice." Despite his best efforts, a
few hot tears escaped.

Farleigh shook his head, as if saddened by something Dennis couldn't see. Then he turned and hobbled back to the front
of the stage.

Dennis headed back to the lobby. At the door, he stopped
for one last look at the stage. There, on the lower set, he saw
the young man Farleigh had been seated next to, now striding
about issuing wild-armed directives to the actors Mercedes had
referred to as "the peasants below." Could this be the boy
wonder?

There *was* something familiar about him. That jet black
hair, shaped in a wedge like a bicycle helmet; the curve of that
neck; those brown, wiry arms; above all, the slightly spasmodic
walk, both hurried and tentative at the same time. Dennis stood,
one foot through the door, and combed through his memory,
but couldn't place where he'd seen the young man before.
Some post-show party? An awards ceremony? A fund-raiser?
Where?

He drove home, sullen and silent, and more fearful than
ever of his future.

At home, he considered unburdening himself to Christos,
but was greeted by the sound of Victoria de Los Angeles singing
"Io son l'umile ancella" at about two decibels shy of Challenger
blastoff level, and gave up immediately. He considered how
good it would feel to wash this miasma of failure and humiliation from him with a refreshing dip in the pool. But then he
recalled how clotted with algae the pool was, and instead sank
onto his bed and sulked.

Two minutes later, he shot up again.

My God. That was it. That's who the young director was.

Farleigh's goddamn pool boy!

chapter
14

Dennis paced the hallway so maniacally that Christos spat at him like a cat and fearfully scooted out of his way. He stopped every ninety seconds or so to check the clock, willing Farleigh to arrive home so he could explain this—this—*thing* he'd set in motion.

Six eighteen.

Six twenty-two.

Six twenty-five.

Six twenty-nine.

God damn him, where *was* he?

The phone rang. If it was Farleigh with an excuse . . .

It was Lonnie. "So, you watch?" he asked.

Dennis wrinkled his brow. "What?"

"You watch the news? Missed it myself—but I threw a tape on. See, I *knew* Paulette would call at exactly six o'clock, pretending she just wanted to gab, but really to prevent me scanning the tube. She knows I'm on to something, right? So she didn't want me to see her boyfriend blitzing the media."

Lonnie's conspiratorial glee was no longer infectious. "I didn't see it, no," said Dennis, carrying the cordless phone into the kitchen so he could nose through the refrigerator. When Christos saw him, he formed a crucifix with the forks he was using to debone a salmon, and said, "*Back, spawn of hell.*"

"*Turn down the stereo,*" Dennis barked back.

"What do you mean, you didn't watch?" asked Lonnie indignantly.

"Got more important things on my mind," Dennis snapped as he rummaged through the refrigerator's bottom shelf. He turned over a vat of cottage cheese to check its expiration date.

"Well, excuse me, Dr. Jonas Tightass Salk," sniffed Lonnie. "Didn't mean to interrupt your hard work saving humanity with anything so crude as dish."

"I'm not saving fucking humanity, I'm . . . you know. It's that Farleigh shit goin' on." Sometimes, when he and Lonnie butted heads, it was Lonnie who adopted a nelly attitude, and Dennis who came off as butch. Go figure.

"Still that, huh?" asked Lonnie.

"Still, and worse." The cottage cheese was two days past its freshness deadline. Dennis scowled and put it back on the shelf.

Christos appeared behind him, looming like an obelisk. "How long you figure on holding that door open?"

"Listen," said Lonnie, "if it's that bad, why don't you come over to my place, and we can watch my tape of the Spanker together? Get your mind off your troubles."

"I've got whipped cream setting in there," said Christos, tapping Dennis on the shoulder. "Made from *scratch,* thank you very much."

Dennis reached to the back of the shelf, where he thought he spotted a tub of fat-free chocolate yogurt. "My troubles are the *last* thing I want off my mind," he said to Lonnie. "Got my mad all worked up now, so this is exactly the time to confront Farleigh." The tub of yogurt turned out to be a small jar of black olives. He plunked it back on the shelf.

"If you don't close that door right now," said Christos, "I'm going to cut off your head, stuff the neck with garlic, and invite the neighbor's cat over for supper."

Dennis awarded Christos a glare so filled with ire that the daunted cook stumbled back a few paces and said, "Fine. Take whatever you want. Just be aware I can pee in your wineglass anytime I want." He went back to the salmon and sulked.

"Sounds like you're goin' at it already," said Lonnie.

Dennis, now feeling guilty for his rudeness, grabbed a lump of tinfoil and resolved to eat whatever was wrapped inside it. He shut the refrigerator door and headed back to the foyer. "That wasn't Farleigh, it was Christos playing TV mom. Don't know where Farleigh is, exactly. Which is no small part of the problem." He sat down again, peeled back the tinfoil, and to his horror found that it contained exactly three boiled russet potatoes. Not even a sprig of cilantro to brighten the prospect of eating them. Nevertheless, he grimaced, picked one up, and commenced.

"Well, listen, you want me to keep giving you updates on this Spanker thing, or what?" asked Lonnie. "I mean, if you're up to your neck in bad nastiness on your home court, maybe you don't need a bunch of bullshit from the bleachers."

"Thanks, but I *am* interested," said Dennis, suddenly humbled by the cold earthiness of the potato in his mouth. "Really, sorry I snapped. It's Farleigh I'm mad at, not you."

"Well, be mad at Farleigh, then," said Lonnie. "You've got a right. Fuck, if I didn't yell and swear and break a few lamp shades every now and then, I don't think Dierdre'd have any respect at all for me."

"Don't know if it's quite *respect* she feels when you do that," said Dennis, feeling a little shiver of arousal at the thought of Lonnie running wild through the living room, like a rogue stallion. "But anyway, listen. Gotta run. You're too much of a distraction; I need to concentrate on fanning the flames of my anger."

"Whatever," said Lonnie. "Later, then. Break a leg. Preferably Farleigh's."

They hung up, and when Dennis had finished the last of the potatoes, he balled up the tinfoil and defiantly threw it at the front door, so that Farleigh, who hated anything out of place, would not only see it but have to step over it. Blazing with merry hatred, he sat and smiled.

Christos, passing on his way to collect flowers from the window box to grace the dining room table, stopped in his tracks at the sight of the discarded tinfoil. "You stinking smear of filth," he said to Dennis. "Don't think I'm picking that up!"

"I don't care if it sits there forever," snarled Dennis. But when Christos returned with the flowers and studiously avoided looking at either Dennis or the foil as he passed, Dennis felt that perhaps his point—whatever it was—had been made, and so crept over to the tinfoil, plucked it up, and deposited it in his pocket.

Then he slumped back into his chair, hurled his arms across one another, and glared at the door. Christos, in anticipation of Farleigh's arrival, had shut off his music, so Dennis could now hear himself think.

Farleigh, he rehearsed mentally, this kind of childish subterfuge is beneath you. It's a betrayal of everything we've shared, and I'm furious with you. I expect an explanation.

Better yet: Farleigh, did you really think I wouldn't find out? Do you really think so little of me that you treat me like trash and expect me to *take* it? Kick me aside for the goddamn *pool boy* and expect me to bow out gracefully? I *demand* an explanation.

Even better: Farleigh, you scum. You slime. You smirking, sneaking, skulking seducer. You monster of ego. Give me one good reason I shouldn't break your fucking neck for what you've done. Have you no decency? Have you no shame? You're not taking one more *step* into this house until I have a *complete* explanation.

The door latch jiggled. Farleigh's key.

Followed, in short order, by Farleigh himself.

At the sight of him, Dennis's anger dissipated like steam, replaced by trepidation. He folded up in the chair, gave Farleigh a crinkly smile, and said, "Hi, sweetie. Tell me about your day?"

chapter
15

Christos had brought out the platter of poached salmon and left it for Farleigh and Dennis to serve themselves. Farleigh poured himself a glass of Sancerre and then filled one for Dennis. The candles were lit, the lights were low, and in the background Dawn Upshaw was singing Canteloube's *Songs of the Auvergne.* And Dennis was as nervous as a rabbit.

"So," said Farleigh, placing the bottle in an ice bucket and picking up his fork. He lifted a hunk of salmon to his lips and, before taking it into his mouth, glanced at Dennis and smiled.

Dennis made himself smile back. "So," he said, consciously mirroring Farleigh's maneuvers with the food.

Moments passed; Farleigh made a little grunt of pleasure, then took another forkful of salmon. "Succulent," he said in admiration.

Dennis, who wasn't the salmon lover Farleigh was, nonetheless assented. "Is that dill I taste? . . . Yup. Dill." He nodded as if this were terribly important to know, then took an embold-ening swallow of wine.

Farleigh chewed in silence, staring off to his left at something no one else could see. Dennis waited a few moments for him to snap out of it, then started gently clinking his knife against his plate to jar him back to reality.

He turned, smiled at Dennis again, and said, "*So.*"

Dennis wasn't about to start *that* again. He decided that since Farleigh was apparently not going to willingly give him the promised explanation, the best course of action was perhaps to act as though the explanation *had* been given, and then treat it as a matter of small importance.

"Pool's getting slimier every day," he said nonchalantly as he wiped his lips with his napkin. He lifted his fork again and took a stab at a wedge of radicchio in his salad. "Any plans to hire a new pool boy? Now that the old one's been promoted and everything." He popped the radicchio into his mouth and tried to keep his left leg from shaking.

Farleigh sat back and shrugged. "Suppose I ought to," he said. "No use having a pool if you can't use it."

Dennis continued eating politely, but Farleigh remained silent, staring again at something unfathomable.

Finally, Dennis, having finished off his first glass of wine and poured himself another, cleared his throat and said, "Interesting that you've got him working with you on the production. Not the usual career path for a pool boy."

Farleigh snapped his head at him and, eyes narrowed, said, "What's that supposed to mean?"

Dennis tried to shrug off the anxiety he was feeling. "It means most pool boys don't make the leap to theater. Or maybe I'm wrong. I wouldn't know, really."

"I'll have you know that Jasper"—Jasper! Dennis couldn't even remember having heard the boy's name before—"is perfectly competent for the role I've assigned him."

Dennis put down his fork and chose his words carefully. "I didn't say he wasn't. I simply said his being assigned it was the kind of thing that doesn't happen every day."

They stared at each other for what seemed a very long time. Farleigh seemed to be weighing each of Dennis's phrases for any hint of bitterness or venom. Finding none, he puffed out his cheeks and said, "Well, yes. That's true."

"Assistant director. Isn't that his title?" Dennis asked, reaching for his wine again. He noticed his hand shaking violently, and so let it drop to his fork instead.

"Yes, yes," said Farleigh, a bit testily. "What of it?"

"Well, yeah, *what* of it?" Dennis said. "I mean, something he said or did must've impressed you enough to give him this chance. I'm a little surprised you never mentioned it to me, is all. It's a very . . . I don't know. Charming story. Like an old movie, or something."

Farleigh quarter-turned his head and mumbled, "Yeah, well, you haven't exactly shown a high degree of interest in the production." Dennis suspected that Farleigh had rehearsed a much more accusatory reading of this line, but Dennis's non-confrontational manner had pulled the stinger out of it.

He took a great risk and reached over to Farleigh, putting his hand on his forearm. Farleigh, to his great relief, did not immediately remove it. "Sorry, honey," he said. "Been preoccupied with this employment thing lately. Which is, like, a whole alien culture I have to figure out. *Not that I won't,*" he added hastily. "But of *course* I'm interested in the play. I even got a copy and read it." A whopper of a lie; he knew he'd better say something quick before Farleigh called him on it. "And of course, I'm *always* interested in the pool, so . . ."

Farleigh laughed—actually laughed! Then he leaned forward, crossed his arms over the table, and said, "I never know what to make of you anymore."

Dennis, for the life of him, couldn't think of a response to that. He stared at Farleigh, his wheels spinning, until Farleigh sat back again and said, "Oh, hell. Not like there's anything wrong with it. Not like I've broken any law."

Dennis reached for his teaspoon and began to fiddle with it nervously. He didn't want to look at Farleigh.

"Thing is," said Farleigh, reaching into his cast to scratch in vain at his instep, "I was at the pool a couple weeks ago, taking notes on *Lady Windermere.* Just, you know, looking for some way I could make it—different, new. Fresh. Chicago audiences . . . well, this is a provincial town, I've always said that; so I've got to put on one of the old warhorses every other season or so just to get people to come out. But the problem I was having was, how do I make Oscar Wilde as subversive today as he was back then? I thought about modern dress, you know— setting it in the late eighties or something. But Wilde's characters aren't like Shakespeare's; they aren't far enough removed from the present day to make it workable. Then I thought, I could do it with the genders reversed. But what would that say, exactly? Besides, Cloud Forty-two's done something similar with their all-male readings of *The Women*, which makes wonderful sense, and I wouldn't want to be accused of stealing and then diluting their idea.

"Well, all the time I was sitting there on the deck chair, jotting down ideas and then rejecting them, Jasper was there, too, just quietly sweeping the bottom of the pool. And I guess I must've muttered something of my displeasure, because after he'd worked his way around to where I was, he stopped and asked what was wrong."

Farleigh stopped scratching and sat back again, putting his hands behind his head. "Well, believe it or not, I was so dispirited, I actually told him. I told my pool boy about my creative difficulties. Something I've never even discussed with you. But like I said, I was desperate and feeling it. And Jasper surprised me by sitting down, looking right into my eyes, and telling me how the idle-rich characters in Wilde's plays actually lived off the sweat and blood of a sprawling global empire filled with oppressed Third World peoples. Then he said, a really socially committed director would find a way to put that across, rather than just find a cute new way to mount another creaking revival of an ancient piece of imperialist flotsam.

"Well, I couldn't completely agree . . . I mean, to me, Wilde is anarchy, he's subversion, he's everything imperialism *isn't*. But the trappings—the economics of his time, the social structure—I mean, it was all there. I'd just never seen it before. I said as much, and then Jasper recommended I read Edward Said's *Culture and Imperialism*, specifically the analysis of Jane Austen's *Mansfield Park* and its nearly invisible subtext of systematic economic exploitation in Antigua.

"Well, what can I say? I was stunned, just *stunned* by this boy's erudition and learning. I mean—how old can he be? Nineteen? Twenty?"

"Oh, *surely* he's older than that," Dennis said desperately.

"But he has the intellect of a much older man, combined with the unique perceptions of youth. It's a very appealing mix, I tell you." He took one hand from the back of his head and used it to rub his stomach in satisfaction. "And I thought, Why am I wasting this boy on menial tasks around my swimming pool? A mind like this . . . I want it working for me!

"So we put our heads together and came up with the device of the divided stage, with the upper stage reserved for a traditional production of the play itself, and the smaller, darker bottom stage for a kind of *tableau* of East Indian peasants slaving away in rice paddies."

"I think it's *Japanese* peasants who slave away in rice paddies," said Dennis, eager to show off the minuscule fruits of his own learning.

Farleigh waved a hand at him. "Whatever. Jasper's handling the research on that. It'll be authentic, whatever it is. We'll even have a real cow. Funny, though, I'd originally hired him to direct the lower stage goings-on, in counterpoint to what was happening up top, but he had so many good ideas as the weeks passed, so many instinctive insights into line readings, blocking, propping—well, I thought I'd just let him direct the whole bang shoot. Keep my input to just producing the thing. And that's about when you walked in. Cast and crew haven't warmed up to him as yet, because the device—the East Indian counterplay—well, it still isn't pulling together like it should. I hear snickers . . . I'm sure they're ridiculing him behind his back." He shrugged. "Let 'em. It's my production, and I say Jasper gets his way."

Dennis, stupefied and angered by Farleigh's helplessness before a youthful blush and a glib tongue, now stammered out, "B-but, that East Indian thing—the whole idea—it's nothing but irony! Just a big dollop of it! You always say irony is the device you hate the most in theater, and now you're basing an entire *production* on it."

Farleigh narrowed his eyes, pursed his lips, and said, "I've only lately begun to realize how completely certain situations lend themselves to an ironic perspective."

Dennis was chilled by the tone of that remark. It was obviously supposed to *mean* something to him—but what?

He had no time to figure it out, for Christos chose this moment to stick his head into the room and call out, "Ready for dessert yet?"

Farleigh looked up mirthlessly and said, "Whatever. Why not."

He sallied forth to clear away the plates, and when he saw the dinner resting virtually uneaten on them, he cried, "What's wrong? Didn't you like the salmon?"

Farleigh took his fork and attacked his instep with renewed gusto. "Oh, sure," he said, "I liked the *salmon.*"

Dennis realized that veiled insults are the cruelest kind; instead of letting the listener hear how awful he is, he has to *infer* it. He has to *work* to be offended.

Well, enough was enough. He got up, letting his napkin fall to the floor, and without a word, went out for the night.

chapter

16

He found himself at Lonnie's place.

Lonnie, of course, lived with Dierdre Diamond, who had the entire second-topmost floor of a Gold Coast brownstone. (She craved the topmost like a fish craves water, and longed for the day its owner—a retired restaurateur who lived alone except for an aged chimpanzee—would die so she could snap it up at auction.) But it was part of Lonnie's arrangement with Dierdre—an arrangement kept secret, of course, from *tout* Chicago—that he had a separate apartment on the same floor, installed by Dierdre and connected to her own by a single door that could be locked from either side. It consisted of just four rooms: living room, bedroom, kitchenette, and bathroom—but it was enough to give Lonnie the space he felt he, as a male animal, needed. It had, as well, a separate entrance from the main apartment, so that he could come and go without Dierdre's knowledge.

Dierdre put up with this because Lonnie always came when she called. And besides, she had fourteen rooms, all meticulously, if not richly, appointed; how could he ever regard those four tiny rooms as home when all this opulence awaited him

just beyond the door? Let him stake out his boundaries like
some dog lifting its leg in its yard; she knew—or, rather, Lonnie
led her to believe she knew—that his real home was in her
realm, as her pet.

All the same, Dennis felt a little skittish and shy ringing the
doorbell to Lonnie's apartment, lest Dierdre Diamond herself
hear it through her own nearby door and step out into the
elevator vestibule to investigate. Too many of the walls separat-
ing the War Room conspirators' lives had fallen already, what
with Lonnie playing pizza boy for Farleigh and the Spanker
becoming headline news. Dennis certainly didn't want a con-
frontation with the formidable Ms. Diamond to complicate matters any further.

He needn't have worried; Lonnie answered the door in a
matter of moments, wearing nothing but denim cutoffs and a
paisley kerchief over his head. "Hey, man," he said, smiling
and slapping Dennis on the shoulder. "Change your mind
about the tape?"

Dennis tried not to be sensually distracted by Lonnie's naked torso, and so glanced down at his own fingernails. "Uh,
no," he said. "Actually, I just sort of walked out on Farleigh,
and I need a place to chill for a while." He looked up into
Lonnie's deep, amber eyes. "That okay? I only chose you 'cause
you've helped me with Farleigh before, and—well—I guess the
ugly fact is, I don't have anywhere else to go."

Lonnie gave him a commiserating hug and said, "Don't go
getting pathetic on me. Just come on in. I may have to drop
everything if Dierdre calls, but even if I do, you're welcome to
hang here. Long as you want, in fact." Was it Dennis's imagination, or did Lonnie's eyes flash when he said this?

Lonnie opened the door wide and gestured him in. He entered, feeling suddenly nervous and silly, like a kid on a first
date. If only Lonnie would put a shirt on! But no, he shut the
door, traipsed over to his refrigerator, and pulled out two Becks.
He tossed one to Dennis, who clawed at the air girlishly before
catching it.

Lonnie pried off the cap with his bare hands, something
Dennis had never been able to do. He handed his bottle back
to his host and said, "If you please. Some of us may soon be

paying for our own hand cream, and we must needs be careful."

Lonnie laughed, opened Dennis's bottle, then handed it back to him. "Right, cheers," he said, taking a first, quick gulp. Then he wiped his mouth on his wrist, and his wrist on his chest. Dennis felt a little zap of erotic energy.

"Long as you're here," Lonnie said, his eyes bright with deviltry, "come look at the tape. It's worth seeing."

They sat together on the small leather couch in Lonnie's dim-lit living room. They were uncomfortably close—at least, Dennis was uncomfortable. At this proximity he could smell Lonnie's hair, his skin, even his feet. He could also feel his warmth, oozing out from him as from a steam-heat radiator.

The TV was already on; Lonnie had been watching something loud on the Comedy Channel. Now he grabbed the remote from the arm of the couch, pressed the Play button, and let himself drop lazily back into the cushions. Dennis tried to watch the screen, but kept sneaking glances at Lonnie's gently heaving, smoothly muscled chest as it expanded and contracted with each breath. Surely no one this beautiful could be *completely* straight.

With one finger on the remote, Lonnie fast-forwarded through a block of commercials, then said, "Here it is."

A fierce-looking anchorwoman in a red Chanel jacket, with hair like something out of a Mad Max movie, eyed the camera and with extreme gravity said, "Supporters of Representative Patterson Dance have carried their protests over the Republican congressman's retirement plans right to the lawn of his Evanston home. We join our correspondent, Brock Taunton, live."

The scene cut to a generic-handsome anchorman-in-training in a beige trenchcoat, standing outside what must be the palatial digs of the politico in question. Behind him, an impressive rabble—some thirty persons, maybe more—held placards with slogans like DANCE DON'T GO and WE WON'T DANCE WITH ANYONE BUT DANCE, which Dennis thought was fairly witty.

"Thank you, Anita," said the reporter, who then dropped his voice to address the camera. "Dozens of supporters have been gathered here, just outside the grounds of Congressman Patterson Dance's home on the Evanston lakefront, for the better part of the day. All of this is in response to Dance's plans, announced this morning in a radio interview, to retire at the end of the coming term. And while potential replacements are wasting no time jockeying for his seat, many Illinoisans aren't quite ready to give him up just yet."

The screen switched to a close-up shot of an extremely obese woman with two pigtails, one on either side of her head. "He's been good for Ill'nois," she told a microphone with alarming fervor; did politics really stir up these kinds of passions? Dennis felt suddenly like he was from another planet. "He's kept jobs comin' here and inves'ments. We trust him, we don't wan' anybody else comin' in to replace him, and that's it, *period.*"

Back to the reporter. "But Dance remains firm, as he makes clear in a statement taped earlier today." Cut to Dance—slim, patrician, but rather bloodless in Dennis's eyes—standing at what appeared to be his front door, next to a largish, well-coiffed woman who must be his wife. She bore the expression of someone afraid that the cameraman might lunge over and bite her.

"I've nothing else to say," said Dance in clipped, polished, prep-school tones. "My family come first." (Ah, the singular British "come" instead of the plural American "comes," thought Dennis; how *did* this elitist become such a crowd pleaser?) He put an arm around his wife—a rather calculated move, Dennis thought—and added, "I'm grateful for the outpouring of support, but I believe this country would be a far better place if each man made his wife his chief constituent." Dennis pursed his lips and thought, Nice sound bite . . . the hypocrite.

"Mrs. Dance," said the reporter from off-camera, and the woman flinched as though a shot had been fired at her, "do you feel that you're taking your husband away from public life before he's had a chance to fully serve the state and the nation?"

She shook her head—or was it just nervous trembling?—and mouthed a few words that sounded something like, "It's better that, uh, what he, uh, we first wants for him, uh," before

looking desperately to the congressman for rescue. He, no fool,
stared steadfastly ahead.

The scene cut back to the reporter for a wrap-up, but before this could be delivered, Dennis said, "Oh, hey, there's
Paulette."

Lonnie shot up. "What? Where?"

Dennis was a bit alarmed by Lonnie's reaction; he wanted
to say, Jesus, get a life. Instead he said, "Rewind. Just to the
reporter's left, for about a half second."

Lonnie rewound the tape, then replayed the transition from
Mrs. Spanker to Anchor Wannabe in slow motion. "My God,
you're *right*," he giggled as Paulette's unmistakably ivory mop-
top tried in vain to dart out of the frame. "Couldn't stay away,
could she? That brazen hussy!"

Brazen hussy. Dennis shivered. Surely no straight man would
use a term like that! An odd feeling of erotic expectancy welled
up in his loins.

Lonnie turned off both the tape and the TV, then crossed
his legs on the couch and faced Dennis. "Gonna be pretty hard
to pretend we don't know about any of this," he said, grinning
happily. He sucked the last of the beer out of his bottle and
said, "You up for another round?"

Dennis, who had scarcely touched his, said, "No, no. I really
should be getting back. Try to thrash it out with Farleigh. But,
thanks."

Lonnie cocked his head. "Well, if you want. But I usually
find these things go better if you sleep on them first."

Dennis's head nearly jumped off his shoulders. "You
mean—like, me stay *here*?"

Lonnie shrugged. "Whatever. You're welcome to."

"Well. Okay, then!" He patted the leather cushion beneath
him. "Seems pretty comfortable."

Lonnie punched him in the arm. "Hell with that! I've got
a queen-size bed, just waiting for a queen." He laughed. "You
can have half of it." He checked his watch. "Fact, since Dierdre
hasn't called yet, I can safely assume she's drunk herself into a
coma for the night. So that means I'm free to pack it in, too."
He winked. "Follow me."

Dennis's heart was pounding as he and Lonnie made their way across the living room to the adjoining bedroom. "You can have the bathroom first," Lonnie said as he stretched lazily and scratched an armpit. "Th-that's okay," said Dennis as he began, rather demurely, to undress. "You go ahead."

While Lonnie was in the bathroom, gargling loudly, Dennis slipped out of his clothes and slid naked beneath the sheets. A few minutes later, Lonnie returned, the bathroom light spilling over his head and shoulders, as if anointing him with holy oil. He spotted Dennis tucked beneath under the covers and said, "Oh, hey, I didn't take too long in there, did I?"

"No," said Dennis. "I'm just kind of tired, so I thought I'd skip the prelims and just hit the hay."

Then Lonnie unbuttoned his cutoffs, unzipped the zipper, and let them drop to the floor.

He was wearing crimson bikini briefs.

Well, thought Dennis, almost relieved, *that* settles the issue. No gay man in America would be caught dead in crimson bikini briefs.

Lonnie jumped into bed, said, " 'Night, now," and within four minutes was snoring.

He left the bathroom light on, too, thought Dennis in distress. He's not just straight, he's *pathologically* straight.

In the morning, they had Lucky Charms in whole milk, served in mismatched ceramic bowls and eaten while standing up. Just before Dennis left, Lonnie moved aside a Chinese screen (obviously a Dierdre gift), and proudly showed Dennis a ham radio set that took up the better part of the living room. But by now Dennis had no illusions left about him, and so was able to ooh and ahh and act suitably impressed.

When Lonnie hugged him goodbye at the door, any lingering erotic charge had fizzled. It was like hugging a beautiful but rather dopey golden retriever.

chapter
17

Christos, wearing a sequined baseball cap and a rose-colored union suit, was dusting the baby grand when Dennis returned to the house.

"Where's Farleigh?" he asked.

Christos propped his feather duster on his hip and stared at him. Then—an unprecedented thing, for him—he went over to the stereo and turned it off. An unlucky soprano had to suddenly swallow a thorny coloratura.

Christos faced Dennis, and in the sudden, cavernous silence, said, "What? What was that? Did I hear you right? Did you just say, 'Christos, I apologize for being such a petulant little shrew-bitch from hell last night, please forgive me, and oh by the way where's Farleigh'? Is that what you said?"

Dennis bit his lip so he wouldn't laugh. "Yes, that's what I said."

"I thought so." Christos smirked and resumed his duties. "All right, then, I forgive you. And Farleigh went out."

"Out?" Dennis looked at his watch; it wasn't yet nine o'clock. "Where'd he go this early?"

Christos ran the feather duster up the full eight octaves. "I imagine he found someplace. Anywhere to be away from *you,* Lady Macbeth Thing."

Dennis felt the room close in on him. "I—but—*he* was the one who started . . . oh, this is ridiculous." He threw himself into a nearby chair, angry and confused.

Christos sat down and played the first bars of Beethoven's Ninth Symphony—the "death rapping at the door" measures. Then he looked up at Dennis and said, "Sorry, that's all I know of it. Wanna hear 'On the Atchison, Topeka and the Santa Fe'? It doesn't fit your mood, but at least I have it memorized. Lyrics, too."

"Thanks, but no," said Dennis. He slung one leg over the arm of the chair. "I've been stupid, haven't I? I'm just *hurling* Farleigh into the arms of that goddamn pool boy." He picked absently at a loose button on his shirt. "Not that he hadn't worked up a decent trajectory on his own."

Christos frowned. "What pool boy? *Our* pool boy?"

"Our pool boy that was," said Dennis. "Now he's the director of an innovative new production of *Lady Windermere's Fan,* featuring several additions to the original cast, including a beast of burden."

Christos put his hand over his mouth. "Oh, my God. I had no idea."

"Makes two of us."

"That son of a bitch Farleigh!"

"I know, I know."

"How am I supposed to run this household if he's spiriting away my staff and not telling me?"

Dennis narrowed his eyes, and in clipped syllables said, "I think the larger issue is his not telling *me.*"

Christos looked suddenly abashed. "I meant that, too," he said with a sheepish grin. Then he hopped off the piano bench and scuttled over to Dennis. "You must feel like hell, girl," he said soothingly, dropping to his knees and giving the seated Dennis a bear hug.

"I feel—I feel—I don't know. I don't think I'm feeling anything at all right now. No . . . defeated. That's how I'm feeling." The olive scent of Christos's skin, however, was starting to make him feel something quite different.

Christos squeezed his knee. "Don't you *dare* feel defeated. Don't you *dare* give up. Farleigh is your man, you fight for him!" Dennis cocked an eyebrow. "*You* didn't." "Yeah, well, I didn't love him, did I? Not really. Not in a fighting-for-him kind of way. Not like you do." Dennis sighed and let his head drop back against a wall. "I *wonder* if I do. Part of me is just so tired. I want to say, fuck it, and go off and live somewhere by myself."

Christos nodded impishly, then said, "And pay for it exactly how?"

"Ah. Yes." Dennis rubbed his eyes, as if awakening from a momentary dream. "The little details one forgets."

Christos got to his feet and tousled Dennis's hair. "I'll do whatever I can to help, sweetie. But you have to confide in me. I didn't know what was goin' on with you last night, or I'd have *let* you throw a screaming diva fit. You should've told me." His eyes clouded over. "I mean, bad enough I'm the third wheel here—the hired help in a house that was once half mine. If all of a sudden *you're* keeping things from me, and *Farleigh's* keepin' things from me—then, hell. I'll just walk. Don't think I won't."

Dennis sighed, and said, "It's not like that. I didn't tell you because . . . I guess because I was just so ashamed. I felt, you know—so *low*. Like, if I'd told you, and you made one smart remark or laughed at me, I'd have self-destructed."

Christos, affronted, gasped. "I'd never have done any such thing!" Dennis looked at him dubiously, and he said, "Oh, well, maybe I would've. But I wouldn't have *meant* it."

"All right," said Dennis. "I'm sorry. Friends forever?" He got up, and the two men embraced. Then, feeling a little emotional, Dennis said, "I just wish you *could* help me. But I don't know what anyone can do. I don't even have the slightest idea what *I* should do now."

"Probably read the note," said Christos matter-of-factly. When Dennis looked at him blankly, he said, "Didn't I tell you about Farleigh's note?"

Dennis slapped him on the arm. "Silly-ass cleaning lady!"

"Sorry, I got distracted by the juicy pool boy gossip! It's in the breakfast nook."

Dennis loped happily to the kitchen and found the envelope Farleigh had left for him on the sun-drenched table. He
tore it open eagerly and read the following.

Dear Dennis,

*On reflection, I can see how my recent actions may have upset you
and how I personally have been insensitive to both your position and
your feelings. I know I complained that you, too, are insensitive to my
involvement with the play, but I must remind myself that I am the more
mature of us two, and that from the start I have thus had the greater
responsibility with regard to conduct and deportment.*

"Mighty fuckin' white of you," murmured Dennis, not
meaning it as harshly as it sounded.

*But your own behavior last night was nothing short of exemplary.
Despite having ample grounds to accuse me of having violated the tacit
terms of our commitment, you took great pains to be patient and understanding, until I pushed you beyond the limits of your endurance.
Even then you didn't attack me, but most reasonably and commendably
absented yourself from my presence. My only hope now is that I haven't
driven you from my life completely, and that wherever you spent the
night was not so agreeable to you as your bed and board here with me.
Part of the reason I think I behaved towards you as I did, is that
Jasper*

"Uh-oh, here it comes . . . man the shit screens."

*is that Jasper is able to coexist with me on that artistic and intellectual
plane that I have always longed to inhabit with you. But he has not
your beauty, or your charm, and I do you both an injustice by comparing
you. Believe me when I say you have no cause to be jealous of Jasper.*

"Right," said Dennis. "And the check's in the mail, and the
injection won't hurt."

*I'm dining tonight with Jasper to discuss aspects of the production
that are not yet refined to my satisfaction. If you return in time to read*

*this note and join us, please do. Cornelia's, eight o'clock. I truly do
want you to be there.*

All my love,
Farleigh

Dennis read through the note a second time, then folded
it and put it back in the envelope. Despite the cynicism he'd
forced himself to feel while reading it, he found himself now
strangely happy. He danced out to the sitting room, where
Christos had moved on to dusting the tops of an impressive row
of books.

"Everything better now?" the housekeeper asked as he sent
a spray of motes spiraling off Gore Vidal's *Duluth.*

"Well, things aren't hopeless anymore," said Dennis as he
executed a little series of pirouettes around the room. "Farleigh
says Jasper's just business, and he doesn't have my beauty or
charm."

Christos gazed on him with such incomparable sadness that
it stopped Dennis in mid-twirl.

"You poor, naive thing," he said. "You better learn one
thing, and learn it fast: Jasper doesn't need beauty or charm.
He's got *youth.*"

chapter

18

Cornelia's was situated smack in the heart of the gay ghetto, which meant it was virtually impossible to park anywhere near the place—not only because of the popularity of the neighborhood, but because so many gorgeous boys caught Dennis's attention that he couldn't bear to keep an eye out for open spaces. The restaurant did, however, have a valet, and Dennis eventually gave up and entrusted his precious Saab (really Farleigh's, but Dennis felt it was spiritually his) to the dull-eyed attendant and scooted, late, into the restaurant.

He found the place filled with an almost exclusively male clientele, which made picking out Farleigh and Jasper somewhat difficult. Then he caught the unmistakable whinny he'd spent fifteen years hearing passed off as a laugh, and when he turned toward its source he found Farleigh seated at a table right by the window. Surely he'd seen Dennis come through the door! Why hadn't he called out?

Dennis let the slight go and approached the table. Farleigh lifted his head and said, "Oh, *there* you are." And it was only then that Jasper, who had his back to Dennis, rose from his chair and turned around.

At this close proximity Dennis could see that the former pool boy was somewhat more attractive than he'd remembered (or, rather, with his disdain for hired help, *allowed* himself to remember). Luminous skin, flushed cheeks, silken hair, long eyelashes, and clear, sparkling black eyes. Not exactly a beauty, but, as Christos had said, he had youth aplenty, and it was undeniably attractive. In fact, he seemed to *spill* youth all over the restaurant, indiscriminately . . . unlike Dennis, who had to hoard and cultivate what little youth he had left.

"I believe you've met Jasper," Farleigh said after giving Dennis a perfunctory kiss.

Dennis shook Jasper's hand—his hot, eager, *young* hand. "Yes, of course," he said.

Jasper grinned expansively. "Haven't seen me since I left the pool, though. How you been? Boy, that pool must look pretty shitty by now, huh!"

Dennis grimaced. "Well, now that you mention it."

"I keep telling Farleigh he should hire someone new, but you know how he is . . . got his nose in the production, so the rest of the world can just go screw."

They stood awkwardly for a moment, till Farleigh gestured at the chairs and said, "Let's sit, shall we?"

After they had done so, Dennis fussed over his napkin and his fork and knife for a few moments, to give himself time to consider how to react next. But before he could decide, Jasper leaned over to him and said, "We already ordered wine. I hope you don't mind."

Dennis was caught by surprise. "Uh, no. It's all right."

"See, I don't like Italian whites, just reds, and the French whites on the list aren't so impressive. What is it they've got, like, two bottles?" This last was to Farleigh, who shrugged. Jasper turned back to Dennis. "So we got a Californian. There's a Sauvignon blanc here we like a lot. We always order white here 'cause Farleigh always gets the pork tenderloin stuffed with garlic cloves." He laughed. "Then I send him home to you! I know—'Thanks a lot.'"

He and Farleigh laughed and winked at each other, and
Dennis felt for all the world like he was having his first dinner
with an old married couple. Now thoroughly abashed, he
picked up his menu and said, "Well, let me just have a look
here, since you two obviously have the bill of fare memorized."
He tried to say it offhandedly, but it came off sounding just a
touch sarcastic. Even though he had his eyes on the menu, his
peripheral vision caught Jasper and Farleigh exchanging concerned glances.

Dennis stared at the menu for a good three minutes while
his dinner companions exchanged quiet little asides about
nothing. Dennis found himself listening to each one as though
it might contain the key to untold revelations. Eventually he
realized he'd never be able to concentrate on the actual menu,
so he put it aside and tried to smile. "It all looks so good," he
said to Farleigh. "What do you recommend?"

Farleigh was about to respond when a waiter appeared with
the bottle of wine. He displayed the label to Jasper, then
opened it and poured a splash into a glass for Jasper to taste.
Jasper. *Jasper* tasting wine instead of Farleigh. In fifteen years
Dennis had never been allowed that privilege. He began to feel,
quite literally, hot under the collar. Sweat beaded up around
his temples; he had to daub his forehead with his napkin.

Jasper approved the wine, so the waiter proceeded to pour
for the table, then set the bottle in a bucket of ice and said,
"Are you ready to order?"

Dennis was about to say he wasn't when Jasper blurted out,
"We'll have an order of risotto for the table to start, thanks."

The waiter nodded and departed. Then, as though Dennis
had suddenly vanished, or had never even arrived, Jasper leaned
across the table toward Farleigh and said, "I'm still having trouble with Mercedes."

Farleigh nodded. "I know. The bitch."

"She just won't listen to me. Period. *Will not listen to me.* I'm
sure you've seen her do it. She's reading Mrs. Erlynne like she's
playing the Roman Coliseum. I'm sure they can hear her up in
Bucktown. And when I tell her to tone it down, modulate her
voice, she looks at me like I'm some kind of lower life form. I
won't even *tell* you what she's called me."

"Ignore the Tourette's," said Farleigh, "it's not her fault. But I know what she's up to." He stuck a fork down his cast and started scratching. "She disapproves of your innovation, so she's trying to ride right over it. Suck all the attention away from the East Indian tableau. And, by God, she's the kind of actress who can actually do it. But there *are* ways of handling her."

"I've tried everything," Jasper said, running his hand through his incredibly thick, heavy hair. "Really laid down the law with her. I mean, to the point of almost getting angry. But she always acts like I'm some insect no one's had the decency to kill yet. So I always end up having to come to you. One word from you, and she snaps to attention."

Farleigh made a grimace as he made one last scratch, then pulled out the fork and said, "Goddamned cast." He took a quarter-turn as he said this, but because of his lazy eye it was impossible to tell whether he'd looked at Dennis or just glanced somewhere in his vicinity. He then pulled his chair up to the table, folded his arms over his plate and said, "I was hoping you could get Mercedes to toe the line on your own, but hell, you're new at this. And to be fair, respect has to be earned, and in her eyes you haven't done that yet. I'll tell you how to handle her, if you want. Easiest thing in the world."

"Tell, tell! I've given up."

Farleigh took another swallow of wine. Dennis, sitting ignored, had nearly finished his.

"The thing to do," Farleigh said conspiratorially, "is *co-opt* her."

Jasper paused for a moment; then his face lit up as though he'd been graced by sudden enlightenment. "Of *course!*" he said, slapping his hand to his forehead.

Dennis, who had no idea what Farleigh was talking about, took the bottle from the ice bucket and refilled his glass.

"All actors are basically insecure," Farleigh continued, "and Mercedes is aging in the bargain. She's bound to have her defenses up. So If you want to achieve some kind of authority over her, it can't come from above." He gestured over his head. "It has to come from *below.*" He dropped his hand to table level.

"Flatter her, you mean," Jasper said. "Treat her like I'm her biggest fan."

"Exactly. Tell her every morning how beautiful she looks, how youthful, how majestic, whatever. And if she's too loud, say something like, 'Could I get a sense of hushed intensity on that last line? I know it's a lot to ask for, and I wouldn't ask just any actress, but I know a pro like you can do it.' "

Jasper laughed. "My God! Yes! She'd give me 'hushed intensity' just to show off!"

Farleigh nodded excitedly and started toying with a matchbook. "Exactly. Now, tomorrow, you show up with a bouquet of roses. Not too sweet, but with the kind of meaty smell older women like . . . you know what I mean? Tell her you're sorry you got off on the wrong foot with her, but that you're so in awe of her you've been afraid you'd be unable to hold your own against her will. And now that you've seen that her instincts are inevitably the right ones, you're willing to work with her and learn from her."

"She'll lap that up like cream," said Jasper with a giggle.

Dennis, bored, went back to examining his menu.

They were all able to order entrees not much later, and this was the only time Farleigh and Jasper interrupted their shop talk. It wasn't till midway through dessert that Dennis's mind, now seriously wandering, was snapped back to the chatter at hand.

"—because of goddamn Patterson Dance," said Farleigh angrily.

"What?" Dennis blurted. "What about Patterson Dance?"

Farleigh, as if noticing him for the first time in hours, refilled his wineglass (they were on their third bottle) and said, "Bastard just announced he's going to run again after all. His wife caved in under pressure and gave her consent. Which is bad news for us, 'cause he's one of those Contract With America types who's determined to abolish all arts funding." He put the bottle back into the bucket, then turned and scowled. "Thought we'd have a chance to get a moderate in his seat."

"Well, hey," said Jasper. "Maybe the guy won't win."

"Oh, he'll win, all right," growled Farleigh. "And all his comrades-in-arms will win, too. They'll just keep on winning till there's no way for young playwrights to have their work read before an audience in this town, or anywhere else. Which means, in essence, no more young playwrights. Which means I go on doing Oscar Wilde for the rest of my life. Or Shaw, or Shakespeare, or Tennessee Williams. Or if I want to get really cutting edge, Sam Shepard." He grunted in disgust.

"Uh, gee," said Dennis, his face burning with guilt. "Maybe it's not so bad. I mean—if someone's talented, you can bet he'll get noticed eventually. Like—like—" He was grasping at straws, or he wouldn't have gone on to say what he did. "—like, look at Jasper, here. No stage training, no moving up through the ranks, yet here he is. Because of sheer talent, he's directing a major show. See what I mean?"

All Dennis had wanted to do was roll back, in Farleigh's mind, the dastardliness of Patterson Dance, and thus roll back in his own mind his culpability in the matter of Dance's revived career. But he'd apparently done far, far more, because both Farleigh and Jasper were now looking at him with quite incredulous expressions on their very different faces.

Finally, Jasper, his eyes moist and his young lips almost trembling, said, "Thank you, Dennis. That's really . . . I mean, we don't even know each other, really, so it's—it's just flattering that you'd have such faith in me."

And Farleigh!—Farleigh cleared his throat and said, "Sometimes I remember why it is that I love you."

Dennis, a bit bewildered by this unintended wave of gratitude and affection, sat silently and blushed for a while. Till the meal ended, actually, and Farleigh picked up the bill.

As he drove home, he replayed the scene over and over in his head. He'd clearly scored a point with Farleigh, despite Jasper's domination of the whole evening . . . the vile little lickboot. The only discomfiting thing—the only burr beneath the saddle—was the subtext to what Farleigh had said: "Sometimes I remember why it is that I love you."

Meaning that most of the time he had no idea.

chapter
19

Having procrastinated as long as he dared, Dennis called the employment agency where he'd listed with Cindy Bassey-Esterhazy. He got another agent on the line and said, "Hi, my name's Dennis Racine. I used to be one of Cindy Bassey-Esterhazy's, uh, clients, or whatever you call them. And I understand she's not coming back, so I was hoping I could get someone else to work with. To get a job, I mean." He was sitting by the pool, sunning in the unseasonable, almost freakish warmth, and sipping a Fruitopia; he hoped his cry for help didn't sound too achingly insincere.

The agent—he sounded like a friendly, middle-aged black man—said, "Well, let's see here. I know we divided up Cindy's active files among those of us who haven't yet run off to become island princesses." Dennis heard the rustling of paper, then the agent asked, "What did you say your name was?"

"Dennis Racine. R-A-C-I-N-E."

More rustling, then a short silence. "Hmm." Another silence. "I don't know what to say. I've got the list here of who got which of Cindy's people, but I don't see your name anywhere on it. How long had you been working with Cindy?"

"Not long at all. I actually only met her the day she left on her trip."

"Ah. Well. She must've just misplaced your application in all the excitement. Tell you what. My name's Frank Franklin. Why don't you come in when you get a chance and see me? Fill out some new forms, and get your search going again."

Dennis thanked Frank Franklin, then hung up and put his head between his knees in embarrassment. He knew instinctively what had really happened. The agents had gone through Cindy Bassey-Esterhazy's file, dividing up her applicants, till they came to the thirty-one-year-old man whose last job had been manning a cash box at the age of fifteen. They'd had a laugh over that one, then dumped it in the trash. They wouldn't have known about its mitigating connection to Farleigh Nock, because Dennis hadn't revealed that till Cindy had completed the application and stuck it in a file.

Well, he couldn't go back to that agency, not now. As soon as he related his work history anew, they'd all realize he was the Cash Box Boy, and although Dennis usually relished any kind of attention, he drew the line at being the focus of an in-joke among office dweebs.

Even worse, he'd have to endure the humiliation without even wanting an actual job. He still believed his only chance at any sort of future was to restore himself to Farleigh's favor. But to do that he needed to placate Farleigh on this job issue.

There was only one thing left to try. Something he swore he'd never, ever do, even if the world should stop spinning on its axis and the mountains come tumbling down.

With a sigh he set down the empty Fruitopia bottle, sat up, sneered at the algae-encrusted pool (it had come to symbolize all his failures), and went inside to don a jacket and tie.

After all, one had to look presentable when throwing oneself on the mercy of one's family.

It was a long drive—more than an hour—from Chicago to Huntley, the small agricultural community where his brothers, Jameson and Harold Racine, ran the furniture store they'd inherited from their late father. Now, Jameson, the older of the two, boasted a bevy of young girls and was thinking of changing the name of the business from Racine & Sons to Racine &

Daughters. Last time Dennis had spoken to him (how many years ago was that?), he'd been planning to bring his eldest, Kristin, on board as soon as she finished college.

It was that kind of place. Family smeared on toast. That's why Dennis thought he could, if he prostrated himself with enough humility, get some kind of "if-when" commitment from his brothers. Nothing they might accept, God forbid—no humiliating jobs walking the sales floor—but maybe some kind of offer to do their advertising or public relations, necessitating a once- or twice-a-week visit to the store, at best. They'd eventually turn him down, of course; too expensive, and Dennis had no experience. But all he needed was to get them to consider the matter; that would hold Farleigh for a little while.

It wouldn't be easy, though. He hadn't seen either of his brothers in more than two years, and had played the haughty city sophisticate at the time. Harry had come close to throwing him out of his house.

It was mid-October, but the temperature was creeping into the eighties. Indian summer of a particularly ambitious kind. Of course, this *would* happen on the one day Dennis had decided to wear a tie. As he zipped through Huntley, keeping his eyes peeled for anyone driving anything to compare with his Saab (he childishly loved having the finest car on the road), he began to feel pangs of nostalgia at the sight of his charming childhood hometown being replaced by a succession of strip malls and video huts.

It wasn't till he'd parked at Racine & Sons and was approaching the door that he realized he should've called first. Too late . . . he was here.

As he entered, he tugged at the sleeve of his jacket, the better to reveal the Rolex he'd taken out of his safe-deposit box for the trip. He'd also brought out a diamond ring and a gold collar clasp. He didn't want his brothers thinking he actually *needed* their help.

He made his way through the showroom—still filled with the same kind of overstuffed pastels and innocuous prints he remembered from his youth—and unceremoniously stuck his head through the office door with JAMESON RACINE emblazoned on it.

Jamie was at his desk, eating from a bag of Doritos and reading a local newspaper. He looked up at Dennis and stared for a few moments, not recognizing him. And Dennis did likewise, for he could have sworn, for one brief moment, that he was seeing his late father come back to life. Jamie hadn't just taken over the old man's business; he appeared to be taking over his skin.

"Denny?" he said, Dorito crumbs tumbling from his lower lip.

"Hey, Jamie." Dennis smiled, entered, and extended his arm.

His brother rolled his chair back, got up, and shook Dennis's hand with both of his own. Then he stood back and said, "Look at you! Gettin' to be an old man."

Dennis winced—apparently visibly, because Jamie laughed and said, "Still the same vain Denny!"

Dennis poked him in the gut. "Vanity not being an issue on your end, it seems."

Jamie patted his protruding stomach. "On the contrary. This is a work of art, I'll have you know. Years of care and craft gone into it. Sit down, sit down." Dennis sat. Jamie was about to lower his own bulk into a chair when he paused and said, "Uh . . . seen Harry yet?"

Dennis shook his head no. He knew exactly what was behind Jamie's trepidation. He and Harry were engaged in an ongoing practical-joke war of some twelve years' duration. It had started innocently enough—salt in Harry's sugar bowl, erotic singing telegrams to Jamie's house on Sunday morning—quirky, irksome ways for emotionally stunted brothers to express affection. But they were a competitive duo, and the pranks had rather quickly grown spectacular, often achieving the status of legend in the town. People still talked about the homecoming game played at the local high school the year Kristin was queen; it had been Jamie's honor, as her father and a businessman of some repute, to present her and her court at halftime. But Harry forestalled that by releasing ten thousand crickets, purchased at no small expense from a bait store in Crystal Lake, into the bleachers, causing instant chaos and usurping Jamie's big moment.

This might have caused acrimony between lesser siblings,

but Jamie and Harry viewed each new prank as a challenge to be met and topped. Dennis often found himself feeling pangs of jealousy over this bizarre brotherly bond; even now, as he reassured Jamie that he was not in league with Harry in some prank against him, he almost wished he were.

But, no, this was silliness, middle-aged brothers sticking pins in each other at the end of the world. Dennis was an urbanite, an A-list homosexual, a fixture on the Chicago theater scene. He had no interest in this blighted life he'd left behind.

But for the moment he must pretend he did.

Jamie, leaning back in his chair, extended the open bag of Doritos to Dennis, who shook his head and said, "How's business?"

Jamie shrugged. " 'Bout the same as ever. New outlet mall over in Woodstock hasn't hurt us as much as we'd feared. No real competition there for us, thank God. Still, something might open up and bite us in the ass. Never know. Got Kristin on board now; she graduated summa cum . . . summa cum something from college, and we're lucky to have her. Started her out in sales, to see how she does. Gotta get new blood in the place. Wait forever for Harry to settle down and pop out some infinks. You know he broke up with that sweet little Gretchen, don't you?" Dennis nodded, although he had absolutely no recollection of any Gretchen. Jamie reached for his can of Pepsi, then snapped his fingers and said, "Shock of seein' you knocked my manners out of me. Coffee? Soda?"

Dennis said, "Sure. Diet anything would be great."

Jamie craned his neck over the intercom and said, "Kristin, honey, come see your Uncle Denny, dropped by to surprise us, and while you're at it, bring him one of them fag sodas." As soon as he'd said this, he blushed crimson, looked sheepishly at Dennis, and said, "Sorry."

Dennis laughed heartily and said, "Hey. Call it like you see it." Then he cleared his throat and said, "Actually—you just mentioned new blood. See, I was thinking maybe . . . you know, I haven't been too close to the family, an—"

Jamie interrupted him with a bark of assent. "No shit," he said, and he popped a Dorito into his mouth. "Runnin' off at fifteen'll do that. How's—what's his name? Farleigh?"

"Farleigh's fine. Sends his regards. He's busy mounting a new production of Oscar Wilde's *Lady Windermere's Fan*."

Jamie stared at him blankly. "Don't think I know that one."

Dennis bit his tongue, then continued. "Well, anyway. As you so sweetly mentioned, I am getting older. And I kind of miss the family in ways I never thought I would. And I was thinking, maybe there's a way I can—I don't know—become involved with the firm on some level." He paused a moment to let this sink in before going on to offer his advertising or P.R. skills. Jamie would then politely offer to sleep on it, and Dennis could get Farleigh off his back about the job thing for a while.

But instead of seeming uninterested, Jamie's face distorted into something unreadable and rather frightening. He looked at the Rolex on Dennis's wrist, at the diamond ring on his right hand, and went quite white. "My God, Denny," he said, and his voice was hoarse. "You don't know how many times I've tried to work up the nerve to just call and *ask* you."

"You . . . you have?" Dennis asked incredulously.

"I've got *plans*, see," he said, and suddenly he was a whirl-wind of motion, flinging open desk drawers and producing a roll of blueprints. He leaned over the desk and started unrolling it. "Knock down a few walls, build a new showroom . . . *expansion*'s the key word here."

At that moment Kristin appeared in the doorway, holding a Diet Sprite and beaming an almost hungry smile at Dennis. He suddenly remembered that from her early childhood, Kristin had always had a huge crush on him.

"Hi, Uncle Denny!" she said, setting the can of soda before him and nervously smoothing out her pink blouse and gray skirt, as though they were betraying her with their wrinkles. "I didn't know you were coming! These aren't my best work clothes or anything!"

"Kristin," said Jamie, his face now flushed red, "Uncle Denny is thinkin' about *investing* in the business, now how do you like that!"

She clasped her hands together in sheer joy. "Oh! Oh! Would you be a partner, too, like Uncle Harry?"

"A silent partner," said Jamie rather too quickly. "He still wants to live in the city, don't you, Denny? But we'd surely run everything by you, every decision. Look here." He propped open the roll of blueprints with a telephone, an ashtray, and his can of Pepsi, then, finding no other object of weight, grabbed Kristin's hand and placed it firmly on the fourth corner. He pointed at some lines on the paper that Dennis couldn't make head or tail of, and started babbling about inventory and projected volumes and market trends and all sorts of terms Dennis had hoped never to hear addressed to him during his lifetime.

In the end, he had to pack up the blueprints under his arm and promise to look them over in detail and carefully consider Jamie's proposal. It staggered him that it was he, not his brother, who wound up repeatedly saying, "I'll sleep on it."

As Jamie showed him to the door, one hand on his shoulder in an ecstasy of renewed filial affection, he asked, "So, Denny, what're you driving lately? Still got that BMW?"

"Oh, *God*, no," said Dennis. "Farleigh sold that in ninety-three. I'm driving a Saab convertible now."

Jameson whistled, and behind him Kristin cooed in awe. Then he said, "I just got myself a Chrysler New Yorker. And when I say just, I mean two days ago. Come on out and have a look at it."

"Sure, whatever," said Dennis, trying to keep the unwieldy blueprints balanced under his arm. As they exited the store, they met Harry on his way in.

"Denny?" he said, astonished. "Is that little *Denny*?"

"Where've you been?" asked Jamie, smacking him on the shoulder. "Denny and I've been havin' a *great* conversation. Tell you about it later."

"Hello, Harry," said Dennis. The roll of blueprints slipped from his arm, and he bent over to pick it up.

"Little *Denny*," said Harry, who had begun to go bald and looked at least ten years older than the last time Dennis had seen him. "To what do we owe this very great honor?" A bit sarcastically, this last.

"*Tell you later*," snapped Jamie, forestalling any comments that might offend his prospective investor. "Right now I'm walking Denny out to see my New Yorker."

"Oh," said Harry gleefully. "Let me accompany you!"

The three brothers, tailed by the ebullient Kristin, walked outside to the row of parking spaces in front of the store. Jamie looked around with increasing concern and said, "Where's my New Yorker? Kristin, did you take Daddy's New Yorker?"

"No, sir, I did not," said Kristin, alarmed at the accusation.

"Oh, *I* see it," said Harry, a musical lilt to his voice.

Jamie looked down the row of parking spaces again. "What? . . . Where?"

"Heavens—you're cold."

"What?"

"You're *cold.* I said you're *cold.*"

Jamie snapped his head toward Harry.

"Ah!" said Harry. "Now you're getting warmer!"

"*Where's my New Yorker?*" said Jamie through gritted teeth, lowering his head menacingly.

"*Colder,*" said Harry. "*Colder.*"

Jamie turned to Dennis. "I'm sorry about this, Denny. Harry can be a real—"

"Ooh, *freezing,*" interjected Harry.

Despite himself, Jamie started to grin; he turned and began scanning the immediate area. "Oh, *cold,*" said Harry with almost juvenile delight. "Sub-zero. Arctic. *Ant*arctic."

Finally, Jamie looked up. "Oh, my God," he said flatly.

"*Hot!*" cried Harry. "*Sizzling! Scalding!*"

Dennis and Kristin followed his gaze.

The brand-new New Yorker was sitting primly on the roof of Racine & Sons.

There was a terrible, suspended silence.

"How the *hell* did you get it up there?" said Jamie at last, his voice small.

Harry giggled. "Ah, now if I told you how I got it *up,* you'd know how to get it *down.*"

"You asshole. You fucking asshole." This was said without a trace of animosity . . . quite the contrary; almost with admiration. "You'll pay for this. You *asshole.*"

Dennis rolled his eyes at Kristin, who shrugged her shoulders. He winked at her, quietly crept over to his Saab, slipped into the driver's seat, and, while Jamie and Harry traded threats, sped away.

chapter
20

When he got home, Dennis dumped the blueprints in the trunk of the car and took the elevator up to the house. He could hear Christos in the kitchen, singing along with something bombastic in Italian as he prepared the evening meal. Dennis snuck down the hallway and up to his changing room, to slip out of his jacket and tie.

He found a package awaiting him there, with no return address. He opened it, and found a bottle of gold-label Veuve Clicquot with a note that said *Thank you!—Paulette.*

The gratified glow of the acknowledged Samaritan rouged his cheeks; then he got nervous and tore up the note, lest Farleigh find it and somehow be able to supernaturally infer its relation to the upward swing in Patterson Dance's destiny.

He stripped down to his boxer shorts, then went to the master bedroom, intent on a little nap before dinner. He found the bed still unmade, but didn't mind that Christos hadn't got to it yet. It reminded him of the night before, when Farleigh had at last rejoined him beneath its sheets. During rehearsals Farleigh historically took his rest on the daybed in the guest room, as though he were a monk whose concentration was most

effectively honed by asceticism. But Dennis's impromptu pany-
geric to Jasper's talent during last night's dinner at Cornelia's
had apparently so moved him that he slipped into the bed
somewhere around two in the morning (startling Dennis, who
almost conked him on the head with an ashtray) and cuddled
until late morning. It wasn't quite the sexual reconquest Dennis
had planned a few weeks earlier, but it was enough of a victory
to give him a surge of confidence. It had also inspired him to
pursue the employment trail again; he didn't want to lose the
ground he'd gained with Farleigh over laziness in that area.

He curled up in the bed and had a catnap—how long, he
couldn't quite say. But the whir of a blender was what awakened
him, which meant that Christos was still in the kitchen, so too
much time couldn't have passed.

He slipped on some khakis and a denim shirt, then rinsed
his face and went down to the kitchen to chat.

"Oh, *there* you are," trilled Christos, who today was wearing
an open-neck tuxedo shirt, electric blue Lycra biking shorts,
and flip-flops. Dennis didn't dare comment. "Little package
came for you today, by messenger."

"Saw it," said Dennis. "Already been upstairs." He yawned.
"Had a nap."

"How exhausting it must be, being you," said Christos, a
bit snappishly, and he stirred a pot filled with something that
looked oddly vegetal, but smelled anything but. "I hope me
working my cheeks off here in the kitchen didn't wake you."

Dennis pinched one of the cheeks in question. "No, but
Miss Misery Guts did," he said, tossing his head in the direction
of the kitchen speakers. "Who is this, anyway?"

"Montserrat Caballé as Aida. The 'Ritorna vincitor' aria.
She's just realizing she has to choose between her country and
her lover."

"Which one does she settle on?"

"Both, in a way."

"Good for her! Happy ending, then?"

"*Hell*, no. I just said she *chose* both. I didn't say she got them.
Her old man screws that up for her."

"Old men'll do that." Before Christos could attach any
meaning to that remark, he stuck his head over the pot and

said, "Smells delicious. What is it?" He extended a finger toward the mixture, but Christos slapped his hand with a wooden spoon.

"Key lime pie filling," he said. "In honor of Indian summer. No tasting."

Dennis shook his smarting hand. "A simple 'Don't' would've done the trick."

"I know you," said Christos, resuming his stirring. "Pain is the only admonition you understand."

"I can't *imagine* who told you that." He checked his watch. "Aren't you supposed to be picking up Farleigh about now?"

"Yes, I am," he said tersely, "but honestly, this filling hasn't set yet, and I don't dare leave it. Think you could call the theater and ask him to get a ride from Debbie tonight? Or cab it? I'd really appreciate it."

Dennis shrugged. "Hell, why don't I just go get him myself? Got nothing else to do."

Christos beamed at him. "Oh, if you'd do that for me, girlfriend, I'd do *anything* you asked in return." He bounced his eyebrows up and down suggestively.

"You'd do that anyway. But yeah, I think I'll go. I want to talk to him, so it kind of works out." He loped back upstairs, slipped into some loafers, grabbed his car keys, and took the elevator back down to the garage.

He sent the Saab careening out into the still warm dusk, feeling carefree and happy. He *did* want to talk to Farleigh, to tell him that he'd met with his brothers today, and had discussed with them the possibility of some connection with the family firm. He just wouldn't mention that the connection they desired was a fat cash investment, not a job. And if Farleigh asked for specifics . . .

Well, he'd lie.

He didn't like lying, but it was getting to the point where survival took precedence over ethics.

He parked right in front of the Pruitt, turned on the hazard lights, and dashed inside. It was five minutes past Farleigh's regular pickup time; he'd be impatient to get on the road.

In the outer lobby Dennis ran into Mercedes St. Aubyn, who was wearing an ancient mink stole with two actual mink heads still attached, peeking over her shoulder like they were preparing to ambush her breasts.

"Oh, hello, Mercedes," he said as he tried to sweep past her. "Just come to pick up Farleigh."

She grabbed his arm and brought him to a halt. "Oh, how lovely to see you again," she said. "But I'm mortified—I've forgotten your name."

"Dennis," he said, smiling as politely as possible; he was eager to be on his way.

"Dennis, of course! You're too late to see the rehearsal. Ended some time ago. I'm just awaiting my driver." Her head twitched violently. *"Epicene!"*

"Ah, well," said Dennis, not knowing how to respond to any of this.

"A shame you missed it," she said, completely ignoring his obvious desperation to be away from her. "Everything's going so swimmingly now. Really coming together."

"Great, great," said Dennis, eyeing the corridor to the office.

"Bound to be a great success, and controversial too, what with the innovations of our boy wonder."

Dennis paused long enough to note that the phrase "boy wonder" had been shorn of any trace of scorn or derision; indeed, it now sounded laudatory, almost like an honorific.

"Such a clever lad," Mercedes continued, still not deigning to release Dennis's arm. "Such depths in him! Takes one a bit of time to actually plumb them."

So, Dennis thought, Farleigh's little flattery scheme must have been an immediate success. He wondered how much butter Jasper had had to smear over the old girl's ego.

Just then an obviously hired Lincoln Town Car pulled up in front of the theater and parked behind Dennis's Saab. "Ah, there's my ride!" said Mercedes, and she released her iron grip on Dennis's biceps. "So lovely to see you again, dear." As she turned to head for the door, she barked out, *"Catamite! Gunsel!"*

Dennis rubbed his sore arm and made for the back office. When he reached it, he found Debbie Stebbe sitting before the door, as if guarding it.

She was poring over some chicken scratches in her ever present yellow notepad, with such intensity that she didn't notice Dennis until he was almost toe to toe with her.

"Hey, Debbie," he said, not wanting to sound overly friendly to her. "Farleigh ready?"

Her head snapped up; she looked at him in sheer horror. "What are *you* doeen here?"

At first Dennis thought she might have mistaken him for someone else; those glasses of hers were so thick they were almost opaque. He leaned forward so she could see him better and said, "I'm here to pick up Farleigh."

"I thought Christos was pickeen him up," she said, her voice growing more shrill. "I'm supposed to tell Christos to wait in the car!"

"Well, Christos was busy, so I came instead." He tried to squeeze past her—actually put his hand on the doorknob—when she propelled herself out of her little folding chair and blocked him. Her notepad—the precious notepad—fell noisily onto the floor.

"*You can't go in there!*" she said, more shrilly yet—almost screeching.

"Don't be ridiculous. I'm here to pick up Farleigh. We *live* together. Who exactly do you think you're protecting him from?"

She said nothing, but, gasping for breath, spread her chubby arms across the width of the door and went rigid with fear.

They stood staring at each other for a good fifteen seconds; then Dennis said, "This is absurd. Let me through."

"He's not in there," said Debbie, her voice now something of a croak.

Dennis laughed in exasperation at this obvious lie. It was ludicrous. If Farleigh wasn't in the office, why was she so insistent that he not enter it?

Realization struck him like lightning, seared him like lightning, too.

Farleigh wasn't in there alone.

He craned his neck over Debbie's shoulder, wanting to get

to the bottom of this. *"Farleigh?"* he called out. *"It's Dennis. You in there?"*

There was no reply. Dennis could almost hear Farleigh holding his breath.

A second bolt of lightning: Farleigh was in there with Jasper. With Jasper, behind a closed door, with his flunky standing sentry.

Dennis almost put this to Debbie—almost looked her in the eye and said, "He's in there with Jasper, isn't he? With orders not to disturb them for any reason." But as much as he disliked her, he didn't relish seeing the look of suicidal failure he knew would wash across her face.

Instead, his own face a mask of stony impassivity, he said, "My mistake. So sorry."

And he returned to the Saab and he drove home, where he went to bed without dinner . . . without even any key lime pie.

It took him a long time to fall asleep, and when he did, he didn't sleep well; he thrashed about in an agony of hurt and doubt until two in the morning, when he dropped off to sleep from sheer exhaustion. Then his hunger kicked in and woke him up again. He dozed only fitfully after that.

At seven-thirty, he found himself lying in bed, wide awake, staring at the ceiling and listening to the clock radio. The news was being reported. Bombings in the Middle East. Property tax hikes. Sports scores. The discovery of a planet orbiting a distant star. It all registered with equal weight to him; it was all random, unreal, a kind of Dadaist symphony of sheer sound.

At eight, he sat up, swung his legs over the side of the bed, and rubbed his eyes.

The trauma of the night before, which had loomed over him so powerfully during the night, now seemed smaller, more manageable in the white light of morning.

The first thing to do was establish whether his hunch had been on target. And that was easy enough. All he had to do was go down to breakfast.

If Farleigh greeted him with a rebuke for leaving him stranded at the theater, then followed by demanding a report on his job hunt, then Dennis would know he'd imagined the whole thing; Farleigh hadn't been in the office screwing Jasper, Debbie Stebbe's behavior had just been characteristically insane, and the whole scenario was just a product of Dennis's hair-trigger imagination.

On the other hand, if he went down to breakfast and Farleigh was charming and considerate and attentive, then he'd know he was right; that Farleigh *had* been in that office screwing Jasper, that he *had* heard Dennis outside calling his name, and that he was now trying to drown Dennis's suspicions in a deluge of sweet talk and nice-nice.

Dennis threw on a terry-cloth bathrobe and went downstairs to the kitchen.

Farleigh was seated at the breakfast nook, reading the paper. He was wearing the sweater Dennis had given him for Christmas—the one he'd said he didn't like. When he saw Dennis, he put down the paper, smiled, and said, "Morning, sunshine!" Then he lifted a pitcher and said, "Passion-orange-papaya juice?"

Dennis stared at him mutely for a few dull seconds, then turned around and went back upstairs.

He sat on the bed and called the number of the apartment the Spanker kept for Paulette. She answered sleepily. " 'Lo?"

"Hi. It's Dennis."

He heard sheets rustling; she wasn't out of bed yet. "Hiya, pal! Oh, boy, do I owe you big!"

"Well, good, 'cause I'm collecting. War Room—today. Soon as it opens."

She clicked her tongue. "Shit. Bad nastiness, huh?"

"Bad nastiness. Got to call Lonnie now. You'll be there?"

" 'Course I will. Always, for you."

He hung up and made the same request of Lonnie, who despite sounding groggier than usual, also agreed.

Then he locked the bedroom door, got back under the covers, and managed to get a few hours of real sleep at last.

chapter
21

The War Room opened its doors at three o'clock, and Paulette somehow managed to have a drink in her hand, half downed, by the time Dennis arrived at 3:04.

"Thought you said you'd be here when it opened," she said when he joined her at the table.

"My God, Paulette, they're still sweeping up," he said with a laugh.

She took a mouthful of ice along with her next swallow, and crunched on it nervously. "So, what's the big crisis? Spanker's expecting me back in an hour. And I've got, uh, some accouterments to buy before that."

A yawning waitress in a granny dress plunked a dish of peanuts between them; Dennis noted with admiration the serpent tattoo coiling up her forearm and under her sleeve; then she turned and sauntered away insouciantly.

"Wait till Lonnie gets here," he said, and he immediately started pillaging the peanuts.

Lonnie dragged himself through the door at 3:13, rubbing his reddened eyes and looking completely disheveled—still adorable, but somewhat seedier, like a Ken doll after a soak in boric acid.

"Morning, stud muffin," chirped Paulette.

Lonnie dropped onto a stool and propped his head up with both hands.

"I said, good *morning*," she repeated.

"*Mglahh*," he replied.

"This won't do," said Dennis, shaking his head. He poked Lonnie's shoulder. "Hey. *Hey*. Come on, buddy! I need you alert!"

"Journalism awards thing last night," he croaked. "Dierdre got some big gold lifetime whatever." He burped dramatically. "Don't think I've ever had that much champagne."

"Oh, what label?" asked Dennis, suddenly envious.

Lonnie ignored him. "I know I've said Dierdre can drink me under the table—but, man. Last night she did it *literally*. I woke up at four in the morning, under the buffet in the ballroom." He shivered in disgust at the memory. "Entire place was dark, and I couldn't move my legs for almost three whole minutes. Scared the fuck out of me. Tried to call for help, but nothing came out. I started to freak, till I realized that I had almost an entire mouthful of Napoleon still sitting on my tongue."

"Eww," said Paulette. "Did you swallow it?"

Dennis rapped on the table. "Ex-*cuse* me," he sang out; "this is *my* emergency, remember?"

"Take a pill," said Paulette, who then turned solicitously to Lonnie. "How's big ole Dierdre doin'?"

"Dunno," he said, running his fingers through his hair. "Wasn't home when I got there. Bed hadn't even been slept in." He puffed out his cheeks, as though he might throw up, but then sucked them in again without incident. "Ooh," he said. "I feel awful."

Paulette sat back and looked concerned. Then she snapped her fingers at the waitress, who was languishing by the cash register as if fatally ill. "Get you a little hair of the dog," she said to Lonnie. "Just the ticket."

"Now, just one minute," said Dennis tartly. "We're supposed to be here for me!"

"Oh, stop being so selfish," snapped Paulette, cupping Lonnie's limp left hand in hers. "Our friend here is in real pain!"

"*Selfish?*" Dennis said in an almost morally affronted tone. "My God, Paulette, that's the *last* thing I need to hear from *you*."

She immediately stiffened. "What's that supposed to mean?"

"Well, for Christ's sake," he said, flicking a peanut shell onto the floor. "I helped get your congressman daddy out of his career spiral, only to find out that Farleigh hates the guy's guts because of his anti-arts funding stance. So I've essentially put my relationship on the line for you—because if Farleigh ever finds out I helped you, I'm toast. Now tell me again that I'm selfish, please."

Dennis suddenly felt Lonnie kicking him sharply under the table. But it was too late for any warning; Paulette was staring at him through menacingly squinted eyes. "How," she asked flatly, "do *you* know the Spanker's stand on arts funding?"

Dennis gulped; he was well and truly busted. He turned to Lonnie for aid, but Lonnie was rubbing his nape and wincing painfully, clearly playing for pity. Dennis angrily decided to take his cowardly friend down with him. "Lonnie told me," he said.

Lonnie, recovering miraculously, whirled on him. "You *swine*."

"What?" screeched Paulette. "What's going on here?"

"Oh, for God's sake," said Dennis, laughing in disbelief and turning his palms upward. "We're all friends, here, right? Can we just agree that we're all friends?" The two others looked at him expressionlessly. "So, if we're friends, what's the big deal about us knowing that the Spanker's really Patterson Dance? You said yourself we'd probably figure it out. You *said* that."

Paulette's nostrils flared. She angrily tapped a Tiparillo out of her cigar case and lit it. "Figuring it out," she said, after taking one furious puff, "is pretty goddamn different from actively looking for it. Which, correct me if I'm wrong, is exactly what you fuckers did."

"*I* did," said Lonnie nobly. "Denny's innocent."

"*This is not a war crime*," said Dennis with as much urgency as he could muster. "We're friends! We're friends! We're friends! I'm going to keep saying it till I make you both believe it!"

Paulette puffed away at her cigar. "Well," she said at last, "fine. For now I'll forget about it. But I reserve the right to bring this up again later."

Dennis threw his hands over his head in sheer exasperation. "Yes, Madame fucking Chairwoman. May I now please address the tribunal before we move on to the fucking minutes from last month's fucking meeting or whatever?"

At this point the waitress appeared at the table and stood before them with a pencil poised over a pad. "You want something?" she asked Paulette dully.

"Well, yeah, I did when I called you over here," Paulette said with a sneer, "but in the intervening eon I changed my mind." She turned to Lonnie. "Buy your own champagne, Sherlock."

Lonnie looked at the waitress sheepishly, and, turning on his charm, said, "Coffee. Shot of rum."

The waitress grunted as though she got this request ninety times an hour, then turned and sauntered away.

"All right, then," said Dennis, determined to allow nothing else to interrupt him. "Here's the thing. Farleigh's dumping me and shagging the pool boy. Oh, and he wants me to get a job to pay my bills."

Paulette put down her Tiparillo as if she couldn't find the strength to hold it up any longer. "Shit. Oh, shit. I'm sorry. I had no idea it was this serious. I thought you just broke a nail or something." She hopped off her stool, then trotted over to Dennis on her stiletto heels and gave him a good, hard, Paloma Picasso–scented hug.

"Wow," said Lonnie, his face scrunched against his wrist. "I didn't know about the pool boy."

"Yes, well," said Dennis, smoothing out his clothes after Paulette's hug. "I wasn't sure about it, either. But there's no doubt now. He's even made the kid director of his new play."

Paulette gave him a mock shove. "Get out! You should've said something earlier!"

He shrugged. "Well, I couldn't . . . not with your situation still up in the air."

She pouted prettily. "I vewwy sowwy I caww you seffish." She pressed one of her talon-like fingernails into his chest and twisted it. "I a bad, bad giwl."

"Apology accepted," Dennis said. He was feeling a little lump in his throat. "You guys are really all the hope I have. I love you."

"We wuv you, too," said Paulette, and she hugged him again; even Lonnie lurched over to enfold them in his damp, alcoholic embrace.

When they came out of the hug, Dennis, fearing his voice might break, needed to make a brief getaway to recover his cool. "Oh, this is such a *Hallmark Hall of Fame* moment," he said. "We need some music to complete the picture. And I'm afraid only Barbra will do."

"Oh, great," said Lonnie. "Then I really *will* hurl."

"It's my crisis, I'll play Babs if I want to." Without another word he fled to the far side of the bar, where he inserted a dollar in the machine and chose "Evergreen," "Stoney End," "Enough Is Enough," and "Love Theme from the *Eyes of Laura Mars.*"

When he returned to the table, Lonnie was sipping his just delivered rum-laced coffee.

"Well, the obvious solution," said Paulette as she puffed on her cigar, "is for you to get Farleigh out of town so you can work on him alone without this pimply little distraction of his."

"Jasper doesn't have pimples," said Dennis, sitting down and shelling another peanut. "His skin's actually pretty beautiful. And anyway, Farleigh won't leave town while rehearsals are going on."

"Why not?" asked Lonnie. "You just said he's not the director. The pool boy is." He took a sip of coffee, and his eyes drooped in relief; it was as though he'd just been given a much needed elixir of life.

Dennis popped some of the shelled peanuts into his mouth, and swallowed them almost without chewing. "Yeah, yeah, but he's obsessed with this kid . . . he'd never even *think* of planning a trip right now."

"So, *you* plan it," said Paulette. She crossed her leg and started wiggling her foot; she was obviously thinking about her imminent rendezvous with the Spanker.

Dennis looked at her, angry that she was taking his problem so lightly. "I'm sorry, Paulette. I'm not following you."

"I said, *you* do it. Plan the trip, buy the tickets, give them to him as a gift."

"Ridiculous. I've never given Farleigh a gift before."

"Even better. He can't possibly refuse it, then." She checked her watch. "We done here now?"

"No, we're not done," said Dennis harshly. "The plan sounds fine, except for one thing: I'm broke."

They looked at him as though he'd just announced his affliction with leprosy.

Then, amazingly, Paulette put down her cigar and took his hand. "Okay, sweetie. You were prepared to finance my spinsterhood if push came to shove, and fair's fair, or so I hear tell. You don't have money?" She shrugged this off. "*We've* got money."

He looked at Lonnie, who was nodding in agreement. "The Dierdre Diamond fortune is at your command. At least for this one trip."

Dennis was almost reeling; the eyes of his caring friends bored into him, while in the background Barbra Streisand wailed like a banshee about how she never wanted to go down the stoney end.

Later, he would wince when he remembered the embarrassingly Dickensian thing he said next, his wit and intelligence having failed him utterly:

"Oh—oh—you've made me so happy!"

chapter

22

Well, Ace," said Fatima as she wiped the residue of her last chug of Evian from her lips, "that's it for a couple weeks. Not gonna go shirkin' your workin' while I'm gone, are you?" She snapped a sweat-damp towel at him.

He dodged it, then borrowed the bottle from her and had a swig. He gave a little appreciative gasp, then handed it back to her and said, "Actually, Fatima, I'm thinking of going away myself."

She punched him in the shoulder, much too hard. "Get out! Where?"

"Greece," he replied casually as he slipped off his weight-lifting gloves and tried to look nonchalant.

She whistled. "Way to go, Ace! That boyfriend o' yours takin' you?"

"Actually, other way 'round. That's what I wanted to talk to you ab—"

"Ooh! Ace!" she cried suddenly, doubling over. "Agck! Got a cramp!" She dropped the Evian and grabbed her leg, which almost kneed Dennis in the groin as it shot into the air. "Help me out—help me out, here!"

Dennis took Fatima's massive ivory leg in his hands. "What—what should I—"

"Stretch it out, Ace . . . come on!" She grimaced in pain.

He tried to extend the leg, but it was like trying to unbend a collapsed steel girder. "Christ," he muttered. "It's not giving!"

"*Harder,*" Fatima bellowed.

He gave her lower leg a terrific yank, with the result that she lost her balance and toppled heavily to the floor. And she didn't just topple; she flailed her arms as she went, and made a loud, long, cartoon-character noise: "*WhoaaOOAAH*"—and when she hit, "*OOOF!*"

"*Oh, my God,*" Dennis cried, clutching his face with his hands. *"Fatima, I'm so sorry!"*

She gulped down a few breaths, then said, "S'okay . . . better down here. Stretch me out *hard,* now."

He grabbed her leg anew and, while she arched her back to help him lift it, he threw his weight into the task and unbent her knee, then left her foot hanging over his shoulder and pressed down on her kneecap to straighten the leg. During the procedure she grunted and barked as though she were giving birth; but finally she said, "Oh—okay—that's okay! Oh, yeah. Oh, yeah, Ace. That's the way to do it."

This sounded so uncomfortably post-orgasmic that Dennis took a wary peek around the weight room to see if anyone had heard it. Not only had everyone done so, but the entire contingent of iron pumpers was standing in dumbfounded amazement at the scene. Dennis giggled nervously and said, "It's okay . . . she's fine."

Fatima was now sitting up and flexing her leg confidently. "Oh, Ace. You're the best. Thank you. Thank you."

No one appeared ready to turn away and resume his or her circuit training.

Dennis decided to ignore them; he crouched at Fatima's side and said, "Some partner you are. Gonna cripple yourself if you don't cripple me first."

"That's crap," she said, gingerly getting to her feet. He rose and extended an arm to help her; she accepted it with a smile. "I just pushed myself too far. I knew the risks. As for you— you're lookin' better already from when we started. We're a good team, Ace. Hate to lose the time while we're away."

He stole a quick glance around the training room again; the spectators had begun to drift back to their various stations. Dennis then lowered his voice and said, "Actually, Fatima, I don't have my tickets yet. I was hoping you could get them for me this afternoon."

"Tickets to Greece? In one afternoon?" She picked up her towel and her now emptied Evian bottle, then faced him and said, "You know you'll have to pay a premium—like, thousands of bananas."

He shrugged. "Well, you know. That's okay." And it was; he'd gotten a virtual blank check from both Paulette, who had the Spanker around her little finger now, and Lonnie, whose reappearance had caused floods of delight in Dierdre Diamond (she'd spent the entire post-awards night at a police station, trying to organize a search party for him).

Fatima shook her head in amazement. "Must be nice, bein' rich."

He blushed and said, "Come on, I'm not rich."

"Hell you're not!" She started for the locker rooms. "What do you call it, then?"

He scampered after her. "Well . . . wealthy."

She yelped a laugh. "What's the difference, Ace?"

He grimaced, thinking hard. "Wealthy . . . wealthy is when you can afford to buy the things you want."

She stopped at the door to the women's lockers. "And rich?"

"Rich is when you can afford to buy things and *then* decide if you want them."

She laughed and said, "Okay. Fine. Learn somethin' every day. Call me in an hour with the dates you want." She wrapped the towel around her neck and headed for the showers. He reached out and grabbed her cement-pillar arm.

"Oh, one more thing, Fatima."

She half turned and raised her eyebrows. "Yeah?"

He smiled nervously. "Uh . . . listen. It's possible that some-one might call the agency and ask if I work there."

"What? What do you mean?"

He decided that the best gambit was the truth, so he forged ahead: "Well, Farleigh wants me to get a job, but I don't want to get one. And I know he'd never agree to go to Greece with me if he knew I was unemployed. So I want him to think I'm working at a travel agency and that I got the tickets as part of my job there. Okay?"

Fatima looked at him as though she had never seen him before. "Huh?"

He shut his eyes and tried not to become exasperated with her; he needed her far too much. "Look, it's like this," he said. "If someone calls you at your office this afternoon and asks for me, just pretend that you're my secretary, and tell him that I'm on vacation for a while. Okay?"

She stared at him, mouth agape, then said, "But I'm *not* your secretary. You *don't* work at my agency."

He leaned into her. "I know that," he said in a conspira-torial whisper. *"Lie."*

She opened her eyes wide and said, "Oh, *lie*." Then she looked down at her hands and said, "Listen, Ace. I'm sorry, I can't do that. I can't lie. Sorry."

He took a deep breath, trying to quell his irritation, then said, "Okay. I understand. I shouldn't have asked you, really. Sorry."

"No, *I'm* sorry. It's the way I was brought up." She shrugged.

"That's okay." He started to turn away, then whirled back and said, "So, anyway, leg's okay now?"

"What? Oh, yeah." She extended it toward him and flexed it. "Feels fine."

"Great." He grinned winningly. "Good thing I was here, isn't it? I mean, think how fucked you'd have been if I wasn't! Everyone else here is so freaked out about your looks, they probably would've been too scared to help you out. You might've ended up in a hospital, or something. Maybe even

crippled. Oh, well, happy ending all around." He winked at her.
"You have a good vacation, now!"

He started toward the door to the men's locker room, and
had actually taken one step through its frame when he heard
her call, "Ace, wait!"

He backed up a step. "You call me?"

She looked enormously agitated; she kept shaking her arms,
as though they'd fallen asleep or something. "Look," she said,
"I'll do it once. If someone calls and asks for you, I'll do the
lying thing *once*. That's all, okay?"

He pursed his lips to stop himself from smiling. "You're a
good friend, Fatima," he said as soberly as he could. Then he
went and took a long, hot, satisfying shower.

chapter
23

Seven hours into the flight, Dennis was well and truly
blotto. A nervous flyer at best, he'd taken every opportunity to ask the flight attendants to refill his glass of
champagne, and had sipped his way happily through the CNN
newsreel, an old episode of *The Abbott and Costello Show*, and
the feature film, *Ace Ventura: When Nature Calls*, which even
drunk he didn't find funny. But at least it kept his mind off his
altitude.

When he realized he was the only one in the first-class cabin
watching the movie, he took off his headphones and settled into
his seat for another nap. He nestled his head against Farleigh's
shoulder, then looked up at him to see if this was all right, but
Farleigh was still leaning against the wall of the plane, staring
aimlessly out the window.

"Still worried about Jasper, hon?" he asked, squeezing Farleigh's knee.

Farleigh glanced at him. "No. Not anymore." He paused.
"And I'll be back in six days, anyway. What can happen in six
days?"

"Nothing," Dennis said, but he thought, Everything.

"And it's not like we won't be in constant phone contact," he added, as if trying to convince himself that all was well.

Dennis snuggled up to him. "Well, then," he said with languid satisfaction.

But Farleigh remained as stiff and unyielding as a board.

Dennis decided to pretend not to notice this until Farleigh turned and said, "Actually, I have a little something to get off my chest."

Dennis's heart played a quick round of hopscotch. He sat up and said, "Nothing serious, I hope," a little laugh coloring his voice.

"Serious to me," he said. "See, I didn't believe you when you told me you were working at that travel agency. Especially when you produced the tickets for this trip and said you paid for them yourself; it all seemed too sudden, somehow."

He sighed. "Farleigh, we've been through this. I've been working there for a while now. I just didn't want to tell you till I was sure I wasn't going to be fired. With my job history, do you blame me?" Just then a blond, large-faced flight attendant passed by; Dennis called out to her, "*Champagne, please.*"

Farleigh looked at his fingernails and started rubbing them with his thumbs. "Well, yes. And I should've just believed you. But I couldn't. I called the travel agency myself. Got your secretary, who said you'd be out of the office for a week, and could she take a message." He grimaced. "I just feel like such a heel for that. I feel like a heel for doubting you."

A red haze of shame spread its way through Dennis's contentment. He dropped his gaze and said, "Well, I haven't exactly given you much cause to trust me," he said in a low voice.

Farleigh whirled. "That's more like *my* line, isn't it?"

Dennis smiled at him. "We're quite a pair."

"Maybe we belong together."

"Whaddaya mean, 'maybe'?"

The large-faced flight attendant reappeared with a bottle of Moet; as she poured into Dennis's glass, she said with barely concealed disapproval, "You certainly have a taste for this!"

The plane skidded over a bubble of turbulence. Dennis snatched the bottle from her, smiled sweetly, and said, "Have a few more chilling."

He delayed his nap long enough to down this latest bottle, then lowered himself back onto Farleigh, who had relaxed and softened considerably. Feeling calmer and more sure of himself than he had in weeks, Dennis lapsed into a bottomless, drunken slumber.

When Farleigh shook him awake, it took time for his eyes to focus, and even longer for him to realize that this was because the sun had set. The cabin was nearly completely dark, although little overhead lights were switching on row by row as a pair of flight attendants moved through them, dispensing dinner trays.

"Meal service coming," said Farleigh gently as Dennis sat up and ran his fingers through his hair. "Didn't think you'd want to miss it."

Uh-oh, thought Dennis; he'd had so much to drink that he felt the odds were about even he'd have to throw up. And of course the flight attendants were blocking the path to the lavatories.

He decided to sit it out and wait. Everything would depend what kind of food they put in front of him. The sight of fish or ham would almost certainly trigger his gag reflex. He wondered why it was you never found airsick bags in the seat pouches anymore.

He was in luck; not only was the dinner service a hearty, aromatic slab of beef bourguignon, surrounded by carrots and a deviled mashed potato, but it was served to him by an adorable, straw-haired male flight attendant.

"May I offer you a little merlot with that, sir?" the attendant said graciously.

Dennis tried to look his most attractive, which was probably useless since he knew he had a bad case of sleep hair, and said, "I think you'd better."

The merlot was of course domestic, but wasn't bad. Farleigh had a glass as well, and they ate together hungrily, barely speaking.

They'd nearly finished when the flight attendant returned and said, "What would you gentlemen like for dessert? We have fresh berries in zabaglione, lemon meringue pie and, if you're feeling adventurous, a delicious rum-flavored flan."

"The flan," said Dennis at once; then he asked, "How much rum exactly?"

"Gosh, I don't know. We get them pre-made."

"I'll have it anyway."

Farleigh asked for the berries, but without the zabaglione.

As he was leaving, the flight attendant winked at Dennis and said, "I had a hunch you were the adventurous type."

When he'd moved on, Farleigh leaned into Dennis and said, "Do cute young boys flirt with you *everywhere?*"

"Oh, come on, he wasn't flirting," said Dennis with a tsk, which was as good a way as he knew of saying yes.

Mere moments later, Christos appeared, crouching in the aisle next to them. "Hi," he said cheerfully. "What are they feeding you up here?" He swiped a stray piece of meat from Dennis's tray, dunked it in the sauce, and popped it in his mouth. "Bourguignon, right? Passable, too." He scowled. "You know what we get back in steerage? *Burritos.* I kid you not. Plus, I had to pay six dollars for a *tiny* bottle of wine, and all they have are chardonnay and merlot. The merlot's not bad—oh, you're having it. Are you guys gonna finish here . . . ? Farleigh, you got any food you don't want there? I couldn't bring my-self to finish that damn burrito." He twisted his mouth into a strange configuration, then said, "I think I have cilantro stuck in my teeth. What are you getting for dessert?"

The large-faced flight attendant reappeared from the crew station and said, "Sir . . . sir . . . you're not allowed up here!" She waved a finger at him.

He said, "It's okay—I work for this man." He pointed at Farleigh.

"I'm sorry, but you're still not allowed up here." She started down the aisle toward him.

"I'd better go," whispered Christos. "She looks like she might eat me." He got up. "Let me have a dinner roll, at least!"

Dennis tossed him a partially devoured knot of bread. As he scurried away from the flight attendant, he sniffed it and said, "Mmm, rosemary!"

Dennis turned to Farleigh to comment on Christos's sur-prise visit, and found Farleigh smiling at him in a way he hadn't seen in what seemed a century—his lips partially open, one side of his mouth screwed up in merriment. Then they both started laughing . . . not loudly or with great hilarity, but with an easy, refreshing companionability. It was like they'd found each other all over again.

Jasper the pool boy seemed very, very far away.

And in fact, he was.

Within two hours, they were staggering off the plane and into the Athens airport.

chapter
24

Farleigh sent Christos on to Mykonos to open up the house. Then he and Dennis spent the next two days in Athens, just enjoying themselves.

Farleigh had, at his own insistence, had his cast removed before the trip, but his doctor insisted in return that he walk with a cane, to keep undue pressure off the newly mended bone. So Farleigh's progress around the city was necessarily somewhat slowed. But strolling actually seemed to be the order of the day; the air was warm and heavy, and Dennis felt pleasurably lazy. There also wasn't much to do in Athens, anyway; most of the city was dirty or at best inelegant. They spent most of their time rediscovering their favorite pockets from previous visits.

On their first day, they dumped their luggage at the hotel and took in the Archaeological Museum, and had fun finding all their favorite old bronze and marble sculptures. Farleigh mused aloud about how little the concept of male beauty had changed over the millennia, as opposed to female beauty, which boomeranged from Nefertiti to Titian to Kate Moss and all points in between. And they spent a lot of time trying to find their favorite statue of Antinuous, the Emperor Hadrian's boy toy-turned-martyr, only to realize in the end that they'd actually seen it up in the mountains, at the Delphi Museum.

They grew tired rather quickly, partially because of jet lag and partially because the museum itself was a chaotic jumble; some galleries simply defeated their efforts to make sense of them. There was something to be said for good old American showmanship, and Dennis in fact said it, then tweaked Farleigh's behind in tribute.

That evening, they attended a concert by a beautiful young Greek singer named Eleftheria Arvanitaki. Farleigh had bought several of her CDs on their last visit after hearing them played in a restaurant and becoming enchanted with her birdlike soprano, put in the service of mesmerizingly melodic Greek folk ballads. It was the sheerest coincidence that she should be performing on the night of their arrival . . . not to mention that they should actually stumble across a poster telling them so (although it took some translating on their part). And it was uncanny that there were tickets still available—albeit not very good ones. Even so, it all seemed to form one of those happy confluences that augur well for everything that follows.

The concert was a joy. Dennis liked Greek concerts of this kind because they reminded him of old American TV variety shows; the headliner occasionally stepped aside and let a guest performer have the spotlight. On this night the ethereally lovely Ms. Arvanitaki gave her stage over to a band of regional musicians who played some kickass bouzouki, and later to a much older woman who sang what must have been a comic song, since much of the audience laughed in the same spots. Dennis didn't understand more than a few words of Greek, but he found himself laughing along, out of sheer high spirits.

After the concert, they took in a very late dinner at a restaurant called Bajazzo, in the Kolonaki district, not far from their hotel. It had always been their favorite restaurant in Athens, and they were delighted to find that it was still up to snuff. Dennis had, however, forgotten that the place was decorated rather exhaustively in a clown motif, with clown masks, costumes, and dolls tucked into every available corner. It was a little disorienting at first, but his sea bass was so fine that he soon grew oblivious to anything else.

After dinner, they took the nearby funicular to the summit of the hill called Likavitós that made up the southern edge of the district, and sat drinking from a cheap bottle of ouzo while they surveyed the panoramic view of the city. Athens, an ugly smudge during the daylight hours, looked almost pretty at night, as so many things do; and of course, the sight of the fully illuminated Acropolis, in the midst of it all, was breathtaking.

The next day, they rose late, skipped breakfast, and wandered the Plaka district looking for bad souvenirs to take home. Dennis found a set of plastic coasters decorated with sexually explicit scenes from Greek vases (authentic, the cashier assured him rather unconvincingly), and he purchased them with great delight. Farleigh found a CD store and bought Eleftheria Arvanitaki's most recent releases.

In the street outside, Dennis was swarmed by a group of Europe's notorious "sleeve-petter" gypsy women, and when he managed to disentangle himself from their grasp, more than a little unnerved, he made a quick check of his pockets and discovered that almost all his cash had been filched. This provoked the first wrong note in the trip; Farleigh grew angry and scolded him for not having got traveler's checks as he'd been told. Dennis remarked that he'd only had several hundred thousand drachma on him, and that he'd planned to use credit cards wherever possible anyway.

"That's ridiculous," snapped Farleigh, "you'll get raped by the interest rates. I've got plenty of traveler's checks; just let me pay for everything."

Dennis cocked his head and thought, Hey, works for me.

They had lunch at a small taverna. They ordered Greek salads (*real* Greek salads—not a leaf of lettuce in sight) and braised lamb shank, and washed it all down with retsina. Dennis, who had been quite a retsina aficionado during his previous visit, took his first sip and gasped, "My God! How young *was* I when I could drink this stuff?" But his palate, spoiled by smooth, drinkable French and Italian wines, rapidly acclimated itself to their crude Hellenic cousin, and by the end of the meal they had finished off a second bottle.

After that it was well into mid-afternoon, so they staggered back to the hotel for a nap.

Dennis thought, It's now or never.

They undressed; then Farleigh drew the curtains and slipped into bed. No sooner had he done so than Dennis was on him like an affectionate puppy.

"Hey," said Farleigh, laughing, "watch it with that tongue! You'll get me all smelling like garlic."

"You already do," said Dennis, not slowing down a bit.

"Cut it *out*, now," Farleigh ordered him. "I'm tired and I'm drunk and I'm in no mood." But he didn't sound like he meant it, so Dennis ignored him and pressed on; and before long, they'd reached a kind of fumbling reciprocity that yielded, not terribly quickly, a pair of almost simultaneous orgasms.

As they panted in exhaustion in the moments following, Dennis searched for some way of consolidating this small victory—something he could say, short of a turgid "I love you," to cement this groping alliance into something stronger. But before he could do so, Farleigh grabbed the reins from him.

"Now I'm *really* tired," he said genially but unhelpfully. He kissed Dennis on the nose and said, "Thanks, honey."

The next thing Dennis heard from him was a full-bore snore.

chapter
25

Disaster struck that very night. After waking up refreshed, they started packing their suitcases, getting ready to check out and leave Athens on the ferry.

Farleigh sat down on the bed, winded from having moved all his bags to the door with the help of his cane. He said, "I think I'll call Jasper and see how things are going."

Dennis nodded agreeably, but his pulse started thrumming. This was the first mention of Jasper since the plane, and although he knew some contact with the erstwhile pool boy was inevitable, he'd hoped it was at least a few days down the line.

While Farleigh dialed slowly, constantly checking the crumpled slip of paper on which he'd written the instructions for calling the States, Dennis casually ambled into the suite's adjoining room, then carefully picked up the extension on the suite's desk. If Farleigh was going to speak to Jasper, he needed to listen in; the tone of a single "I miss you" would be enough to tell Dennis how tough a road he had ahead of him.

The connection was made, rather clunkily; then the ringing started. Once; twice; thrice; four times and then five.

Finally, Debbie Stebbe picked up. "Farleigh Nock Productions," she said breathlessly.

"It's me, Debbie."

"Farleigh! Where are you? I've been calleen your house for two days."

"We're still in Athens. Christos should be there, though; he must've been out running errands when you rang. There are more than a few to run. How's everything? Is Jasper handy?"

"Jasper's not here."

"He's not? What time is it there, anyway?"

"Four-thirty. Listen, Farleigh, we've got big troubles."

A beat. "What?"

"Well, you know how the Ross Foundation only agreed to put up the money for the production if they could examine the theater in advance for structural—"

"Yes, yes," said Farleigh testily. "They always do that. So what?"

"So they found termites."

A longer beat. "You're joking."

"I'm not. Apparently the theater's infested with them."

"Their inspection was *months* ago. Why are we only hearing about it now?"

"Who knows? Some memo somewhere got lost on someone's desk—I don't know. It could be anytheen."

Farleigh sighed. "All right. Fine. Have the management company exterminate."

"I called them, but all they said was that they'd get around to it; I couldn't get them to commit to a date. And in the meantime, the foundation has pulled its money."

"What?"

"They pulled out. I'm not kiddeen, Farleigh. We're in real trouble."

"Listen, go ahead and order an extermination yourself. Pay for it out of petty cash. We'll get the management company to reimburse us."

"I did, I did that—the exterminator's comeen tomorrow. But it's too late; the foundation says they think the termites have already done too much damage. They won't back the show as long as it's in the Pruitt."

"I can't believe I'm hearing this."

"It gets worse."

He half laughed. "All right. Let me have it."

"Well, the foundation never actually sent us their first check."

A virtual explosion. "Those bastards! We've been on the phone with them half a dozen—no, a *dozen*—times and they always assured us the check was cut and on its way!"

"Well, they lied. They were waiteen for the building inspection before they cut it."

"But that was months a—"

"Months ago, I know. I'm tryeen to get to the bottom of it, but I can't get anyone at the foundation to return my calls."

"I'll call them. You better *believe* I'll call them."

"That would be a big help. But in the meantime, without their check, we couldn't exactly meet payroll."

"Oh, my God."

"So the crew walked off, and the cast has mainly stopped shoween up till we pay them."

"Oh, my God."

"Judy Shapiro actually took another job. Flew to Minnesota to shoot a commercial."

"The *bitch.*" A long, tension-soaked moment. "I can't believe this. I should never have left. This is the kind of thing I could've cleared up in an hour. *Damn* it."

Dennis felt his face drain of color; he'd taken Farleigh from the play at a crucial moment, and now he was going to pay for it.

"All right," said Farleigh at last. "Here's what I need you to do. Contact my attorney, Byron Pratt . . ."

"I know Byron," said Debbie a bit defensively.

". . . and tell him we want to sue the Pruitt's management company for loss of revenues incurred by their negligence. Then call the Illinois Arts Council and whatever other arts organization you can, and see what kind of help we can get from them. *Any* kind of help. Then call around to the other theaters in the area, and see if we can cut a deal. Try the Varsity Playhouse."

"That's in Evanston!"

"I don't care. We're desperate. That cyberpunk comedy of theirs closed early last month. See if we can cut a deal for their space. Keep the foundation people in on this. And as far as the actors go . . . have Byron look into what our options are regarding Judy. I'd love to haul that bitch's ass back from Minneapolis. As for the others, tell them to—to—actually, it's probably best to have Jasper handle them. Where'd you say he was?"

"I don't know. Gone."

The longest beat yet. "What do you mean, 'gone'?"

"He said that since the play fell through, he was going away somewhere. He wouldn't say where. He treats me really bad, Farleigh. He knows I'm your assistant, but he treats me like I'm notheen."

"All right, all right." Farleigh sighed. "If you should happen to see him, tell him from me that he'd better fucking call me, that's all. We'll be at the house on Mykonos, unless I can get a flight out of here right away."

"Okay, Farleigh, don't worry. I know what I'm doeen."

"No, you don't. I haven't told you how to handle the cast yet."

"Oh, yeah. Sorry. What should I do? Everyone's threateneen to quit except Mercedes."

"You just give them my personal assurance that we'll have a space—and *cash*—by the end of the week, and tell them I'm on my way back to take charge again. And that if I hear about any one of them giving you any undue trouble, I'll see to it that whoever it is never works again in this state in anything better than a theme park. Got it?"

"Got it. Let me get on the phone right now. I'm feeleen much better about everytheen, Farleigh. I'm so glad we finally connected. I'll call you at the house when I've got sometheen to report."

The conversation seemed to end there, so Dennis hurriedly (but quietly) replaced the receiver. Then he grabbed a discarded pair of jeans from the floor, folded them over his arms, and, summoning up all his courage, returned to the bedroom. "Something the matter?" he asked as he tucked the jeans into his suitcase. "You sounded kind of edgy on the phone just now."

Farleigh was scratching madly at his instep. "Yes, something's the matter," he said tersely. "Whole production's falling to pieces, and my director's up and disappeared." He sat upright, grabbed his cane, and with one violent sweep struck the lamp from the bedstand. The light went out at once, but the lamp itself was such a sturdy thing, it didn't even break. "*Christ*, this is aggravating! I should *never* have let you talk me into this trip!"

Dennis quelled his fear enough to allow him to go to the bed and sit by Farleigh. "I'm so sorry," he said. "I just thought, we haven't been to the house for three years, and this seemed like the perfect time to do it, since everything was going so well. I had no idea I was taking you away at the worst possible time. Forgive me." He put his hands on Farleigh's neck and started rubbing the pressure points just behind his ears.

Farleigh visibly softened. "Listen, I'm not angry at you," he said as he warmed to Dennis's massage. "It was sweet of you to want to take me away, sweet of you to buy these tickets with your own hard-earned money. I should've known better than to say yes, that's all. I'm really angry at myself." He hesitated. "And, of course, at Jasper."

Suddenly Dennis thought that maybe this wasn't such a disaster, after all. His sole purpose in whisking Farleigh off to Greece was to dissolve his attachment to Jasper. But Jasper had apparently done that much more effectively himself, by disappearing at the first sign of trouble.

Farleigh took Dennis's hand from his neck, kissed it, and said, "Maybe you'd better go on to Mykonos without me. You have a little holiday on your own, with Christos, okay? I'll just stay here and try to arrange a new flight out as soon as possible. Tomorrow morning, if I can."

Dennis shook his head. "My place is with you. Besides, you're walking with a cane now. Who'd carry your suitcases?"

Farleigh beamed at him. "Oh, my lovely boy." He wrapped his hands around Dennis's head and kissed him twice on the lips. "What would I do without you?" He smiled sadly. "You and Debbie—all I have left."

Being lumped in with the unappetizing Ms. Stebbe took some of the sheen off the moment, but Dennis accepted this tribute gratefully all the same.

Farleigh spent the next half hour on the phone, trying to arrange a flight out of Athens for the next day, then the day after, with no luck. He was put on several waiting lists, then called the hotel's front desk and asked to extend his stay. But that worked out even less well; the room was booked, he was told, and he must vacate. He called some of the other premium hotels in town, but none had any rooms available. He was just at the point of trying some of the lesser hotels when Dennis stepped in and said, "It's not likely we'll get a flight out till the day after tomorrow at least. Why sit in Athens suffering when we can wait it out on Mykonos? I know it's a schlep, but they have an airport on the island; we can be back in Athens in an hour, if you want. Plenty of time to catch the first flight that becomes available."

Farleigh, looking shrunken and defeated and suddenly very old, said, "You're right." He sighed, and sat up straight. "Very well, then. Let's get the hell out of here and see if we can catch that bloody ferry."

chapter
26

Farleigh was silent during the cab ride to Piraeus, and was visibly irritated that the ferry was late. They waited on the pier for fifty minutes, staring at the stars and trying to avoid the jabber of the dozens of American and German tourists who surrounded them. Dennis offered to make a run for some small bottles of ouzo, to make the time pass more pleasantly, but Farleigh declined; he was obviously intent on being miserable.

When the ferry at last arrived, there was a mad scramble to board, and Dennis somehow got separated from Farleigh. Since Farleigh was still walking with a cane, he felt no small alarm at this, and pushed his way against the flow of bodies until he found where Farleigh had been left behind; he was cowering behind a steel girder, looking ashen and afraid. Dennis had never seen him look so old. He gave him his arm, smiled, then led him aboard the ferry, brandishing the cane so that rude Europeans would get out of his way. (Americans, he noted, had far less trouble staying in line—probably all that early training at Disneyland.)

There were several levels to the ferry. The topmost contained the cheap seats, set up in rows, and the throngs of students made their way there almost immediately. Below this was a sort of salon with big, red circular banquettes, two billiards tables, and a lengthy bar. The banquettes were filling up rapidly when Dennis and Farleigh passed through. Below that were the cabins. Since their cruise would last all night, Dennis had booked one of these. He held his ticket in his hand, lest anyone question him in Greek, and led Farleigh to their assigned berth—Cabin 13. Why hadn't he noticed that inauspicious number before?

He swung open the door, and the place stood revealed in all its grimness. It was clean, certainly, but very tiny, and very drab. A sink, a mirror, a chair, and two sets of bunk beds were all it contained.

"Well," said Dennis merrily, "I guess we don't need to look for a chocolate on the pillows."

"I don't care," said Farleigh, edging his way past him. "My foot is killing me, I'm tired, I'm angry, and all I want to do is curl up and pass out." He proceeded to do just that.

Dennis sighed, shut the door behind him, and threw their luggage on the bottom bunk opposite Farleigh's. Then he unlaced Farleigh's shoes, slipped them off his feet, placed them on the floor, and climbed up to the top bunk, where he lay with his face mere inches from the ceiling.

And then he tried to sleep.

But he couldn't. The ferry hadn't yet pulled away from the pier, and for some reason the anticipation of that event was keeping him wide awake.

Half an hour passed. He decided it was ridiculous to keep lying there, staring at nothing, waiting for the engines to start humming again. He hopped down to the floor, donned his loafers, and stole out of the cabin, intending to have himself a nightcap.

Just as he did so, he heard the engines start to stutter and purr. Figures. Well, he'd come this far . . . he might as well have a drink anyway.

He clambered up the stairs to the bar level, where he found all the stools taken by sodden tourists leaning over watery gin and tonics and bad scotch whiskies. He waited for one of them to show some signs of moving; none of them showed signs of even breathing.

"Fuck it," he muttered. He'd buy a bottle of wine anyway, and drink it up on the deck, where he could enjoy the breeze.

He managed to catch the bartender's attention, but, alas, the man's English was only marginally better than Dennis's Greek. (Why have him serving on a ferry, then? thought Dennis, miffed.) Dennis managed to convey that he wanted wine, but didn't recognize any of the names the bartender tossed back at him. Panicking, he nodded at one of them, purely randomly, and received in return a rather yellowish white wine in a green bottle, with a label he couldn't read because it was in Greek. He thought, *How bad can it be?*, threw down several thousand drachmas, and signaled the bartender to open the bottle for him.

This done, he took the bottle and a glass to a pillar just adjacent to one of the billiard tables; he leaned against it and poured himself a mouthful. And drank it.

Or tried to. In truth, it was close to undrinkable.

He must have made a face conveying this, because he heard shrieks of laughter erupt from somewhere off to his left. He turned and saw two college-age girls, spread out with their enormous backpacks on a banquette, holding their mouths and quaking with glee. They were unmistakably American: their full, healthy faces, butter-brown complexions, and uninhibited manner were as clear an indication as if they'd had Old Glory emblazoned on their sweatshirts.

He gave them a long-suffering shrug, as if to say, What can you do?

One of them—the taller of the pair, with shoulder-length hair and sporting a pair of Mary Janes—leaned over to whisper to her companion, then turned back and said, "We'll help you with that! We're so broke we're ready to drink *anything*."

Dennis clearly couldn't drink it himself, and he didn't fancy sitting up on deck with no alcohol to soften the chill wind, so he shrugged and thought, What the hell.

He went over to the banquette, and the taller girl roughly knocked her backpack to the floor to make room for him. She gave him the kind of guilelessly rapacious smile only Americans can still manage and said, "Hi, I'm Tracey, and this is Rose-anne."

Roseanne, smaller, more timid, with shorter, darker hair and much longer eyelashes, sat up as well, and said, "Hi." Then she shot Tracey a look that clearly said, *Is this wise?* Dennis could already tell that Tracey was the ringleader, Roseanne the voice of caution.

"I'm Dennis," he said, following their lead and leaving off his last name.

Tracey scooted in and patted the seat cushion beside her. "C'mon in," she said. While Dennis maneuvered himself into place, she raced on, babbling like a brook. "We didn't see you on the pier! Were you on the pier? At Piraeus? We were looking for cute guys on the pier."

"*Tracey,*" said Roseanne in a stage whisper.

Dennis plunked the wine on the table and said, "Yeah, I was on the pier. With my boyfriend." Better to get this out in the open.

Tracey whirled and slapped Roseanne's shoulder. "See? See? I *told* you he was gay!"

"I never said he wasn't," said Roseanne, still in a stage whisper. Did she think Dennis couldn't hear her? "It's just . . . you think *everyone's* gay."

"All the cute ones *are.*" She turned back to Dennis. "Rose-anne has a fiancé back home. Four years they've been together. So she's a little out of practice. I can tell a gay guy like *that.*" She snapped her fingers.

"Pour the *wine,*" urged Roseanne, and the implication was, Shut *up.*

Tracey clicked her tongue. "Into what? We only have one glass. Besides, it's really bad, right?" This to Dennis.

He nodded. "Bottomlessly awful."

She winked at him. "Let me slide out for a minute."

He did so, then resumed his seat. Roseanne grinned nervously. "Where are you headed?" she asked.

"Mykonos. You?"

"Naxos," she said with a small smile of relief. "Which comes first?"

"Mykonos, I think."

That pretty much exhausted their conversation, so they turned to watch Tracey. She had bopped over to the bar and struck up an animated conversation with the bartender, who appeared enchanted by her.

"Does she speak Greek?" Dennis asked.

Roseanne shook her head. "Not a word."

Tracey jabbered on, gesticulating wildly, till the bartender handed her three cans of soda pop and two more glasses, and said something to her in return. She raised her shoulders coyly, winked at him, then skipped back to the banquette.

She made Dennis move over to make room for her, so that now he was trapped between her and Roseanne's enormous backpack. "I got us some Sprite," she said, setting the cans on the table and immediately popping one open. "We can make wine coolers."

Dennis was dumbstruck by the girl's sheer genius. He'd been ready to dump the wine overboard.

"You didn't *pay* him," said Roseanne, whispering again.

"He wouldn't let me," said Tracey as she released a fizzy flow of Sprite into a glass. Then she wrapped her tongue around her cheek and topped it off with Dennis's wine. "There," she said, and she shoved the cup over to Dennis. "How's it taste?"

He took a sip. "Delicious," he enthused.

Tracey made two more makeshift coolers for herself and Roseanne, then they all raised their glasses and toasted. "To the islands," said Dennis.

"To a fun time," said Roseanne.

"To hot island guys," said Tracey.

They thudded their glasses together and took a big gulp.

And then, as travelers will at times like these, they began to exchange life stories. They only broke twice, when Dennis was forced to return to the bar for more Sprite and also for two more bottles of the exact same wine . . . he took the first one back empty to make sure the bartender got it right.

By two in the morning, he'd heard all the dirt on Tracey and Roseanne's families, old boyfriends, and dizzying experiences at Drake University in Des Moines, Iowa. And it was *his* turn to divulge.

Well, he was stone drunk, and on cheap wine at that. Cheap wine and *Sprite*, for God's sake. What that lethal combination did to him, he never knew, but he must have told quite a tale of woe about himself, because by the end of it Tracey and Roseanne were very nearly bawling.

"Oh, my God, you are *so* making my eyeliner run," said Tracey as she daubed it on the sleeve of her sweatshirt.

"And you made up this *story?*" asked Roseanne, leaning over the table at him, gazing at him intently, tears streaking down her ample cheeks. "This *lie* to get him away? Just so you could keep your one true love from falling for another *man?*"

"Well, yeah, tha's basic'ly it," said Dennis, suppressing a burp.

Roseanne put her hands over her mouth, then removed them and said, "That's the most incredibly poignant thing I ever heard in my life. Oh, my God, you should be *with* him! Right *now!*"

"You should *so* be with him," agreed Tracey as she lay down on the banquette and rested her head on her arm.

"I should," said Dennis as his head lolled on his shoulders. "I really should."

But he didn't get up and go back to the cabin, because Roseanne started a story about a friend of hers who had a similar situation except that it was different in some way Dennis only vaguely grasped, and the next thing he knew, there was noise all around him, and sunlight streaming into the banquette, and he started in alarm, realizing he'd fallen asleep.

All around him, people were milling about, as if preparing to disembark.

Farleigh! he thought.

He lurched up, plowed through the crowd, raced down the stairs to Cabin 13, then knocked open the door and stumbled in.

Farleigh was awake, at the sink, washing his face. "Well, well," he said.

Dennis's head was pounding. "Oh, hi," he said, his shoulders drooping in relief.

"Good morning. Might I ask where you spent the night?"

Dennis collapsed onto the bunk Farleigh had vacated. "Oh.

Oww. My head hurts." He rolled over and faced the wall. "I was up all night partying with a couple of college students."

There was a long silence. Then Farleigh said, "I see," with a tone in his voice that almost put frost on the porthole pane.

Dennis knit his brow. What was the problem?

Ah. *That.*

He rolled over again and gazed lovingly at Farleigh. "You'll have to meet them. Lovely girls."

Farleigh, drying his face on the thin, bristly towel, turned and raised his eyebrows.

"Yes, Farleigh, *girls.* Rosy-cheeked, full-bosomed American coeds. I told them all about you. Say, did we pack any Advil?"

chapter
27

D ennis, his head throbbing, slung their bags over his shoulder, then lent Farleigh his arm again and guided him into the line of people queuing up to depart. Once he was safely in place, Dennis excused himself, loped over to Tracey and Roseanne's banquette, and found it now occupied by a family of five who were transparently happy to have snatched it. He let his shoulders slump in disappointment.

He glanced up the staircase to the upper deck; the girls had probably made their way up there, the better to check out the cute male students in the now abundant sunlight. Well, Dennis wasn't about to race after them.

He tried not to feel hurt that the girls had given up on him so quickly; after all, he'd sort of unceremoniously dumped them first. He slouched back over to Farleigh, his hands in his pockets. The line hadn't yet begun to move.

"Where are the coeds?" Farleigh asked him.

He shrugged. "Dunno. Not where I left them." He gave Farleigh's shirtsleeve an affectionate twist. "Kind of a shame. I really did want you to meet them."

"Hmm. How sad." Farleigh pursed his lips and stared straight ahead. Dennis thought, He doesn't believe me; he thinks I was involved in some kind of teenage boy orgy.

The line jostled to life, and Dennis thought, Well, then, he can just lean on his fucking cane instead of me.

But after Farleigh limped several yards at his side, he softened and gave him his arm.

The pier was teeming with persons and autos and souvenir vendors. Farleigh said, "Keep an eye out for Christos. He's supposed to meet us here."

After a few minutes, the crowd thinned a little, and Dennis saw not Christos, but Tracey and Roseanne, nearly crushed beneath their backpacks, wandering around aimlessly. "Oh, look!" he cried, pointing. "It's them! *Hey, guys! Over here!*"

The girls heard him, waved back at him, and started lumbering his way. When they reached him, Tracey unstrapped her backpack and let it fall to the ground. "I hate that thing," she said. "I'm gonna buy some totally impractical designer suitcase while I'm here."

"You can't afford it," said Roseanne, who kept her own backpack on but leaned it into a lamppost and heaved a sigh. "My feet hurt already."

"What are you doing here?" said Dennis, wondering how the girls could look so fresh-faced while he felt like death warmed over. "Weren't you going to Naxos?"

"Yeah, but we were having so much fun with you, we decided we'd try Mykonos first," said Tracey, glancing occasionally at Farleigh. "We want to meet this incredible boyfriend of yours, for one thing."

Dennis stepped aside and displayed Farleigh as though he were first prize at a carnival shooting gallery. "Well, here he is! Farleigh, meet Tracey and Roseanne. Guys, this is Farleigh Nock."

The girls' smiles froze on their faces. "Pleased to meet you," they said, their tone suddenly hushed and reverential. They were obviously taken aback by Farleigh's age and apparent infirmity.

"The pleasure is all mine," said Farleigh in a tone that said exactly the opposite. He shook their hands, then said to Dennis,

"Where the *hell* is Christos? I called him last night and told him to be here." He started to scan the pier. "Where's there a telephone?"

Tracey's and Roseanne's faces drained of color. They looked longingly back at the ferry, as though they were considering dashing back aboard before it was too late.

"We got here late," said Dennis, trying to calm Farleigh down. "Christos has probably already been here and left. Be patient. He'll be back."

"I'm going to call the house," he said stubbornly, and he started across the pier to a distant phone booth. "You watch the bags."

The girls watched him go, making slow progress with his cane. Then Tracey turned and said, "Uh . . . wow. He's really hot."

Dennis found himself laughing aloud. "He has other qualities," he said gaily. "You don't have to pretend he's a stud."

Roseanne put two fingers on her chin. "Wait a minute. That's the guy who you had to get out of the country because a twenty-year-old rival was after him?"

He nodded. "After him *big*-time."

The girls were silent for a few moments. Then Tracey said, "Gee. And I thought *Europe* was weird."

Dennis laughed again.

"There's some Nutella in my pack," said Roseanne. "Dig it out, okay?"

"Oh, yay," said Tracey, clapping. She slipped behind Roseanne and unzipped her voluminous backpack. "We both bought jars in Athens," she explained to Dennis, "but I ate all mine waiting for the ferry."

"I *told* you you'd want some later," said Roseanne as Tracey produced the desired jar. "And now you don't have any."

Tracey held the jar, aghast. "What—you mean you're not going to share?"

"No. Why should I? You ate all yours and didn't let *me* have any."

"But I'm *hungry.*"

"Too bad. Give that to me."

Tracey darted a few steps out of the way, then screwed open

the lid, broke the paper seal, and dug out a whopping fingerful of chocolate-hazlenut ooze. "Mmm," she said as she stuck it into her mouth.

"Oh, that is *so* not fair," Roseanne said, seething. She pushed herself away from the lamppost and started hobbling after Tracey, who continued to gorge herself. But before she could get very far, she noticed that her belongings were spilling out of her backpack onto the grimy cement; she was leaving a little trail of underwear, socks, and magazines. "Oh! You *jerk!*" she shrieked at Tracey. "You didn't zip me back *up!*"

Tracey, her finger in her mouth, had to turn around to hide the fact that she was giggling at her friend's distress.

And Dennis, giggling too, bent down to help Roseanne pick up her belongings, until one look at the girl's face showed him beyond doubt that she'd be mortified by his touching her underthings.

He stood back up and was about to apologize when Farleigh reappeared with Christos. "I found him," he said, exhausted by the walk. "Just as I was dialing the phone."

Dennis expected Christos now to spew forth a litany of melodramatic excuses, occasionally punctuated by gasps of mortification or by a pause to press the back of his hand against his forehead in indignation. But no such song and dance occurred. Instead, Christos merely stood there, in faded, floppy jeans and a sleeveless flannel shirt, and chewed a toothpick in silence.

"*Kalimehra*, Christos," said Dennis, remembering now that the houseboy reverted to stoic Greek machismo after even a short spell in his home country.

He nodded back. "*Kalimehra*, Dennis. You ready to go?"

At the sight of Christos's broad back, bronzed skin, and chest hair, Tracey and Roseanne had snapped to attention. Tracey now handed the jar of Nutella back to her friend, who was still trying to stuff her belongings into her backpack without actually removing it, and traipsed up to Dennis's side. "Hi!" she said, smiling brilliantly.

Dennis nodded at her. "Christos, this is my friend Tracey, from America. And over there is my other friend, Roseanne." Roseanne, turning in circles while she bent her arm unnaturally to work the zipper, managed to gasp, "*Hello.*"

Christos gave them a deep nod; Dennis could almost see their pulses quicken. He said, "*Kalimehra,* ladies."

"What's that mean?" Tracey asked brightly.

"It means, 'Good morning.' "

"*Kollammerra* back atcha, then!"

Roseanne at last lurched over, smiling desperately, and said, "Kolla—kol—uh . . . hi."

Farleigh was growing visibly impatient. "Nice to have met you, girls," he said. "Dennis, grab the bags. I want to get to the house as soon as possible, so I can call Debbie and see if there's anything new to report."

"*Oh,*" said Tracey, even more brightly than before. "You have a *house* here?"

"Yes."

"Sweet!" She was all but begging for an invitation. Farleigh couldn't not realize this; all the same, he turned away from her and nodded to Christos.

"Lead the way, please. I'm getting tired of standing."

Dennis, deeply embarrassed by Farleigh's behavior, dug into his pockets and, as Farleigh and Christos made their way across the pier, he handed the girls all his remaining drachmas.

"Here," he said. "I know you're broke. Take this and get a hotel."

Tracey looked appalled. "Whoa! I'm only broke till I can wire my dad for some money."

"Then pay me back when you get it." He winked. "See you guys around town. I hope."

"Us, too. You're way fun, Dennis."

"Thanks."

"How old is Christos, anyway?" She looked after him winsomely.

"Old enough to be your father. Gay enough to be your mother."

Roseanne snickered. "I *knew* it." She turned and strode away, giggling.

Tracey picked up her backpack and followed her. "Like hell you did. *You* never think *anyone's* gay . . ."

Dennis looked after them a moment longer, then raced to catch up with Farleigh and Christos.

chapter
28

Dennis sat in the back of the Jeep and held onto the luggage while Christos barreled across the island, weaving between the farms and fields and tiny grottoes that made up the rustic interior. Only occasionally would the jagged line of the landscape be broken by a dilapidated house, or a well, or one of those tiny two-person chapels the islanders were so fond of.

Christos had regressed so completely into primal Hellenic masculinity that he now whipped out a pack of horrific Turkish cigarettes, lit one up, and let the strangulating smoke drift back to assault Dennis's nose and throat. It was ridiculous; at home in Chicago, Christos couldn't even wash a dirty ashtray without gagging.

Farleigh was silent for the duration of the ride; he sat with his cane across his lap, looking out but not seeing anything. Dennis knew him well enough to know that he was just biding his time till he could get to the house and start making phone calls to America. Straighten out the *Windermere* mess.

And maybe, just maybe, he was mourning his little fling with the pool boy. Well, let him. That was dead and buried, if anything in life was certain. The little twink had run out in a moment of trouble. Farleigh, being Farleigh, could *never* forgive that.

Christos barreled around a corner and the house came into view. It was smaller than Dennis had remembered it, but it could not be more breathtakingly perched. It sat on a cliff top overlooking the island's gay nude beach, Super Paradise (unfortunate name, Dennis reflected; every time he said it, he felt like he was an extra on *Star Trek*). It was large by island standards, but quite a bit smaller than their brownstone at home; Dennis and Farleigh shared a room that could barely contain Dennis's things alone. Still, it had an incredible dining room overlooking the Aegean, and a spectacular sun porch, and Dennis relished seeing it again after all these years.

As they approached it, he peeked over the side of the Jeep, down at Super Paradise, and saw a number of frolicking brown bodies at play. Wouldn't be long before he was down there himself, letting it all hang out. First time he and Farleigh had strolled that beach (Farleigh, of course, wearing not only Bermuda shorts but a cotton shirt and canvas shoes), the young, lithe, naked Dennis had drawn every eye on the beach. He affected not to notice, but he did . . . and he especially noticed *Farleigh* noticing. With any luck, a repeat performance would help seal their renewed bond. He knew only too well the quirk in Farleigh's character that made him value his possessions only to the extent that they were valued by others.

They pulled up in back of the house, and Christos brought the Jeep to a screeching halt. Then he leaped over the door, flicked his cigarette into the bushes, and trotted around to open the passenger door for Farleigh. Dennis was left to fend for himself; he climbed out over the back of the Jeep and started unloading the bags.

Farleigh took Christos's hand, maneuvered himself to the ground, then said, "House open?" Christos nodded, and Farleigh hobbled in without another word to anyone. When Dennis and Christos entered the house later, shouldering the various bags, they could hear Farleigh on the phone, yelling.

They carried the bags to the tiny master bedroom, then dumped them on the bed. Dennis puts his hands on his buttocks and arched his back. "Ooh," he said. "Glad I won't be carrying those damn things again for a while. What'd we pack? The Encyclopedia Britannica?"

Christos didn't even crack a smile. He just flipped open Farleigh's suitcase and started unpacking it.

So *that's* how it was going to be, eh? Suddenly he remembered how he'd passed the lazy hours last time they were here, three years before: by trying to trick Christos into a shriek or a cry or a whine, or some other involuntary expression of his great big girlish soul. Hadn't managed it, not once. This time, though, he was determined.

He threw himself on the bed. "Sweetie, why don't you unpack my stuff, too, when you're done? So tidy and neat. Love ya." He rolled over and grabbed a magazine from the drawer of the nightstand; he was fully expecting an explosion of shrill "I-ain't-yo-slave-Miz-Scahlet" theatrics from Christos.

Nothing.

He rolled back over. Christos faced away from him; he was placing some of Farleigh's shirts in a dresser drawer. Dennis sighed and lowered his head onto the pillow. "Oh, hey, look at this," he said, "an issue of *Us* magazine, from December 1993." He flipped it open to the contents page. "And look here. 'Opera's Next Reigning Queen.' Page fifty-four."

Christos had shut the drawer and was standing with his hands on the knobs, not moving, his back to Dennis. There was clearly an inner struggle of some magnitude going on. Dennis flipped through the pages. "Ah," he said. "Here we are. *Diva of the Decade?* splashed across the page. Gee, I don't recognize her name. Guess they were wrong about her . . . pretty thing, though . . ."

Christos slowly dropped his hands to his side and walked out. "Think I hear Farleigh calling me," he said, his voice barely audible.

Poor Christos. If he'd only given in to his hidden queeniness, he'd know by now that Dennis wasn't reading an old copy of *Us* at all, but one of Farleigh's back issues of *The Atlantic Monthly*. As far as he knew, there was no copy of *Us* in the entire house. It pleased him, though, to think of Christos snooping around later, trying to find the one Dennis had invented.

He dropped the magazine back on top of the pile, then

rolled off the bed and onto his feet again. Best to continue unpacking.

The minimal exertion it took to sort, hang, and stash his belongings started to weary him fairly quickly. So stuffy in here, he thought, and he threw open the doors that opened onto the terrace. A small red lizard scampered away at the sight of him. Amazing view here—Homer's "wine-dark sea." Not that Dennis had read Homer, but every time they came here Farleigh went on interminably about the "wine-dark sea" and "rosy-fingered dawn." Well . . . let him. The sea *was* wine-dark. And the way the cliff sort of sloped gently down to the beach was almost in the way of an invitation. Dennis couldn't wait to strip off all his clothes and throw himself into those ancient, inspirational waters.

But it was best not to leave until he'd gauged Farleigh's mood after his various phone calls. He was dimly aware of his voice droning on and on and on from several rooms away. Couldn't tell from his tone whether things were going well for him or badly.

Christos had swept the terrace and brought out several deck chairs. Dennis took off his shoes and socks, dropped lazily into the first available chair, and settled down for what he thought would be a refreshing little snooze. . . .

The air had a slight tang to it when Farleigh awakened him by giving his chair a bit of a kick. His face felt tight and flushed. "Oh, wow," he said, sitting up in alarm. "How long was I out?" He ran his hands through his hair. The sun, he noticed, had galloped across the sky and was hovering, almost tauntingly, over the western horizon.

"Few hours," he said. "Closing in on two-thirty now."

"You mean I missed lunch?" He rubbed his eyes and looked up at Farleigh, who, he noticed for the first time, was smiling broadly and carrying two tall glasses of champagne.

"Christos is whipping up a spread of cheese and organ meats," he said as he took the deck chair next to Dennis's. "Lots of unhealthiness to help us get acclimated. And to help me celebrate."

"Celebrate?" Dennis repeated, his eyes wide with hope. "You got everything straightened out?"

"Not *everything*." He settled into the chair, then swung his aching leg onto the footrest with some difficulty. "What, do you think I'm Superman?"

" 'Course I do!"

"Well, let's toast to me and my genius for management, first," he said, extending his glass toward Dennis. "Then I'll tell you all about it."

"Here's to you and your genius." They tapped the glasses together; a dull clank was the result. No crystal for the Mykonos house; here, they were roughing it.

The champagne was delicious; it went down like liquid diamonds. "La Veuve?" asked Dennis.

"None other. So, anyway, I made a few calls, and it's all arranged now. Secured a commitment of four weeks from the Varsity Playhouse in Evanston, and the Ross Foundation agreed to come back on board pending a site inspection. The actors have all been recalled, and we even got Judy Shapiro to come back before she's finished filming her commercial shoot. She'll be angry, but tough. We weren't bluffing; we'd have sued. Debbie's on the phone now calling all our subscribers one by one and assuring them that the only thing that's changed is the venue; the production is going on as planned. Even the same opening night."

"Amazing," said Dennis, leaning back and staring at him adoringly. "See? I was right. Superman!"

Farleigh laughed, then blushed a little at the compliment. He scratched his instep and said, "Well, not exactly. There are still two little problems I have to deal with."

"Which are?"

"First, the Varsity Playhouse is a smaller space than the Pruitt. So that's going to present problems in mounting the East Indian tableau. But even worse than that, I have no one to *handle* those problems. I've lost my director. Debbie says Jasper hasn't even phoned."

"The bastard," said Dennis. "The *bastard.*"

Farleigh sighed and looked out at the Aegean. Suddenly, he looked old again, almost like a latter-day Homer himself.

Dennis nudged him. "I think we'd better toast your genius again," he said.

And they did.

chapter

29

Farleigh intended to return to Chicago as soon as possible, to prod the rescued *Windermere* back into life, and also, reluctantly, to take over the directorial reins. And since an opening on a flight might occur as soon as the morning, he decided to treat Dennis and Christos to a night on the town, so that Christos wouldn't have to cook. Christos almost let out a little squeal of delight on hearing this, but at the last second managed to sidetrack it into a cough.

They chose Nikos's, one of their favorite tavernas from years past. It was a noisy place, managing to be terrifically smoky even though it was practically open-air, with windows swinging free on all sides, and as Dennis watched, a cat from the alley outside jumped in and walked regally across one of the empty tables. But this was Greece, and Dennis had learned long ago to leave his Yankee expectations at the door and just dive into the experience.

The proprietor—whom one assumed to be Nikos, although he had never introduced himself—not only recognized Farleigh, but greeted him as though he'd just seen him the night before. "Hello, Mr. Nock," he called out with a nod as he plunked a bottle of wine onto a table surrounded by tourists. "Table for what, three? Come on over here." He pulled out a chair at a corner table. "Right here."

Christos flicked his foul-smelling cigarette to the floor and ground it into the tiles, then followed Farleigh to the table. Farleigh was even walking better, so happy was he over his having snatched victory from the jaws of termites.

Dennis followed Christos to the table—or would have, had someone not grabbed his wrist and squealed, "*Hi!*"

He turned to find Tracey and Roseanne's radiant, fresh-scrubbed faces smiling at him. He clapped his hand over his mouth and said, "Oh, my God! This is so great! I didn't think we'd run into you again! Where are you staying?"

"We don't know," said Tracey. "A hotel. We can't read the name of it."

They giggled, and Roseanne hit her arm. "We do so! The clerk said. It's called the Helena. Or something."

"That's fabulous," he said. "Nice?"

"*Really* nice," they said in perfect synch; then they turned and laughed at each other again.

Dennis felt eyes on his back and turned to find Farleigh, Christos, and Nikos staring at him. Dennis said, "Oh, hey, you remember Farleigh and Christos, don't you? Guys, look who I ran into!"

Nikos said, "Ladies want to join the party? No problem, Mr. Nock. I get two more chairs."

Dennis, remembering Farleigh's complete disenchantment with the girls when they met on the pier, said, "No, no, that's all right. I was just saying hello."

But Farleigh astonished him by saying, "Don't be ridiculous, Dennis. What kind of travelers would we be if we left our countrywomen to their own devices?" He bowed to them and said, "Please do join us. We're celebrating tonight, and I want you to be my guests."

Tracey and Roseanne needed no further invitation. In fact, they were out of their seats before Farleigh had uttered his last syllable—or rather, Tracey was. Roseanne took a bit longer because the strap of her purse got caught on a window jamb. "This always happens to me," she said morosely.

When they'd taken their seats at Farleigh's table, Nikos reappeared carrying two extra chairs aloft so that they sailed above the heads of his other diners; this disconcerted many of them, who ducked as he passed. Only a bored French couple glanced up at the chairs in disdain, saying nothing and taking long drags off their Gauloises.

Nikos dropped the chairs next to Roseanne, and everyone sat. Tracey seemed a bit unnerved that Christos was placed next to her; despite her obvious attraction to him, she apparently still found him a little frightening. And he was certainly doing nothing to put her at ease. He leaned back in his chair, scratched his stomach, and settled into a good, long frown.

"This is really nice of you, Mr. Farleigh," said Roseanne. "I mean, like, *so* nice."

"Just Farleigh, please," he said, smiling broadly. Then he turned to Nikos and said, "Bottle of Boutari to start."

"Certainly. Coming up."

"But we can only stay for, like, one drink," said Tracey. "Or two, maybe. See, we're having dinner with this guy we met, an—"

"My *God*, you work fast," said Dennis, shaking his head. "You Hellenic *hussy*."

Tracey turned crimson, but appeared rather flattered. "I wish!" she said. "We can't make up our minds if he's gay or not."

"He's not," said Roseanne.

"Is so," said Tracey. "Anyway, we met him on our way to our hotel, because he stopped to ask us directions just before *we* were gonna ask *him*. So it's kind of funny. But he's American, and he's here to see his grandmother because she just turned a hundred or something."

"Cute?" asked Dennis.

Tracey rolled her eyes, then rubbed her chin.

Dennis nodded. "So—is that a yes?"

Her shoulders slumped, and she looked at Roseanne. "He doesn't remember." She turned back to Dennis. "Don't you remember, on the ferry? Our secret code for if we saw a cute guy?" She rubbed her chin and winked at him.

"Oh, *yeah*," said Dennis, the memory filtering through that night's alcohol-induced fog. "Yeah. Man. I *wondered* why my chin was so sore this morning."

The whole table laughed (except, of course, Christos). Then Farleigh, his generosity more expansive than Dennis had seen it in years, leaned over to Tracey and put his hand on her forearm. "Your young friend can join us when he arrives, as well," he said. "As I said, we're celebrating, so the more, the merrier."

Tracey and Roseanne had a silent consultation on this, in the form of a split-second glance. Then they smiled happily and said, "Okay!"

Nikos was suddenly hovering over them. "Boutari," he said, and he plunked two bottles onto the table. One was already open. He pointed at it and said, "Some other people, they tried it but didn't like it." He held his nose and extended a pinky, as if to say, Snooty bastards. "You like the wine, you can have the rest. Just opened half an hour ago. No time for bugs to get in."

Dennis was about to balk, but then he thought, Greece. Plunge.

Apparently Farleigh felt the same way, because when Nikos poured him a glass from the already-opened bottle, he unhesitatingly took a swig and said, "Fine. Fine. A perfect, earthy Greek wine. Let's get lots of salty seafood to go with it."

"Octopus today is like a dream," said Nikos.

Dennis put down his menu; he needed to hear nothing more.

Tracey and Roseanne, however, looked less enthralled at the prospect of a table full of tentacles. Tracey wrinkled her nose and said, "Could we have a few minutes?"

"Sure, sure," said Nikos. "I bring you salads and, what— bread? Americans like bread."

"That'd be great," said Farleigh.

Nikos ambled off to greet two new arrivals, and the girls started poring over the menus. "Do they have lamb?" Roseanne asked. "I want lamb."

"You've had lamb every meal you've been here," said Tracey. "Be adventurous."

"I want lamb. I *like* lamb."

"The specials are on the board, there," said Farleigh as he

donned his spectacles. He looked behind him at the maze of characters scribbled on the blackboard over the bar.

"I can't read any of that," said Tracey. "Roseanne, do you have the dictionary with you? I can't read any of this."

"Just a second," Roseanne replied; she was already busy digging through her purse. "It was here this morning. This always happens to me!"

"What's the triangle? The triangle is an L, right?"

"No," she said, producing the book at last. "The triangle is a D. A triangle without a bottom is"—she flipped the book open—"yes, *that's* an L."

"Okay, turn to the restaurant section and see wh—"

"The first special," said Christos, now leaning into them and speaking in a deep, throaty voice, "is the grilled octopus. The second one," and here he pointed his hairy, muscular forearm at the chalkboard, "is sea bass. The third is eel. Sauteed." He put his arm down. "Those are the specials."

Tracey and Roseanne stared at him in fascinated terror, scarcely breathing. Dennis had to choke down a laugh. If only they could see him in a kimono, swooping around the kitchen pretending he was Joan Sutherland in *La Sonnambula!*

"M-maybe we'll just wait till our friend gets here," said Tracey, looking at Farleigh apologetically. "So we can all order together."

"*He's here,*" hissed Roseanne, tugging excitedly on Tracey's sleeve. "*He just walked in!*"

Dennis twisted around in his chair, eager to see the young American stud to whom the girls had taken such a shine.

And at the sight of him he felt the floor fall away. Reality seemed to swallow itself up in one big, anomalous gulp.

He reeled, and gripped the arms of his chair.

It couldn't be.

It *couldn't* be.

But somehow—some way—it was.

Jasper!

chapter

30

After he recovered from the initial shock, Farleigh got up, grabbed Jasper's arm, and hustled him out of the restaurant. They disappeared around the side of the building. Jasper offered no resistance; he looked more than a little stunned himself.

"You know Jasper?" said Tracey, thunderstruck by this revelation.

"He used to be our pool boy," said Christos with just a hint of breathlessness. Not even his macho pose could withstand an intrigue like this.

"He's the guy I was telling you about," Dennis said, almost whispering; he wanted to determine whether he could hear Farleigh and Jasper through the open windows.

"*What* guy?" asked Roseanne.

"The guy who—the guy I brought Farleigh here to get away from."

Tracey and Roseanne looked at each other in disbelief. Then Tracey turned back and said, "Okay. Wait a minute. So, you're, like, this totally hot guy, who has to steal this old man away from another totally hot guy. Is that, like, basically what's going on here?''

Dennis blushed. "Well . . . maybe in an excessively flattering sense, yes.''

"And, like, you and Jasper never thought, gee, maybe you should be, y'know, hot for each *other*?''

He gave her a disappointed look. "I thought women were supposed to judge men by what's inside instead of by their looks.''

"Not this woman!'' She grinned wildly and had another sip of wine.

Roseanne, peeved by her friend's attitude, jerked her thumb at her and said, "I keep telling her. Looks don't mean anything.''

"Easy for you to say. You've got Hank.''

"*His* looks have nothing to do with it.''

"Not *now* they don't.'' She turned back to Dennis. "That's another thing I don't get about women. Okay, so you get this total babe to love you, right? And every other woman in the world is just like *so* wild with jealousy. Then what do you do? You take him home and start force-feeding him until he's this monster potato, and all the other women who used to want him are suddenly looking at him and going, 'Whoa, narrow escape.' ''

Roseanne slammed her glass onto the table. "That is so unfair! Hank is only a little overweight.''

"But it's all in his *stomach*,'' said Tracey. "He's got no *hips*. That party we were all at before we left, Georgia Meek and I made a deal that we had to do a shot of tequila every time Hank hitched his pants up. By the time we left, Georgia couldn't even walk. I was lucky—I puked most of mine up in Vinnie Pressman's terrarium.''

Roseanne's nostrils were flaring; she was clenching and un-clenching her fists. "He has a perfectly *adorable* tummy. I can't *believe* you and Georgia would do that to me.''

"We didn't do it to you, Hank did it to us. Hitch, hitch, hitch!''

Dennis thought he heard a voice raised in anger, some-where outside the restaurant.

Roseanne was close to tears. "I don't know why I put up with you. You're so mean to me."

Tracey looked as though she'd been struck. "I . . . I am?"

"Yes. You treat me like dirt. You always do. You always have."

Now Tracey's eyes were welling up. "I'm sorry. I don't mean to. Do you hate me? Am I evil?"

Roseanne broke into a full bawl, completely drowning any noise from the street. *"Of course you're not evil! You're my best friend!"*

Tracey lunged into her and hugged her. *"I know! You're mine! I'm sorry, Rosie!"*

"Ahu-ahu-ahu!" they sobbed together.

Dennis looked at Christos in exasperation. Christos wasn't able to return the glance, however; he was too busy refilling his glass of Boutari. Dennis noticed that both bottles were now almost completely empty. Since no one else at the table had had much of a chance to drink any, he could only assume that Christos was, in the vernacular, goin' to town.

Tracey and Roseanne were now drying their tears and sniffing contentedly, their little rinsing rainstorm of emotion blown over. Dennis once again craned his neck toward a window and listened.

"Okay, then!" said Nikos, reappearing suddenly and clapping his hands so hard that Dennis actually jumped. "We ready to order yet?—Hey, where's Mr. Nock?"

"He'll be back," said Dennis. "Look, we're probably going to need a few more min—"

"Octopus," said Christos, lighting up another cigarette. "We'll all have octopus."

Tracey and Roseanne were too afraid to contradict him. They stared at him with pale, fascinated faces.

"Excellent choice!" said Nikos. "You will never have them fresher! Just in this afternoon. One of them I even killed myself!" He smiled proudly, then turned on his heel and marched away.

"This is getting ridiculous," said Dennis to the table at large. "What's keeping Farleigh?" He threw his hands into the air, then let them drop noisily onto the table.

"You should go check," said Tracey, now completely re-covered.

"No, no," said Roseanne. "Tracey, you don't have a relationship; you don't know."

"Oh, fine, rub it in."

Roseanne turned to Dennis. "This is *so* a test of your trust. You have to sit here and wait even if it takes till, like, doomsday."

"Oh, please," said Tracey. She tried to freshen her glass of wine, but found nothing left in either bottle. She turned to Dennis. "Um, I'll pay for another bottle of wine, if we get one."

"Farleigh's paying," he said through clenched teeth. "Oh, you'd better *believe* he's paying." Having borne quite enough of this, he slapped his hands on the table and stood up, knocking his chair behind him.

Roseanne reached across the table and tried to stop him. "Wait! Wait, Dennis! Believe me, I know what I'm talking about! Once, like, a year ago, Hank went to dinner with his old girl-friend, Lois Sienkiewicz? And I let him? Because he was all, 'She's like a sister to me now.' And I'm, 'Okay.' And everyone, including Tracey, was like, 'Oh, go to the restaurant in disguise and watch them.' And I'm, like, *so* no way. Because first of all, what are the odds of Hank, y'know, recognizing me? Like, *mega*. Okay? So, second of all, what would that *say*, exactly? 'Oh, hello—I, like, don't trust you?' Thanks, but no thanks. And third," she said, sinking back into her chair, "third, you're a great guy, and maybe, like, it's time you let Farleigh realize that and come after *you*. Okay? Maybe it's time you just, y'know, say, 'Okay, Farleigh. Here I am. Your call.' Because, sometimes you *so* have to."

He was immediately overwhelmed by Roseanne's innate wisdom. He hesitated a moment; then, feeling shaky, he sat down again. "Well," he said, his voice trembling, "yes. Yes, I see what you mean. But, it's just—it's just *youth*, you know. I'm old, and Jasper's young. I can't compete with that."

Roseanne put her hand over his. "Well, who says you have to? And if you do, who says it has to be about youth? Why can't it be, like, shared history or something? Or, y'know—whatever?"

Tracey started bawling again. "Ohmigod, that's so *totally* beautiful."

Christos flung an arm into the air. Everyone else at the table jumped.

"*Another bottle, please!*" he snarled, and they realized he was calling out to Nikos. "*In fact—two.*"

Dennis grimaced at him, then turned back to Tracey and Roseanne. "You girls are great," he said. "You really are. I'm glad I met you." They blushed in acknowledgment of this. "But, I mean, I'm not stupid. Farleigh and Jasper get five more minutes. That's all. Then I go out there a-gunnin'."

Roseanne nodded. "Five minutes? Well. Okay. I mean . . . you are a guy, after all."

"More or less," he said, and he winked at Christos, who once again missed the gesture; he was too busy picking his teeth with his fork. Christos, who at home refused to use any floss that wasn't waxed and flavored spearmint.

Nikos brought the next two bottles of wine, and a buxom waitress followed with a tray of Greek salads. "To keep you busy till Mr. Nock returns," he said.

Dennis pursed his lips. "That's it," he said. "Even the staff has noticed." He stood up and strode away from the table before anyone could offer an objection. He headed for the door, and before he knew it, he was out in the street.

It was a busy night in Mykonos town. A procession of black-clad grannies was filing into a tiny chapel. A souvenir store was filled with Japanese tourists. A local couple were outside a disco, arguing frantically about something or other. And in between flowed streams of people. Happy, smiling people, smelling of liquor and excess sun.

Dennis made his way around the side of the building where he'd seen Farleigh and Jasper disappear.

It was dark here, darker than he thought. The only light came from the stars.

"*Hello?*" he called out. "*Hello . . . anybody?*"

He could hear a muffled noise—like a cat coughing up a hairball, or a fratboy with the dry heaves.

He stood still, till his eyes adjusted to the darkness. Then he could make out—just barely—Farleigh's rotund form, in sil-

houette, against the luminous sky. And in Farleigh's arms, collapsed like a marionette . . . well, it could only be Jasper. The
hacking sounds were coming from him. Crying. Jasper was crying. Almost violently. No—*absolutely* violently.

"*Farleigh?*" said Dennis. *"Everything all right?"*

"It's fine," said Farleigh in a voice clear and strong and
confident. "Go back inside. We'll rejoin you in a moment."

chapter
31

"H ello?"

"Lonnie, hi. It's me. Dennis."

"Dennis? Wha—wait a minute? Where are you?"

"Greece. Listen, I—"

"Greece? What the fuck time is it over the— Jesus, kiddo, it's eleven o'clock here. Over there it must be—"

"Four or five in the morning. Or six. I'm not sure. Can we talk? Did I wake you?"

"Yeah, yeah . . . but I wasn't out for the night. Just fell asleep on the couch watching Jay Leno. What's up?"

"He's here."

"What? Who are you talking about?"

"Jasper. The pool boy. He's here. Turned up at dinner tonight."

"Whoa. *Whoa.* Let me shake myself awake, here."

"Sit up. Turn off the TV. I need you. Can we conference-call Paulette, or something?"

"I don't know about that. Saw her at the club today; told me the Spanker surprised her with a big, new Gold Coast apartment to thank her for rescuing his career from death-by-Florida.

Said they were going out all day shopping for furniture, then out to dinner. And if they did all that, she owes the Spanker some serious fucking right about now. Wouldn't call that number if my life depended on it."

"Damn it. *Damn* it."

"Well, you've still got me, buddy. Give it a shot."

"I don't know. You sound all—weird. Fuzzy-tongued. You been drinking?"

"Little. Dierdre and me had a celebration tonight."

"Oh, fine. Let's everybody have relationship pinnacles but me. What now? You getting married?"

"Good as. Turns out, she was seriously freaked when I went missing. You remember, when I passed out and rolled under the buffet table? And didn't wake up for about six hours? Well, apparently at the party Dierdre was . . . let's say she was *allowing* certain parties to be rude to me and snub me and even make little comments about me. Y'know? Nothing I haven't learned to put up with a long time ago. But apparently it was a little worse than usual that night—not that I noticed. Too drunk. But Dierdre noticed, and when all of a sudden the party was over and she couldn't find me, she thought I'd walked out on her because of it."

"Really? Well, you know that's not all bad."

"No shit! She spent all night calling everyone in the world looking for me, trying to get the police to search for me. They just laughed at her. A real nightmare. And when I turned up all disheveled in my tux and told her what happened—"

"Right, right. I remember this part. Glorious reunion. Trumpets and choirs of angels. What next?"

"Just a palimony agreement."

"Get out! Dierdre *Diamond* gave you a *palimony* agreement? She's worth about a bazillion dollars!"

"No, *we're* worth about a bazillion dollars. Signed the papers this afternoon. So we came home and had a little champagne and fag food to celebrate. Then a quick shag, then Dierdre dropped off to a light snore, and I came back to my place to watch Leno. Then you called. You are now officially caught up."

"Yeah, and how wonderful. Congratulations. Now, Mr. Bazillionaire, can we concentrate on how to keep me from home-lessness and poverty?"

"I'm sure it's not that bad."

"Wh—what was that? What did I hear?"

"Nothing."

"I heard a slurp. I *distinctly* heard a slurp. Are you drinking again?"

"Just popped open a beer, is all. Wash the taste of cham-pagne out of my mouth."

"How dare you drink when my life is in crisis?"

"It's either drink or puke. Your choice."

"God. God, I'm doomed. I should just throw myself into the Aegean right now."

"Look, maybe you could save the melodrama for our next local call. Am I right in thinking that Farleigh's paying for this?"

"Jesus—yes. Thanks. Last thing I need is him waving a big transatlantic phone bill in my face. All right, down to business. The pool boy's here, and Farleigh's all over him like a wet T-shirt."

"What's he doing there? Isn't he supposed to be handling the rehearsals and everything?"

"Oh, brother. I forgot you hadn't heard. Okay, the produc-tion pretty much fell apart after Farleigh left."

"Ooh . . . bad! Pool boy's fault?"

"I wish! But he didn't help matters. He panicked, and fled. All the way to Greece."

"Whatever for?"

"Well, he says it's because he couldn't bear to tell Farleigh about it over the phone; he had to come and make his confes-sion in person."

"And Farleigh forgave him?"

"After all those hot tears flooding his rosy young cheeks? After he batted his eyelashes and begged for mercy? *Forgave* him? How about, forgave him and invited him to come stay at the goddamn *house* with us till he gets over the trauma of his first theatrical disaster?"

"He did not!"

"He did so. 'Course, the kid's sleeping in Christos's room,

while Christos takes the couch, but you should've seen me in
bed with Farleigh afterward. Like there were scorpions sleeping
between us. He couldn't get far enough away from me."

"Well. Well. This is serious business. What are you going to
do?"

"That's what I'm asking *you*. If you could stop slurping up
that beer for a moment. Didn't anyone ever teach you how to
swallow without noise?"

"Sorry. Let me think about this for a minute . . . You know,
one thing I don't get is how a pool boy could come up with the
money for a trip to Greece, just like that."

"Oh, yeah. I asked Farleigh about that, too, just before we
went to bed. Apparently, Jasper has a grandmother who lives
on Santorini and who just turned a hundred. His mother's been
begging him to go see the old broad before she dies. She can't
go herself because she's in a wheelchair, so Jasper was supposed
to go to the big birthday bash in her place and pay the family's
respects. Anyway, Jasper wasn't into going—kept finding reasons to put it off. Missed the party and everything. But when
the play fell apart and he knew we were in Mykonos, he hit his
mother up for a ticket to Greece, and implied that it was to see
the grandmother. Mom whipped out her credit card, Jasper
hopped a plane, and here he is. He just changed the final des-
tination from Santorini to Mykonos."

"Clever kid. Reminds me of you."

"Never . . . *never* say that."

"Jesus, buddy. Only kidding."

"I hope so. Anyway, that's the situation as it stands. I
couldn't sleep all night from worrying. Got up as soon as the
sun rose. I'm calling from out on the patio, so my voice won't
wake anyone else up."

"Is that the crashing of the surf I hear? I thought we just
had a bad connection."

"Never mind the connection. *Help* me, Lonnie."

"I'm thinking, I'm thinking . . . This grandmother thing
intrigues me. His mother's mother?"

"Appears that way."

"Is he going to see her? Did he say?"

"I don't know. All I know is what I got from Farleigh last

night. Which wasn't very much. Acted like he was offended by my even asking. Son of a bitch."

"Okay. Here's the way I see it. The kid put it off this long —well, there's got to be a *reason* for not wanting to see the grandmother. So I say, make sure he sees her. And make sure you and Farleigh go along."

"Ugh! What do I want to go to some horrible hut in the middle of some island for?"

"First of all: what if he's lying? What if there is no grand-mother? What if he got the money some other way and just doesn't want Farleigh to know?"

"Uh-huh. Interesting . . . Okay, I'll bite. And what if I force the issue, and it turns out there *is* a grandmother?"

"Well, that's up to you. Size her up, gauge your opportu-nities. Been my experience that nothing kills a budding infat-uation more than a face full of family. Let Farleigh get a dose of the old bitch; maybe it'll be enough for him to look at Jasper and think twice."

"Yeah, and maybe not."

"Like I said, it's up to you to pay attention and, y'know, help it along. You know how to do this, party boy. Don't tell me you don't."

"All right. I accept your homage to my gifts."

"And until then, make sure you play it cool with Jasper. Treat him nice, make sure he feels welcome. Last thing you want is for Farleigh to suspect you of something."

"For him to suspect me of something would mean he'd have to think about me for more than two seconds at a time. So no big worry there. But thanks, Lonnie. I mean it. I'll report back, okay?"

"Okay. Listen, I gotta go. Think I hear Dierdre calling. Must've woke up and missed me."

"Huh. Suddenly, I don't envy you anymore. You go play. And, Lonnie—I *owe* you."

chapter
32

"My God, what a day!" said Farleigh, standing on the patio in his silk dressing gown and gazing in wonder at the sun pouring pleasure onto the earth. "Feel that breeze! And that heat! That's it. We're going to the beach."

Dennis, who had fallen asleep on one of the deck chairs, the phone hanging limply from his hand, roused himself and rubbed his eyes. "The beach?" he repeated, incredulous. "You hate the beach!"

"Don't be silly," he said, slapping Dennis on the shoulder, as if he were a coworker at a body shop or something. "Why would I have bought this house if I didn't like the beach?"

Dennis wanted to say, Because *I* like the beach, but decided against it. Farleigh had apparently forgotten that he'd bought the house for Dennis, and wouldn't take kindly to being reminded.

"We'll get Christos to put together a basket for us," Farleigh continued, rubbing his ample stomach and basking his face in the sunlight. "Sandwiches, cold beers. Make a day of it. We're not here for long, so we might as well enjoy ourselves."

Jasper appeared at the door to the patio, looking bleary-eyed and adorable, his hair pointing in five different directions. "Uh, morning," he said tentatively. He was wearing only boxer shorts. His nipples were the size of cocktail coasters. "Anything for breakfast here?"

Farleigh turned and beamed a smile at him. "Ask Christos. He should be in the kitchen. What'd you have in mind?"

"I dunno. Cereal?"

"We can probably do that. Oh, and would you mind telling him to prepare a picnic basket, because we're going to the beach today?"

"You are?"

"*We* are. The three of us." He patted Dennis on the head like he would an obedient dog.

"Okay," said Jasper excitedly. "Great. That'd be great." He disappeared into the house.

Farleigh turned back to Dennis; he spotted the phone and his smile disappeared. "Who'd you call?" he asked.

"Office," said Dennis, thinking quickly. "Wanted to check in, make sure everything was okay."

He scowled. "I'm not aware of too many travel agencies open that late at night."

"I know. Forgot the way the time thing works. Thought they were seven hours ahead, not behind. I just left some messages for people."

He nodded but appeared unconvinced. "Well. Whatever. Go easy on the international charges, though."

Dennis felt a sting of pride. "Don't worry. I'll certainly pay for any calls I make."

"No need for that. Just be careful, that's all." He took a deep breath, then reentered the house.

Dennis sat on the patio seething. It was clear to him that Farleigh's only reason for heading down to the beach was so that he could watch Jasper frolic naked for the better part of the day. And from what Dennis had seen of the boy in his boxers, you could scarcely blame him. Body as lean and taut as a ripcord—and effortlessly so. Dennis, thanks to Fatima, hadn't been in better shape in years; still, he knew that his physique looked different from Jasper's—almost *tortured* into shape. Farleigh couldn't help making the comparison.

He heard laughter inside the house—unfamiliar laughter. Jasper's. His face flushed with anger and jealousy. He decided to stay right here until the time came to head for the beach. It wasn't as though he needed to shower or anything; he'd be throwing himself into the Aegean. And he didn't need to change. In his jams and T-shirt, he was perfectly dressed for the trip down to the beachfront. At which point he'd be stripping down to nothing, anyway.

So he sat and sulked until, some forty minutes later, Farleigh appeared at the patio door and said, "We're on our way now, Dennis. Coming?"

"Yeah, yeah," he said sulkily, and sat up.

"If you're not feeling up to it, it's all right if you stay. Jasper and I will just go down alone."

I don't *think* so, he thought, and he leapt to his feet. "No, no, I'm up for it. I really am." He galloped to the door, gave Farleigh his widest smile, and said, "Let's roll."

Farleigh handed him a stack of towels and a beach umbrella, then led him through the house to the front door. There they found Jasper, already waiting, carrying the picnic basket, a backpack over his shoulder. "All right?" he asked eagerly.

"All right," said Farleigh, pleased to be so indulgent.

Jasper scampered on ahead. Farleigh followed, and Dennis, burdened by the bulkiest load, brought up the rear. He had to keep setting down the umbrella and shifting it to the opposite shoulder, so that by the time he reached Farleigh and Jasper, Jasper had already stripped off his clothes and was cavorting naked on the sands.

The sight stopped Dennis in his tracks. Brown, lean, and youthful as Jasper was, nothing could have prepared him for the boy's nether parts. The buttocks were so round and white, they might have been carved out of the new-fallen snow. They practically *invited* despoilation. And that cock . . . ! Thin at the base, thickening as it extended outward, and curving deliciously leftward near the tip. It was a cock with *personality*. Dennis imagined he could spend hours just perched on his elbow, *talking* to that cock.

Then he caught himself admiring his enemy, shook himself
back to reality, and plunked the towels and umbrella on the
sand next to Farleigh.

"Spot's good as any," Farleigh said in approval. "Set the
umbrella up here."

A spasm of rage passed over Dennis. "I paid my own way
here," he said through gritted teeth. "I'm not a fucking servant.
Set it up yourself." Then he ripped off his jams and T-shirt and
raced naked to the water, his feet pummeling the sands like
pistons.

The water was warm, and swallowed him up almost eroti-
cally. He felt his own cock grow hard; it was like reverting to
the womb . . . a comforting, nurturing sack of amniotic fluid.
And wasn't the Aegean kind of a cultural womb, anyway? He
wouldn't mind dying here. There was something almost poetic
about it. Maybe he should just make things easy for Farleigh
and everybody else, and just go under and not come up. . . .

But then he caught sight of some of the magnificent naked
bodies strutting the sands before him, and hope reasserted itself
in his breast. Where there was beauty, there was always hope. A
piano sonata, a classic haiku, a perfectly muscled abdomen
splayed with golden hair—all were reason enough to want to
go on living.

He took a deep breath, then swam freestyle back to the
beach. He crawled out of the water, shook his hair dry, then
padded back over to where Farleigh, in his sun hat and silk
trousers, was struggling ridiculously with the umbrella. "*I'll* do
it," Dennis said as he grabbed it out of Farleigh's hands and
rammed it into the sand. "Just stop taking me for granted,
okay?"

Farleigh merely nodded; his face was red and he kept his
eyes downcast—very much the demeanor of a deservedly
chided child.

Dennis spread out a blanket and threw himself onto it, then
huffed out the rest of his anger and lay awhile, waiting for his
heartbeat to slow and the thrum of his pulse to leave his ear
canals. Beads of water ran from his temples down the bridge of
his nose, tickling and calming him. Eventually, his temper restored, he lifted his head and turned to Farleigh.

"Where's the boy wonder?" he asked.

Farleigh was sitting under the umbrella, reading a biography of Lillie Langtry (an intimate of Oscar Wilde, Dennis later learned, thus explaining his interest). He didn't raise his eyes from the book, but merely said, "I'm not certain. I'm sure he'll be back."

But Dennis could see Farleigh's lips turning white from the pressure with which he brought them together. His idyllic day at the beach was off to a rather bumpy start. He'd offended his current lover, and the next-in-line was off gallivanting naked somewhere out of sight on a beach filled with gorgeous, libertine gay men.

It was about to get even worse for him. From several yards away came a husky, bellowing cry: *"Farleigh! Ahoy,* there—Farleigh *Nock!"*

Farleigh put down his sunglasses and stared down the beach in disbelief. "I don't believe it," he said. "What in the seven hells is *she* doing here?"

Dennis propped himself up and followed Farleigh's gaze. A tall, bronzed, somewhat elderly woman with a bandanna and a ponytail was making her way toward them, her ankle-length black beach robe flapping wildly behind her. She carried a canvas bag in one hand, and was waving wildly with the other. "Who is it?" Dennis asked, shading his eyes to better view this startling apparition.

"Talent agent from Chicago," said Farleigh, marking his page with a bookmark and setting the book aside. "You've met her before. Jennifer Jerrold."

"Oh, yeah," he said, a dim memory growing brighter as he focused on it. "I think I remember her. Wasn't she the one who was married to a qu—"

"*Yes,*" hissed Farleigh, interrupting him. He put his finger to his mouth and shushed him just as Jennifer descended on them like a lioness.

"*Far*leigh Nock," she declared with finality. "What *are* you doing here?"

"Hello, Jennifer," he replied politely. "I have a house here." He pointed to where the house in question sat perched atop the cliff.

"I know that," she said, pulling her robe taut about her fanny, then dropping into the sand beside him. She wiggled herself into place, then exposed her leathery upper chest to the sunlight. "What I meant was, what are you doing here when *Lady Windermere* is in rehearsals? Especially with the production in some sort of trouble—or so rumor has it."

"No trouble, Jennifer. Just a change of venue."

"Oh. I see." She seemed almost disappointed; then she rallied. "Say, have you seen Kyle around? You remember my husband, Kyle, don't you?"

"Very well. And I haven't seen him, no."

She sighed, and fondled her enormous lapus necklace. "I've been looking for him for the better part of an hour. Don't know *how* he slipped away from me. Ah, well." She shrugged. "He can't get too far. I've got *these*." She reached into her canvas bag and pulled out a pair of filmy blue swimming trunks.

Dennis took a quick glance at the throngs of naked men cruising each other on the beach, and bit his tongue; he wanted to say that Kyle might not *get* very far, but he could *go* all the way. Still, he had not as yet been acknowledged by the rather imperious Miss Jerrold, and if possible he preferred to remain unnoticed for the duration of her visit.

Alas, Farleigh would have none of that. He turned and said, "I think you remember my companion, Dennis Racine."

Dennis rolled over on his side and smiled. Jennifer lowered her sunglasses, gave him an unembarrassed appraisal, head to toe, and said, "Yes. Yes. How do you do."

"Very well, thanks. Good to see you again, Jennifer."

She pushed her sunglasses back up her nose, then stuffed Kyle's swim trunks back into the canvas bag, and in their place brought out a bottle of Evian and a small ceramic cup. "May I offer anybody a drink?" she asked.

"None for me, thanks," said Farleigh.

"Suit yourself." From the pocket of her robe she produced a silver whiskey flask, which she unscrewed and nearly emptied into the cup. "So, tell me," she said as she screwed the cap back onto the flask and slipped it back into her pocket. "Whom did you ever find to play Mrs. Erlynne? Anyone I know? An out-of-towner?" She opened the bottle of Evian and splashed some water into the whiskey, then picked it up and knocked back a hearty throatful of the mix.

Farleigh watched her in what appeared an equal measure of amazement and admiration. "Actually, I found a local actress who fit the bill quite nicely. I don't know if you know her. Mercedes St. Aubyn . . . ?"

Jennifer nearly spat out her drink; it dribbled down her chin while she pounded her chest so that she wouldn't choke. When at last she could speak again, she said, "Surely—surely you don't mean the *Tourette's.*"

"It's an affliction, not an identity," said Farleigh. "And it only affects her social speech, not her line readings. She's really quite wonderful."

Jennifer regarded him with her mouth half open, as though waiting for him to admit he was making a joke. When it became clear he'd do no such thing, she rolled her eyes and said, "Yes, well, I suppose you know what you're doing."

He laughed out loud. "No, you don't, Jennifer. You don't suppose anything of the kind."

She narrowed her eyes at him and gave him a mock punch on the shoulder. "So sue me for being polite. Well, I *do* hope she works out for you. You'll let me know, won't you?"

" 'Course. Say, what are *you* doing here, anyway? Who's running the store?"

"My office manager. A real go-getter. Left everything in her hands. Kyle and I just came over for a bit of a holiday." She took an enormous chug of her drink, finishing it off. "How long are you here, darling? We should have dinner."

Hastily, Farleigh said, "Well, we're probably leaving tomorrow. Can't spend too much time away from rehearsals."

She put the cup back in her bag. "It'll just have to be tonight, then. What time is good for you?"

"Oh, gosh, Jennifer," he said, digging his toes into the sand as if trying to gain purchase there lest Jennifer attempt to drag him off to a taverna right now, "tonight's out. Sorry. Other plans. Perhaps back in Chicago . . ."

She sighed, then gave up and collected her bag. "Crap, is what I say. Why do these arrangements never work this side of the Atlantic? I'm just *dying* to talk to someone besides Kyle."

There followed a slight, uncomfortable pause while she gazed out at the horizon, and seemed for a moment inexpressibly sad. Then she turned and said brightly, "Till Chicago, then. Now, I really must go and find that bad boy of mine."

As she got to her feet, Dennis noticed that Jasper had emerged suddenly from the water and was running up to them, carrying an enormous seashell. With the sun behind him, accentuating his leanness and turning each bead of water that flew from his hair into a brilliant, temporary diamond, there was something almost mythically beautiful about him. Dennis felt his scrotum tighten.

The boy loped across the sands until he was standing, panting and wet and beautiful, before Farleigh. He extended his hands, displaying the shell, and said, "Look, Farleigh! I found it for you. Look at the colors!"

Jennifer, who had only just collected herself and was preparing to move on, now noticed Jasper for the first time, and when the full force of his youthful splendor hit her, she dropped her canvas bag and stared at him, slack-jawed.

Farleigh, noticing this, said, "Oh, Jennifer, I don't believe you know Jasper Batton, my *Lady Windermere* director. Jasper, this is a fr—a colleague from Chicago, Jennifer Jerrold."

Jasper said, "Hi," and smiled widely, and Jennifer was hit by another erotic whammy. She burbled out a hello of her own, then picked up her bag and hobbled off, looking dazed.

Dennis noted well the look of amusement on Farleigh's face. There was no mistaking it: it was the extremely satisfied look of a man who's just seen his prized possession openly desired by another. And that's how he thought of Jasper, it was clear—as his possession. All he had to do was make room on the shelf for him. By taking down something that didn't belong there anymore.

Dennis, for instance.

There was still fight left in Dennis, though; he wasn't about to give up easily. Remembering Lonnie's advice, he turned on all his charm and, reaching his leg over to tweak Farleigh's love handles with his toes, said, "I think you were teasing her just a little, honey."

Farleigh looked at him in some surprise. "How in the world

did you know that?'' he asked. "I never told you about her wanting to play Mrs. Erlynne!'' He turned to Jasper and said, "That lady—Jennifer—let it be known all over town that she wanted to make her big comeback in our show. But she never approached me directly, so I never bothered calling her. Damned if I'll go crawling to her for the favor of an audition. Anyway, just now I was singing Mercedes's praises to her, and obviously making her more than a little uncomfortable.''

Jasper laughed along with him. But Dennis shook his head and, casually straining sand through his fingers, said, "That's not what I meant. You told her we were leaving tomorrow. You can't really have meant that.''

"Why not?'' Farleigh stopped fondling the seashell Jasper had given him and arched an eyebrow at Dennis. "I spoke to the airline this morning. We're all on standby for the afternoon flight.''

Dennis shrugged and said, "Well, think of poor Jasper.'' At this Jasper, who was busy drying himself with a towel, stopped and looked at Dennis with a hint of alarm. "He's come all this way to see his poor old grandmother. We can't just abandon him now.''

Farleigh slapped his forehead. "My God. I'd totally forgotten.'' He turned to Jasper. "Of *course* we'll come with you.''

Jasper was giggling in what was clearly panic. "Oh—oh, hey. You guys don't have to—I mean—look, I never really intended to *see* her. That was just my excuse to get the ticket.''

Farleigh gave him a sidelong glance. "Now, don't tell me you were planning to deceive your poor mother. Were you? You weren't going to go back home without having fulfilled your part of the deal. Don't tell me you're that kind of man.''

" 'Course he's not, Farleigh,'' said Dennis. "He's obviously just kidding you.''

"Well, he'd better be. Now, where did you say your grandmother lived? One of the other islands, wasn't it?''

Jasper was visibly trembling. "S-santorini. It's pretty far from here . . .''

"Nonsense!'' Farleigh shook his head. "A hydrofoil to Paros, a ferry from there to Santorini—it's a matter of hours at best. I've done it many times.''

"She's—you have to . . . Farleigh, my family here is very rustic," Jasper said desperately. "They won't be able to put you up, or, or, or show you a good time, or—"

Farleigh waved him into silence. "Lots of hotels on Santorini. We'll book one this afternoon." He turned to Dennis. "Remind me."

Don't worry, thought Dennis.

"We'll go tomorrow," Farleigh continued. "I'll change our flight to the day after. Now, if there are no other silly objections . . . how about lunch?"

Jasper stood, eyes wide as a fawn's, completely at his wit's end. Farleigh didn't notice; he was too busy digging with gusto into the picnic basket.

chapter
33

Jasper was quiet and jumpy through the rest of the day, and partook of more than his fair share of wine at dinner. It certainly didn't help that Dennis kept bringing up (totally innocently, of course) the fun they'd have visiting "family" on Santorini the next day. "I hear it's really beautiful there," he kept repeating. Once, he leaned serenely into Jasper's table space, perched his chin atop his knuckles, and asked, "How long has Grandma Batton lived there?"

Jasper paused only long enough to say "Batton is my father's name. My grandmother's name is Ioannou, and she's lived there all her life," before downing another entire glass of Boutari.

Dennis was certain there was something terribly wrong here. Terribly wrong *and* exploitable. That night he slept better than he had in months.

The next morning, however, Jasper pretended to have a bad cold.

"I don'd know how I god id, Farleigh," he said, his acting execrable by any definition. He sat at the breakfast table and held his head in the crook of his arm. "I dust woge ub feelig awful."

Farleigh, of course, had the approximate sophistication of a tree slug in these matters, so he swallowed this bunkum whole. He even moved Jasper into the master bedroom and insisted he stay there all day, quiet and under the covers, intruded upon only by Farleigh with successive bowls of Christos's homemade chicken soup, which he dutifully spooned into the boy's mouth.

Dennis, infuriated by both Jasper's playacting and Farleigh's naiveté, sulked around the house, his hands in his pockets. As luck would have it, the day was overcast, gloomy, and chilly; even Super Paradise was virtually empty, with the exception of a few fat Scandinavians who by their very ethnicity had no concept of cold.

By two o'clock, after a terse lunch with Christos in which neither one of them spoke a word, Dennis crept to the door of the master bedroom and lurked outside it, listening to Farleigh's sick-making bedside manner as he nursed the clearly phony invalid.

"There," he said, practically cooing. "That's the last spoonful. Now, have some more water . . . that's it . . . plenty of fluids. Wisdom in those old wives' tales. How are you feeling now? Any better?"

"Oh, Farleigh," said Jasper, his voice so adenoidal he sounded like a Saturday morning cartoon character, "how could I nod feel bedder with you being so sweed?"

"It's my very great pleasure," said Farleigh.

"I'b so sorry for ruiding your day. I didn'd mead to ged so . . . so strepdocockeyed."

Farleigh laughed—one of his genuine, full-throttle, from-the-gut whinnies—and Dennis realized that he hadn't heard that kind of reaction from Farleigh in years. He also realized that he himself would *never* have thought up a pun like "streptocockeyed." A cold, hard hatred for Jasper settled over him, like a cloak, or a mantle. It was a turning point.

That boy must go, he thought to himself. *If I have to push him into the Aegean myself, I will.*

But what chance would he have? Farleigh had made it clear

that he had no intention of remaining in Greece . . . not with *Lady Windermere* rescued from the scrap heap and in need of his guiding hand. And Jasper had successfully wriggled out of the last full day they'd have here. The goddamn pool boy had won. He'd beaten Dennis at his own game. Tomorrow they'd be on a plane back to the States, and no one would ever know what old Granny Ioannou might have brought to the party.

In a fury of frustration Dennis stormed down the hall and cornered Christos in the kitchen, where he was washing the plates from their lunch.

"I don't *believe* it," he snarled, pacing around the table like a jungle cat. "Farleigh can't *possibly* believe that lying son of a bitch is really sick. He's *got* to know the kid's just pretending so he can get out of going to Santorini. Hasn't he felt his forehead? What kind of moron is he?"

Christos, the ever present Turkish smoke hanging from his lower lip, turned and regarded Dennis over one shoulder, then shrugged and resumed his soapy scrubbing.

Dennis felt something snap in his head. He stormed over to Christos and gave him a thwack on the back. The housekeeper whirled in astonishment; his cigarette even fell in the dishwater.

"And I'll tell you what *else* I can't believe," said Dennis, his nostrils flaring. "I can't believe that back in the States, you made this big weepy scene about me keeping secrets from you, and *insisted* that I take you into my confidence; then as soon as we get to the goddamn Greek islands, you turn into a goddamn Greek *statue*. Big macho Christos. Well, I'm in *trouble* here, okay? So can Anthony fucking *Quinn* just take a fucking *hike* and let the *real* Christos out for *one* fucking *second?*" He finished his tirade and stood trembling with fury.

Christos stared at him as though they'd never met, then muttered something in Greek that Dennis couldn't understand, and went back to his dishwashing.

Dennis felt his moral center suddenly begin to wobble in the storm of his emotions. He would gladly have killed someone right then. Farleigh. Jasper. Christos. Himself. It didn't much matter who, as long as there was blood, and lots of it.

Suddenly frightened, but no less angry, he fled the house,

hopped into the Jeep, and drove away at something less than light speed but considerably more than a tear.

He hadn't taken a jacket, and the chill wind whipped through his hair. He could have put up the windows, but he refused; the wind felt good. Sharp, like his anger. In some way he felt that it *fed* him.

An endless vista of farmland and rock mounds hurled past his head, and then he found himself in Mykonos town, wandering under the dreary, oppressive, late-afternoon sky. All around him, the islanders and the tourists paraded by, oblivious to him, mindless of his suffering and his anger, which, if they only looked into his eyes, might have stopped their hearts with its intensity.

He barely noticed them. The features of the island—its uneven streets, its whitewashed facades, its brightly colored awnings and shutter boards—barely registered on his conscious mind. He was walking in a daze, lost in an elaborate fantasy in which he, Iago-like, poisoned Farleigh's mind against Jasper and brought them both to ruin.

He bumped innumerable shoulders; he knew two separate Greek expressions for "Excuse me," but used neither of them.

And then he saw it: a sweets shop. Baklava in the window, brown and oozing, the crust flaking off into the tin trays that held it. THEMI'S, it said in the window. Dennis could read that much. THEMI'S something-or-other. Shop? Or café? He didn't know and didn't care. It was just THEMI'S in his memory.

He and Farleigh had been here. Long ago, on their first trip to Mykonos. After a grueling night of lovemaking on the ferry from Piraeus. Three separate climaxes—and that was Farleigh! Farleigh, who was now lucky if he could manage one a month. They'd missed breakfast; they'd ended up throwing on their clothes and dashing from the ferry, laughing, at the sound of the whistle.

Where to eat? After so much activity, after so much love.

They'd wandered the town—this town, the one Dennis was walking alone now—and they'd found Themi's. Here, tucked away somewhere between a postcard shop and someone's dingy residence. Themi's, where the proprietress—Themi herself?— was standing outside the door in fluffy slippers and a very dirty

Jackson 5 apron, smoking a cigarette, looking insouciant and glamorous and dangerous, like a latter-day Carmen.

Well, Farleigh had fallen in love with her. In his halting Greek he'd asked her if she had any pastries they could have for breakfast.

She'd looked at him, then at Dennis, and blown a hot, thin stream of smoke in their faces. "Sure," she said in perfect English. "Come on in. Take your pick."

There wasn't much of a choice. It had been baklava for both of them. Sticky and almost sickly sweet; the perfect post-coital love food.

And twenty-five minutes later, Farleigh presented him with the house. The house on the cliff. Overlooking Super Paradise.

"It's for you," he'd said, parking in front and beaming at Dennis, who was mute with shock. "I only wish I could give you the entire island."

Could that really have been this world? This earth? This millennium?

Dennis stared at the window of Themi's, shaken to his bootstraps, until Themi herself appeared at the door and raised an eyebrow at him. "Can I help you?" she asked in English, obviously recognizing him as American, but not recognizing him as the boy from long ago. But then, why should she? The truth was, he almost didn't recognize *her*. Her hair was now ivory white. Had it been that many years? That *very* many? Had everything aged and faded so *much* since then? Grown hoary and anomalous and irrelevant?

Maybe it had. Maybe there was something about Dennis himself that proclaimed the passage of time—not as starkly as Themi's white hair, of course, but to those who knew him, inescapable. Something slight and subtle, that all the same said, *Here is an artifact. Here is a remnant of times past.*

Oh, God, it was depressing. A relic at thirty-one.

He turned on his heels and resolved to plunge headlong into the first bar he encountered.

He hadn't gone far when he heard the trilling of familiar laughter. He scanned the street ahead of him and discovered Tracey and Roseanne coming his way gaily, accompanied by two virile-looking Greek youths. Or rather, *Tracey* was coming at him gaily, hanging on the arm of her newfound beau, who wore a black Urge Overkill T-shirt; she was chattering away at him madly, while he returned her good humor with a wide grin that verged on a leer. But Roseanne, behind them, walked somberly, her arms folded; a compact car could've driven through the space between her and the other Greek youth, who kept glancing her way expectantly over the rim of his Revo knockoffs.

Dennis felt his ill humor disappear in a little puff, like powdered sugar off a donut. These girls were exactly the tonic he needed. Smiling ear to ear, he galloped over to them and said, "Hey!"

At the sight of him, they awarded him their usual big-eyed, overwhelmed, fulsome-sounding "*Hiii!*" It made Dennis feel like he was exactly the person they'd been longing to see. Tracey even trotted over and hugged him, and although Dennis knew she was doing so, at least in part, to make her new boyfriend jealous, he was still flattered. When she broke away, Roseanne rolled her eyes at him, as if to silently indict Tracey for excessive girlishness; then she pulled her hair back and gave him a peck on the cheek.

"What are you *doing* here?" Tracey asked, as though she had no idea he was even in Greece.

"Spending the day away from the others," he said, trying hard to be honest. Lying to these open-faced girls would be nothing short of degenerate. "It's a small house, you know. And after a while it gets to you, having people on top of you all the time."

Tracey hunched her shoulders and said, "Ew. I can imagine. Anyway, this is my new friend, Andreas. Andreas, this is Dennis Racine . . . *Den*-nis. Understand? And Dennis, this is Roseanne's new friend, um . . ." She wrinkled her nose and turned guiltily to Roseanne.

"His name is Evagoras," Roseanne said tartly. "And he's not my friend, he's Andreas's." She turned to Dennis. "I don't *have* boyfriends," she explained. "I have a *fiancé*. As someone here knows perfectly well. Although if she meets two cute Greek guys on the make, she, like, somehow manages to forget it in a hurry."

Dennis looked uneasily at Evagoras, who smiled at him

pleasantly until Roseanne said, "Don't worry, he doesn't understand English. Neither does Andreas, though you'd never know, the way he laughs at everything Tracey says."

"You're such a *pill*," said Tracey, clutching Andreas's arm even tighter. "You just can't enter into the spirit of things, can you? This is supposed to be an *adventure*. What else are we here for?"

"To get some sun and relax and to experience the local culture," Roseanne retorted at once. "Wasn't that, like, what you said when you talked me into coming with you?"

"Yes," said Tracey, unabashed. She rubbed her arm against Andreas's and said, "So let's *experience* it, all right?"

Tracey narrowed her eyes, then turned back to Dennis. "I'm only going along with this so I can look after her. I know you probably could care, but I just want *someone* to know."

"I understand," said Dennis. "You know, I was just on my way to get a drink somewhere. Why don't you guys join me? My treat."

Roseanne clearly liked this idea, but turned in deference to Tracey, who grimaced and said, "Oh, you know—I'm kind of sorry? But I promised Andreas I'd spend the afternoon with him."

"How could you do that?" asked Roseanne sharply. "You don't speak Greek."

"We worked it out in sign language while you and Evagoras were settling the lunch bill." She made an apologetic face at Dennis. "Don't hate me, okay?"

He was crestfallen, but decided not to show it. "That's okay. Maybe me and Roseanne and Evagoras can go."

Roseanne shook her head. "I don't care *what* she promised that guy. I am *so* not letting her out of my sight." She jerked her thumb in Evagoras's direction. "But you can take my 'friend,' if you like. *I* don't want him around."

Dennis looked at the olive-skinned boy, with his shock of black hair and his enormous hands, and it was a measure of how desperate he was that he almost agreed to the proposition. But after a moment's reflection he realized that Roseanne had been making a joke, and that the likelihood of Evagoras leaving some potential pussy to go off with an over-thirty American queer was somewhere close to nil.

"Well," he said, shrugging his shoulders, "maybe next time."

Andreas started tugging at Tracey; he was trying to tell her that this little interlude had gone on long enough. She said, "Sure, next time. We'll have lunn—" Andreas pulled her away, forcing her to swallow the word.

Roseanne said, "So long, Dennis," then followed glumly, and Evagoras trotted along beside her.

Dennis watched them go, watched them until they turned a corner and disappeared down a side street. Then he stood awhile longer, in case Roseanne doubled back and waved him along. But of course she didn't; he felt humiliated that he'd actually thought she might.

He was feeling abandoned and hopeless and old and sad.

A stray mutt wandered up to him and sniffed his leg.

"You don't want anything to do with a loser like me, pal," he said. And the dog, as if understanding this and agreeing, padded off without further ado.

Dennis sighed. "Now," he muttered, "about that drink."

It was only four o'clock in the afternoon, so it took some doing to find a bar that was actually open. But since he had nothing to do but search and all the time in the world to do it, he eventually found a second-story disco whose doors were open, and although the place was virtually empty, the bartender—an incredibly wrinkled man with mutton-chop side-burns and at least nine gold chains, two of which bore yin-yang symbols—agreed to serve him.

"Bottle of retsina," Dennis said before he could stop himself.

The first glass was the hardest, as always; harsh like acid—but warm acid. Friendly acid. *Mellow* acid. In fact, it wasn't harsh at all, was it?

The second glass . . . a bit brusque. That was all.

The third glass? Rather drinkable, actually.

The fifth glass? . . . Smooooooth.

Alas, five was all the bottle offered him. He was now, unfor-

tunately, stone drunk. It would be all he could do to pay the
bartender and be on his way.

But what's this? Not the same bartender? No—the same bartender. But now he was smiling. Now his wrinkles weren't showing. Now he looked, somehow . . . *do*able.

Dennis suddenly noticed how dark it was in the bar. He
wondered what time it was, and checked his watch.

Seven forty-one.

He'd been here more than three hours.

Well, how long did it take one to down a bottle of retsina
by one's self? Three hours and forty minutes was about the
minimum survivable time.

Dennis caught the bartender's eye and made a little motion
with his thumb and forefinger, as though he were writing in
air. Universal sign language for "Check, please."

While he waited for the check, he swiveled (rather unsteadily) on his stool, and looked at the bar.

How astonishing to find it crowded!

Well, not crowded, but nearly filled. And filled with people
of purpose, too. Not like the few lingering deadbeats with whom
he'd started drinking hours earlier. These were young people.
People who stood in clusters and drank and laughed and
danced. There was music playing, he noted now. What was
wrong with him? How had all this happened behind his back?
What kind of pit had he fallen into that he could so lose
himself—almost *literally* lose himself—in a bottle of retsina?

He recognized the song that was playing. A remix of
Blondie's "Call Me." *Who says the Greek islanders are out of touch?*
he thought. There was a woman on the dance floor—her hair
an almost certainly store-bought red—who was shaking herself
convulsively. Her face resembled a knot of pain. Tilt her horizontally and put her on a bed, she could be having a seizure.
She had a pierced eyebrow and a pierced nostril.

Dennis watched her for a few moments and thought, She is
so cool.

The bartender reappeared. He handed Dennis his bill, then
winked at him and went to attend to someone else.

There was a man behind Dennis—he didn't actually see

him, he *felt* him looming over his shoulders—who was just waiting for Dennis to pay his bill and vacate his stool. So, he thought, this must be the hour that things start really rocking here. When stools become a commodity, what else do you call it?

He was just about to slip off—his butt cheeks had actually slid forward—when he realized something.

The "sleeve-petter" gypsies in Athens had made off with most of his cash. And he'd given the rest to Tracey and Roseanne so they could get a hotel room.

He was sitting here, absolutely flat fucking broke. With a bill for several thousand drachmas staring him in the face.

The man who wanted his stool practically had his own butt cheeks on it by now.

Dennis slid back abruptly, knocking the would-be pretender out of the picture. Then he flailed out his right arm and brought the bartender running back.

"Yes?" the bartender said, with another wink.

Dennis didn't even attempt any phrases in Greek. He pointed to the empty retsina bottle and said, "Changed my mind. Same again."

The bartender nodded, and returned with a new bottle in almost nothing flat. Now the speakers were blaring R.E.M.'s "Losing My Religion." People were dancing wildly. *America is a way big town*, thought Dennis.

He poured himself a new glass of retsina, took a drink, and thought, Cotton candy. Then he turned and surveyed the bar; it was even *more* crammed with people now. They must have *teleported* in. It was hard for him to focus his eyes after so much wine, but he knew he had to. His first, most crucial task now was, find someone to pay his bill.

He thought for a moment that he'd caught the attention of someone who might do just that, but the man—a surly type, who looked shockingly like Quentin Tarantino—was glaring at him in a decidedly unfriendly fashion.

Must be the joker who wanted the stool, Dennis decided.

He continued to scan the bar for a potential savior. There weren't many. In fact, there weren't any. This was clearly a het-

erosexual bar catering to an almost exclusively Gen X crowd.
Scarcely any Greeks, even. What chance of finding some polite,
elderly gay gentleman to assume Dennis's paltry debt?

He was about to give up and sneak out without paying when
he spotted a likely suspect. He hadn't noticed him before, but
when he looked toward the door, to gauge how far he'd have
to bolt without the bartender spotting him, he happened to
catch sight of a fortyish man in a gray houndstooth jacket, with
lots of billowing blond hair and a scraggly beard. The second
Dennis laid eyes on him, the man snapped his head in the
opposite direction.

So. He'd been watching him. And Dennis had *caught* him
at it.

A sort of confident calm spread over him. He had sighted
his quarry; he knew what to do from here.

He leaned against the bar. He kept his eyes locked on the
older man, knowing that he'd turn and look at him again. It
was inevitable. In fact, unless he missed his guess . . .

There. He'd done it. Looked back. For a split second. Long
enough for Dennis to smile at him.

Wait a little longer now. Glass in hand, at the ready.

Wait for him to get his nerve up. Just a little longer . . .

There.

Dennis raised his glass in salute and smiled, then tossed
back a swallow.

Mmm. Retsina.

What a fine, fine night.

The stereo was now playing "Revolution Earth" by the
B-52s.

Whoop! Got too wrapped up in the song. Almost missed
that. More eye contact.

And here he was now.

Here he was.

Dennis gripped his retsina. Tossed back another swallow.

"Bonjour," said the stranger.

"Hi," said Dennis. "You're French?"

"Oui. Yes. You are American?"

"Yes. Dennis Racine." He stuck out his hand.

The Frenchman shook it. "Alain Bertholde. You will excuse my English."

Dennis shook his head. "It's *perfect*."

"I may buy you a drink?"

"Actually, Monsieur Bertholde . . ."

"Alain. Please to call me Alain."

"Actually, Alain, you could buy the ones I've already had." He looked a bit panicked. "Ah. Yes."

Dennis put on his most pitiable expression. "I wouldn't ask, but I'm in dire straits."

"Please . . . ?"

"Real trouble. See, I left all my cash at my house on the other side of the island. I've just been looking for a Prince Charming to come rescue me."

"Prince Charming, eh? Like in your Disney films."

"Yes, yes, that."

The crowd was thickening. A heavyset local man bulldozed his way through the crowd, and as he did so he knocked Alain into the space between Dennis's knees. Alain did not immediately move back. Dennis pressed his knees against his thighs.

"Are you here on holiday?" Dennis asked.

Alain, who was holding his own drink, downed it in one gulp, then slammed it onto the bar. He was breathing heavily now. "No, I come to look at property here. I have property on Crete. I am living on Crete."

"Property on Crete! You must do very well for yourself."

"I am doing well. Yes." A pause. "And you?"

Dennis smiled slyly, then handed him his glass of retsina. Alain took one gulp, then made a face and handed it back to him.

"It's an acquired taste," said Dennis.

"Pardon?"

"It takes time to get used to it."

"Ah. Yes."

"Anyway, to answer your question . . . I have a house right here on Mykonos."

"You are, then, native?"

"No. I live in America. But I'm here on holiday."

"Ah." Alain looked across the bar, as if contemplating an escape route. Dennis pressed his knees against him even harder, and handed him yet more retsina.

He drank it.

When he gave the glass back, he said, "You are a very beautiful man."

Dennis laughed out loud.

"Why are you laughing, please?"

"You—it's just—the way you get right to the point." Alain stared at him as though not understanding this; his gaze was so intense that Dennis began to squirm beneath it. "So," he said jovially, "do you always come into bars like this to pick up men?"

"Only if the men are first staring at me," he replied, his eyes still smoldering. "So no, I do not much often pick up men. I am too old; I hear no thank you too much. So mainly I give it up, and now I am coming into places like this just to drink."

Dennis looked at him hard and said, "Alain, I know what I'm about to say next is the only thing you've left for me to say, but I want you to know that's not the reason I'm saying it; the truth is, I mean it, I mean it profoundly, when I tell you that you are *not* too old."

Alain looked at Dennis for a very, very long time. Then he reached into his jacket, pulled out his wallet, and produced a sheaf of drachma bills. He tapped the shoulder of the woman on the stool next to Dennis, and when she turned he said, "Excuse me. I would like to buy this stool from you," and handed her the wad of bills.

Dennis doubted that the woman understood English, or even French, by the look of her, but she understood drachmas. She took the money, slipped gracefully off the stool, and minced away.

Alain sat down and smiled at Dennis. "If I am paying your bill, I insist I must be sharing your wonderful wine."

"Fine," said Dennis giddily. "We can get you your own glass."

"Not necessary." He took the glass from Dennis's hands and took a healthy swallow, then handed it back.

"An acquired taste," said Dennis. "Just like I told you."

Alain put his hand on Dennis's knee, and said, "I do not mean to frighten you, but this is what I must say now: I am taking a ferry back to Crete in one hour. My luggage is sitting on the pier even now, with my valet, who is looking after it. From then on I will not be back in Mykonos for some weeks. It is so sad to me that I must be meeting you now, when I am leaving. But I am thinking, you are young. You perhaps make decisions with swiftness, and perhaps have a daring spirit. Will you come with me to Crete? I would love to be showing you my house there. You can stay with me as long as you wish. This is my offer to you."

Dennis began to sense that Alain's hand on his knee was drawing some attention, and none of it very friendly. He gently lifted the hand and put it back on Alain's own knee, then said, as kindly as possible, "I'm sorry, I'm not as young or as daring as you think. Much as I might like to, I can't just leave in an hour. Disrupt my entire life like that."

"Ah," said Alain, sitting back. "But of course, there is someone else. You have fought, eh? You are angry. So you are coming to this bar to drink and be even more angry. And to flirt with a man who will pay your bill. But even though I offer you much more than that—everything, everything I offer now—even so you will be returning to the man who so angers you. Yes? Because you love him." He grinned sadly, then took the glass of retsina and finished it off in one gulp.

Dennis sat with his eyes wide open, nearly reeling with surprise. This man, who had known him for, what—five minutes? —had looked into his soul and seen what was there with an accuracy Farleigh had never even approached.

"Uh . . . I . . . I don't know what to say." He giggled, then nervously smoothed his pants legs and said, "Alain, you are an incredible man. I don't know what I'm doing. My lover doesn't want me anymore, he's up at the house with someone new, he doesn't even care where I am, and—and here *you* are—handsome, and kind, and generous—and *French*, for God's sake, and you're offering—offering me—" He put his hands over his mouth, to stifle a sob. "Why am I going back to *him*? Why am I saying no to *you*? It doesn't make any sense."

Alain shook his head; suddenly, he *did* look old. "Love never does make sense, my friend."

Well, that was that. Before he could stop himself, Dennis was bawling. *Bawling.* Like he hadn't since he was a baby. His face had twisted itself into a ball, and the sobs and wails were just gushing out of him, like lyrics to a song he knew by heart.

He couldn't even see, but he could feel, suddenly, Alain's strong hands on his arms, feel his quivering, heaving body being lifted from the stool and virtually carried outside, where the cool night air hit him in the face like a slap and brought him out of his crying jag in an instant.

He was still weak, so he let Alain help him down the steps to the street. Neither of them said a word; Dennis was still unable. He was too busy catching his breath, regaining his composure.

At last, when they had reached a busy corner, Dennis looked at him and said, in a paper-thin voice, "Did you pay the bill?"

Alain shook his head. "They were about to throw us out anyway. Let them be eating it, as you Americans say."

Dennis shook his head and hugged him. "I hope I see you again."

"That is not likely. But perhaps." Then, boldly, brazenly—in full view of the crowds on the street—he tipped back Dennis's head and kissed him full on the lips. Then he stood erect and said, "I do not even know your name."

"Dennis. Dennis Racine."

"Goodbye, Dennis Racine. I wish you luck. I wish you love." He winked, then ambled off in the direction of the pier.

Dennis, faintly aware that he was being stared at, watched him go for only a moment, then turned and headed off on his still unsteady legs to where he'd left the Jeep.

He sat at the wheel for a while before starting the engine, trying to empty his mind of everything . . . of the surprise he felt at the enormity of his own revealed feelings, and at the equally enormous opportunity he had just given up in consequence.

Then he drove back to the house, back across the very empty, very dark, suddenly very cold island. He was drunk, he was exhausted by his emotional cloudburst, and so he kept the

top down all the way there. The wind flapped his hair around
his forehead and occasionally into his eyes, but at least it kept
him alert and awake.

The house was dark when he pulled up. He crept in and
found that the couches Farleigh had assigned Dennis and himself were empty.

He tiptoed to the master bedroom. The door was partially
shut; there was a mist of dull yellow light seeping through.

"To hell with it," he thought, and he swung the door wide
open.

Jasper was lying in bed, asleep, with a washcloth across his
forehead. There was another washcloth across the lamp, which
accounted for the dimness of its glow.

And Farleigh was asleep in a chair at the side of the bed,
his biography of Lillie Langtry hanging open in his lap.

Somehow, the innocence of the scene made it even worse.

Dennis checked his watch. If he hurried . . . that ferry to
Crete . . . Alain . . .

But he knew better about himself now. He returned to the
living room, lowered himself onto his couch, and let uncon-
sciousness overtake him.

chapter
34

Worse luck: the next morning, Dennis himself awoke with a cold—and this a real one. His head was pounding, his throat dry, and his sinuses clogged; no sooner had he taken his first breath on awakening than he began coughing, and he couldn't stop.

He staggered to the bathroom, hacking all the while, realizing that this would wake the rest of the household and not caring. In the bathroom he spat some phlegm into the sink, then drank a tall glass of mineral water from the bottle by the soap dish (he never trusted tap water outside the States). He thought this might make him feel better; of course it did no such thing.

He stared at himself in the mirror; his eyes were like ping-pong balls. It was like staring at a reflection of Kermit the frog. Part of his problem, he realized, was that he had drunk well more than a bottle of retsina by himself the previous night. But he had also driven back to the house, damp with emotion, the windows open and cold air washing over him. And once indoors, he'd slept on the couch, barefoot, without a blanket or a quilt or cover of any kind.

Now he was paying for it. He tried to take a deep breath and feel strong, but his nasal passages felt like they were filled with Jell-O. He groaned in exasperation, went back to the couch and lay down.

Farleigh had just come in, tucking in his rumpled shirt. "What's the matter? Where were you last night? What's with all the coughing?"

"I caughd our liddle friend's coad," he said as he curled up into the fetal position. "Thangs so buch for bringing hib up here."

"Typical of you," Farleigh said with a sneer, "blaming someone else for your misfortunes."

"So sorry," he said, narrowing his eyes and glaring back at him. "I'd sure I didn'd catch id from Jasber ad all. I'b sure I caughd id from some villager I passed for two seconds lasd nighd."

"All right, that's enough." Farleigh sat on the opposite couch and ran his hand through his hair. "You didn't say where you were last night."

"No, I didn'd." He coughed heavily into his hand for a moment. "Jusd oud of curiosidy, how long was id before you realized I wasn'd here? Waid—led me guess: it was the momend you needed somebody to clead up Jasber's puge."

It was Farleigh's turn to glare. "Jealousy doesn't become you."

"Abandonmend doesn'd becub me, either. Rejectiod doesn'd becub me, either."

Farleigh averted his eyes; guilt colored his voice when he said, "Stop being so melodramatic."

"Melodramadig?" said Dennis, sitting upright in a fury. "Ogay, I won'd be. On one conditiod. You jusd go get a big bowl of soub, and sid by my side all day long, staring ad me with big doe eyes, and spooding id into by bouth. *Thed* I won'd be melodrama—" A wad of phlegm caught in his throat, and set him off on another spate of coughing.

Farleigh got to his feet. "That's disgusting," he said, backing away. "Turn away from me when you do that. And while you're at it, get a grip on yourself. You can't just lie around here all day. We're going to Santorini. Unless you'd rather stay behind."

"Sandoridi?" Dennis almost laughed. "We're still goig to Sandoridi?"

"Of course. I won't allow Jasper to shirk his duty."

"Whad aboud his code? Don'd tell me the boy wonder has had a sudded recobery."

"He's sitting up in bed and feeling fine, thanks for asking. And—ah, Christos." The manservant had just walked into the room, buck naked, scratching the back of his head and yawning widely. "Jasper is feeling better today. Fix him something to eat, will you? Then we're off to Santorini for the day. You're welcome to join us."

Christos nodded and padded off to the kitchen.

"*No bregfast for me, thangs,*" Dennis hollered after him. "*Jusd a liddle garlic and baybe some heroid.*"

"I can't stand to be around you today," Farleigh said, poised at the door to the bedroom. "You're just spewing germs and sarcasm. Maybe you *would* be better off staying home."

Dennis smiled at him evilly. "Stay hobe? Nod a chance! I wouldn'd biss Sandoridi for the world!"

chapter
35

Jasper's recovery was indeed remarkable. He ate two bowls of shredded wheat and some kippered herring (a combination that made Dennis shudder), then bolted out for a quick swim in the Aegean before setting out for Santorini. Why, one might think he'd never been sick at all. Unless, of course, one was laboring under the stupidities of lust.

But something was wrong with the scenario. After all, the boy had shaken in his boots at the mere idea of going to Santorini to see his grandmother, and now he was acting positively eager for the trip, shouldering his backpack and merrily swinging it into the back of the Jeep. What was going on here? . . . And why was he constantly checking his watch?

Dennis checked his own watch; it was nearly ten o'clock. He was sitting on a deck chair on the patio, a stadium blanket covering him from head to toe, and shivering like mad. Even the heat of the sun wasn't warming him, although he certainly was sweating as though it did.

Farleigh was on the patio, too, sitting placidly in his panama hat, reading yesterday's *Chicago Tribune* and sipping coffee.

Jasper was running around the patio being young, when

suddenly he stopped behind Farleigh and checked his watch again.

Dennis, noticing this, checked his own watch.

Ten o'clock on the dot.

The phone rang.

Aha, thought Dennis. *The answer at last.*

Christos appeared at the door. "Farleigh, it's Debbie," he said, then disappeared again.

Farleigh sighed, put down the paper, and picked up the receiver. "Farleigh here," he said. "Yes, Debbie. I'm . . . what? No, I'm not coming home today . . . Yes, that was the original plan, but Jasper got sick, and . . . yes, Jasper's here . . . Well, we've tagged two more days onto the trip, is what that has to do with anything, and don't take that tone of voice with me . . . Yes, well, two more days isn't going to put anything at risk . . . What do you mean, I don't 'sound like' myself? Why are you so panicked? Is something wrong? What time is it there, anyway?" Here he looked at his own watch. "Nothing's wrong? Then why are we having this conversation? . . . No, Debbie. I will not change my mind. I'm coming ho . . . I said, *I'm coming home the day after tomorrow.* I've already confirmed with the airline. I'll talk to you then. Goodbye."

He dropped the receiver into its cradle and turned to Jasper, who suddenly looked terrified again. "Well, that was the *strangest* call," he said, rubbing the bridge of his nose. "Debbie, all panicky that I'm not home yet. I said, 'Is anything wrong?' and she kept saying 'No, but,' and there was never anything after 'but.' I swear, she must be having a nervous breakdown."

"M-maybe you'd better go back, then," Jasper said with an earnest nod. "If she's, like, incapable of . . . you know . . ."

"Don't be silly." He turned back to the paper. "No one tells me what to do. And I have no intention of letting you out of honoring your promise to your mother. As soon as Christos is ready, we're going to Santorini."

Jasper went white as a sheet, then dashed into the house.

Dennis's sixth sense kicked in; the back of his neck started to tingle. Although his cough had largely cleared up, he pretended to suffer another attack just now, and so had an excuse to get up and hobble into the house.

Once inside, he fell silent and listened, and sure enough, he could hear the hiss of heated argument coming from the kitchen.

With aching precision he slowly passed into the adjoining room without attracting the attention of either Jasper or Christos; he, however, could see both of them quite clearly.

Jasper was frantic, practically pulling his hair. He paced behind Christos, who was finishing the last of the breakfast dishes.

"I thought we had an *agreement,*" the boy whined. "You were gonna convince Debbie to get Farleigh back *immediately.*"

Christos turned, with menacing slowness, and wielded a spatula at him. "We had no agreement," he said through clenched teeth. "You told me you thought Farleigh was doing too much with his leg. You said you didn't want him island-hopping because he wasn't fully healed yet. You said the production needed his attention, too, and then you begged me to call Debbie and tell her all this and ask her to call Farleigh home." He jabbed the spatula at Jasper, poking him in the shoulder. "And I did because I care about Farleigh, and I thought you did, too. And if it turns out he thinks he's okay to go on, that's all I need to know."

Jasper was nearly gasping from frustration. "But all the way to Santorini . . . all that hiking and . . . and . . . *hiking* . . ."

Christos pulled the plug from the sink, sending the water gurgling down the drain. "I don't know what you're up to, but face it, kid: we're on our way. Get ready to kiss Grandma hello."

Jasper emitted an odd, strangulated noise from somewhere near the back of his throat; then he darted out of the kitchen and across the house to the bedroom, where he slammed the door shut behind him.

Now Dennis faced the task of creeping back outside himself; he didn't know if he could manage it, especially since he felt a cough coming on. But he had to try. He stood stock still between the wall and a china chest and waited for Christos to turn his back.

After what seemed like fully half the lifespan of a fruit fly, Christos did just that, then opened a cabinet and began putting away plates.

Dennis, the tickle in his throat now like a contained nuclear

explosion, crept with great care across the dining room, and
had almost reached the door and sweet freedom—freedom to
cough, more than anything else—when Christos, his back still
turned, said, "I know you're there, you know."

Dennis, thinking that he might be talking to himself,
stopped dead in his tracks and put his hand over his mouth.
The cough was ready to blow.

Christos turned and, wiping his hands, eyed him without a
trace of surprise. "I saw you when you crept in. Between the
two of you boys, you've got enough espionage goin' on to revive
the Cold War."

Dennis let go of the cough; it burst forth with so much force
that he thought it might jar his brain out of its pan. Then he
whirled on Christos and said, "Why didn't you say something,
you fucking jerk? Make me look like a fool trying to creep out
of here without coughing." He coughed again.

Christos threw the dishtowel onto the counter and said,
"For some reason that kid doesn't want to go to Santorini and
see his grandmother. I don't know why, and I don't care. I just
don't like him lying to Farleigh."

"Me either," said Dennis. "And I think we sh—"

"I *also* don't like you leaving without telling anyone and
staying out half the night," he continued, interrupting him.
"Farleigh's life is Farleigh's to live, but anyone who hurts him
has to answer to me."

Dennis, wounded by these words, said, "I'd never hurt him.
I love him. You know that." He swallowed another cough.

Christos looked at him with one eyebrow cocked. "Well, if
you love him, stop playing games. Stop this schoolgirl shit."

"I'll stop the schoolgirl shit when he stops mooning over
the pool boy."

Christos shook his head. "When I told you to fight for him,
this was *not* what I meant." He marched out of the kitchen,
buttoning up his shirtfront. "Get dressed. In five minutes we
hit the road."

chapter
36

At its appointed departure time, the hydrofoil shuttle had not even arrived at the pier yet, which was pretty much the way things operated on the island, so Farleigh felt comfortable simply dropping his bags and going off to a seaside bar for a drink. Jasper and Dennis accompanied him; Christos stayed with the bags, ostensibly to watch them, but really so he could stretch out on the gravel and bask in the sun.

The cold, windy ride in the Jeep had brought back Dennis's cough in force, and stopped up his nose, too. Farleigh eyed him in irritation every time he as much as sniffled or cleared his throat. So in the bar—a dark, narrow, mint-smelling place with a Greek music video station playing on a monitor—he ordered a little hair of the dog: retsina, in hopes that it would clear his afflicted head.

"Bit early for that, don't you think?" said Jasper.

Dennis gave him a look that would have frozen an industrial fire. "Don't know," he said in a low voice. "I'm not accustomed to island practices. I'll have to ask your grandmother."

That shut him up. He turned and stared dumbly in the opposite direction.

Farleigh was oblivious to all this; he was busy counting his money after having paid for a plate filled with fatty Greek pastries. "Could've sworn I had an extra forty thousand in here," he muttered, rifling through his wallet again. "Ten . . . twelve . . . seventeen . . ."

Dennis sighed, and turned his gaze to the avenue outside. Feeling tired and sweaty and sick and unattractive, he let himself tumble into a little fantasy about Alain Bertholde, with whom he would now be basking in the Cretan sun if he'd only had a little bit more nerve.

He was in the midst of a particularly stimulating part of this fantasy when a small section of the blur of colors and shapes in the avenue pierced his reverie and demanded his attention. He focused on it, and it coalesced into Tracey and Roseanne, coming down the slope as if one person, Roseanne's arm draped around Tracey's shoulders.

Tracey, he saw a moment later, was crying.

Alarmed, he jumped off his stool and raced out to see what was the matter. He heard Farleigh give a little call after him, but ignored it.

He was breathless when he reached the girls; his cold had sapped most of his energy. He said, "Tracey! What's wrong? What's happened?" and he tenderly touched her chin, to try to get her to look at him.

She shrieked and leapt back a step.

He was so startled, he did the same thing, then held his hands high and said, "Hey! It's only me! It's only Dennis!"

Roseanne, who was hovering over Tracey like a she-wolf, said, "It's okay, hon. Everything's okay." Then she swept her hair away from her face, gave Dennis an exhausted look, and said, "We had, like, a trauma, is all."

"I'm so sorry," he said. "Is there anything I can do?"

"Th-that pig," said Tracey through her tears. "He—he was so nice all day yesterday, and th-then today, he . . . that *pig*." She started crying anew.

Dennis looked at Roseanne. "Andreas?"

She nodded. "We all took the boat to Delos this morning.

Day-trip thing. Not many tourists, so we thought we were lucky. But we—"

"We—we were *all alone* . . ."

"That's right, hon. Had the island almost to ourselves. Anyway, Tracey and Andreas went running up this big hill . . . you know it? . . . and left me and Evagoras trudging behind. Well, anyway, we *so* lost them. And the next thing I know . . ."

"He had his h-hands all over me," said Tracey with sudden fierceness. "He ripped my blouse!" Dennis noticed, for the first time, that she was holding her shirtfront together.

He doffed his windbreaker and gave it to her, while Roseanne continued. "Like, the next thing I know, I hear this scream? And I go tearing up in the direction I came from, and what do I see . . ." Here a little grin crept across her face. "What do I see but . . ." Her hand flew to her mouth, too late to hide a sudden smile.

"What is it?" Dennis asked.

She shook her head and refused to reply. Her eyes were bright.

"It's not *funny*," said Tracey.

"It is, *kind* of," said Roseanne, who was clearly feeling some relief from the day's tension. She turned to Dennis and said, "Well, what do I see but Andreas rolling around on the ground, holding his balls and, like, *moaning*, and Tracey hopping around on one foot and going, '*You asshole, I think I broke my toe.*' "

Through her tears, Tracey started laughing now, and soon both girls were howling. Dennis joined them—so much so that he nearly doubled over.

"What . . . what happened to the creep?" asked Dennis when he could get a breath.

Roseanne was holding her stomach. She gulped down her last bit of laughter and said, "Oh, Evagoras stayed with him. But when Tracey and I ran away, we could hear him cursing Andreas in Greek like you wouldn't even *believe*."

"The *pig*," said Tracey, but there was more merriment in the word this time.

By now a crowd of old women in black stockings and scarves had gathered a discreet distance away to watch the shameless bellowing and shrieking display by young American girls. Dennis felt it prudent to move them inside. "Come with me," he said. "I think you both need a drink. Farleigh's treat."

When they entered the bar, Farleigh saw at once that Tracey was in a state, and Roseanne only slightly less so, so he welcomed them to join him at once. After a brief explanation of their plight, he insisted, as Dennis knew he would, that he buy them both a brandy. They ended up with little shot glasses of some terrible Greek liqueur that the bartender had recommended to them instead, which to Dennis meant simply that he didn't have any brandy in the house.

Tracey rolled up the sleeves of the windbreaker and had a sip; she made a face and then stuck her tongue out, but it was clear she was feeling immeasurably better. Then she turned to where Jasper was sitting, sullen and uncommunicative, and said, "Hey, gorgeous. Miss us?"

Jasper gave her a quick, dark look, then nodded perfunctorily.

Tracey and Roseanne both cast inquiring looks at Dennis, who shrugged in reply.

Farleigh finished paying the bartender, then slipped his wallet back into his jacket pocket and put his arm around Tracey. "There, now," he said in his most paternal manner. "Better, everyone?" He tweaked Tracey's cheeks. "Farleigh's Lesson Number One for Young Ladies: men are absolute shits."

Roseanne lost part of her drink through her nose at this, and they all laughed at her.

Christos appeared at the door. He nodded manfully at the girls, then turned to Farleigh and said, "Hydrofoil's here."

Farleigh thanked him, then patted Tracey on the back. "I wish we could stay and make sure you're all right. Or barring that, I wish you could come with us." He winked at her.

She winked back. "I'm fine now, Farleigh. Thanks for everything."

Suddenly, Jasper came to life. He stopped tearing threads from the fraying edge of the bar buffer and turned to Farleigh. "Why *can't* they come with us?"

Farleigh and the others were too taken aback by the question to answer it. They all stared at Jasper quizzically.

He shrugged and continued. "Well, they were all ready to

spend the day on Delos, and now they can't. Or don't want to, whatever. Why don't they come to Santorini with us? It's just a day trip."

"Well, actually," said Farleigh, "it's more like a day and night. So as not to have to rush. I'd planned on us not returning till tomorrow." Before Jasper could raise an objection, he said, "I've already booked the hotel."

"Yes, but . . . I . . ."

"We'd love to come," said Tracey suddenly, surprising everyone—even Roseanne. "We'll get our own hotel room and everything, too, so you don't have to worry. My dad wired me some money this morning!"

"There, you see?" said Jasper, flinging his arms in the air. "Perfect solution for everyone."

"*Tra*cey," hissed Roseanne, "we don't have a change of *clothes*. We don't have *tooth*brushes."

Tracey had already set down her glass of liqueur and was slipping off her stool. "We can buy some new T-shirts and tooth-brushes on Santorini. Jesus! What's wrong with you? We've got to seize these opportunities, you know? We're here for adventure!"

"I've had quite enough adventure for one day, thanks. My feet hurt."

"Oh, *come* on, Roseanne," pleaded Jasper. "Come with us! It'll be fun! Just like our first day here on Mykonos." He gave her his most winning look, and his blue eyes, raised up in entreaty, were fairly irresistible, Dennis had to admit.

Apparently Roseanne thought so, too. "All right," she said reluctantly. "But we're on the first boat back in the morning!"

Jasper appeared dizzy with pleasure; he was now fairly ushering the party out the door and to the pier. What was going on here? Dennis was bewildered. The boy dreaded seeing his grandmother, that much was clear, had even descended to subterfuge to try to get out of it. But now that he'd talked Tracey and Roseanne into going, he couldn't wait to get moving.

What was going on in that tousled head of his?

And why did Dennis have the sinking feeling that any hope of keeping Farleigh had now vanished?

chapter
37

Dennis and the others seemed to be the only Americans aboard the hydrofoil; indeed, the rest of the craft was occupied almost entirely by the members of an extended Dutch family, all of whom appeared lost in outrage and several of whom were berating in severe tones a sullen, clearly unrepentant adolescent boy. Dennis couldn't imagine what the boy had done to offend eighteen to twenty people at least three times his age, but the berating—and the constant shaking of heads and tut-tutting—went on all the way to Paros. Dennis caught the boy's eyes once, and gave him a sympathetic wink and a thumbs-up; it didn't seem to have much positive effect on the kid's mood.

The boat hit a wave and was suspended aloft for a moment, then came crashing down with more force than Dennis would've liked. He stood up and peered to the fore, where Farleigh and Jasper were seated snugly by the window with Tracey and Roseanne. Farleigh and the girls were laughing, and Jasper was leaning against Farleigh's shoulder as though he had no other choice, given the close quarters. What a little creep.

Dennis and Christos had unluckily managed to get behind

the Dutch clan when boarding, and so were squeezed all the way in the back, next to the open cabin door. Occasionally, water would spray in and lick Dennis's face. He wished he had his windbreaker back, but he could scarcely ask Tracey for it, with her blouse ripped so revealingly. Oh, well . . . if his cough came back because of this exposure, he didn't suppose it'd make any difference. He could contract bubonic plague and be no less attractive to Farleigh.

He sat down again and turned to Christos, who was, as always, smoking his foul Turkish cigarettes. "So," he said, "what d'you suppose is up with the pool boy? You heard the way he practically insisted that those girls come with us, didn't you?"

Christos, his eyes droopy-lidded with unconcern, shrugged.

"Well, I just think it's funny, that's all. He tries every trick in the book to kill this trip to see his grandmother, then all of a sudden the two girls are coming along, and it's a big fucking lark. Doesn't that seem funny to you?"

Christos blew a mouthful of smoke from his lips; the onrush of air from the door immediately sent it sweeping behind his head. "I don't know," he said, tapping some ash onto the floor. "If I bothered to think about it, I might find it funny." He turned away from Dennis and took another puff.

Dennis felt a sudden urge to strike him. "Well, you were pretty fucking 'bothering to think about it' this morning. I heard the way you went off on that kid."

Christos gave him a lofty, irritated look. "So what exactly is your point?"

So many furious responses to this crammed themselves into Dennis's throat all at once that not one of them made it out. He commanded himself to take a few deep breaths, then he poked Christos roughly in the shoulder and said, "I'll tell you what my point is. My point is, you're a big fucking hypocritical faggot, and a bad friend, too. Yes, a *bad friend*. And I'm not forgiving you this time. Every time we come to Greece, you magically turn from Zsa Zsa to Zorba, and act like it's no big deal. Well, it never was before . . . I even found it kind of silly and cute before. But I'm in trouble now, and you're *sitting* there like you're rehearsing for a role in some Italian neorealist film, ignoring me or barely tolerating me, and I just want to say, fuck you. *Fuck you.*" He was aware that he was drawing a modicum of attention away from the naughty Dutch boy; he didn't care. "If all it takes for you to abandon our friendship is a change in the landscape, then our friendship was no big shit to begin with. So just stay out of my way, all right? Not just here, but when we get back to Chicago. Presuming I make it back to Chicago, at this rate. But if we do, you just stay out of my way. I don't like you anymore, I think you're ridiculous and stupid and a big fucking traitor, and I don't want to know you. I don't want to know you *at all.*"

To his credit, Christos at least looked stunned by this outburst; all the same, Dennis gave him no time to reply. He leapt to his feet, made his way across the boat to the toilet, locked himself in, and coughed violently into his fists for nearly seven solid minutes. Fucking boat. Fucking weather. *Fucking Christos.*

When he'd finally passed through the worst of his coughing spell, he rinsed the tears from his eyes; then, as wobbly from physical fatigue as from the motion of the boat, he went back out and found a spot far from Christos, just behind a seat where two enormous Dutch women were shaking their heads sadly and comparing notes on their young relative's appalling character traits.

When the boat arrived in Paros, Dennis waited till Christos had got off, then disembarked himself. He stood apart from the other passengers and spoke to no one. And he wore on his face such a look that no one dared speak to him.

When Farleigh and the others were at last on the pier, he reluctantly went over and joined them. Farleigh was jabbering excitedly to Jasper and Christos. ". . . piece of good luck," he was saying as Dennis came within earshot. "The afternoon ferry to Santorini wasn't scheduled to leave for another three hours, but of course, this being Greece, the *morning* ferry hasn't left yet." He pointed across the pier to the enormous vessel, which was still taking on one or two more automobiles before casting off.

"Let's hurry and get on it," said Farleigh, taking the tickets from his breast pocket and distributing them to everyone. "We'll get to Santorini early enough to have some dinner and drinks before going to bed. Jasper, give me a hand." He was so excited that he didn't even think about the impropriety of asking Jasper to help him to the boat instead of Dennis. But it didn't do him much good, anyway. Because just as they all turned to head over to the ferry, the Dutch family got the same idea, and started bustling over there, en masse.

Tracey saw this and shrieked, "*We have to beat them! Run!*" And she and Roseanne went galloping away. After a moment Jasper, caught up in their high spirits, bolted after them, before even helping Farleigh walk a step.

A feeling of quiet triumph settled over Dennis. He calmly went over to Farleigh, who was looking confused and hurt, and took his arm. "Come on, hon," he said. "I'll see you get there."

"It's . . . it's just, my foot still hurts a little," said Farleigh, his pride wounded. "I have to go easy."

"I know, I know."

Christos appeared on Farleigh's opposite side, the bags slung over his shoulder. "Need help here?" he said, offering Farleigh his own, muscular, hairy arm.

Dennis craned his neck past Farleigh and snarled, "Just do your job and see to the luggage, *boy*."

Abashed, Christos fell back and left them alone.

"What was that about?" Farleigh asked as they approached the steps to the ferry.

"Nothing," said Dennis, maneuvering Farleigh to the handrail. "I just get sick and tired of his stupid macho act. Okay, now. I'm right behind you. Up we go . . ."

Farleigh mounted the steps with some small trouble; he seemed suddenly ten years older than he had mere minutes ago, when he'd confidently advised everyone to bolt for the ferry. It was as if Jasper gave him renewed vitality and strength, and as soon as the boy left his side, it all drained away. Dennis could almost hate him for that, but hating him wouldn't do any good. And helping him might.

The ferry was absurdly crowded. It was obvious that theirs had not been the only hydrofoil whose passengers had arrived on Paros and decided to take advantage of an available ferry. (After all, in Greece one never knows when the next one might arrive.) There was a stink of sweat and smoke and alcohol all through the lounge, as though people had been waiting hours for departure. "Don't worry," he said to Farleigh, "we'll find you a place to sit."

But that had been a bit overconfident of him. Every chair was taken, every banquette was filled, and there were elderly and infirm persons here who had clearly been searching for a seat for far longer than Dennis, with no greater luck.

Finally, when Farleigh's face had turned a rather frightening shade of gray, Dennis took matters into his own hands. He pulled a large ashtray stand from behind some chador-clad Arab women, who clearly wouldn't be needing it. Then he overturned it, scattering ashes and stubs before plunking it solidly on the carpet.

"There," he said, rocking it to see if it would support Farleigh; it didn't budge. It was wedged into the red shag. "Park it right here, sweetie."

The base of the stand was just wide enough for Farleigh to get a little of each butt cheek onto it. When he'd done so, he took a handkerchief from his front pocket and mopped his forehead. "Thank you, love," he said, and Dennis thought, *Love!* "I was beginning to feel a bit faint, there."

Dennis crouched in front of him and looked into his eyes. "You okay now?" he asked, tweaking his cheek. Some color came back into it. Farleigh nodded, and stuffed his handkerchief back in his pocket.

"I could do with a glass of water," he said.

"Leave it to me," said Dennis. He hopped up, and had shimmied several feet into the crowd when he had to double back and say, "Uh—maybe I should have a little cash. Just in case they ask me to pay for it."

Farleigh nodded distractedly, then reached into his pants pocket, produced his wad of drachmas, and handed the whole thing to Dennis. *Better and better,* Dennis thought.

He was indeed charged for the water—and exorbitantly charged for the lukewarm Coke he bought for himself. The bartenders clearly knew they had the upper hand with this captive crowd.

Dennis made his way back to Farleigh, more than once being bumped almost to the point of spilling both drinks—fucking rude tourists! When he returned to Farleigh, he found him lazily scratching his instep while chatting amiably in English with one of the Muslim women.

Dennis handed him the glass of water, and the woman turned away and resumed chattering in Arabic with her friends.

"How'd *that* conversation start?" Dennis asked.

Farleigh released his itchy foot, then took a sip of water and sighed in relief. "Oh," he said, leaning back into the wall. "I just offered her my seat."

"You did?"

"I was feeling better. And, you know how it is . . . being brought up a gentleman . . . but she said no thank you. Said she wasn't even supposed to talk to strange men, much less take a seat from one . . . but she talked quite a bit, actually. Kind of an adventure for her, I suppose . . . They charge you for the water?"

Damn, thought Dennis, who had counted on Farleigh not thinking of this. "Yeah," he said. "And I got a Coke for myself." He dug into his pockets and returned the wad of cash. "Here you go."

Farleigh returned the cash to his breast pocket, then took a deep breath and shut his eyes. Dennis waited for a moment, then said, "Farleigh? You be all right here for a bit? Just thought I'd better try to locate the others."

Farleigh nodded without opening his eyes.

Dennis waited a moment longer, to make certain he didn't change his mind; then he plowed his way through the crowd (Taste of their own medicine, he told himself), and scooted up a short flight of stairs and out onto the deck.

The fresh, cool air hit him in the face and helped restore him from the enervating effects of the claustrophobic lounge. He leaned against the railing, and saw that the ferry had slipped its moorings and was now moving away from the pier. The din in the lounge had been so dense that he hadn't even heard the engines turn over.

He stood for a while, enjoying the breeze and letting it wash over him, like a kind of spiritual bath. Then he felt his first chill and hugged his arms to his chest. He was wearing only a T-shirt, but he couldn't very well ask Tracey for his windbreaker back, even if he knew where Tracey was.

He set out in search of her and the others. He especially had it in mind to find Christos and apologize. That "boy" remark had been a little more offensive than he'd intended. But he'd have to make it clear to Christos that he stood by the gist of his complaint, and that he still considered their relationship redefined forever: their friendship was over, and that was that.

As sardine-close as it was in the ferry's interior, the outer decks were comparatively free of traffic. Apparently the gorgeous cherry-red waters of the afternoon Aegean were considered resistible by most of those who'd booked passage here. Dennis, however, found the sight, and the sounds, and the slight vibration of the motors, soothing in a very real and almost sensual way. He wandered the decks, hugging himself for warmth, the urgency of his search dissipating with every passing minute. Despite the chill, his sinuses seemed to be clearing. The sea, *this* sea, was magical indeed.

He found himself almost at the prow of the ferry before a rather handsome midshipman turned him back with a flurry of commands in Greek. Dennis tried flirting with him, just to stay in practice, but it didn't do much good; the sailor sent him packing.

His cough returned as he made his way back aft, and he decided that maybe it was a good idea to get back inside where it was warm, anyway. Farleigh might be needing him, and maybe some of the others had already found their way to him.

He was about to duck back through the door down to the lounge when he spotted Tracey and Jasper standing by the railing at the very back of the boat, watching the island of Paros recede into the horizon. Dennis scanned the scene for Roseanne, but she didn't appear to be on hand; funny. He'd grown accustomed to thinking of the girls as inseparable.

He started across the back deck to ask them where Roseanne had gone, when all at once Jasper put his arm around Tracey, and she leaned into him and put her head on his shoulder.

Thunderstruck, Dennis stopped short and stood at attention, his eyes wide, watching this impossible thing that was happening.

Then Jasper whispered something in Tracey's ear, and when she giggled, he bit her earlobe.

Dennis actually shook his head and took another look, as if all this might be some kind of mirage.

He wanted to stay put and see what else occurred, but a cough threatened to erupt from him, and he had to race below deck before he was seen.

Back in the lounge, he started hacking wildly, so much so that people moved away from him, as though he were spraying bullets, not germs. When he'd partially recovered, he took a tissue from his pocket and blew his nose; it had been colder out on deck than he'd thought. He was starting to feel sick again . . . even delirious.

Had it *been* delirium, then? What he'd just seen?

He made his way back to where he'd left Farleigh, and found him still seated on the upturned ashtray, only with Roseanne seated cross-legged on the floor next to him. They were talking happily, Farleigh gesticulating in that expansive manner of his, when Dennis interrupted them.

"Hi," he said, not knowing what else to say.

"Oh, hello," said Farleigh. "Look who found me! Christos, too," he said, pointing at the bags next to him; Dennis hadn't seen them till that moment. "I had him leave the bags and go look for you and the others. Did you see him?"

"No," said Dennis truthfully.

"What about Tracey and Jasper?" asked Roseanne. Dennis read her face for some sign of suspicion, but found none. "Somehow I got separated from them."

Yeah, *somehow*, he thought; like, how about they *ditched* you?

Dennis strove to find a truthful reply, and settled on, "I'm not sure I saw them." This was true; he was still convinced it might be some kind of hallucination induced by his head cold.

"Well, they've been missing a very good time down here," said Farleigh brightly. "We've been having a fine chat! Roseanne's got wonderful instincts and is very well read. I'm trying to convince her to come and work for me when she's graduated."

Roseanne shook her head. "I told you, I'm, like, studying to be a nurse."

"Well, I'm an old man. I'll need a nurse."

She winked at him. "You're not old. And Dennis takes good care of you, I'm sure."

He beamed at Dennis. "Well, yes. But I'll never let him stick a needle in my arm!"

They all laughed at that, and then Christos rejoined them. Dennis tried to catch his eye, but he avoided his gaze.

"Any luck?" Farleigh asked.

"I thought I saw the two of them," said Christos. "I even called out their names, and I thought they heard me. But when I got to where I thought I saw them, there was no one there." He shrugged.

Dennis stared at him, and wondered how *much* he had seen.

Unfortunately, thanks to his outburst on the hydrofoil, he wasn't exactly in a position to ask.

chapter
38

The Hotel Ariadne was small but plush, and reeked of tourist money. Everywhere in the lobby he turned, Dennis found his reflection staring back. Taking advantage of a mirrored column, he discovered a fleck of pastry stuck in his teeth, and so took a flavored toothpick from the registry desk and attacked it.

Farleigh was busy negotiating a third room, with Christos as translator. Tracey and Roseanne stood by them dutifully; the room was, after all, to be theirs. This left Dennis and Jasper in the background with idle hands.

Dennis retreated to the lobby entrance and looked at an array of Santorini guide brochures fanned out on a table. They were all identical, except for their alphabets. One was English, one Russian, one French, one Japanese, one Arabic . . .

He picked up the Arabic version and flipped it open. He liked looking at Arabic, liked thinking that there were people in the world who could convert such a trail of delicate, decorative wiggles into words. He stared hard at a short interior subhead as though its brevity might make it easier to decipher, then furrowed his brow and brought the brochure close to his face. And then closer yet . . .

Someone tapped him on the shoulder. He whipped the brochure back onto the table, embarrassed.

It was Jasper. "I didn't know you could read Arabic," he said, an impish but irresistibly handsome grin on his face.

Dennis frowned at him. "Yeah, well. There's a lot you don't know about me."

Jasper's smile drooped, and he nodded sagely. "I'm sure, I'm sure. Hidden depths. Well, I . . . uh . . . I hope maybe we can get to know each other better, Dennis. I really do. Listen," he said, suddenly deadly serious, and he stepped right into Dennis's personal space. Dennis could smell the strangely apple-scented sweat on the boy's skin.

"What?" he asked, backing away.

Jasper shrugged nervously. "I want to ask a favor of you, that's all." He tried to smile again. His blue eyes brimmed and sparkled; if Dennis hadn't disliked him so very much, it might have been difficult to deny him anything. "It's just that . . . well, I don't get along very well with Christos. God knows I've tried, but I think he doesn't like me. Back when I took care of Farleigh's pool, he was always pretty much lording it over me, but now—well, he barely speaks to me, and when he does it isn't pretty." He gave a wry little laugh. "So, anyway . . . I was wondering if maybe you wouldn't mind a room switch, is all." Dennis's eyes opened wide in horror at the suggestion, but the boy barreled on. "I just don't like the idea of having to bunk with Christos for the entire night. Kind of gives me the creeps." He made another vain attempt at a grin; it looked more like a grimace. "I'd really appreciate it."

Dennis was just about ready to blow; how transparent could this kid be? He was obviously trying to have it both ways: be able to sleep with Farleigh *and* have it be partly Dennis's idea! Such skill at manipulation was almost frightening.

But then, Dennis was no slouch at manipulation, either, and he now conceived a truly wicked scheme. He rolled it over in his mind for a moment, then reached out and squeezed Jasper's shoulder in reply. "Sure," he said with a wink. "It's the least I can do. Hell, I've been having troubles with Christos myself."

"What?" Jasper asked, a hint of surprise on his face as Dennis broke away and headed for the front desk. Farleigh was just signing the registry; the girls were running excitedly up the stairs, and Christos was following them, the overnight bags slung over his shoulder.

"Farleigh," said Dennis, "we have a favor to ask." Farleigh turned just as Jasper lurched onto the scene, his eyes wide with confusion.

"What is it?" Farleigh asked, still holding the pen poised over the book.

"Well, Jasper asked if I could room with him instead of Christos, and I told him yes. I knew you wouldn't mind, but I'm checking just in case. You don't, do you?"

Farleigh looked completely flabbergasted; Dennis could almost see the wheels turning in his head as he tried to figure out what could be behind this sudden alliance of his boy toys. And as he hesitated, Jasper let out a pair of small, frustrated noises; he couldn't actually correct Dennis, because that would mean revealing his real purpose in suggesting a switch. But he couldn't do anything else, either. He was trapped.

Farleigh shrugged and said, "No, I guess I don't. You . . . you boys room together, if that's what you want. Christos can stay with me."

Dennis slapped Jasper on the back and said, "There you are, roomie. We're in! Let's go have a look at our digs." He grabbed Jasper by the arm. "You got a key for me?" he asked Farleigh as he started dragging his quarry away.

Farleigh stared hard at him, his brows knit. "Christos has all the keys," he said. "You're in Room 219."

"Right. Thanks."

He pulled Jasper up the stairs and into the second-floor hallway. "Isn't this great?" he enthused. "Now we really *can* get to know each other. Just like you wanted!" There was a hint of sarcasm creeping into his voice; best to keep that out. He wanted Jasper to believe he was sincere about this.

They passed an open door—Room 216. Inside, Roseanne and Tracey were standing at the open window, looking out over the pastel rooftops and chattering like magpies.

Dennis felt Jasper's momentum slow at the sight of Tracey,

so he gave him another good yank. "We're just a few doors
farther down," he said.

When they reached Room 219, they found the door hanging open, and Christos inside, unpacking his bag on one of the
beds.

At the sight of Dennis, Christos straightened up and gave
him a severe look. "Yes?" he asked frostily.

Dennis decided to match frost with frostbite. "There's been
a change of plans," he said flatly. "You're staying with Farleigh
tonight. You may bring my clothes to me here in this room."

Christos stared at him a moment, then at Jasper; if he was
feeling anything, his face didn't betray it.

Then he brusquely scooped all his belongings back into his
knapsack, and proudly left the room without looking at either
of them.

When he was gone, Dennis looked at Jasper and heaved a
contented-sounding sigh. "Excuse me for a moment, okay? I've
got to freshen up." He slipped into the bathroom, opened the
faucet, and splashed some water on his face.

Refreshed, he stood up and looked himself in the eye.

"Okay," he muttered. "I got him away from Farleigh and
here under my thumb." He leaned in closer, until he was nose
to nose with himself. He squinted meaningfully at his other half,
as if it might hold the answers to questions he himself couldn't
plumb, and said, "*Now* what?"

chapter

39

Jasper sat in one of the room's two chairs and pretended to be absorbed in a dog-eared Greek guidebook. Dennis had long since unpacked and was now flipping in frustration through TV stations so quickly that it looked as though he were watching a slide show. He'd tried, but couldn't get anything out of Jasper but an occasional reading of one of the book's more intriguing passages. "Did you know Santorini is also known as Thira?" Jasper said now. "And that it might be the basis for the myth of the sinking of Atlantis?" Dennis rolled his eyes and kept channel-surfing.

When this had gone on much longer than long enough, Dennis flicked off the set, leapt to his feet, then sulked down the hall to Farleigh's room. He rapped on the door and stood waiting, arms akimbo.

Christos answered the door, which momentarily threw Dennis for a loop. "Oh . . . hi. Listen, it's eight-thirty." He checked his watch. "Eight-*forty*. Are we going to dinner, or what?"

Christos gave him a blank look, then, maddeningly, turned back into the room without opening the door any farther. Dennis could hear him mumble a question; then came a mumbled reply from Farleigh. Christos turned back and said, "Farleigh's tired. He says to go eat without him."

He tried to shut the door, but Dennis stuck his foot into it. "Hold on a min—*ow! Christ!*" Christos had really slammed the door. "You big fucking gorilla! Watch out!"

Christos reopened the door and looked down as Dennis retrieved his foot. "I thought people only did that in movies," he said as Dennis hopped up and down, clutching his throbbing instep.

"Just let me see Farleigh," Dennis said with as much of a snarl as he could muster. He felt a stab of murderous fury as Christos again turned and consulted with Farleigh first; then he turned back and said, "Okay. You can come in."

"Fuck you very much," said Dennis as he hobbled into the room.

Farleigh was lying on the bed, scratching his instep listlessly. "Hey," he said as Dennis approached, "*I'm* the one with the limp."

"Sympathy pains," said Dennis with a grin. He sat on the bed beside Farleigh and felt his forehead; it was cold, and slick with sweat. "You feelin' poorly, Farleigh-boo?" he said, dredging up his old pet name for Farleigh—dormant now for several years, at least.

Farleigh smiled, and there was something alarming in the purity of that smile, something that almost smacked of the deathbed. "Took on too much today, Denny-rimple," he said, recalling his own long-unused name for Dennis. "All this island-hopping. Getting too old."

"Rubbish. The islands are older, and they're still putting up with it." He turned to Christos and said, "Get me a wet wash-cloth, please."

"No, no," Farleigh said, suddenly agitated. "I just told Christos to go to dinner. Keeping everyone waiting like this— it's inexcusable. Have to apologize. All I want to do is sleep right now. Rest this damned leg. You go, too, Denny-rimple. Get some yummy in your tummy." He squeezed Dennis's hand.

"I don't understand this," Dennis said, squeezing back. "You were fine this morning."

"Did too much," he repeated. "Also, called Debbie when I

got to hotel." He was dropping articles—a sign of his fatigue. And his eyes were fluttering shut. "Bad news from home. Set crew won't work at Varsity Playhouse till I sign contract." He gave a tremulous sigh. "Should never have come here. But have to see this through; this far now. Shame to turn back. For Jasper's mother. Don't want him lying to her." This was turning into a bit of a ramble. "Fly out day after tomorrow. Take care of everything."

"Yes," said Dennis, feeling nervous in a way he'd never felt before. He wiped the sweat from Farleigh's brow with his bare hand, then wiped his hand on his trousers. "It'll all be fine."

And with that, Farleigh was asleep. Dennis waited a few minutes longer, to make certain that he was breathing steadily. Then he turned to address Christos, thinking that he might as well take this time to apologize to him, but Christos was gone.

Well, he thought, everyone *else* might abandon Farleigh, but *I* won't.

He sat with him for ten minutes . . . twenty . . . twenty-five. And then he could bear it no longer. He was hungry, he was bored, and Farleigh was so deep in slumber that he clearly wasn't going to come around and need anything anytime soon.

So he left.

He stopped back at his own room, and found Jasper gone, presumably to dine. Christos must have stopped by and told him that it was every man for himself tonight.

He went across the hall and knocked on Tracey and Roseanne's door. No response, and of course there wouldn't be. When Jasper was cut loose from duty, he'd naturally head here and corral the girls to be his dinner partners.

That left Dennis alone and adrift. And suddenly melancholy.

Farleigh was lying alone in a strange hotel room, Dennis himself was out on the streets of a suddenly very foreign place, and there was so much between them . . . acres, it seemed, of emotional rubble. All surrounding this Jasper person. Who didn't even care enough to stop in and see how Farleigh was. What was his hold over Farleigh? What could make Farleigh abandon a troubled production for some ridiculous jaunt to Santorini just for this boy's sake? Jasper himself didn't want to be here. It was Farleigh, Farleigh insisting . . . it just didn't make sense. What did he care if Jasper lied to his mother? If Jasper snubbed his grandmother? Farleigh had *Lady Windermere*—and an imperiled *Lady Windermere*, at that. Was there any real competition, there?

Not with the Farleigh he knew. There wouldn't—couldn't ever—be.

Well, it remained to be seen what the visit to Granny Ioannou resulted in, tomorrow. If Jasper was so keen to avoid it, it could only mean trouble for him.

But strangely, Dennis was now rather averse to the visit himself. If it would hurt Farleigh . . . for *whatever* reason . . .

He slouched past several restaurants and tavernas, all filled with American and European tourists, guzzling wine and eating with the kind of gusto inspired only by sea air. His hunger, however, had suddenly gone. Maybe he'd spent too much time being devoured by doubts for him to devour anything in turn.

He found a bar, called the Amazing Parrot Club, and without even stopping a moment to wonder what that could possibly mean, he went inside.

It was a small place: a twelve-foot bar, stools all along its outer edge, and a strobe-lighted dance floor taking up a bit more space than that. A Pet Shop Boys tune was just ending. Dennis sat down and ordered a retsina from the frizzy-haired female bartender.

And where would I be now if I'd gone with Alain Bertholde? he wondered as he drank. And where would I be now if Christos hadn't hired the goddamn pool boy in the first place? Where would I be now if I'd learned to take care of the fucking pool myself? Where would I be now if I hadn't been so selfish, if I'd really treated Farleigh right? Where would I be now if Christos had really loved Farleigh? Where would I be now if I'd stayed home and done my social studies homework instead of crashing that disco bash where I met Farleigh? Where would I be now if I only liked girls?

Someone on the dance floor lost control of herself, lashed out, and struck him in the head, bringing him out of his miasma of melancholy conjecture. He'd felt the force of the blow, but not the blow itself; his head was far too numb. He suddenly realized that he was very, very drunk—even for an experienced sot like himself.

"Sorry," said the dancer.

He grinned at her. "S'lokay," he said, his tongue filling his mouth like a water balloon.

He checked his watch: ten after one. One in the *morning*.

He decided he'd better leave. He pushed away his nearly empty glass (there were another two next to it that obviously hadn't been collected yet; how many had preceded them?), and reached into his pocket for some cash.

And then he remembered.

"Goddamn *sleeve-petters*," he cursed under his breath.

The bartender appeared; she'd evidently seen him shove his glass away. "Another, then, love?" she asked as she picked up his three empties.

He nodded his head. "Pleezsh."

She cocked her head at him and grinned. "Wow, you're really something," she said in a British accent that Dennis hadn't noticed before. "Know how to put 'em away, don't you?"

Dennis didn't know how many he'd had, but he nodded and tried to look proud.

When she turned away, Dennis slipped off his stool and tried to race out of the bar. Unfortunately, his sense of balance had been shot to hell by too much retsina, and on his way to the door he banged his left hip and thigh against the jukebox, and ended up limping painfully for the second time tonight. This one worse. He'd have a nasty bruise to show for it tomorrow, he could tell even now.

Worse still, the night air had brought with it the usual chill, and by the time he'd limped halfway to the hotel, his cold had kicked in again. When he reached the door of the Ariadne Hotel, his sinuses were blubbery with mucus, and he hadn't anything even close to a handkerchief on him.

The lobby was dark and quiet when he entered. He ripped a feathery page from the guest book, blew his nose into the names of some Scandinavians and Argentines, and then started the long, lonely limp up the stairs.

He reached the landing, and hobbled down the corridor toward his room. But just as he was about to step from a darkened stretch of hallway into an area in which the ceiling light actually worked, he was stopped in his tracks by the susurration of a whisper.

"—otta go, Roseanne will be missing me." This was clearly Tracey speaking under her breath.

Dennis flattened himself against a wall and peered down the corridor to where Tracey stood, just outside his room, her forearm gripped tightly by Jasper, who stood in the doorway wearing only a pair of boxer briefs.

"Roseanne is probably asleep," Jasper whispered back. "Besides, what do you care what she thinks anyway?"

"She's my friend," Tracey said, and she shook her arm in what was clearly a token gesture of defiance. "She watches out for me."

"Don't let her watch out for you too much," Jasper said impishly. "We don't want her stumbling onto this little thing we got going, do we?"

Tracey gave him an affectionate slug in the shoulder. "What's the matter? You afraid of her?"

"Who? Pipsqueak? Chance in hell of *that*."

Tracey snickered, then leaned into him and gave him a kiss; the angle was just askew enough for Dennis to be unable to see how serious it was—whether, for example, any tongues were involved. Then she jumped away from him, fluttered her fingers in a wave, and bolted across the hall, so mirthful and giggly that she didn't even see Dennis.

Jasper stepped out into the hallway, his chest gleaming with sweat, and watched as Tracey fumbled with her key and then shut herself tightly into her room. Dennis could actually hear the dead bolt drop.

Then the boy smiled in satisfaction and padded back into the room.

Dennis waited for what seemed an eternity before making another move; he didn't want to spoil the almost incredible luck he'd had in not being noticed by the two youngsters. Could their hormones have really been so overpowering that they didn't see him not six yards down? He struggled to remember his own youthful longings and decided, yes, they could.

But Jasper—! What could one make of him? Putting the

moves on Tracey, then letting her flutter away the next? It was a puzzlement. Like everything else about the boy.

When his knees began to give way, Dennis decided he'd better move again.

He limped to the room, then produced his key from his pocket and opened the door.

It was quiet inside, and dark. By the light of the moon streaming in through the window, he could just see Jasper in bed, still and silent; if he hadn't known better, he'd have presumed the boy asleep.

But he'd seen him in the hallway only minutes before. How could someone go from that state of arousal to the depths of slumber in so short a time? Dennis shook off his sweatshirt, kicked off his loafers, and stumbled over to Jasper's bed.

I really am drunk, he thought without alarm as he sat next to the pillow.

"Hey," he said, in a normal conversational volume. "Hey. Sleeping Blooty. Wake up. If you're rilly ashleep, that is." He shook Jasper by the shoulder. Jasper didn't respond. Dennis bent over to the boy's ear. "*Hey. Jazhper.* Shake Mr. San'man from your byootiful eyelashes and lissen up. Y'hear? *Hey.* You *in* there?"

Jasper finally consented to give up the act. He rolled over on his back, looked Dennis in the face with a measure of fear, and, without the slightest trace of sleep in his voice, said, "What?"

Dennis leaned back in an achingly obvious pretense at surprise. "Oh!" he said. "Did I wake you? Never ever did I mean to wake you! Say you'll forgive me or I sim'ly shan't ever rest."

"What do you want?" asked Jasper flatly.

Dennis lay down next to the boy and cuddled up next to him; he felt him go rigid beneath his sheets. "Jus' this," he said, whispering in his ear. "Whatever it is you've got up your sleeve for Tracey, an' I don't even preten' to know what sick thing that could be, jus' remember this, okay? You're a good kid. You're good for Farleigh, okay? You check on him when you got back tonight?"

"You're drunk."

"Answer the question."

A slight, anxious pause. "No."

"See, tha's *bad*," Dennis said, shaking his head. "He *depen's* on you, an' when you let him sit and *fester* like that . . . well." He took Jasper's chin in his hand and turned his head roughly so that their eyes were boring into one another's. "Here's the thing," he said. "If you hurt Farleigh in any way, I . . . man, I don't know what weird shit you got goin' with Tracey, but if it hurts Farleigh, then *I* hurt *you*."

"Is that a threat?" asked Jasper, his nostrils flaring.

Dennis smiled almost beatifically. Then he shook Jasper's chin and said, "Yesh. It's a threat. It's a *big* ol' threat. A big ol' fucking *evil* threat from big ol' evil me. What'choo gonna do about it, huh? Twinkie-boy?" He released Jasper's chin, and Jasper's head snapped back to its original position, facing away from Dennis.

With some difficulty Dennis rose from the bed, took two awkward steps, and fell into his own bed, where he lay, face-down, in the pillow. *Christ*, he thought; I must be fuckin' *plastered*. I just ordered my rival not to leave my lover!

He was just beginning to contemplate the sad, sick irony in that when sleep overtook him like a pouncing leopard.

chapter
40

The next morning, Dennis awoke to the sounds of a married couple arguing in French in the next room. He sat up in bed and held his head between his hands as though it might drop off his neck if he let go.

Jasper was already up and gone, his bed a tangle of unmade sheets.

While Gallic epithets assailed his ears, Dennis tried to dissipate the mists in his brain and remember what it was he had said to Jasper last night, in the thick of his drunk. He'd confronted the boy about *something*, that was certain; he could remember being close to him, the *smell* of him . . . But that was a sensually distracting memory. Put it aside and get to the crux.

Something crashed against the wall, and the French couple upped their volume to the level of all-out shrieking.

Dennis crawled out of bed, noticed for the first time that he was still fully dressed (although he'd managed not only to divest himself of his shoes but to get them somehow across the room), then made his way gingerly to the bathroom, where he ran the water for a very long time, shuddering over the sink until it was ice cold. He then splashed it on his face, said, "Oh,

God," a few times, and wondered if he might throw up. When he was reasonably sure he wouldn't, he went back to the bed and began undressing for a nice, long sleep. He had just let his pants fall when someone knocked on the door, causing his head to ring like a tuning fork.

He tried to say, "Don't come in," but his tongue was too slow; before he could even get out the first syllable, Farleigh swung open the door and peeked in. "Morning," he said. "Oh, good, you're dressing. We're about ready to go. I've sent Christos for a car, and I'm just on my way to pick up a trinket of some kind to present to Granny Ioannou as a birthday gift. Want to come with me? I've sent Jasper off to pick up some breakfast pastries we can eat in the car."

Dennis stared at him with horror, his pants gathered around his ankles.

Suddenly, Farleigh noticed the state he was in. "Well," he said. "Looks like *you* did some celebrating last night." His tone was mock-offended, but his face bore an elfin smile. He came into the room, sat on the bed beside Dennis, and placed the back of his hand over Dennis's forehead. "No temp. Your cold must be over. So I'd say you're just hungover, kiddo. Serves you right for living it up while I was out cold with . . . whatever it was. Looks like *you* feel like *I* felt. Grand, ain't it?"

Dennis was still concentrating on trying to produce his first words.

Farleigh, clearly feeling *much* better, reached between Dennis's legs and grabbed his crotch. Dennis yelped and rose a good two inches off the bed; when he came down again, he considered reassessing his previous conclusion about the possibility of throwing up.

"Listen," said Farleigh, laughing, "you just stay here today, okay? Sleep it off. That's all I needed: a good twelve hours. Made me right as rain. No need for you to have to sit in some bumpy rental car while we drive across the island. And it's really Jasper's business, not yours."

Dennis's will suddenly underwent a kind of power surge. He straightened his spine, took a deep breath, and looked Farleigh straight in the eye. "I'm coming," he said in a voice that invited no argument. "I want to see more of Santorini. I've heard it's the most beautiful place on earth. I'm not staying in a hotel room and missing it."

Farleigh shrugged. "Well, great. I'm sure Jasper'd love to have you along. Your suddenly flowering friendship, and all." He quickly eyed the pair of unmade beds, but a tad suspiciously, as if this were some kind of red herring provided for his benefit.

Dennis got to his feet and pulled his pants back on. "Just let me change my socks," he said. "I'll be right out."

Farleigh pushed himself back to his feet and took his leave; when he turned to pull shut the door behind him, he looked at Dennis, who was rifling madly through the contents of his suitcase. "My word," he said, "I thought you knew how to pack better than that."

"I do," Dennis replied, his head pounding. "I'm just in a hurry."

"I don't mean the suitcase," he said. "I mean the clothes you're wearing. Looks like you *slept* in them." He winked, then departed, closing the door behind him.

Dennis found a pair of white socks to replace his day-old ones and made the switch, then, willing himself to be up to the day, he left the room and headed down to the lobby. A Spanish family was standing at the desk checking in; the parents were in quiet conversation with the desk clerk, while their young son gripped his father's pants leg and sucked Coca-Cola through a straw. Dennis smiled at the boy as he passed the desk, and found Farleigh just beyond, in an earnest conference with Jasper, who was holding a fat-soaked paper bag, presumably filled with pastries.

"—ooked all over," the boy was saying. "There's no sign of them."

Farleigh appeared unconcerned. He was picking his teeth with one of the flavored toothpicks. "I don't understand the big fuss," he said, working his way past a bicuspid. "They're big girls. If they've changed their minds about joining us, it's their business. Let them stay in town and shop, or whatever."

"But they *said* they wanted to come along. They *both* said." Jasper appeared nearly frantic.

Farleigh shrugged his shoulders. "Well, what do you want me to do? We can't *force* them to come along." He stuck the

toothpick far into the gap behind one of his bicuspids. In order
to do this, he had to contort his face so that he looked as
though he were casting upon Jasper a grimace of displeasure.
In spite of himself, Dennis took this as a good omen for the
day.

"Let's wait till they show up," the boy pleaded. "I'm sure
they'll be back in no time. We can't just leave without even
checking if they want to come. Their feelings will be hurt . . ."

Before Farleigh could reply, a noise at the base of Dennis's
skull suddenly grew louder, and pushed its way into his con-
sciousness. He recognized it as the sound of the French couple
arguing. It was coming from behind him, so he turned to see
what this pair of savages could look like.

To his amazement, he saw a pair of tiny, rather round persons well into their dotage reach the bottommost landing of the
staircase, and stop there to harangue each other briefly before
continuing their descent. Their argument was by now so violent
that the old woman, red in the face with the force of her shrieking, lashed out and knocked off the old man's dapper little hat.
He reached up above his head, wildly trying to prevent this, and
when the hat went sailing beyond his reach he regarded the
woman with fury and screamed back.

This performance had of course attracted the attention of
all half-dozen persons present in the lobby, and Dennis turned
to Farleigh to exchange an amused and astonished glance that
such roiling passion could exist in such withered breasts. But
before he could catch Farleigh's eye, the old man stunned the
onlookers by reaching out and pushing the old woman down
the last flight of stairs. She emitted a piercing cry of fright, then
rolled heavily down the dozen or so steps till she came to rest
heavily on the floor.

She didn't move. No one watching made a move, or said a
word; they were transfixed by horror.

That horror was doubled when the little old man raced
down the stairs and, upon reaching his fallen companion, began kicking her in the stomach.

This time the hotel's desk clerk leapt into action; he raced
over and stood between the woman and her assailant, flailing
his arms and shouting wildly in Greek. A housemaid appeared,

and the desk clerk spat a few commands at her; she dropped her load of towels and rushed to the desk, where, despite trembling fingers, she dialed the phone and then, after a pause, began loudly and plaintively crying into its receiver.

The desk clerk had by now taken the old man by the scruff of his neck and led him in a corner, where he stood guard over the scowling and unrepentant-looking little monster.

The woman lay yet still.

The entire incident had so splashed the onlookers with disbelief that it was a moment before anyone could find his voice, much less move.

Except Jasper. When Dennis, badly shaken, turned to ask Farleigh if they dared approach the woman and ascertain her condition, he noticed that while Farleigh himself stood with his mouth agape, and the Spanish couple and their child stood likewise (the mother with her hands covering all her face save her eyes), Jasper . . . well, Jasper was looking out the hotel's front door in an agitated state. Not as though he was seeking escape from too emotionally wrenching a scene, which was Dennis's first thought; no, Jasper's demeanor suggested something else.

Then it hit him. The boy was still worried that Tracey and Roseanne hadn't yet returned! Despite the horrendous scene that had been played out here before them, Jasper's focus had never strayed very far from that. Why? What in God's name was so important about the girls' accompaniment?

He couldn't think about that now. He looked at Farleigh, who again appeared ashen and frail as he had the night before. "I think I'd better go have a look," he said, nodding his head in the direction of the old woman.

Farleigh nodded. Dennis tiptoed to the foot of the stairs, and peeked over the woman's badly twisted shoulder to see what he could see on her face. If her eyes were open, then nothing more need be done . . .

They were fluttering. Even better, she emitted a long, low moan of agony.

He let a sigh of relief slip from his chest, and realized he was trembling.

He lowered himself into a crouch and was about to press

his hand to the space between the woman's jawline and her neck—why, he couldn't say, but he seemed to remember having seen that done on TV medical shows.

But before he could provide this questionable service, there simultaneously appeared an official-looking gentleman in a tie from the staircase above, and an assemblage of concerned citizens from the street outside; they swarmed immediately around the woman and began gabbing in Greek. The desk clerk, still standing guard over the sullen old man, shouted information to them from across the lobby.

All of these men ignored Dennis utterly, so he was able to slip away from them and rejoin Farleigh and Jasper. As he did so, he gave a little nod to the Spanish family, and they seemed to understand that this meant the old woman was alive. The father draped his arms over his wife and child, and ushered them quietly out of the hotel.

"She okay?" asked Farleigh, the toothpick still drooping from the two teeth between which he'd stuck it.

Dennis nodded. "Think she's conscious."

Farleigh released a long, loud sigh. "What a world," he said.

Jasper apparently decided he should make some token comment on the incident. "Yeah," he said, "there's heterosexuality in a nutshell for you." When both Farleigh and Dennis whirled on him, and regarded him with clear distaste, he changed his tone. "Terrible, and everything, though," he said. Then, he brightened. "Say, Farleigh, if you're too upset by everything, maybe we'd better not go."

Farleigh's eyes widened; it was evident he had no idea how to respond to this.

A siren from down the street announced the arrival of an ambulance. Farleigh said, "Let's get out of their way," and herded Jasper and Dennis outside before the medics could pull up and start piling into the hotel.

Outside, Dennis noticed that the hotel windows were thronged with people, most of whom had their hands and faces pressed there, spying on the aftermath of the scandalous scene inside.

"Christ," he said. "News travels fast!"

The ambulance barreled up to the hotel and slammed on

its brakes; so reckless was its progress that it nearly sideswiped a car trying to back into a parking space across the narrow street. Dennis regarded that car to see if the driver reacted at all. He saw that it was Christos at the wheel.

He waved. "Christos! Over here. You won't believe what hap—" He stopped himself, suddenly remembering that he and Christos were not on speaking terms. He turned around and looked back into the hotel as the medics streamed inside carrying leather bags and a collapsible stretcher.

Christos crossed the street and joined them. "What's going on?" he asked, his voice hushed with presentiment.

"Some old guy pushed his wife down the stairs," said Jasper matter-of-factly. "Say, you didn't see Tracey or Roseanne anywhere, did you?"

chapter
41

Despite the upsetting event at the hotel, and Jasper's entreaties to reconsider their expedition in light of it, Farleigh insisted on going ahead with the day as planned, even to the point of first shopping for a gift for Granny Ioannou. He set out to do just this, after bidding Christos to wait by the car for their return. The unspoken command was that he should also keep an eye on the hotel in case there were any interesting postscripts to the assault; an arrest, for one thing, was almost certain to follow.

Farleigh gave Dennis his arm, and Dennis helped him down the narrow side streets of Santorini town while Jasper walked a few paces ahead, his hands in his pockets and his head low. He scuffled as he walked.

"That boy is *cold*," said Dennis when Jasper had got far enough ahead of them to be reasonably out of earshot.

Farleigh let this accusation sit for a few moments; then he said, "He's young, Dennis. Outbursts of passion don't strike him as remarkable, the way they do you and me."

Dennis almost choked at this. Did youth excuse *everything*? "Farleigh," he said, "that's absurd!"

"It's not, really," he said. "Not if you think about it. How many persons in their thirties or forties are willing to die for love? Hmm? And I mean really *willing.*" He stopped before a small jewelry store. "It's something we outgrow. We're able to abstract our affections more; we're able to place them in an emotional context, because we've had more familiarity with them. We know them better. Not like the young. To them everything is hot and new." He pointed his cane at the window of the store. "Call Jasper back, I want to go in here."

Dennis complied; the boy, now a full half block away, turned, frowned at him, and began backtracking.

Farleigh opened the door and let Dennis guide him into the shop. "You know, in spite of the terrible nature of what that man did," he continued as he entered, "in a way, I almost envy him. To be that age, and to feel such stirrings of emotion that . . . well, that anything is possible! Even atrocity." He reached the counter and came to a rest; Dennis released his arm. "I suppose it's something uniquely French."

The bells above the door jangled to life again, and Jasper shuffled in. "You're going to buy my grandmother *jewelry?*" he said derisively. "Farleigh, she's a hundred years old!"

"Never underestimate female vanity," he said with a smile. He rang the service bell on the counter. "It survives age, frailty and, I'd be willing to bet, even death."

A trim, middle-aged clerk in capri pants came through the door to the shop's back rooms. She had half a pear in one hand, and was wiping juice off her lips. "I'm so sorry," she said, "we don't open for twenty minutes yet."

Dennis was amazed that all the island natives knew to speak to them in English. Were Americans really that distinct from other peoples? While he pondered this, Farleigh turned on his charm and said, "Oh, dear, that's such a shame; we're off to visit my young friend's grandmother, and I hate to arrive empty-handed. She just turned a hundred, and we missed the party."

"A hundred!" said the clerk, surprised. "Oh, my, that is very old!"

"Yes," said Farleigh. "May we all have such long life. Well, thank you very much for your time, and we're sorry to have troubled you." He turned to go.

"Oh, sir, please wait," she said, putting down her pear and wiping her hands against each other. "For such an occasion I will gladly make an exception."

"*Epharisto,*" said Farleigh winningly.

"*Epharisto,*" the clerk countered, a big jack-o'-lantern smile now lighting up her face.

While the clerk showed Farleigh her wares, Dennis took a sidelong glance at Jasper, who stood, as ever this day, staring out into the street as though he might by chance catch sight of Tracey and Roseanne. He still didn't understand the motivation behind this; could his flirtation with Tracey be genuine? The boy could perhaps be bisexual. But if so, why would he risk Farleigh's discovery of it by mooning over Tracey's absence like a road-show Romeo?

"Oh, now *that's* quite beautiful," said Farleigh suddenly. Dennis turned back and found him pointing through the glass of the display case at a silver necklace with a reproduction of a Greek coin affixed to it. "Who is that, Athena?"

"That is Aphrodite, sir, the goddess of love. And may I say what fine taste you have." She took the necklace from the case and draped it over one of her hands, which she extended to Farleigh so that he might have a better look at it. "This coin is of course not genuine, but it is the work of the finest craftsman on the island, who only produces such pieces twice or thrice a year."

Dennis rolled his eyes, and pictured hundreds of these things rolling hourly off a conveyor belt in Taiwan.

Still, Farleigh seemed taken with the necklace, even if he wasn't taken in by its reputed history. "May I feel its weight?" he asked.

The clerk placed it in his cupped hand. "Notice how the chain coils into a very small space," she said. "That is the mark of quality."

Farleigh's eyes twinkled; Dennis inferred from this that he was enjoying her bogus sales pitch. He was certainly gallantly playing along. "Yes, it's fine indeed," he said. "It's very simple, and very pretty, and very Greek." He smiled. "May I have it gift-wrapped?"

"Of course, sir." She smiled as she took the necklace back

from him. "How will sir be paying for this beautiful necklace?"

"American Express," Farleigh said with mock pride in his voice; he sounded as though he might actually salute. Dennis coughed into his hand to dispel the urge to laugh.

The clerk took Farleigh's card, then disappeared with both it and the necklace. When she had gone, Farleigh looked at Dennis and shrugged. "Well, it *is* pretty. And I don't want to embarrass Jasper's grandmother with anything too extravagant. I'm assuming she's a woman of slender means." He turned to Jasper. "Am I right in that, Jasper?"

Jasper raced from the store.

Farleigh looked after him, completely dumbfounded. "What in the world . . . did I say something I shouldn't, or—"

"I'll go after him," Dennis offered. He was, in fact, eager to know himself what had set the boy off.

He flew out of the store and ran up the street, hot on Jasper's trail. Almost immediately he spotted him; he had, incredibly, discovered and cornered Tracey and Roseanne, who were carrying shopping bags and sipping mineral water from plastic bottles and looking, all in all, contentedly American.

Dennis hurried to join them. When he arrived, Tracey was saying, "I'm sorry, hon, but Rosie and I never actually thought you wanted us to go all the way to your *grandmother's* with you. We just thought you wanted us along for the trip to the island." Behind her, Roseanne nodded avidly. "And we *so* just want to go up to the roof of the hotel and get some sun today. They have a big deck up there, and everything. Oh, hi, Dennis."

"Hi, Tracey. Hi, Roseanne."

Jasper flashed him a look of irritation, then took Tracey's hand—a bold step, indeed; he was essentially abandoning any subterfuge about the flirtation. "*Please,*" he said, "it won't be any fun *at all* without you."

"I'm not sure a visit to one's centenarian grandmother is *supposed* to be fun," said Dennis, enjoying his role as gadfly.

Jasper gave him another murderous look, and Dennis, remembering what Farleigh had said about the young being capable of any atrocity for the sake of love, decided maybe he'd better back off a bit.

Tracey was grinning with pleasure; Dennis had never seen

a girl who so enjoyed being courted. But it was also clear that
she had no real desire to ride into the wilds of Santorini to visit
peasant folk, either. It would be interesting to see how she
would choose.

She looked imploringly at Roseanne, who said, "It's up to
you, Trace, but I'm going up to the roof, with or without you.
My feet hurt."

Even Dennis knew she didn't mean this; she'd follow her
friend to the ends of the earth, whether her feet hurt or not.

Jasper squeezed Tracey's hand and, allowing his eyes to go
liquid and irresistible, said, "Just come with me today. I promise
you, as God is my witness, it'll be the last thing I ever ask of
you. But it's—it's . . ." He scowled at Dennis, then said, "It's
an important part of . . . what we talked about."

"It is?" asked Tracey, surprised.

"Yes. *Please.*"

Whatever willpower Tracey possessed was no match for
those entreating eyes. She shrugged, let out a little laugh, and
said, "Oh, hell. Sure. Whatever."

Jasper's face erupted into an aspect of joy; he leaned in as
if to kiss her, then perhaps thought he shouldn't go quite that
far in front of Dennis, and pulled back.

As Dennis had predicted, Roseanne relented as well, allowing Tracey to persuade her to come along with only a token
show of resistance. On their way back to the jewelry store,
Tracey said, "So, what's new with you guys? We miss anything?"

"No," said Jasper, grinning at her.

Dennis felt his face redden with offense. "Actually," he said
in cold, hard tones, "quite a lot happened. An old man as-
saulted a woman in the lobby. Pushed her down the stairs and
kicked her in the stomach. An ambulance had to be called."

Tracey clicked her tongue. "What a creep," she said. Moments later, she was describing what she and Roseanne had
bought that day.

Dennis thought, *My God. Farleigh's right.*

chapter
42

When they got back to the car, Christos reported that the old Frenchman had indeed been arrested, and had gone quietly. Maybe the assault on his companion had drained him of aggression. Despite himself, Dennis was a little disappointed.

They piled into the car—a Fiat Tipo—and set out on their journey. Since Christos hadn't anticipated Tracey and Roseanne being along, he hadn't requested a larger vehicle, and the seating arrangements were rather snug. Roseanne squeezed between Christos and Farleigh up front, and in the backseat Tracey snuggled in between Dennis and Jasper.

The drive across Santorini's hilly length was conducted largely in silence; Dennis was now not on speaking terms with either Christos or Jasper, and Roseanne was ignoring Tracey to protest the abandoned day on the rooftop. Even Tracey herself seemed withdrawn; now that she was in the car, she seemed to resent Jasper's having persuaded her to join him.

And if internal tensions hadn't silenced the lot of them, Santorini's great, scalloped beauty might have. Dennis found himself staring in trancelike awe at the way the roadside occasionally gave way to sheer plummeting cliff sides—cliff sides so close that as Christos drove alongside them (entirely too quickly), Dennis could feel the backs of his arms prickle with raw terror.

And all of this violent assemblage of rock was drenched in the most delicate colors . . . a palette of pastels, spread like gouache over everything. The rocks themselves were the kind of pink and rose and white Dennis associated most closely with human flesh; within every cranny and crevasse was a lick of gorgeous greenery, like pesto sauce drizzled onto a pile of cavatappi.

Dennis lost track of time; so much gorgeousness passed his eyes that he began to feel overfed, and to desire the aesthetic equivalent of a burp. This came soon enough, as Jasper leaned past him and into the front seat, and said, "I think this might be it. Up ahead. I remember it mostly from pictures, but . . ." His mouth flashed an involuntary tic, and he turned around to squeeze Tracey's hand. Farleigh, in the seat ahead of him, didn't see this.

Dennis did.

The town they were approaching was beautiful in its own crazy-quilt way. A sunny, indolent fishing village, it filled the upper portions of a spectacular cliff side in a chaotic, dizzying way, as though someone had poured all the houses haphazardly onto an acres-wide foundation of warm caramel.

"This *is* it," said Christos, reading a sign as they drove past. "Ia."

"Ia," repeated Dennis. It sounded, somehow, so . . . Hellenic. So pre–Ottoman Empire. He felt a cozy sort of affection for the place already.

They had to leave their car outside the perimeter of the village, because in fact the place *was* a crazy quilt; the roads stopped short and became sidewalks and staircases and dirt paths that wound up and down and over and sometimes into each other, and in places even stopped short, or came to an end on someone's shingled roof.

"Jesus," said Dennis. "Imagine what it must be like to deliver the mail here."

"You must have to be born into the job," said Farleigh merrily as he descended a sudden swirl of steps that led to a cobbled walk. "Spend your youth in apprenticeship."

"Like royalty," said Tracey.

Farleigh scoffed. "Hardly."

They stumbled onto a wide expanse of sand and tile and stopped to look out over the massing of roofs and patios below them. "It's pretty, in a way," said Roseanne. "Like a bunch of pebbles on a beach."

"How are we supposed to know where we're going?" asked Jasper. "I haven't been here since I was six. This was a bad idea right from the start."

"What's your grandmother's name?" Christos asked him.

"Huh? Oh. Ioannou. Lina Ioannou. Why?"

He didn't answer, but instead leapt over a low wall beneath the veranda of a small brick house behind them. He cupped his hands over his mouth and called out something in Greek.

"Oh, God," said Tracey beneath her breath, "he is *such* a stud!"

A moment later, a middle-aged woman in a pink jogging suit came out on the veranda and answered him in an inquisitive tone, and within twenty seconds she and Christos were exchanging Greek like gunfire. Dennis couldn't follow any of it, but the woman spent a great deal of time pointing in various directions, and Christos echoed every gesture in a manner that suggested he was seeking her approval. Eventually Christos said, "*Epharisto*," and the woman replied, "*Epharisto*," and Dennis knew this meant the interview was over.

The woman returned indoors, and Christos leapt back over the wall and rejoined his party.

"Okay," he said. "I know where Lina Ioannou lives." He started back the way they'd just come, and the others scrambled to keep pace with him.

"It's that small a community here?" asked Farleigh as Dennis helped him back up the steps.

"Well, it's *pretty* small," Christos replied as he turned down another path they'd chosen not to take earlier. "At least, there aren't many permanent residents. Lot of vacationers and summer leases, apparently. This way . . . down here."

They followed him for several minutes, their conversation

consisting mainly of continued amused observations on the patchwork nature of the town, and of sympathy for Roseanne's tired feet. At one point they came upon a repair crew shoring up a collapsed brick wall. Since there was nothing in Ia that could properly be called a street, no automobiles could enter it; thus the load of bricks and mortar mixture was slung over the back of a donkey.

"Oh," cried Roseanne, "the poor thing!"

One of the workers, who apparently spoke English, looked at her and laughed, then whispered to the other worker, who laughed at Roseanne as well.

She pursed her lips and turned away with a contemptuous snort. "I don't think it's a bit funny. Animals have rights!"

"Says the woman who had octopus her first night here," Christos observed teasingly.

Roseanne surprised everyone by giving him a playful slap in the arm. "That's only because you ordered for me and I was too afraid to contradict you!"

"And do I frighten you now?"

"Nah," she said, shaking a fist in his face, which loomed an easy five inches above her own, "I could take you out easy."

Everyone laughed, and Tracey held her hand over her heart. "I don't know where she gets it," she said to Jasper, within Dennis's earshot, "but every once in a while she shows what she's made of. Now you see why I let her look after me."

"I wish you'd let me do it for her," said Jasper.

Tracey clicked her tongue, then scampered ahead of him.

Dennis shook his head. I wish I could figure out his game, he thought; maybe the visit to Granny will clear the air. . . .

And then they were at Granny's door.

chapter
43

Jasper knocked; big flakes of red paint fell from the door
as he did so. The house was small, lopsided, and in an
advanced state of disrepair. It looked as though it had
been some years since it had last had the requisite island white-
washing.

Through a grimy window a face appeared for a moment; it
looked masculine . . . beyond that, it was impossible to determine anything about it.

A moment later, the door swung open and a gray-haired,
brown-skinned man in khaki trousers, a black rayon shirt, and
house slippers stepped outside. Dennis felt a shiver of fear, but
then the man smiled.

"Jasper?" he said. "Little nephew Jasper from America?"

Jasper took a step back in alarm. "Uncle . . . Uncle Kostas?"

Apparently this was exactly who it was, because he scooped
Jasper into a bear hug—a hug the boy was visibly unwilling to
endure. "Your mother called and said you'd be visiting," he
said as he released his hold; Jasper wobbled uncertainly before
regaining his footing. "We thought to see you before now."

"I . . . was . . . uh, busy on Mykonos," he said, staring baldly at his uncle. "With . . . my friends, here." He reached out and pulled Tracey over by the hand.

Kostas nodded to the rest of the party. "Ah," he said. "So, you get your mother to send you to Greece to see your dull old family, and you turn it into a holiday with friends." When Jasper blushed, he ruffled the boy's hair with his grizzled hand and said, "Just like your uncle."

Jasper feigned an amused laugh, then said, "Yes, well . . . this is Farleigh Nock, my—my associate in a . . . theatrical . . . uh, play. And Dennis Racine. A . . . friend. Christos Mistaras, who's Greek, too. Born on—where was it, Christos?"

"Kithnos."

"Kithnos. And this is Roseanne DiStanislau. And *this*," he said, squeezing Tracey's hand, "is Tracey Helmerich."

Dennis noticed that Farleigh did a double-take at the squeezed hand. Could he really just be noticing now?

"Everybody, this is my Uncle Kostas. My mother's brother." He turned back to Kostas, who beamed a smile.

"Very proud to know you all," he said. "Do you need a place to stay? Any friends of Jasper are welcome here."

"No, no," Jasper said, "we're at the Hotel Ariadne, in Santorini town. But, Uncle, I thought you lived in England." He turned to Farleigh. "That's how my mom met my dad. She went to Liverpool to visit Uncle Kostas."

"My little English nephew," Kostas said affectionately. "Come in." He ushered the group through the door, and as they entered the house he said, "My prosthetics business went bankrupt two years ago. I expanded, you see: fake limbs for animals. You cannot imagine the magnitude of my failure there. Little Scotch terriers and corgis, all over Britain, chewing off their synthetic legs. I was lucky to get out of the country alive." He laughed ruefully. "Also, I divorced your aunt even before that, and your cousins Stephanie and Helena had gone to live in America, just like your mother. Boston. So I had nothing to keep me in England anyway. I came back here to look after your granny."

Jasper, not releasing Tracey's hand, said, "I never knew that."

"Ah, you did," Kostas said as he shut the door behind him,

"your mother told you all about it. But she says you pay no heed to family news."

Jasper blushed again.

Dennis, enjoying the boy's discomfort, yet managed to tear himself away to see if he could spot some sign of the elusive, centenarian granny. The house, however, appeared empty— though crowded with worn furniture. The air in the room, though, wasn't close at all; it was dank. He almost felt chilled.

As he continued to survey his surroundings, he noticed that the walls were filled with icons and crucifixes and cheesy pastel portraits of the Virgin Mary. More than a dozen of these last, in fact . . . one in which she looked disturbingly like Kathie Lee Gifford.

Kostas invited everyone to sit down, which was difficult to manage, because there weren't enough chairs. Farleigh and Dennis seated themselves on a low-backed sofa that faced a little altar on a table on which stood a statue of the baby Jesus, dressed in whatever robes were appropriate for this liturgical season; he held a scepter and a globe and, all in all, looked like a more than respectable drag queen.

Christos, knowing his place, dropped to the floor and crossed his legs. Roseanne and Tracey took two of the remaining chairs; Kostas took the other one. Jasper, momentarily at a loss, squeezed into Tracey's chair and put his arm around her; neither looked comfortable with the arrangement. Farleigh was staring at them, his brows knit.

"So how is my sister Maria?" Kostas said. "How fares she in that wheelchair?"

Jasper shrugged. "Okay. She's been in it for twelve years, Uncle Kostas. Used to it by now."

He shook his head and wagged his finger. "See how little you know? So young . . . you just don't care. I speak to your mother but twice a year, and even *I* know. In her dreams, she tells me, she still walks. Did she ever tell you that? And runs. And dances. In her dreams Maria still *dances*. Don't tell me she is used to the chair!"

Jasper, who by now had his blushing routine down just about perfectly, gave forth with another performance.

Kostas grinned and looked at the others for a moment,

then, with the barest evidence of a facial tic, said, "Perhaps we should drink to Maria's health. I ought to offer you drink, anyway; where are my manners?" He got up. "I'm sure this rascal has told you what to expect of me: just a dissolute old man."

"*I didn't tell them what to expect,*" Jasper called out as Kostas disappeared around the corner, "*because I thought you were still in England.* And besides," he continued, more softly as Kostas was now rounding the corner with a bottle of wine and seven juice glasses in his hand, "the last time I saw you, I was just a kid. And you had black hair."

Kostas set the bottle and the glasses on the table gently, then ran his hand through his ashen locks. "Well, time has sapped all my youth and given it to you, eh? What an ungrateful boy." He appeared more jovial than he had just moments before; clearly, the prospect of wine had brightened his spirits. Dennis noticed that the bottle had already been opened.

"Excuse me, Mr. Ioannou," said Farleigh, "where *is* Jasper's grandmother, if I might ask? I've brought her a belated birthday gift."

"Why, she's at mass," he said as he pulled the cork from where it had been reinserted into the bottle neck. "As she is every morning and every afternoon and every evening. That is Granny's hobby. She likes to nag God." He laughed uproariously at this, then poured everyone a few swallows of the wine; he gave himself the lion's share.

He held his glass aloft and said, "To Maria in America, and to her son here in Greece." The others echoed this in mumbled tones, then drank; Dennis found the wine bitter and raw, and set down his glass without finishing.

He sat back and stretched, and noticed, set primly on a lace tablecloth atop a bookshelf, a yellowed photograph of a raven-haired beauty. She was cradling her throat with her hands, and the hands themselves were clothed in satin gloves. It looked like an ancient film-studio glamour shot. Dennis asked Kostas who the subject was.

"Ah, well," he said, pouring himself a new glass of wine without offering anyone else any. "That's Granny. You remember that shot, Jasper? That's Granny in the late twenties." He slugged down some more wine. "She was a big star back then. But of course, you've heard this."

"I don't think I have," said Jasper.

"You have; you don't listen." He waved a hand at him dismissively. "Ah. I'll tell your friends and you can hear it again. Granny was a big star in those days, in Greek movies. She made period pictures, mostly."

"Ancient Greece?" Roseanne asked.

Kostas shook his head and wiped his mouth onto his sleeve. "Eighteenth century. What in England they call 'potboilers.' I don't know why. I don't know why the English say half the things they do, and I lived there for twenty-eight years. Anyway, they wanted Granny to do movies they could ship to America. Make her the next Greta Garbo."

"Oh, I *do* remember this," said Jasper, trying to wrest his thigh from where Tracey had pinned it the last time she shifted her weight. "She wouldn't show cleavage, right?"

He nodded, and poured himself yet a third glass of wine. "They wanted to put her in low-cut gowns and to play prostitutes and adulteresses. She said she wouldn't do such filth, and she walked out of the studio one day, just like that. Pfft." He made a little gesture with his hands. "Her film career was over. She met your grandfather, a fisherman here on Santorini, and married him, and came to live here in Ia. He died six years later, leaving her with two children and no income. God knows how she's made it work. But however she did it, she's still here." He raised his glass again. "Here's to her, then. Eh?"

The outside doorknob began to rattle at exactly that moment. Kostas leapt to his feet, slopping wine over the side of the glass. "O Sacred Head of Christ," he hissed, "she's back! Give me your glasses! *Quick!*"

Stunned, Dennis and the others somehow managed to fumble their glasses into Kostas's arms; he summarily scuttled out of the room.

And then Granny Ioannou came in.

chapter
44

Oh, what Dennis wouldn't have given to understand Greek for just the five minutes that followed! By Granny Ioannou's gestures and gesticulations—had she acted in *silent* films?—he knew that even his wildest inferences couldn't come close to the mark. Her body language made Sarah Bernhardt look like a Buckingham Palace guard.

She literally brought Kostas to his knees. But might that have been just so he could be at eye level? She couldn't have been more than four-foot nine. And yet in imperiousness, no queen or empress stood taller. A hundred years old? She looked, quite the contrary, ageless. Strands of coal black hair lay, still sleek, among the mass of wiry gray ones; that can't have been vanity. Just part of her ruined beauty, still all there under her black scarf, naked and unashamed of itself; beauty that once ravished on its own merits, and now had to ravish by its tragedy.

Dennis was mesmerized by her. Instantly.

She'd flung open the door, taken two infirm steps into the house with the use of a cane at least four inches taller than she was—larger even than Farleigh's!—then raised her head and eyed her unexpected guests with a flash of surprise followed by a spine-stiffening defiance. Then she called out, "*Kostas!*" in such a way that Dennis thought everyone in the world bearing that name might appear immediately at her side, gasping for breath.

Her son galloped into the room, already babbling what Dennis was certain were fulsome apologies; it was then that he sank to his knees before her and took her free hand. He pointed at Jasper and said his name; at this, Jasper squeezed Tracey's shoulders even more tightly, until the girl squealed in pain and elbowed him in the ribs.

Granny Ioannou smiled at Jasper with gold-rimmed teeth and called him over to her. With a nervous smile he approached her; she clutched his arm and started chattering away.

"Could—could you tell her I don't speak Greek?" Jasper asked Kostas.

He motioned toward a high-back chair, its leather seat well worn. "She's asking you to escort her to her chair," he said. "You'd better do it."

Jasper led the old woman to the chair, and made an attempt to help her into it. Offended that he considered her to need *that* much aid, she rapped him on the skull with her cane, then climbed onto the seat and sighed. Her feet didn't reach the floor.

Farleigh ambled over to Dennis and whispered, "She's magnificent!"

"I know," he whispered back.

Kostas, overhearing this, said, "You may speak up if you wish. Granny does not understand more than a handful of words in English. And even if she did, she is not at all averse to praise."

Granny, suddenly angry at a conversation being conducted that did not involve her, barked her displeasure at Kostas, who made haste to explain to her what was being said. Verbatim, apparently, for Granny turned to Farleigh and Dennis and bestowed on them a brilliant smile and a slight nod of the head.

Then she tapped Jasper's shoulder with the cane and said something to him that sounded very like a command.

"Could you, like, *tell* her, Uncle Kostas?" Jasper said, exasperated. "That I don't do Greek?"

Kostas laughed. "She wants to meet your friends, that's all. I will introduce them for you, how would that be?"

"Whatever." Jasper's intolerant tone couldn't hide the fact that he was covering fear with bravado. He edged back to Tracey's side and took her hand.

Farleigh raised an eyebrow and looked suddenly abashed; Dennis wondered if this was what he'd really wanted by coming here. He'd hoped that this visit would bust up Farleigh's romance with Jasper, but he'd never wanted it to happen at the expense of Farleigh's heart. Farleigh was supposed to leave here feeling disdain for the boy, not rejected by him. What was the little fool *up* to with that girl?

Kostas was going around the room, pointing out Jasper's visitors and naming them, then following this with a brief explanation in Greek. Kostas stumbled a bit when he came to Dennis; no doubt he'd forgotten what Dennis's connection to Jasper was. Probably because there wasn't one. He frowned in embarrassment.

When Kostas pointed out Tracey, Jasper squeezed her hand and gave her a little peck on the cheek. Tracey giggled and said, "*Quit.*"

Farleigh turned to Dennis and whispered, "What do you know about this? Is there something going *on* between those two?"

Dennis stared at him in terror; he couldn't bring himself to reply. He eventually managed a single shrug.

Granny had now set her cane beside her chair and was appraising Jasper, offering some kind of commentary that had Kostas in stitches.

"What?" Jasper asked. "What's so funny?"

"Nothing," Kostas said, drying his eyes. "Granny says you are very grown up. Very much bigger than when she last saw you."

"*Duh,*" said Jasper. "Like fifteen years won't do that."

Granny said something else, and Kostas cracked up again.

"Look, she's making fun of me, and I want to know why." He was trembling; this was apparently taking all his courage.

Kostas was clearly bursting to tell him, and so allowed himself to be persuaded. He pointed at Jasper and Tracey and said, "Granny says you both look so soft and powdered, she wonders which one is the girl."

Roseanne compounded the offense by joining Kostas in laughing at the crack, before she could catch herself and cover up her mouth. Jasper, however, found it much less funny; his nostrils flared, and he said through clenched teeth, "Tracey knows who the man is. If she has no complaints, it's no one else's business."

"Oh, *ho*," said Kostas, his eyebrows arched high. He translated this for Granny, who suddenly grew grim and pointed at the couple. She said something low and guttural.

Kostas said, now suddenly sober, "Granny . . . Granny says she hopes very much you aren't engaging in premarital relations. Because that's . . . well, that's a mortal sin." He reddened, as if embarrassed at having to report this.

"*Gross*," said Tracey, shrugging off Jasper's hand. "You can tell Granny that I haven't let Jasper touch me, and I mean, as *if*." Whatever was going on between them, she'd clearly had enough.

Kostas reported this to Granny, who appeared satisfied; Farleigh, however, looked more confused and hurt than ever. He was trying to catch Jasper's eyes, but Jasper was doing his best to avoid even looking in Farleigh's direction. Dennis's own heart started to break for him.

At that moment Kostas said, "Farleigh, is it? . . . Farleigh, my friend, I've told Granny you have a gift for her."

Farleigh approached, and Granny was so distracted by the prospect of a present that Dennis was able to slip away and yank on Jasper's sleeve. "Can I see you a minute?"

"Can't it wait? My grandmother's opening her gift now."

"No, it can't wait," he snapped. He pulled Jasper away from Tracey and over to where Christos was standing behind the group, as befitted his servile station.

"What's going on with this hands-all-over-Tracey business?" Dennis hissed. "You think Farleigh hasn't noticed? You think you aren't hurting his feelings, you little son of a bitch?"

"I *have* to do it," said Jasper, glancing furtively at his grandmother, who was tearing open the gift-wrapped package with some difficulty, but refusing all help from Kostas. "I can't let them know I'm queer."

Dennis was stunned. "Wh—what?"

"You don't know what it's like here," he said. "My Greek relatives in America—you have no idea. It's even worse here. *They can't know.* Period. That's why I'm playing up to Tracey."

"But . . . this has been going on since the boat. I saw you on the boat, kissing her!"

Granny had at last got the wrapping paper off the box. She opened it.

"I had to lay the groundwork early," he whispered, "so on the boat, I said, What fun if we pretend to be a couple. She liked the idea. Just, y'know—role playing. And when we got to the island, I said, Let's keep it up. It's fun."

Dennis scowled. "And she agreed?"

"Well . . . I persuaded her." He looked cagey; he wasn't telling Dennis something, but no matter—Dennis had heard quite enough.

"You manipulative little shit," Dennis said, shaking his head. "I can't believe you'd use her that way."

"*I have to!*" Jasper said as forcefully as he dared. He took a quick glance at his grandmother to make certain she hadn't noticed; in fact, she was contentedly holding up the necklace. Kostas whistled appreciatively at its beauty. Jasper turned his attention back to Dennis. "You don't know what it's like here! Ask Christos." He jerked his thumb at the houseboy. "Why do you think *he* turns all macho when he gets here? He knows what would happen to him if he acted as nelly as he does at home."

Dennis shot a look at Christos, whose eyes were open in surprise, apparently that he'd been drawn into the argument. He looked at Dennis and said, "Don't get me involved in this. I'm not involved."

"No," said Dennis scornfully. "No, of course not. Thanks, guys. Guess I understand everything now." He turned on his heel and said, "Pair of petty cowards, the both of you."

When he returned to the others and stood before Granny's chair, he found her staring intently at the medallion on the necklace.

Farleigh spoke up. "Tell her it's the goddess Aphro—"

Kostas coughed loudly, interrupting him, then turned and said, "Please, Farleigh, do not say that name. It's best if Granny thinks that this is a medallion of St. Anne. This is what I have told her. She won't allow pagan trinkets in the house. Or," he said meaningfully, "persons who *give* pagan trinkets."

Granny was holding up the necklace, regarding the medallion with even greater consternation, as though she couldn't quite bring herself to believe it was in fact of Christian origin. *Good,* thought Dennis, *let her figure it out.* Enough of hypocrisy. It was all sticking in his throat like phlegm.

Granny was just about to say something when the necklace was snatched from her hand.

By Christos, of all people.

Dennis—and the others as well—turned in astonishment to see the houseboy holding the necklace up before the hollow of his own throat.

"*Well,*" he said, the old familiar lilt back in his voice. "If *she* doesn't want it, guess who does?"

Farleigh cleared his throat and said, "Christos, this is not the time."

"It's the right time, the right place, and the *oh*-so-right *bijou,* sweetie." He blew Farleigh a kiss, then traipsed over to Kostas and said, "Here, honey, will you fasten it please? I can never work these silly clasps myself."

Kostas, his eyes as large and yellow as lemons, merely stared at Christos without replying; he appeared to be holding his breath.

Jasper had his hands over his mouth; Tracey was suddenly forgotten.

Dennis stepped forward. "Come here, you saucy vixen, *I'll* fasten it for you."

Christos cried, "Oh, you *darling!*" and sailed over to him.

While Dennis fastened the necklace around Christos's hairy neck, he was surrounded by a silence so enormous that it threatened to swallow him whole. His heart was galloping, and his fingers felt suddenly three times their normal size. But somehow he got the clasp to work.

"There," he said, "done!" Christos squealed with glee,

then whirled around and planted a big, wet kiss on his lips. Dennis tweaked his chin.

Then Christos sashayed over to Granny herself, who regarded him with the exact expression worn by God in Michelangelo's *Last Judgment.* He bent down before the old woman and said something in Greek.

A dark cloud passed over her eyes; she lifted her head with terrible, aching deliberation, and, curling her lip, said, "*Hermaphroditos!*"

Well, thought Dennis, there's *one* Greek word I can decipher.

All at once she sprang out of her chair, grabbed her cane, and started wielding it around her head like a martial artist. Tracey and Roseanne screamed and darted out of the way. Jasper shrieked as well; he dashed over to Farleigh and hugged him for protection.

"*HERMAPHRODITI!*" howled Granny Ioannou. She hobbled around the room, her lethal cane whipping through the air. "*HERMAPHRODITI!*" Kostas followed, trying to calm her, but had to hang back to avoid the cane's trajectory himself.

"Let's get out of here!" Dennis called out, and Christos, laughing merrily, was the first out the door. Dennis stayed behind to usher the girls and Farleigh through—and Jasper as well, alas; he was affixed to Farleigh like a barnacle.

When they'd safely exited the house, Dennis turned for one last look at the chaos he and Christos had caused: Granny Ioannou, like Boadicea among the Romans, knocking over lamps and vases in her fury, and poor old Uncle Kostas, cringing behind her, begging her to stop.

He cackled in glee, then turned to scoot out the door.

And that's when the cane caught him at the base of his skull.

chapter
45

By some miracle, some gift of a benevolent God, he
didn't pass out, but was able to lurch forward woozily,
the sky and the ground flip-flopping before his eyes, till
some six or seven yards into his flight, he fell.

He could hear Granny behind him, her howl of rage distant,
yes, but growing less so. Imperiled, and knowing it, he still
couldn't move. He had dirt in his mouth, and he thought his
lip was bleeding. He couldn't see straight. He held his hand
before his face; he caught only glimpses of it, as though he were
observing it under a strobe light. Strangely, the sight of his hand
brought to mind his manicurist, Martina, who had once confessed to not wearing underwear. Ever. Since then it had been
her defining feature for him; he had never been able to lose
the awareness of her underwearlessness, even for a second, as
she sat for hours pushing back his cuticles and buffing his nails
and talking endlessly about Lisa Marie Presley's bad life choices.

This must be what disorientation was all about, he decided:
the inability to focus on a life-threatening situation because he
was distracted by the thought of his manicurist's aversion to
panties.

Finally, he heard someone from far off say, *"Dennis? Where's Dennis?—Somebody help Dennis!"*

Before he knew it, he was being lifted to his feet. "Come on, honey," said a voice—Christos's voice. "No time to lay about. Granny's on the warpath."

"Just . . . had the wind . . . knocked out of me," he gasped. He tried to plant his feet on the ground. They folded like a marionette's.

"What, she clip you with that cane?" Christos asked while dragging him.

"Yes . . . am I bleeding, or . . ." He lost his breath again.

The houseboy whistled. "No blood, but you got a real goose egg developing back there. Quite an arm on the old girl. Put her out on Division Street, have that gang problem cleared up in no time."

"Is he all right?" Farleigh's voice now. Dennis couldn't quite see him. "Dennis—Dennis!" He felt his face being slapped. "Are you all right?"

He tried to focus on Farleigh. Little bursts of him popped before his eyes like firefly lights, and faded as rapidly. "Stop slapping me," he said.

"Oh, God." Jasper's voice. "Let's go. She's coming. I'm so sorry, everybody."

"Can he walk?" Farleigh again. "Can you walk, honey?"

"I . . . think so . . . yes."

"Then let's go."

He could hear Tracey and Roseanne squealing somewhere in the distance. Dennis tried to run, but Christos held his arm tightly and said, "Take it easy, sister. No need to kill yourself."

"No," he replied. "Granny'll do that for me." His vision was clearing. He saw that they were approaching a long stone staircase that led up to another level of meandering boulevards.

Christos looked behind him and laughed. "This is ridiculous. She won't give up. She's managing about two yards a minute, but she won't give up."

Dennis turned to see for himself, and though he seemed to be viewing the world though water, he could just make out that

Granny was, though far behind them, yet hobbling after them, wielding her cane like a saber. Kostas followed, waving his arms and pleading with her in vain.

"She's a *hundred*," Dennis said in awe. "What keeps her *heart* going?"

"Hatred, what else?" Christos replied while helping him maneuver the stairs. "Good old, God-fearing, faggot-loathing hatred."

"I'll have to try it," said Dennis. "Takes *years* off her." He stumbled, and scraped his knee. "Ow! *Damn* it."

"You all right, sweetie?"

"Yes, yes." He pushed himself back to his feet; or, rather, Christos lifted him. This was quite like the old Christos . . . maternal, helpful, solicitous. "By the way," Dennis said, "thank you. For—you know—back there at the house. The necklace thing."

"No. Thank *you* for pointing out what a hypocritical shit I've been." He grabbed Dennis by the waist and gave him a final shove up to the first landing. "I invite you to spank my bare bottom later, as punishment. In fact, I *insist* on it."

Far ahead, they heard Tracey scream again—this time in even more shrill distress.

"Oh, Christ, what *now?*" Dennis muttered, his skull now throbbing with pain.

They caught up with Farleigh, who, encumbered with Jasper and with his cane, had been making only slightly better progress than they were. They were at a bend in the flight of stairs, and Tracey and Roseanne, who had run on ahead, were now hurling back down, wailing and shrieking.

"Good *God*," said Farleigh, "whatever's the matter with them?"

"Don't ask us," said Christos. "You were here first."

The girls nearly careened into them, and gave every impression of trying to plow right through.

"*Whoa!*" cried Farleigh. "Hold on! Hold *on*, there."

"*Run!*" cried Roseanne, her face white with terror. *"Run as fast as you can!"*

Dennis looked behind them. "Not bloody likely," he said,

for Granny had now reached the bottom of the steps and was starting to mount them. Kostas, pulling on her skirt, was having next to no effect in slowing her.

"Oh, my *God*," Tracey said, looking faint. "*Help!* What's the Greek word for help?"

"What's *wrong?*" asked Christos, shaking her. Then he looked up, and his eyes grew wide. "Oh," he said.

Dennis looked up as well, and saw that there was a herd of some two dozen goats rapidly descending the stairs. There was no room to let them pass; they were at least three abreast, and pushing against both sides of the rock face out of which the stairs had been carved.

Dennis looked behind him. Granny was on the third stair and carefully mounting the fourth, a stream of virulent Greek flowing from her mouth.

Farleigh looked at him; Jasper was clinging to his shirt, sobbing. "So," he said, "do we risk the old woman or the stampede?"

"The stampede," said Dennis. "Definitely the stampede."

"You're *crazy!*" Roseanne said. She balled her fists and beat on his chest. "Let me by! Let me *by*! Don't you understand? *They smell!*"

Tracey clung to her friend's backpack. "*Hurry! They're almost here!*"

"This is ridiculous," said Christos. "They stink and they're rude, but they're not going to harm you! Not like the old harridan down below. Just follow me." And with that, he loped up a few steps and waded into the sea of goats. He moved through them—unsteadily and slowly, it's true, but he did move. When he'd managed several steps, he turned and, waving his arms to keep his balance, called out, "*Come on! You'll be fine!*"

By that time, of course, they had no choice, for the goats were swarming all around them. Tracey and Roseanne emitted shrieks like factory whistles and clung to each other as the beasts jostled and knocked them as they passed.

Jasper, panicking, released his hold on Farleigh and made a lunge into the goatstream. He raised his hands over his head and tried to keep aloft, but the goats were intent on their downward voyage, and gave no thought to any slender boy's footing.

He began to wobble. "*Oh! Oh!*" he wailed. "Somebody stop them! *Farleigh!*"

Farleigh, his breath coming hard, reached out his cane and shouted, "*Don't fall! Whatever you do, don't fall!*"

But of course, he did exactly that. Right onto the back of a filthy she-goat, who turned and bit his arm for good measure.

"*YOW!*" he screamed, and in trying to get away from those gnashing teeth, he managed to wedge his buttocks in between the she-goat and her neighbor, who continued tripping down the stairs without as much as a pause.

At the sight of their friend being borne away from them in this undignified manner, Tracey and Roseanne lost balance themselves, and fell face first onto the back of a single, extraordinarily matted brown goat, who turned, bared his gums at them, and whinnied like a banshee. Fortunately, the herd was thinning at this point, so when the terrified girls propelled themselves away from this hideous apparition, they landed on the stone steps, their pride and their buttocks the worse for wear, but not much else.

Still, there was Jasper to consider; he'd been carried all the way to the bottom of the steps, right into the path of Granny Ioannou and her upraised cudgel.

"*Oh, no!*" said Tracey. "He'll be *killed!*"

However, a hundred-year-old woman, no matter how indomitable, was no match for a herd of determined goats. They scooped her up as well, and bounced her along their backs till they'd reached the clearing below the stairs, where they shrugged off both grandmother and grandson, depositing them onto the cold, bare dirt.

Kostas, at the sight of his mother's humiliation—her black skirt flopped up over her head, her petticoat exposed, and one shoe tossed several yards away—made the sign of the cross, then sped back to the house and slammed the door.

Dennis, who had clung to the rock face while the goats passed with no trouble whatsoever, was feeling a great deal of pain in his head and thus a great deal of irritation at this entire ill-conceived adventure . . . his idea, he had to remind himself —his right from the start.

Determined to have an end to it once and for all, he turned

to the others, who stood on the stairs behind him, hands on their faces or covering their mouths, and said, "Right. Enough bullshit."

He marched back down the stairs and sailed right past Granny, who had by this time righted herself and was looking about for her cane.

Jasper was cringing before her, his hands over his head and moaning in stupefied, milk-pure terror.

Dennis grabbed him by his collar and said, "Get up."

Momentarily dazed by Dennis's appearance, Jasper nevertheless did as he was told. Then Dennis gave him a shove toward the stairs and said, "Get going."

Jasper scooted past his grandmother, who had just found her cane. She lifted it from the ground too late to strike him as he passed, but when she saw Dennis, she smiled in triumph and raised the weapon high, her arthritic knuckles white with fury.

But Dennis returned her a look that made her falter, a look of such unadulterated disdain that she must have sensed she had no power over him. Furthermore, he approached her on swift, sure legs, fists swinging at his side, not a trace of fear in his manner, and she was so taken aback by this unprecedented affrontery and lack of respect that she let her cane drop again.

When he stood before her, he said, in a cold, clear voice, "Someone should've banged you silly while you were still young enough for it to do some good."

Then he started up the stairs, one step at a time.

Almost as if she had understood his words, Granny recovered her temper and began casting threats at him anew. He could almost infer the sense of them: *Beware of me*, they said, *beware my righteous wrath! You have not escaped me yet!*

chapter
46

They climbed into the Tipo for the drive back to Santorini town. Christos took the wheel again, but Jasper piled into the front seat to sit between him and Farleigh. On the drive back, he dared to rest his head on Farleigh's shoulder. Dennis nearly spat at him in disgust.

As it was, Tracey and Roseanne heaped opprobrium on him. "You should be *ashamed* of yourself," Tracey said, seething. "Asking me to play your girlfriend just so you could impress your grandmother! I thought it was all supposed to be for *fun*. You *deserve* what happened."

"He deserves it," Roseanne echoed, her eyes narrowed in ill will.

"Like, I would've said okay if you'd only just asked! But no, you had to go and give me all those other reasons."

What other reasons? wondered Dennis.

"It's unforgivable," said Roseanne, nodding.

But Jasper pulled the rug out from under them by agreeing. "I know," he said, his voice choked with regret. "I don't blame anyone but myself. I've been a complete shit. I'm sor—" A sob swallowed up the last syllable, and Dennis noted with resignation, if not surprise, that Farleigh reached over and stroked the boy's cheek.

He sighed, then leaned forward and whispered into Christos's ear, "So, what did you say to get old Granny so riled, anyway?"

He quarter-turned his head away from Jasper, and said in a low voice, "Ah, I just asked her if she had anything else I could try on."

Dennis barked out a laugh, then sat back in his seat and rested his head against the cool glass window. He gingerly touched the bruise on the back of his head. It was about the size of a golf ball now, and hurt like hell.

Tracey and Roseanne, mollified by Jasper's prostration before them, had turned their attention to the future. "Maybe I should forgive Andreas," Tracey said, twirling a lock of her hair between her thumb and forefinger.

Roseanne was appalled. "Tracey! For God's sake, the guy tried to rape you!"

"Well . . . I did sort of lead him on, you know? We ditched you and Evagoras and ran off alone, and everything. I mean, what did I *expect* him to think? It's really kind of my fault, too, when you think about it."

Roseanne banged her fist against her forehead in exasperation. "I repeat: the guy tried to *rape* you!"

"I know, I know . . . but aside from that, he was kind of cute."

Roseanne looked at Dennis and shook her head slowly. "*Now* you see why she needs my protection?"

Their argument ate up most of the silence that pooled around the others. When they arrived back in town, Farleigh took Jasper to a physician to see to the boy's goat bite (even though the skin wasn't broken), while Tracey and Roseanne, ever resilient, ran off to do a last bit of shopping before the stores closed. As for Christos, he drove the car back to the rental agency. So Dennis found himself entering the hotel alone.

He stopped at the concierge desk and asked for a bag filled with ice. When this had been handed to him by a stern-looking young girl with a bleached mustache, he crossed the lobby and climbed the staircase the old woman had been thrown down only a few hours earlier. Violence and staircases . . . was it a theme for the day, or what? He felt, all at once, very unsafe; it was as though the world had suddenly revealed its random, amoral nature to him, and didn't care what he thought of it.

Back in his room, he sat on the bed and held the ice against his bump. But it was too difficult to maintain the required pose, with his elbow so uncomfortably high; so he gave up, tossed the icebag aside, slipped off his shoes, peeled off his socks, and began to massage his feet.

And then he thought. And thought hard.

If only he'd stage-managed things a little better, he decided, the visit to Granny Ioannou could have been everything he'd wanted it to be. If he'd only revealed the boy's hypocrisy to Farleigh . . . pointed out his manipulation of Tracey, exposed him for a fraud, a coward, a quivering pillar of fear before the judgmental eyes of a mere old woman. (Well, scratch that; nothing mere about Granny. She'd spook the Apocalypse Beast.) And why hadn't he done it? Why had he sat back and let it all rage out of control? Why, when he had exploitable evidence of Jasper's bad behavior in his hands, had he retreated? Why had he, in every sense, aborted his own mission?

He dropped his feet and lay backward on the mattress, careful to let his head hang over the side so no pressure was applied to his bump.

There was only one reason, he thought as he stared at the spiderweb of cracks on the ceiling. One reason only: Farleigh.

He just couldn't bring himself to break Farleigh's heart.

Once he'd seen that Farleigh actually did care for the boy —once he'd witnessed the confusion and hurt that flashed across Farleigh's face whenever he caught a glimpse of Jasper's attentions to Tracey—Dennis's own heart had cracked wide open, like an egg. And he'd grieved for Farleigh. For Farleigh, who had treated him so shabbily these past few weeks!

No . . . not shabbily—as well as he could. He was falling in love with someone new; how else should he treat his old love? With as much respect and consideration as possible, and he'd done that, hadn't he? With lapses, it's true, but then, his concentration had been elsewhere. Still, whenever Dennis had stood on his dignity and demanded his due, Farleigh had given it to him. To the extent that he was able.

So, this was it, then.

Dennis, his head lolling off the side of the bed, looked out the open window, where the curtains were gently being stirred by the easygoing Aegean wind. A clean white wall, clean cotton curtains, and a sky full of clouds; is this what he should be seeing? Now, at the moment of his final defeat? Should he be lying here, fingers down his pants, contentedly grooming his pubic hair while gazing upside-down at a sky too blue for Technicolor?

He sighed. Maybe acceptance of defeat was something that came in increments, so that when it was complete, it lacked any punch, any jolt of disruption. Dennis felt peaceful before this window, looking into eternity; might it not portend something, this vista, at this time? A clear road ahead . . . a future of un- limited possibilities . . . ?

He fell into a light doze, but when he descended into deeper sleep, his head grew heavier; and upside down as it was, it cut off his windpipe when it drooped.

He choked for a moment, woke up with a start, then sat bolt upright.

"Whoa," he said as he waited for the momentary panic to subside and his heartbeat to decelerate.

At that moment Jasper opened the door. When he saw Den- nis sitting on the bed massaging his throat, he paused a mo- ment, then pocketed his key and entered the room without meeting his eyes.

Dennis watched him cross the room, then said, "So. No infections, I take it?"

Jasper sat down and unlaced his sneakers, then placed them neatly by the side of his bed. "Not that you'd care, but no," he said, still not acknowledging Dennis with a look.

Dennis was taken aback. "What's that supposed to mean?"

Jasper rubbed his feet against his ankles. "Hypocrite like me, you know. What do you care? It was pretty clear how funny you thought it was that my grandmother blew up like that over Christos's stunt. Which you as good as put him up to, by the

way." He picked up his guidebook and pretended to resume
reading. "I can't even say I'm sorry she clubbed you over the
head like she did. I know I *should* be sorry, but I'm not."

The little *fuck*. Here Dennis was, gratefully accepting his
fate, accepting Jasper's assumption of his old role, and this was
the thanks he got? A mouthful of abuse from the chief bene-
ficiary of his graciousness?

Well, the hell with that. Dennis looked out the window
again, and this time he could see the noisy, ragtag streets of
Santorini—streets clotted with conflict and tension and guile.
This was the *true* state of the world. What had he expected,
looking at it upside-down? Of *course* he'd get a topsy-turvy view
of things.

This wasn't over. This wasn't over by a *long* shot.

"I'm going to shower," he said acidly. "All I want to do is
wash the grime of this entire experience off me."

He stripped off his T-shirt, and as he pulled it over his head
he caught Jasper's eyes on him. Just for the space of a heartbeat—even less.

Hmm, he thought.

He decided to experiment further, so instead of retreating
to the bathroom for the rest of his undressing, he stood where
he was and dropped his pants.

Jasper turned to the wall and held the book very close to
his face.

Clearly, the boy was fighting the urge to look at him.

Dennis shimmed out of his boxer briefs next, and stood
stark naked in the middle of the room. "Let me know if anyone
calls for me," he said.

Jasper didn't respond, nor did he as much as move his eyes
from the book. But when Dennis turned to go into the adjoining bathroom, he felt the boy's eyes on him. So he whirled back
around, just in time to catch his head in mid-snap. After which,
the boy was once again the picture of literary absorption.

Mm-*hmmm*, thought Dennis again.

As he showered, he decided that Jasper's reluctant appre-
ciation for his body was the key he needed to really put an end
to this farce. Of course, it would mean breaking Farleigh's
heart, really and truly breaking it, but shying away from that

necessity had got him nowhere thus far. And certainly, afterward, he could always paint himself as being just as much Jasper's victim as Farleigh was. "He took us both in," he recited in the shower, as if trying on the line for size, "we were both fools, Farleigh. Let's forgive each other and start over, okay?"

What Dennis had decided was, he must seduce Jasper.

And have Farleigh discover them together.

chapter

47

After he'd showered and changed, Dennis left Jasper behind in the room, still buried in his book, but Dennis noticed that the same color plate of the Elgin marbles was gazing out from it . . . clear evidence that the boy hadn't turned a single page.

Heartened by this sign of his prey's internal torment, Dennis happily went out for a walk. In the lobby, he ran into Christos, who was carrying his overnight bag and heading for the door.

"Christos! Where are you off to?"

He smiled at Dennis and set down his bag. "Oh, Farleigh's sending me back to Mykonos tonight. To close up the house."

Dennis frowned. "Oh, damn. Do you have to go *tonight*? It's been so long since we've had a chance to really talk!"

"Well, you *know Miss* Farleigh Thing when she gets a bug up her butt. Suddenly everything's all 'Gotta get back to Chicago.' Like, the whole brouhaha today with Granny Ninja-Bitch has made him realize how much time he's wasted gallivanting around the islands on a lark."

Dennis raised an eyebrow. "Well. That's something at least. What's his schedule?"

"Well, y'all are to follow to Mykonos tomorrow morning; I'm supposed to meet you at the airport there with all the bags. Then we get on the first flight to Athens, and from there, the first flight home to Miss Libertyland."

"Jesus." Dennis scratched the back of his neck. "He *is* in a hurry."

Christos nodded. "Tell you the truth, I think he'd have tried to leave tonight, only he's not feeling so hot."

A flash of concern. "He okay?"

"A little pale and shook up. All the excitement of the day, is my guess. He's taking a walk right now, get himself a little fresh air. My suggestion. Man's a bundle of nerves."

"Well." Dennis looked out at the door to the street. "I'm headed for a walk myself. Maybe I'll find him while I'm out."

"You look after him, now." Christos swept him into a bear hug. "And I'll see you tomorrow back at the house. Give sloppy kisses to the girls for me."

"I will," said Dennis, hugging back. "Miss you, sweetie."

"It's just till tomorrow." But Dennis knew that Christos was as aware as he was that the restoration of their intimacy was still a fragile thing, and even several hours apart was going to be risky for them. Still, they put on a brave face, walked out to the street together, and, just before Dennis saw him into his cab, had another lingering hug.

Then Dennis wandered through the tourist-thronged streets of Santorini. This new information, that this was their last night, not just on this island but in Greece, made it imperative that he seduce Jasper *tonight*. Once they were back home, and Jasper was on his home ground, it would be next to impossible; it had to be here, where the languid Aegean climate made everything seem just a little unreal.

Even so, it would be difficult to pull off on such short notice; he'd counted on having at least one more day to lay the groundwork for the seduction, so that when it occurred, Jasper would be without resistance.

Still, he was up to the challenge. He might be past thirty, but he was still beautiful, still desirable, and—the one benefit of his advanced age—a hell of a lot more experienced than any twenty-year-old boy. He could get Jasper into the sack without too much trouble. And once he'd got him there, he could arrange for Farleigh to walk in on them. After which, of course, Jasper would be banished, and Dennis and Farleigh could begin comforting each other.

Pleased with this plan, Dennis examined it for potential trouble spots. He ordered a gyros sandwich from a curbside vendor and munched on it while he sat on a bench in a little public square occupied only by a pack of almost wild mixed-breed dogs, who were fighting and tussling and yelping to beat the band.

As the onions, beef, and cream slid down his throat, he decided that the one crucial element to be decided was where the seduction would take place. The obvious answer was in the room he shared with Jasper; they had privacy there, and beds, too. It seemed made to order. But no, if Jasper really *was* attracted to Dennis—if those furtive, admiring glances hadn't been a lie, and Dennis knew they hadn't—then Jasper would be keenly aware of both the privacy and the beds, and would be on his guard against being steered in any direction that might take advantage of either. He wasn't stupid; he'd demonstrated that time and again. He wouldn't risk his grip on Farleigh for a fling with Dennis. So in order to get him in bed, Dennis would have to get him someplace where he wouldn't *expect* a seduction . . . someplace neutral, where neither of them had any real authority. Someplace unlikely. And with a bed.

He crumpled up the wax paper the gyros had been served in, and tossed it toward a wastebasket. It bounced off the rim and onto the ground. Immediately, two dogs pounced on it, gave it a good sniffing, and started fighting over it.

Dennis sighed and got to his feet. He needed to think of a location, and he needed to think of one fast. The only thing that came to mind was, another room in the hotel. But how could he get access to one without actually booking it? And once he had it, how could he get Jasper in there without arousing his suspicions and getting him on his guard again?

Frustrated by his inability to brainstorm a solution, he shoved his hands in his pockets and slouched back to the hotel.

He considered making another transatlantic call to Lonnie or Paulette for advice . . . but there was an awful lot of background he'd have to explain first. Maybe too much.

Just outside the hotel, he ran into Tracey and Roseanne, who were this time accompanied by three strapping, handsome blond boys in shorts. At the sight of them Dennis was jolted out of his funk.

"Dennis, *hiii*," Tracey said, as usual sounding like she hadn't seen him in about a decade. "How *are* you?" She hugged him; Roseanne immediately did the same.

"I'm okay," he said, then rubbed his chin . . . the secret "cute guy" code.

Tracey laughed, pulled one of the boys forward, and clung to his arm. "Dennis, this is Erwin and his friends, Wilhelm and Albert. They're German soccer players, and they're here for some kind of tournament."

"They might be in the *Olympics*," enthused Roseanne, who, Dennis was amazed to note, was herself clinging to the arm of one of the other boys; apparently, the romance of the islands had gotten even to her. It boded well for his task with Jasper.

"They invited us to come watch them practice," said Tracey. "And then to a party afterward. You want to come along? There's, like, one left over for you!"

Dennis laughed in surprise at this, and looked sheepishly at the boys to see if they'd been offended (also to see which one he might have liked), when Tracey added, "Don't worry, none of them speaks English. But I'm, like, fluent in German, 'cause of my dad. And I wasn't kidding about having one for you. I've got some *serious* doubts about Albert."

"No, *Wilhelm*," gasped Roseanne, squeezing her beau's arm. "*This* is Albert."

"Oh, yeah. Wilhelm. Sorry." She beamed at the boys, who beamed back at her; then she turned back to Dennis. "So, you up for it?"

Dennis shook his head. "Sweet of you to think of me, but Wilhelm's on his own. I've got bigger fish to fry."

"Oh, you have, huh?" Tracey said, her voice full of meaning. She rubbed her chin questioningly, and Dennis rubbed his back in reply. "Ooh, good for you!" she squealed.

"Listen," he said, "I hate to bring this up, but . . . well, I might need a little cash to pull it off, and . . . well, do you think you could see your way clear to—"

"Oh, my God!" she exclaimed, and clasped her hand to her forehead. "I never repaid you that money you lent me!"

He felt a sudden onrush of embarrassment. "I wouldn't ask, but it's just that . . ."

"No, no," she insisted as she dug through her purse. "I'm, like, *so* sure I forgot after you were sweet enough to lend it to us. You must think I'm a total bust-off. Could somebody please just, like, shoot me in the head?"

Dennis, watching her suffer such mortification, thought, *Gee—glad I didn't ask for the windbreaker, too.*

She produced a billfold and carefully, audibly counted out several drachma notes to Dennis, which was somewhat unnecessary since Dennis wasn't even aware of how much he'd given her; it had just been a small wad of bills he'd stuffed into his pocket after getting them in change in some forgotten transaction.

Tracey kissed him again to thank him for the loan; then she and Roseanne said goodbye and started up the street. Just before Dennis turned toward the hotel, Tracey called back, "*Oh, by the way, we won't be back for dinner, so don't expect us.*"

He gave her a thumbs-up.

He entered the hotel and bounded up the stairs, thinking all the while. "Won't be back for dinner, huh?" he muttered. "Hmm . . ."

In the hallway, he discovered Farleigh trying to get into his room, fumbling with the key and cursing himself. Dennis hastened over to him and said, "Having trouble with that, hon?"

"Oh. Dennis. Hello. Yes, the damn thing. Christos usually let me in and out, but I sent him back to Mykonos, and now I can't figure out how he made the blasted key work."

"Let me try." He took the key from Farleigh, re-inserted it in the lock, and gave it a turn; it resisted—the lock was clearly either old or of poor manufacture—but with a little pressure it tumbled. Dennis swung open the door.

"My hero," said Farleigh with a wan smile. Now that the light from the room was spilling over them, Dennis could see that Farleigh was looking dead tired again. His skin resembled parchment. It alarmed him; he'd thought that the last such spell had been an anomaly.

He helped Farleigh into the room and sat him on the bed. "How you feeling, Farleigh-boo?" He crouched down before him and rested his hand on his knee.

"Worn out. I just need a nap, that's all. Couple hours. Set me right up."

"You've been having these spells pretty often, you know?"

"Nonsense. Nonsense."

"No, you have."

He shook his head. "It's just from worry. I shouldn't be here when *Lady Windermere's* in trouble. I let this place sap my judgment. Let the island get to me . . . like that employment agent of yours, Brassy Sally Jessy or whoever."

"Cindy Bassey-Esterhazy."

"Right." He lay back. "Well, the old me is back now. I'll be fine. Not pulled in two directions anymore."

Dennis nodded, kissed him on the forehead, and said, "You call me if you need anything. I'm right down the hall." Then, as he got up, a wicked and ingenious idea wormed its way to the forefront of his mind. He stopped just before leaving and said, "Um, listen. If you're up to it, Tracey and Roseanne are having a little cocktail party in their room before dinner. Around seven o'clock. As a kind of thank-you to us . . . well, to *you*, really . . . for everything you've done. They hope you can be there."

Farleigh's eyes remained closed, but he smiled in acknowledgment. "Very sweet of them," he said. "I'm sure I'll feel up to it. Tell them I'll be there."

"I will." He slipped into the hallway and shut the door behind him, then rubbed his hands together in triumph.

He checked his watch. Four-thirty. Better get to work.

chapter
48

When he got to his own room, he tried the door; it was locked. He rapped on it and called out, *"Jasper—it's Dennis. You in there?"*
No answer.

Instead of using his key to get in, he took his wallet from his back pocket, removed his Bloomingdale's credit card, and slid it between the door and the frame till he'd wedged it under the bolt. Then, by flicking the card up and down, he lifted the bolt and unlocked the door.

Grinning in self-satisfaction, he swung open the door and entered the room.

He was momentarily taken aback by the sight of Jasper stretched out on his bed, but soon realized that the boy was sound asleep. The book he'd been reading was lying next to him, open. A few of its pages were crumpled; apparently Jasper had rolled over on them sometime during his nap.

Well, thought Dennis, *saves me the trouble of finding him.*

He considered the situation for a moment, then decided it presented an opportunity for a good opening gambit. He sat on his own bed, propped his elbows on his knees, rested his chin in his hands, and stared at Jasper sleeping. His idea was to wait until the boy woke up, at which time he could pretend to have been caught mooning over him. But as he sat and stared, he found himself doing something oddly close to just that. Jasper's youth—his damned, irresistible youth—was somehow even more potent and fresh-seeming in slumber. His tousled hair, his rosy lips slightly parted, his long eyelashes, the luminous glow of his skin, all gave him an almost Pre-Raphaelite appearance; if Dennis hadn't known any better, he'd have said he looked innocent.

But palpably sexual as well. He'd stripped off his chinos and was wearing his boxer shorts; his long, lean legs were stretched out over the bed at an unconsciously flattering angle. His bulky white socks gathered around his ankles. And his rugby shirt had crawled up his stomach, revealing a warm, white expanse of his midsection, which expanded and contracted with the intake and expulsion of each breath.

So appealing did Dennis find this picture that when Jasper finally did stir, some seven minutes hence, and rub the sleep from his eyes to catch Dennis in the act of watching him, Dennis didn't have to pretend embarrassment; he really was abashed at having been so genuinely taken in by Jasper's nubile beauty.

"What . . . what?" Jasper said, looking at Dennis suspiciously.

"I didn't say anything," said Dennis, leaping to his feet.

"I mean . . . what are you doing?"

Dennis shrugged. "I'm sorry. I was . . . I was just sitting and . . . uh, thinking. I wasn't looking at you, or anything."

"Hell you weren't." He sat up and pulled a pillow over his stomach and crotch.

"Look, I'm sorry. I couldn't help it. Just forget it ever happened." He backed toward the door, and bumped into the wastebasket, which toppled over and spilled its collection of used tissues and cellophane wrap. Dennis said, "Oops," and emitted a high-pitched, nervous laugh. It was too scary; he wasn't acting. *Get a grip, here*, he commanded himself.

Jasper glared at him uncomprehendingly.

He opened the door and said, "I . . . I'm going now. Out for a walk or something, if anyone needs me." He ducked out, then stuck his head back in and, averting his eyes, said, "I don't suppose . . . I don't suppose you'd want to go with me, or anything."

Jasper let a very long pause crawl between them. "You . . . want *me* to go with you?"

"Look, I'm sorry I asked. It was just a thought." He ducked back out and started to close the door.

"No. Wait."

He peered back into the room.

Jasper shrugged. "I'll come. I could use a walk."

Dennis smiled as though this were his chief desire in life, which, right now, it was, but not for the reason Jasper might infer. "Great!" he said. "Thank you!"

The boy nodded his head in the direction of the hallway. "Just wait outside while I get dressed, okay?"

This puzzled Dennis; all he had to do was pull his pants on. Had he forgotten that Dennis had seen him romping naked on Super Paradise beach?

Even so, Dennis complied, and stood in the hallway teasing the nap of the carpet with his shoe until Jasper came out, endeavoring to smile and tucking in his shirt. "All right," he said. "Ready when you are."

When they hit the street, Jasper said, "Where do you want to go?"

"Let's take the steps down to the dock."

Jasper looked momentarily quailed; there must be five hundred enormous steps winding from Santorini town, down the sheer, volcano-stripped cliff side, to the lonely little dock at sea level. When they'd arrived, they'd bypassed the stairs—as did nearly everyone—by taking the funicular straight up to town. Dennis promised Jasper that once they walked to the bottom, they'd ride back up again. The boy seemed somewhat placated by this and agreed.

Dennis soon discovered that he'd underestimated the physical toll this descent would take. Each step was about three feet wide and, aside from that, had settled over the centuries into a downward slope, so that he had to fight the urge to fall face forward and roll the rest of the way. But the late afternoon sun was warm, the skies were deepening attractively, and there was a lot to see on the way down: beautiful outcroppings of rock, unusual flowers, even the odd feral cat staring out at them from the brush.

Jasper was suddenly remarkably chatty. When Dennis remarked on how spectacular the cliff side was from midway down its length, Jasper agreed, and said, "You have to imagine the kind of force that could do this to an island. There's what's left of the volcano out there," he said, pointing past the dock at a lumpish black knob of rock protruding from the water. "You can take a boat out there and walk around it. There are sulfur springs and stuff. If we were staying longer, I'd like to do that. Stand right at the spot where it blew itself to bits. And took half this island with it. But that's not all." He tripped lightly down several steps, then turned and waited for Dennis to join him. "It was like a nuclear explosion, almost. Set off a tidal wave that bombarded Crete. *Crete.* Do you know how far *south* that is? Completely destroyed Minoan civilization. The first great Hellenic culture, and it was wiped out just like that—just by a flick of nature's wrist." Finally, he seemed to run out of steam. He stood staring at the imposing wall of exposed rock that soared above him.

Dennis reached his side and stared up as well. "All I meant," he said, "was that it's very beautiful."

Jasper's face filled with blood. He looked at Dennis, mortified, then turned his gaze away. "You enjoy humbling me, don't you?" he said.

"Not at all. I'm sorry if you think that."

"You do it all the time with Farleigh. You did it several times today in front of my uncle and grandmother . . ."

"Jasper, I said I was sorry. You should know that's never been my intention." He put his hand on the boy's shoulder. He looked at it as though it were a weapon, then met Dennis's eyes with a frightened, excited gleam of his own.

For the rest of the descent, they were largely silent. When they got to the bottom, they leaned on the railing and watched the sky grow darker, watched the water dapple with the diminishing light; then, as Dennis promised, they took the funicular back up to town.

It was growing cool. They headed back to the hotel. Dennis checked his watch; it was now a quarter to six.

Dennis noticed a liquor store. He said, "Hold on a minute," and ducked inside. A few minutes later, he came back out bearing a fair-sized bottle of ouzo. "I just feel like celebrating," he said, resuming their walk.

Jasper looked puzzled. "Celebrating what?"

"I don't know. Life. Love. Seagulls. Dog shit. Whatever's around to be celebrated. Speaking of which, watch your step."

Jasper looked down and at the last moment sidestepped a pile of canine droppings.

"Thanks," he said.

"Don't mention it." They walked on in silence for a time; they passed a chapel in town, from which the strains of a Byzantine hymn floated out to their ears.

"I'm just going to sit in the window of our hotel room and have a drink and watch what's left of the sun disappear," Dennis said. "I don't know what your plans are. But, you know, you're welcome to join me."

They walked at least an eighth of a mile before Jasper responded.

"What the hell," he said. "Sure."

chapter
49

The sun was hanging over the horizon, bright and red as an enormous pimple. At any moment it would duck out of sight, as if it knew it was being watched and was too shy to endure it. Dennis thought about clinking his glass against Jasper's and toasting the beginning of the evening, but on second thought the gesture was too self-consciously romantic; he didn't want to tip his hand just yet.

Although, he'd better get rolling with *some* kind of action. It was well after six now; they'd already downed half the bottle of ouzo and Jasper showed no signs of slowing down. If Dennis didn't act soon, the boy would just pass out and that would be that.

"You know," said Dennis, "this is a pretty dismal view. I think we'd get a much better one from Tracey and Roseanne's room."

"Don't be silly," he said. "They're across the hall from us. You probably can't even *see* the sun from their window."

"Of course you can," he said loftily. "I heard them talking about it earlier."

Jasper shook his head. "Not possible."

"Well, it's easy enough to prove." He pushed his chair back and stood up. "Come on."

Jasper gave him a dubious look. "Trust me, okay? If you want to go check, be my guest, but I'm fine here."

Dennis grabbed him by the wrist. "Don't be such a stick-in-the-mud. Where's your spirit of adventure? Besides," he said, grabbing the bottle from the windowsill, "we can share some of this with the girls, so we don't drink ourselves to death."

He dragged Jasper out of the room and down the hall, and it did require dragging. The boy was clearly offering his full resistance. Dennis's heart was thundering; he didn't dare look back at Jasper's face—best to brazen it out and hope he'd come around.

At Tracey and Roseanne's room, he knocked on the door. He knew full well, of course, that they weren't within, but it was necessary to keep up a pretense for Jasper's sake. *"Hey, guys,"* he called out. *"It's us. Dennis, I mean. And Jasper."*

When no answer came, he looked at Jasper, who shrugged; the boy seemed mildly irritated.

Dennis said, "Well, the hell with it. I want to show you the sunset, and nothing's gonna stop me." He whipped out his wallet, produced his credit card again, and jimmied open the door.

Jasper was aghast. "This is breaking and entering," he said.

"Well, unless you're going to perform a citizen's arrest, it's hardly relevant. Come on." He boldly strode into the room. When Jasper crept in after him, Dennis shut the door. But didn't lock it.

He met Jasper at the window. The boy was staring at a cornice of the building that obscured the setting sun so easily seen on the opposite side. "You see," he said, shaking his head. "I hate to say I told you so . . . but, hell. Common sense."

Dennis lowered his head and plunked the bottle onto the sill.

"Damn," he said. "I could *swear* I heard them talking about the great sunset they got."

At that moment the sun must have set indeed, for suddenly they were enveloped in darkness. The window overlooked an alley—unlike their own, which had a fair prospect of the street—so precious little light from the street lamps seeped in.

All the same, Dennis could just make out the broad, smooth planes of Jasper's untroubled face.

"Listen, I'm sorry about this," he said. "I shouldn't drink. I get all excited, and I make a fool of myself."

"Not at all," said Jasper. "Maybe we should leave."

"It's okay. I just remembered, the girls are at a party with some German soccer players."

"Lucky girls."

He chuckled, but immediately resumed his somber expression. "It's just . . . Jasper, I—I wanted to celebrate—well, to *particularly* celebrate—the beginning of our friendship. Because I hope that's what this is. This whole afternoon. Starting at the steps, and everything."

Jasper's eyes gleamed in the dusk. "Well. That'd be nice."

Dennis smiled, then took a swig from the bottle and handed it to Jasper.

"No, thanks," said the boy. "I won't make it to dinner."

They stood in silence for a moment; it was awkward between them, the air filled with a confused tension. Which is exactly what Dennis had wanted, and why he'd had to get Jasper out of their own room. They were on eggshells, here. They didn't belong here, but here they were; and that made anything possible. Or did, if Dennis played it just right.

"Maybe we should check on Farleigh," Jasper said at last.

"Okay. Just so long as you really don't think I'm a buffoon, or anything."

"No, no." He laughed. "Don't be silly."

"Well, I wouldn't blame you if you really didn't like me. I mean, I haven't made any secret of my jealousy of you."

"Jealousy?"

"Of your relationship with Farleigh. You're so close, intellectually. You have the kind of relationship I could never have with him. It's finally convinced me to step aside."

Jasper shook his head. "You don't understand . . ."

"Don't interrupt. It's taken me a long time to work up the courage to say all this. Now, I know I've been hard on you, I've treated you badly, resented you."

"Dennis . . ."

"And even this morning I blamed that whole misadventure

with your grandmother on you, when it was my fault for insisting we go there in the first place. You knew better all along."

Jasper shook his head more violently. "No, you're wrong. It *was* my fault; I was a coward, a big fucking hypocrite . . ."

"I had no business saying . . ."

"Even Christos knew you were right. That's why he did what he did." He paused. "You're very persuasive, you know."

Jesus, thought Dennis, *I hope I am. I've got to get this kid into bed in exactly twenty-six minutes. Better pour it on.* "All that is beside the point," he said. "I wished you nothing but ill. When you called me on it this afternoon—in the room just afterward, when you told me how much you hated me—"

"I never said I hated you!"

"It was what you implied, though. And it shocked me. It made me see myself through your eyes."

Jasper grabbed the bottle from him and took a swig, then wiped his mouth with his wrist. Dennis's eyes were growing accustomed to the dark. He could see him quite clearly now. "You have no *idea* how you appear to my eyes," the boy said, a tremor in his voice.

"Maybe not. All I wanted to say was, I'm grateful you allowed me to make amends this afternoon . . . just let me, you know, walk with you and talk to you like we've been doing. Getting beyond all the rancor and bitterness. I . . . I think you're a really wonderful man." He shrugged. "It's just kind of ironic. I mean, I'm finally okay about Farleigh being with you instead of me, finally decided to let him go, and now look what happens." He turned his face to the window and trailed his finger along the sill. "I'm starting to fall in love with you, myself."

He kept his eyes on the sill; he held back from confronting what he knew would be the boy's fear and shock at this revelation. But he also knew that, now that it was out, he could massage it into place, woo Jasper just a little longer, and then —have him. Fifteen minutes tops. And once he got him in bed, he'd have no trouble keeping him there for Farleigh's seven o'clock entrance. Dennis knew lots of tricks.

Finally, Jasper said, quietly, "I can't believe you just said that."

Dennis, now that he'd had his cue, looked up and into the boy's eyes.

But what he saw there wasn't fear, or shock, or even hesitation. It was complete surrender.

"Oh, Dennis," Jasper said, his voice roiling with emotion, "this is a goddamn dream come true! You have no *idea*. I've loved you since I first set *eyes* on you."

The next thing Dennis knew, he was being smothered with kisses.

chapter
50

T hey took a tumble, and Dennis found himself pinned to one of the girls' beds. Jasper was ravishing him with incredible energy; it took some doing before he could push the boy away for a moment, gasp a breath, and catch a glimpse of his watch. Six twenty-five! This was all happening way too fast . . . much too far ahead of schedule.

But then Jasper dove into him again, kissing and licking his neck, and under the ministrations of the boy's artful tongue, Dennis began to reach an undeniable level of arousal. His head still clouded by ouzo, he tried hard to sort through what was happening, and he realized that perhaps . . . perhaps the plan simply didn't *apply* anymore. After all, Jasper had said it was him, not Farleigh, that he loved. So Dennis was in no real danger anymore.

Was he?

He pushed Jasper away again and held him there by his heaving chest, so that the boy was hovering over him, panting with desire.

"Wh—what do you mean, you love *me*?" Dennis asked.

Jasper reached out and ran his fingers through his hair, and said, softly, "Always. From my first day on the job, cleaning the pool. I adored you the moment I saw you. Sauntering out there in your briefs, with a cup of coffee, yawning, lying down on a deck chair and falling asleep. Not even noticing me. You were so elegant and sophisticated. And so beautiful. I felt like a worm next to you."

"My God," said Dennis, who had no recollection of this event. "I was probably just hungover."

Jasper started pulling off his rugby shirt. "And in all the weeks that followed, it was the same. You never even seemed to see that I was there. Like I was invisible. My heart would just break wide open and ooze pain. And look at us now!" He yanked the shirt over his head, then flung it aside and renewed his attack.

Dennis tried to push him away yet again. "But, you and Farleigh," he said as Jasper's tongue burrowed into his ear. "I thought you and *Farleigh* . . ."

Jasper laughed, lifted his head, and started working at the buttons on Dennis's own shirt. "Oh, come on," he said. "I know Farleigh cares for me. But he's got to be, what—around sixty? No, that's a business relationship, baby."

"*Strictly* business?" said Dennis as the boy opened his shirt and began pulling up his T-shirt, kissing each inch of exposed stomach as he did so.

"*Strictly* . . . business," Jasper said between kisses. He sat up again, pulled both shirts from Dennis's body, and tossed them to the floor. "I mean, not like he didn't *want* it otherwise. He made plenty of passes."

"But . . . I could've sworn, once, when I came to pick Farleigh up at the theater . . . Debbie Stebbe was on guard outside the office door, and she acted like . . . like . . ."

"Oh, hell, I remember that." He rolled his eyes dismissively as he unbuckled his wristwatch. "He'd just made a *major* pass at me. Nothing happened from it, but when you showed up, he was suddenly all crazy, like it had. He kept whispering for me to be quiet, and I kept saying, '*Why?*' He couldn't see there was no reason for secrecy. It was a big guilt thing." He rolled onto his back, unzipped his fly, and pulled off his chinos, then his underwear, and kicked them off the bed. "But I *never* gave him my body, Dennis. That's always been yours. Whether you knew it or not." He plucked his socks off and knelt over Dennis, naked and young and hard.

Dennis gulped. "And then," Jasper continued as he lowered himself onto his prey, "Farleigh took me away from the pool and I thought I'd never see you again. And I didn't. Till you came to that *Lady Windermere* rehearsal, and it was like you saw me for the first time. The *look* you gave me!" He shuddered. "It withered me; it was so disdainful. I wanted to die right then and there." He unzipped Dennis's fly and reached inside.

Dennis gave a yelp and sat up. Jasper laughed and pushed him down again, then continued his narrative while he maneuvered Dennis's pants down his legs. "Then there was that night Farleigh invited you to come to dinner with us. I was as nervous as a cat. All I wanted to do was impress you, but I was too terrified to even look at you, much less say one word to you. I only remember babbling on and on about nothing, and you not even paying attention to me. But then, unexpectedly, you said that sweet thing about how talented I was, and I dared to hope . . . but, God, I never dared hope we'd ever end up like *this.*" He rolled off Dennis's socks, and then they were both naked as the day they were born . . . if considerably more tumescent.

Jasper fell onto Dennis again and kissed him so deeply and so passionately that for a moment Dennis thought he was trying to suck the breath from him. When they separated, he looked into the boy's eyes, but there was shadow in his face, and he couldn't read what was there.

"So when you followed us to Greece," Dennis said, slowly being won over by Jasper's attentions, "you weren't just following Farleigh . . ."

"*Never,*" the boy whispered. "I was following *you.* I was almost glad when the show fell to pieces; it gave me an excuse. Not that I'll ever need an excuse again, Dennis. I'll always follow you. Ends of the earth." He took Dennis's engorged penis in his hand and started lovingly massaging it.

Dennis felt an erotic jolt, but tried to remain calm. "Then . . . I don't understand. When I forced you to share this room with me, why were you so reluctant?"

"Oh, baby," said Jasper, his lips grazing Dennis's, his strokes growing more insistent, "it was just that you scared me so. From the very second we met again here in Greece, you were so rude to me, you and Christos both. You terrified me. I wanted to share a room with Farleigh, because I knew he'd protect me. When you insisted I stay with you, I was shocked and frightened. I didn't know what to think. I thought . . . oh, God, baby . . . I thought you were out to get me. That night you came in drunk . . . the way you spoke to me . . ."

Dennis knit his brow. "I don't really remember that."

"I don't want to think about it. I only want to think about now. Please, baby . . . let's just think about now . . ."

Dennis was never one to resist a plea like that. He gave himself up to the moment.

chapter
51

And then something happened he could never have anticipated.

Call it . . . cataclysm.

A choir of angels singing a hundred different anthems in a hundred different keys.

An endless bank of wide-screen TVs, each showing a different nuclear explosion.

An infinite hallway where doors flew open, one by one, *bam-bam-bam*, letting in a burst of uncanny, blinding light.

Cataclysm. *Cataclysm.*

That's what it felt like, to be made fully human, at long, long last.

"My . . . God," he said afterward, running after breath but not catching it. "My God." He swallowed hard and looked at Jasper, who lay next to him, sweating, trembling, his skin hot-cold to the touch. "I . . . I really do . . . *love* you."

Jasper lifted his weary head and kissed him full on the lips; it was like the seal on a deed. He was now his.

Then he dropped his head onto Dennis's chest, and Dennis,

truly alive for the first time in his life, sorted through the events that had led him to this realignment, this rebirth.

Everyone I've wronged, he thought, everyone I've hurt . . . if only I could make it right. If only I could fix what I broke. If only I could make it up to them by giving them one transcendent moment like *this* . . .

The sense of stillness . . . of completion . . . it was like nothing Dennis had ever felt before. Not even with Farleigh; he recognized now that what he felt for Farleigh wasn't romantic love at all, but a kind of companionable, pitying love. Even when they'd first met, when Farleigh had been a renowned, wealthy, dashing sophisticate and Dennis nothing more than an urchin . . . he'd known even then that all power in the relationship resided with him, not with Farleigh. And pity came from that.

But this . . . was this what he'd been missing? No. He hadn't missed this; this could only have happened here and now. It was once-in-a-lifetime. A meeting of souls. He'd been biding time till now; that was all. Biding time . . .

But, of course, everything would be very different from here on. It would have to be. Completely different. Different in ways he couldn't even imagine yet.

With all of this rattling around in his skull, he at first didn't recognize the knock on the door for what it was. But when it was repeated, he sat bolt upright, knocking Jasper from his embrace, and checked his watch.

Two minutes after seven!

"Christ," he hissed, "I *forgot!*"

"What?" said Jasper lazily.

"*Tracey?*" Farleigh called through the door. "*Roseanne? It's Farleigh.*"

Dennis leapt out of bed and whispered to Jasper, "Grab our clothes! *Quick!* And follow me!"

He bolted into the bathroom, fumbled open the window next to the sink, and clambered out. Fortunately, he'd noted the fire escape locations when they'd checked in (a habit he'd inherited from his famously pyrophobic mother), and so knew exactly where to access it. *Un*fortunately, the escape itself was an ancient, rusty thing; it scraped against his bare feet.

He turned and helped Jasper through the window, then slammed it shut, leaned against the wall of the building, and sighed in relief.

"I heard the door open," Jasper said as he himself collapsed against the wall, "but I don't think he saw me."

"I just hope he doesn't stick around in there. The place must *smell* like sex."

Dennis felt the back of his head. "Ow," he said.

"What's wrong, baby?"

"I must have hit my head on the sill when I was climbing through. Same place your grandmother clobbered me, and now this on top of it."

"Poor angel. Let me kiss it . . ."

"No, no," Dennis said, laughing. "Grab the reins, okay, honey? We're perched naked on a fire escape outside a room that isn't ours. Let's just deal with that first. You got our clothes?"

Jasper took the bundle from beneath his arms and handed it to Dennis.

It looked a bit small to Dennis, but it wasn't till he'd sorted through it that he really started to panic. "This is *it*? This is all you *got*?" He dangled the clothes from each hand. "Two shirts and three socks?"

Jasper reeled. "It was dark," he said. "I couldn't see! I was rushing . . . I grabbed what I could!"

"Two shirts and three socks?"

"I'm sorry." He crouched by the window and said, "I'll go back and get the rest. Farleigh must be gone by now."

"You can't get back in! I slammed it shut!"

Jasper crouched down and desperately tried to reopen the window, but there was nothing there that would give him sufficient purchase.

"Oh, Jesus," he said in a low voice. "There's no way. We're gonna have to wait for the girls to come back."

Dennis laughed in astonishment. "First of all, they won't be back for hours. And second, are you crazy? We're buck *naked* out here!"

"That's okay. Tracey would dig it. She'd be all thrilled that we finally got together, above all."

"What do you mean? What does she . . . I don't under-stand."

Jasper stood up again and stretched his left leg. "*Ow!* Kinks. Well, the main reason Tracey pretended to be my girlfriend was to make you jealous."

"*What?*"

"Yeah. I mean, I really wanted her to help me fool my grandmother, but I didn't think she'd go for that, and she was getting tired of the whole 'Isn't this fun' aspect of the charade." He stretched out his other leg. "*Ugh.* So the only way I could get her to continue it was to tell her the real reason was to make you jealous. Not that I ever seriously thought a thing like that would work, but *she* dug that idea; she's said all along we were made for each other."

"Huh. Perceptive girl. Still, it doesn't change the fact that she's out for the evening." He shrugged. "We might as well put on whatever we've got. Here." He handed Jasper his rugby shirt, and pulled on his own white T-shirt. Then he held out the three socks. Even though two of them were his, he gave them to Jas-per. "Here, you take the pair. I'll wear the odd one."

"Oh, God, you're so good," said Jasper. "You don't have to do that, baby."

"Just take them and shut up."

"I can't *believe* how much I love you." He sidled up to Den-nis and started rubbing against him.

Dennis, while not finding this unpleasant, gave him an af-fectionate nudge, and said, "Later for that, okay? We're in a jam here." He looked down at the alley below. Fortunately, there was no one there, but neither did there seem to be any access to the ground without dropping the fire-escape ladder, and Dennis didn't know how to do that.

Plus, even if they *did* get down to the alley, what could they do then? Saunter back through the lobby wearing only shirts and socks?

He looked up. "There's a ladder to the roof. That's our best bet. Follow me." He donned his single sock, then started climbing.

Halfway to the top, he called out, "*You doin' okay back there, honey?*"

"*Uh-huh. Just admiring the view.*"

"*What view?*"

"*The one you're giving me.*"

Dennis, realizing exactly what view this would be, grew pleasantly embarrassed, and scooted the rest of the way up.

When he found his footing on the tar-papered roof, he turned and helped Jasper over the side. Then they turned and looked out over the town of Santorini, which from this height was a glittering array of white and pink lights, curving around the inner arc of the island.

"Wow . . . like God's vanity mirror," said Jasper breathlessly.

Dennis hugged him, then said, "I wish we had more time to take it all in, but the sooner we get back to our room unseen, the better." He turned and surveyed the roof. "Ah-ha!" he said, and he pointed in the direction of a small door abutting from the center. "I'll bet that's our ticket out of here."

They hurried across the rooftop—"Careful of nails and stuff," cautioned Jasper as they gingerly sidestepped debris along the way—only to find the door locked.

"*Shit,*" said Dennis as he tugged harder and harder on the knob. "I can't fucking *believe* our luck."

Jasper wrung his hands. "Could you do that trick with the credit card again?"

Dennis pursed his lips and took a deep breath. "Well, I suppose I could, Jasper, but I don't happen to have my wallet on me at the moment."

"Oh, God." He slapped himself in the face. "I can't believe how stupid I am. I'm so sorry, baby. I didn't mean to exasperate you."

"No, no," said Dennis, softening at once, "*I'm* sorry. I shouldn't have snapped at you. You're just trying to be helpful. I'm so evil. Forgive me . . ."

"Only if you forgive *me* . . ."

They embraced each other, and within moments were mashing to beat the band.

Dennis was the first to regain control. He tore himself away, caught his breath, and said, "We'd better stop this. Last thing we need on top of everything else is a couple of hard-ons."

"Too late," said Jasper sheepishly.

Dennis, seeing that this was true, grabbed the boy and tickled him mercilessly until he was once again pointing south.

"Don't *ever* do that again," gasped Jasper, clutching his sides. "I *hate* being tickled."

"That's the point." They smiled at each other; then the realization of their predicament reasserted itself.

"What are we going to do?" Dennis said, shrugging helplessly. "We can't just wait up here to be discovered. Not like this, anyway."

Jasper put his hand on his chin. "You know, if there's a fire escape on that side of the building, I'll bet there's one on our side, too."

"Of course there is. What of it?"

The boy was already dashing across the roof. When Dennis caught up with him, he was peering over the edge. "Yeah!" he said. "See, here's the ladder and everything. Our side of the building has its own fire escape, just like Tracey and Roseanne's does."

"I know, I know. What's your point?"

"Well, we can climb down to our own room from here."

"And how do we get the bathroom window open?"

Jasper smiled at him in triumph. "I *left* it open."

He felt a surge of joy. "You did not!"

"We're in the Greek islands, Dennis. I left *all* our windows open. The sea air is what we're *here* for."

Dennis smothered him in a bear hug. "If I didn't love you before, I'd love you now!"

He giggled. "Let's continue this downstairs," he said.

Dizzy with excitement that their trial was at an end, they started down the ladder.

They were midway to their goal when they heard the first hoots and catcalls from below. "Oh, Christ," muttered Dennis, "I forgot we're visible from the street on this side." He called down to Jasper, "*Hurry*," and redoubled his own speed.

Within seconds, he'd joined Jasper on the fire-escape landing. The calls and laughter from below were growing louder. Dennis didn't dare look down.

"There," said Jasper, "just like I left it." He pointed to the bathroom window, which, just as he had said, was wide open.

Dennis hooted in joy. "After you!"

Jasper smiled, then crawled inside.

Dennis followed immediately; then, mortified at having been seen in so ridiculous a state, he shut the window behind him, and put his hand over his heart.

Jasper encircled his waist from behind. "It's over," he cooed in the darkness. "We're okay now. We're in our own room . . ." He started kissing Dennis on his nape.

Dennis writhed in pleasure for a while, then turned and kissed him back.

They luxuriated in each other for a while, then Jasper took Dennis's hand and led him to the bedroom.

They stood at the foot of the bed and continued their passionate exploration of each other's mouths, their moans of pleasure growing more and more audible, until—

—until someone switched on the light.

There was an elderly woman in the bed, staring at them.

They whirled in horror.

"Th—this isn't our room," muttered Dennis, paralyzed by the realization.

"We must be the next one over," whispered Jasper, grinning in shock. "My mistake."

The woman, who had perhaps feared she'd be confronted by a pair of guns turned on her, seemed infinitely more distressed by what she found pointing at her instead. She let out a scream that rattled Dennis's eardrums so hard, they actually rang.

Dennis and Jasper didn't need to confer after that. Each of his own volition fled to the corridor and skidded one door to the left; this was undeniably their own room.

It was also undeniably locked.

The elderly woman's screams were continuing unabated. At any moment people would start to gather in response.

"*What kind of man leaves the windows open but locks the door?*" Dennis said, breathless and frantic.

"*Don't yell at me!*"

Dennis groaned in frustration, then dove down the hall to Tracey and Roseanne's room. He flung open the door, stumbled in, grabbed his pants, then flew down the hall again. His hands shaking, he retrieved his key from his pocket, then let himself and Jasper back in, at long last.

chapter
52

S afe inside, they held each other for several minutes until they'd given up trembling for laughing. Now that it was over, and their neighbor's screaming had abated, the whole misadventure did seem rather comic.

"What do you suppose those people on the street made of us?" asked Jasper. "Crawling all over the building with only our bare asses hanging out?"

"Don't know," Dennis replied, reaching around and squeezing the boy's buttocks. "Maybe they thought we were mooning the entire island."

"I wonder if mooning is even a concept here."

They laughed again, and somehow laughing led to kissing, and kissing led to lovemaking.

"Much less to take off this time," growled Dennis as he tore off Jasper's rugby shirt.

Afterward, while basking in the glow of love reconsummated, Jasper, idly twirling Dennis's armpit hair around his forefinger, said, "What now?"

Dennis sighed. "Well, for starters, we have to tell Farleigh."

Jasper blinked, and shook his head. "What? After everything we did to avoid him finding out?"

"Well, there are *ways* of him finding out," Dennis explained, drawing him nearer and hugging him. "Finding us naked in bed together is a bad way. Having us sit down and tell him to his face, while reassuring him that we both care for him, is a good way."

"But . . . won't he kick you out?"

"He won't have to. I'm leaving him."

Jasper pulled away, then propped himself up on his elbows and gave Dennis an uncomprehending look. "But—but where will you go? What will you do?"

"I don't know. Build a life of my own somehow."

Jasper shook his head. "You're incredible. All this time I thought you were terrified of Farleigh dumping you."

"All this time I was. But now I realize, I don't love him—not the way I thought I did. Not the way he deserves. I never even knew what real love was, till now."

"Ooh, you sweet-talker." He snuggled in close again.

But Dennis pushed him away. "And I think we have to do it now."

"What?" Jasper's head slipped off Dennis's chest and onto a pillow. "Tell Farleigh *now?*"

Dennis was already pulling on a new pair of boxer shorts and his retrieved pair of jeans. "If we don't do it right away, it's only going to get more and more difficult. Bite the bullet, baby."

Jasper bit his lip. "I know you're right. I'm just scared."

"Of what?" He donned a fresh T-shirt.

"Well, of hurting him, basically. Farleigh's been so good to me."

"Be honest," Dennis said, sitting next to him on the bed and resting a hand on his shoulder. "You're also afraid of being kicked off the production."

Jasper looked affronted for a moment, then nodded humbly.

"It's okay. I'm afraid of being stricken from Farleigh's will, too. It's okay to admit that. But the thing is, if we really care for him, we have to trust him with the truth. And if we really don't want to hurt him, we have to make sure never to play him for a fool . . . never carry on behind his back. Because this will come out someday, you know, no matter how hard we try to conceal it. And the longer we wait, the more it'll hurt.''

Jasper sighed, nodded, slipped out of bed, and started dressing himself in fresh clothes.

Within minutes, they'd put themselves back together. As Dennis was tying his shoes, Jasper combed his hair in the bathroom mirror. "We have to remember to get our other clothes from the girls' room, too,'' he said.

Dennis nodded. "We'll do that on the way back from talking to Farleigh.''

A moment later, there was a knock on the door.

They stared at each other, stock still. Then Dennis called, *"Who is it?"*

"Farleigh. May I come in?"

He leapt to his feet. Jasper came out of the bathroom, his eyes like saucers. Dennis winked at him and gave him an emboldening thumbs-up. *"Coming,"* he said.

Farleigh hobbled into the room and fell into the first available chair. "What's going on?" he said, clearly irritated. "The girls weren't in their room. I thought you said something about a party. I couldn't find you boys either. Something's going on, and I want to know what it is.''

Dennis knelt before him and clasped his hands around Farleigh's. "I'm sorry,'' he said, "it's all been sort of chaotic. No one ever wanted to confuse or hurt you, Farleigh. But the fact . . . the fact is . . .'' He turned and looked to Jasper for moral support. Jasper came up behind him and put his hands on his shoulders.

"The fact is,'' Dennis said, beginning anew, "Jasper and I have fallen in love. Actually, I think we've always been in love, but I, for one, didn't realize it until . . . well, until this afternoon, actually. And it's kind of thrown a wrench in things, as you can well imagine.'' He let slip a nervous laugh.

Farleigh seemed to slump, both physically and spiritually. "Well,'' he said, his voice hoarse, "I can't say I never expected it.''

Dennis was astonished by this reaction. "You're kidding. You couldn't have. *I* never expected it."

"Yes, well. You forget. I could observe each of you impartially. I had plenty of opportunity to note your obsession with each other. Whenever you were in the same room together, there was so much tension coiled up between you that if you let it go, it could've blown the roof off. Even when I was alone with one of you, the other always seemed to be there, an unseen presence. I knew it was only a matter of time before this happened. I dreaded it, but I knew."

Jasper knelt next to Dennis and put his hands over Farleigh's as well. "I'm so sorry, Farleigh."

"You can't apologize for falling in love. You *shouldn't* apologize for falling in love." He sat back, his face more ashen than Dennis had ever seen it. "Falling in love . . . is a victory."

Dennis felt something catch in his throat; he fought back tears. "We still love you, you know."

"I know. I know that kind of love, Dennis." He attempted a smile, and patted him on the head as though he were a favorite pet. "And at my age, believe me, I'm grateful for it."

"Don't be ridiculous! You're not so old."

"I'm old enough to know I'm finished. I'm actually glad to know you two have found each other. Dennis," he said, his eyes reddening, "you were the love of my life. Jasper, you were my last big infatuation. I'm so indebted to both of you. And I'm so happy you'll be together after I'm gone."

"*Stop* it," said Dennis, squeezing his hands. "You're not going *anywhere*."

"I am. Like I said, I'm finished. I can feel it. I've got nothing left. You, you two—you're the inheritors of my future. You're my legacy to the world. You'll accept that, won't you? You'll remember me."

Jasper was bawling now, but Dennis kept his head. "Farleigh, give it a rest, okay? Remember, you *hate* melodrama."

He got to his feet, very unsteadily; Dennis leapt up and helped him. Then he grabbed his cane and said, "We'll all go home tomorrow, and we can talk some more. Christos will help it all make sense. You boys are my life. You be good to each other. I'm tired now. I'm going back to bed."

"But . . . don't you want any dinner?" Dennis said. "I'll have something sent up. We can join you, in the room. Stay with you till you're over this."

"I'm not hungry," he said, a ghost of a smile on his face, "and I'll never be over this." He shook a finger at Dennis, and for a moment a spark of the old Farleigh resurfaced. "You want to help me out? Roll back time. Set back the clock. Make me twenty-eight again. Or forty. I'd even settle for forty." Then his face sagged anew, and he said, "Help me to my room, please."

Each of them took one of his arms and guided him to the door. Dennis said, "I think you *do* need rest." He turned the knob and began opening the door. "When you've had a good night's sleep, you'll feel much bett—"

"HERMAPHRODITI!"

Dennis jumped back at the sight of Granny Ioannou, swaying in the doorway, brandishing an enormous crucifix and spitting gales of venomous Greek at them.

"Oh, for *God's* sake, Granny," said Jasper, "even *I'm* getting tired of this."

Uncle Kostas came skidding around the corner. *"Mama!"* he yelped, then dashed over to her and grabbed her by her tiny shoulders. "Jasper, I'm so sorry. I let it slip where you were staying, and she snuck out to the garage and took off in my car. How could I know she'd do that? She's hasn't driven since nineteen seventy-three! Luckily, I was in the front yard having a drink when she drove off, or I wouldn't have seen her go." Granny was still writhing and spitting, but Kostas held her tightly. "I had to follow her here in my decrepit old lorry! You should see the dents she put in my passenger door. She hit a drinking fountain and two boulders, and that was before she even got to town! My insurance is going to go sky-high." He shook his mother and spoke sternly to her in Greek, his fear of her seeming to have evaporated. *Hell hath no fury like a straight guy whose car gets bashed,* Dennis thought.

As he led her away, Kostas said, "Please forgive her, Jasper, she's a very old woman and not in her right mind. Give my love to your mother and come again when this old harridan is dead."

Jasper shook his head and turned to Dennis. "I don't *believe* that just happened. Are you all right?"

Dennis put his hand over his heart. "Uh-huh," he said. "She nearly gave me a heart attack, though. How about you, Farleigh?"

They looked at him and saw that his face had gone rigid. "Farleigh?" Dennis said. *"Farleigh?"*

His eyes remained fixed in place, and he began to drool from the corners of his mouth. "We'd better get him to the bed," said Jasper. But as soon as they tried to move him, he turned to dead weight in their hands, and with all their strength, they couldn't stop him from slumping to the floor.

"My God," Dennis muttered, "my *God*. Get a doctor!"

Jasper ran from the room.

Dennis undid Farleigh's collar, then slapped his face; he was turning blue.

"Farleigh!" he barked. *"Farleigh! Look at me!"*

He held his face before him, and his eyes bored into Farleigh's, but within those eyes, Dennis could already see Farleigh falling away . . . far, far away.

chapter
53

Paulette was sobbing into her Kir Royale. "I mean can you *imagine*," she blubbered. "*Pregnant* . . . at her age. It's goddamn *indecent*."

"There, there," said Dennis. "She's only a few weeks on. There are lots of things that can happen yet."

Paulette sniffled and looked at him hopefully. "Yeah?" she asked. "Like . . . like what?"

Dennis found that despite himself, he couldn't actually say out loud that Mrs. Spanker might miscarry or that the baby might be stillborn. It was really the only comfort he could offer her, but he couldn't wish it on anyone, not even for Paulette's sake; it was barbaric. Accordingly, he hemmed and hawed till Paulette gave up on him and started bawling again.

Dennis shook his head in distress and looked at Lonnie, who sat with his elbows on the table, clutching the hair at his temples and letting his head loll unattractively. "Help me out, here, please," Dennis commanded him.

"Don't look at me, man. I got troubles of my own right now."

"Oh, for God's sake. What?"

"Dierdre's ex-husband, that's what."

"Her ex-hus— Wow. I didn't know she had one."

"Childhood thing. Married at eighteen. Couple months later, Dierdre finds him humping another woman and loses her shit. Attacks them both with a kitchen knife."

Dennis put down his Pimm's Cup. "You're joking."

"Husband and mistress both hospitalized. Dierdre does a spell in the slammer. When she gets out, they divorce. This must be, oh—sixty-seven. Sixty-eight. Husband goes off to California with the mistress, and that's that. Out of her life."

"And . . . now?"

"He turns up broke. Blackmailing her. Whole stabbing-and-prison thing gets made public unless pillar-of-society Dierdre Diamond forks over big-time. She's totally freaked. *Throwing* money at the guy to shut him up. Had to mortgage the apartment! My allowance has shrunk to nothing. Can't even afford to maintain the Audi. Gears got stripped, and it's just *sitting* in the garage. Had to cab it here. Next time I might not even be able to afford that. And you know what that means."

Paulette gasped, then moaned, "*The buuuus,*" and wailed even louder.

"But you legally own half of everything," Dennis said. "Because of the palimony agreement, right? Dierdre can't touch *your* half of the cash and assets."

Lonnie dropped his head into his arms. "Yeah. But I can't really say no to the old broad, can I? Not after everything she's done for me."

Dennis gave up and turned back to Paulette. "I still don't understand why this baby is such a big deal. Doesn't the Spanker already have children? I'm sure I've heard you mention them. What's so special about one more?"

"Oh," said Paulette, waving her hand in the air, "those kids are from his *first* marriage. Some Bryn Mawr debutante he married fresh out of college who had two kids and died of breast cancer at twenty-three. Spanker's spent the last twenty-five years idolizing her; current Mrs. Spanker never stood a chance. First wife died young, so she's always gonna be beautiful, always gonna be tragic, always gonna be the mother of his children. Second wife means second best, in this case." She blew her nose loudly into a handkerchief. "Now that she's finally got a bun in the oven, it's all changed, of course; his eyes light up when he talks about her. What I don't understand is how she managed it; Spanker said they don't sleep together. Okay, so, did they bump in the hallway, or what?"

There was a short, wet silence, then Paulette and Lonnie looked at Dennis with pleading eyes. "What can we do, Dennis? Tell us what can we do."

He hadn't a single idea; he gazed back at them with an awful feeling of helplessness till a waitress intruded to ask if they'd like another round.

When she'd gone, Dennis said, "I'll give it some thought. I really will. But if, and when, I come to any conclusions, I'll have to let you know by phone. This is my last War Room conference."

Their jaws dropped. "*Dennis!*" cried Paulette. "Oh, my *God,* honey! You can't do this to us!"

He shrugged. "I can't *not.* I've got too many other demands on my time now. I'm running Farleigh's business *and* managing his estate. I never realized how busy that would keep me. And the whole raison d'être of this little society was that we were all in a similar position and could provide moral and emotional support. Well, I'm not *in* that position anymore."

"You fucker," said Lonnie. "You've graduated!"

He grinned, then took both their hands in his. "Listen," he said, "I'm not forgetting you. I'll help you work out your problems if I can, and if I can't, I'll at least make sure you're never down and out. I can do that, you know. I'm *filthy* rich."

They appeared to take some comfort in this.

"Well, if *you* can't be here for us," Lonnie said, a twinkle in his eye, "maybe you could send the pool boy on over."

"Yeah," said Paulette as she lit up a Tiparillo. "Let him take your place in the ranks. It's only fair."

Dennis knit his brow. "You think I'm keeping Jasper?" He frowned at them. "Don't jump to conclusions."

Neither Lonnie nor Paulette seemed to know how to respond to that, and Dennis took the opportunity to excuse himself. He had an appointment with Farleigh's lawyer . . . no, *his* lawyer, now. He had to keep reminding himself of little things like that.

Outside the War Room, he ran into Bix Zimmer. "HEY, DENNIS, OLD BUDDY, OLD BEAN! IT'S ME, YOUR OLD PAL, BIX!"

In a panic, Dennis checked his pockets. Not a quarter—not a coin of any kind—to be found there. Ironic, now that he was more flush than he'd even been in his life. "Bix! Look, I'm sorry, I don't have anything for you today."

Bix patted his shoulder; Dennis resisted the urge to check to see if he'd left grimy handprints on his overcoat. "THAT'S OKAY, PAL! I KNOW YOU GOT OTHER THINGS ON YOUR MIND! I HEARD ABOUT POOR FARLEIGH."

How on earth would Bix have heard? What circles could he possibly travel in that would make news of Farleigh Nock's death? "Well, yes . . . I am quite the bereaved widow at the moment."

"YOU DON'T THINK ABOUT ANYTHIN' BUT GRIEVIN', MAN. YOU GRIEVE AS MUCH AS YOU WANT. DON'T LET ANYBODY TELL YOU TO GET ON WITH YOUR LIFE. YOU TAKE AS MUCH TIME AS YOU NEED. YOU HEAR? YOU TELL 'EM BIX SAYS SO."

"I will, Bix." Damn Bix and his uncanny instincts; it *was* good advice. The trouble was, Dennis was *already* getting on with his life. He couldn't help it. He missed Farleigh, of course he did, but he never seemed to have a spare moment to dwell on it. He supposed grief must have its day, but for the time being, he couldn't allow it any space.

"I tell you what, Bix," he said as guilt overtook him, "I'm going to make some arrangements with my lawyer about you, okay? I'm sure it's what Farleigh would've wanted."

Bix looked as if he might cry; then he lunged forward and enveloped Dennis in a bear hug. Dennis now knew for sure that the coat would need dry-cleaning.

"YOU'RE THE BEST, MAN! THE BEST! OL' BIX DON'T DESERVE FRIENDS LIKE YOU!"

After he'd pried himself free and seen Bix on his way, Dennis strolled back to where he'd left his Saab. It was a fine, crisp, late autumn day; there was a bit of a cloud cover, and to the west the sky was as purple as a bruise, threatening rain; but right here, right now, the air was deliciously cold and clear.

As he walked, he engaged in his favorite pastime: checking himself out in store windows. His hair, his gloves, his lamb's-wool overcoat, the flash of his teeth—he was looking pretty good for thirty-two.

A sudden movement behind one such window made him stop and adjust his focus. That jerky, manic gesture—like a flamingo conducting traffic—didn't that recall someone he knew?

He peered through the window; beyond it lay a restaurant with a tropical decor: palm fronds and bird of paradise everywhere, and rich pastels.

On an impulse, he went inside.

It was late in the lunch hour, so the place was still busy. An enormous black man wearing a chef's hat stood in the door to the kitchen; he was yelling something. Dennis listened.

"—*ell you to them we out of the soft-shell crab, mon. I tell you that yesterday. I tell you that again, trouble is a-brewin'!*"

He disappeared behind into the kitchen, and a petite waitress burst into tears.

A second waitress appeared, proferring a menu. "One?" she asked him.

He met her eye, and was about to say he was only passing, when he recognized her; she'd been the one he'd seen through the window.

"Cindy?" he said.

She took a step back in alarm.

"Cindy Bassey-Esterhazy?"

"Yes." She appeared flustered. "Do I know you?"

"Dennis Racine!" He shook her hand—she was at first reluctant to give it to him—and said, "I was one of your clients at the employment agency!" He laughed. "I never thought the next time I saw you you'd be wearing a sarong and a flower in your hair."

Unlike Dennis, she seemed completely unenchanted by this unforeseen reacquaintance. "Well, yes," she said, "bit of a life change. But I ran out of cash down on the island, so I had to come crawling home and—well, as soon as I get enough saved up, I'm heading back. This time for good."

"But if that's the case," said Dennis, "why are you working here? I'd have thought you'd make a lot more back at the agency than at—"

Two teenage girls entered behind Dennis, and Cindy instantly brushed him aside. "Just two?" she asked. "Smoking or non-smoking? Booth or table?" She barked out the questions as though they were blanks on an application form, then whipped a pair of menus at the girls with such brisk efficiency that a bit more force might have beheaded them.

When she'd shown the girls to their booth and settled them in, she returned to the front of the restaurant and gave Dennis a so-you're-still-here look.

He shrugged. "So you were saying, you're working here because . . ."

She patted the flower in her hair. "I need new skills if I'm going to live in Jamaica. No call for headhunters down there. But a *waitress*, now . . . that's different."

"Well. I wish you the best of luck."

She nodded perfunctorily, and suddenly he noted a look of ferocious desperation in her eyes. He shrugged and said, "You know, I *am* a little hungry. Maybe just a quick bite . . ."

She grabbed him by the arm and dragged him across the restaurant. As they passed an empty booth he said, "Uh . . . this would be fine, Cindy."

"*Not my station*," she hissed.

She plunked him at a table in the middle of the restaurant, where the sun was at just the right angle to flood into his face. Then she loomed over him and barked out the specials with all the relaxed charm of a drill sergeant.

The food was horrible; Dennis left her a fifty-dollar tip.

chapter
54

Byron Pratt didn't look like an attorney; that's because he'd spent the fifties trying to be an actor and had never gotten over it. Back then he looked like Brando; now he looked like Brando. Which might imply a degree of consistency, except we're talking about different Brandos.

He was wearing a large, loud, floral-print shirt that was unbuttoned to mid-stomach, which must be a style he liked, because no one would ever have asked him to do that. He leaned over the open file of papers before him and picked his nose. It was an affectation, this nose picking; in the fifties Brando had scratched, James Dean had scuffled and squinted, so Byron had thought, Great, I'll pick. He was still waiting for this bit of naturalistic body language to enter the actor's lexicon. He hadn't been onstage in twenty-five years, but he was convinced it would somehow be his contribution.

He wiped his picking finger on his trousers and said, "Okay, Dennis. That's about it. You just sign here, and it's official: the Farleigh Nock Memorial Trust for aspiring playwrights. With an annual award of twenty-five thousand dollars to two honorees."

Dennis, in a blinding white terry-cloth robe, leaned across

the desk, flicked the file around to face him, and signed it with
one of Farleigh's—no, correct that: one of *his*—pens. "I have
to thank you for your help in this, Byron. I mean it." He finished, placed the pen back into its holder, then gently shoved
the file back at Byron, who snapped it up and tucked it immediately into his briefcase.

"Don't thank me," he said, averting his eyes beneath his
bushy, expressive eyebrows. "Farleigh was family. We weren't
blood, but we were *blood*, man." He snapped shut the briefcase,
then smiled gratefully, and a bit sheepishly, at Dennis. "Least I
can do for his memory."

Dennis leaned back and stretched his arms over his head.
"Well, I don't know what *he'd* have to say about it," he said with
a laugh and a yawn. "Way I'm spending his money, I'm surprised he hasn't already come crawling out of the grave to put
a stop to it."

"Oh, yeah," said Byron, a thought occurring to him in mid-
pick. "That reminds me." He unclasped the briefcase again,
pulled out his Filofax, and opened it to where he'd jotted pages
and pages full of notes. He flipped to the most recently in-
scribed page, near the back, and ran his finger down a long
laundry list of items. "Just a few things I need to keep you
apprised of. First, the full scholarships you asked for, for misses
Helmerich and DiStanislau."

"Done?" asked Dennis, lazily scratching behind his ear.

"Done. Likewise the scholarship funds you set up incognito
for the children of one Xavier Ybarba. Who's that, if you don't
mind my askin'?"

Dennis shrugged and swiveled around in Farleigh's—in *his*
—chair. "Someone I got into trouble once. Only way I can
think to make it up to him."

"Ah," said Byron, despite clearly being no more enlight-
ened than he had been. "Well. Anyway, it's done."

"Terrific," said Dennis, still making three-sixties in the
chair.

"And the investment in your brothers' furniture store is all
wrapped up, too," Byron concluded, flipping the pad back into
place and sliding it into his briefcase. "We've even had the first
request from them. Your brother Jameson called to ask if you'd

mind very much if he changed the name of the business to
'Racine & Daughters.' He said since that's all he's got, is daughters, it only makes sense." He snapped the briefcase shut, then
turned and put his hands in his lap. "Your brother Harold already gave his okay, but Jameson says he needs permission from
all the partners. Think he got a charge out of saying that—'all
the partners' instead of 'all the brothers.' You've made him
pretty goddamn happy, Dennis."

"Yeah, well," said Dennis dismissively, "whatever. Tell him
the name change is fine." He was now leaning back so that he
was almost horizontal, and was bouncing the chair slightly as he
reclined. "No, wait, never mind. *I'll* call him." He gave a little
kick and bounced back so far that he momentarily lost sight of
Byron behind the desk. "That it for today?"

"Pretty much. Only other outstanding matter is that Bix
Zimmer person."

"You're clear on what I want there?" Another kick, another
dip below desk level.

"Five dollars in quarters any time he comes into the office
and asks for it." He raised an eyebrow quizzically.

"Trust me. It's a Farleigh legacy."

Byron sighed, then picked up the briefcase and put it in his
lap. "Well, buddy, that seems to be all we got to talk about. I
mean, I already told you about the transfer of the Mykonos
property, right?"

"Uh-huh," said Dennis, now bouncing *and* swiveling. "Last
week. Not like it matters to Christos, though. He started knocking out walls and redecorating *before* his ownership was final-
ized."

Byron chuckled. "Yeah. I'll miss that sonovabitch."

"Me, too. But he put in his years of devoted service, and he
deserved it. And anyway, it's not like he won't be back for visits.
There's no world-class opera house in Athens, and he'd already
bought his seats at the Lyric for next season." He suddenly
sprang up to a sitting position, and rolled the chair up to the
desk again. "Listen, no offense or anything, but I'm getting
bored. All this legal business makes my head ache."

Byron got up and extended his hand. "No offense taken,"
he said. "*Hell*, no. Long as it makes your head ache, you're

gonna need *me*, aren't you? Let it ache, is what I say, kiddo."

"Oh, Byron, I'll always need you," he replied, getting up and shaking the attorney's hand.

Then he escorted him to the front door.

"How's Debbie working out for you?" he asked as they walked.

"Who, Deborah?" said Byron. "Oh, great, great. She's been a real lifesaver. A whiz with the books. Thanks for recommending her to me."

No, thought Dennis, thank *you* for taking her off my hands.

They arrived at the elevator. "So where you gonna scatter Farleigh's ashes?" Byron asked.

Dennis pressed the call button and summoned the elevator. While it moaned and groaned its way up to meet them, Dennis said, "Well, at first I thought, the Aegean. Because that's where he died, and he loved it there. But then I thought, no one could be there for it. So we're having a big ceremony at the Pruitt, and I'm going to scatter his ashes across the stage. You'll get an invitation, don't worry. Should be sometime next month."

The elevator arrived and the door slid open. Byron stepped inside, pressed the ground-floor button, and stuck his finger in his nose. "Pruitt's condemned, though, isn't it?" he asked as he picked.

"Yeah," said Dennis, nodding sadly. "End of an era. Gets torn down a few days after our ceremony. But we'll be safe enough."

"I'm not worried about that. Hell. Farleigh *never* played it safe," he said just before the door slid shut and he was carried away.

Dennis sighed, then turned and walked out to the patio for a swim in the pool. At the sliding glass door, he dropped his white robe and emerged naked into the great expanse of sun and cold air.

Jasper, in jeans and a poncho, was pouring a pail of chlorine solution into the pool. Dennis looked at him and said, "Is it okay to go in while you're doing that?"

Jasper looked up at him, astonished. "I suppose so. I can't believe you want to, though. It must be fifty degrees outside. It's *autumn*, Dennis."

"It's my pool," said Dennis. "You don't know how long I've waited to swim in *my* pool." He dove in.

When he broke the surface, Jasper was in the shed, putting away the bucket. Dennis breast-stroked over to that end of the pool, and when Jasper reappeared, he said, "I'm sorry you've had to take over caring for this thing again, like you never left your old job or anything. It's just that I've been too busy settling Farleigh's estate to hire a new pool boy. I don't even have a new *house* boy yet."

"I don't mind," said Jasper, and he dropped into a pool chair and hugged himself to stay warm. "Gives me something to do now that the foundation's backed out of *Lady Windermere*." His eyes lost focus, and he looked momentarily furious. "Fucking money men," he grumbled. "Panicking just 'cause Farleigh died. I could've made that show a *hit.*" Then he snapped back to attention, and added, "Besides, it's too late in the year; be silly to hire a pool boy now. As a matter of fact, the pool should be drained and winterized already. I wish you'd let me close it up."

"One more week, then I promise," said Dennis, treading water.

"One more *week*! Look at you. Your lips are blue."

"Turn up the heat, then."

Jasper sighed in exasperation, then did as he was told.

When he reemerged from the pool shed, Dennis said, "Come here."

The boy looked at his watch. "What now? I've got to go, Dennis. I've got my workout with Fatima."

"Tell her I say hey."

"I will. 'Course, you could just come back to the club and tell her yourself. It's not like you couldn't *use* a workout after all these weeks sitting on your admittedly fabulous ass."

Dennis dunked his head, took in a mouthful of water, then spat it at him. Jasper tried to dodge, but got sprayed all over his right thigh. He shrieked.

"You smart-mouth little tease, you," Dennis said, kicking gently so that he moved away from the side. "And after everything I did for you this week."

Jasper's shoulders dropped. "What? What did you do for me?"

"No, no," said Dennis, treading water in the middle of the pool. "You go on to the club. I'll tell you all about it when you get back."

Jasper actually stamped his foot. "I hate it when you do this. Come on. I'm late. Just tell me."

Dennis took a deep breath, then dropped below the surface of the water. He lazed about on the bottom of the pool, turning slow-motion somersaults and spiraling like a barbecue spit, before running out of breath and having to return for air. When he was six inches from the surface, he could already hear Jasper screaming at him.

". . . ot funny! Not funny at all! Tell me, damn it!" He was standing by the side of the pool, his fists balled, a look of real anger on his face.

"Oh, are you still here?" said Dennis at his most maddeningly ingenuous. "Very well, then, I'll tell you. See, since we still have a contract with the Varsity Playhouse, and I didn't want to take any more of a bath on *Lady Windermere* than I already have, I decided that we'd better keep the space."

"Keep the space?" said Jasper, stunned. "But we've got nothing to put on there!"

Dennis looked at him with feigned alarm. "My God," he said. "You're right. *What have I done?*"

Jasper laughed in angry frustration. "Dennis, come *on.* Just fucking *tell* me."

Dennis started swimming in a little circle, sidestroke. "How's my form?" he asked.

Jasper bit his lip; he'd clearly been pushed to the limit. He started back into the house.

"*All right, all right,*" Dennis called. "Come back. I'll tell." When Jasper was again by the side of the pool, arms folded, he continued: "Thing is, Mercedes isn't just an actress. She's a writer, too, it turns out. And about two years ago she wrote a one-woman show about her life . . . the story of a woman with Tourette's syndrome who nevertheless took to the stage."

Jasper's eyes lit up. "You read it? Is it any good?"

Dennis rolled his eyes heavenward, then let himself drop below the surface. When he emerged again, he said, "It's *phenomenal*. Funny, enlightening, full of pathos . . ."

"And you're doing it?"

"*You're* doing it." He smiled and aimed a splash at Jasper's shoes. The boy didn't even budge.

"What?" he asked, almost voiceless.

"I mean that Farleigh Nock Productions is proud to present a Jasper Batton production, *Tourette Suite*, written by and starring Mercedes St. Aubyn."

Jasper stared at him, his mouth agape. His arms slowly dropped to his side.

"I know it's not much of a directorial debut," Dennis continued. "A one-woman show on a mostly bare stage. But with the financial beating we took after *Lady Windermere* self-destructed, I couldn't very well—"

"Oh, Dennis, thank you," said Jasper, his voice cracking in at least three different places. "*Thank* you. You don't—I don't —oh, God . . ."

"Now, now . . . no tears. You'll get wet. I mean, wetter."

"I thought—I thought you were just going to . . . I don't know. *Keep* me. Like Farleigh kept you. Like a pet."

Dennis shook his head. "Oh, no," he said. "No such luck for you, my lad. You're going to have to *earn* your keep."

Jasper's eyes brimmed with tears; his smile was nearly beatific. He stared at Dennis, and Dennis, treading water, stared at him.

Then he looked at his watch again and said, "I'm *really* late . . . Fatima . . ."

"You run along, then. Give her my love."

Jasper nodded; his chin was quivering with emotion. He gave Dennis a little wave, then blew him a kiss. Then he turned and went back into the house.

Dennis thought, Well. *There's* gratitude.

Then, without warning, Jasper turned and loped back to the pool, his pace increasing so that Dennis realized he'd never be able to stop in time . . .

And then he was in the air.

And then he was in the pool, sending sheets of water cascading onto the deck. And with his heavy, wet poncho floating around him like a lily pad, he grabbed Dennis, pulled him close, and kissed him hard . . . very, *very* hard.

What a sense of drama! Dennis thought as pleasure drowned him. This boy will go *far.*

And he did.

They *both* did.

· A NOTE ON THE TYPE ·

The Typeface used in this book is a version of Baskerville, originally designed by John Baskerville (1706–1775) and considered to be one of the first "transitional" typefaces between the "old style" of the Continental humanist printers and the "modern" style of the nineteenth century. With a determination bordering on the eccentric to produce the finest possible printing, Baskerville set out at age forty-five and with no previous experience to become a typefounder and printer (his first fourteen letters took him two years). Besides the letter forms, his innovations included an improved printing press, smoother paper, and better inks, all of which made Baskerville decidedly uncompetitive as a businessman. Franklin, Beaumarchais, and Bodoni were among his admirers, but his typeface had to wait for the twentieth century to achieve its due.